ABIGAIL

A NOVEL

JESS HEILEMAN

VAGABOND PUBLISHING

For Tim,
the protagonist of my love story.

PROLOGUE

*M*y hand trembled as I grasped the cool, metal doorknob. I drew in a breath to ease the tightening in my chest before pressing open the heavy, wooden door and peeking inside.

"Abigail." Father's voice was quiet, beckoning.

I took in the familiar scene as my eyes adjusted to the dimly lit room. Little had changed since last night: the fire still flickered in the hearth, elongating the shadows dominating the large room; the curtains were still drawn, though the dawn's glow now crept in along the edges; and Father still stood slumped in his place near the bed.

"Abigail," Father repeated, reaching out his arm toward me. "It's time."

I stepped forward, then stopped and shook my head. I didn't have the strength.

Laurence walked to my side, placing his arm around my shoulder. "Come, Abigail, we will go together."

I searched my brother's grief-stricken eyes, feeling as though I was gazing at my own reflection. It was the sorrow we shared that reflected back at me and I blinked away the unfamiliar likeness.

I gave a faint nod, allowing Laurence to guide me forward to the side of the four-post bed where Father waited. The familiar scent of rose-water and fresh-cut flowers encircled me but did little to bring their usual comfort.

As I looked at the woman who lay before me, tears blurred my vision. There was little resemblance left of who she had been only weeks before. Her face was sallow and sunken in, the shadows around her eyes looking as though death had already stolen her from our unwilling grasps. I surveyed the petite shape beneath the blankets, and the eerie stillness quickened my heavy heart.

A slight rise of the covers and the sound of a labored inhale allowed me an odd sense of relief. I had not lost her yet!

"Darling," Father whispered. "The children are here."

Mother's brow creased but her eyes remained shut.

Father stepped forward and stroked her arm. Her eyes fluttered open at his touch. "Darling, the children have come to say their goodbyes."

She smiled weakly at Father before focusing her gaze on us. I forced away my despair as her shaking hand reached out. I intertwined my fingers with hers and sat next to her on the bed, letting the weight of our hands rest on my lap. Laurence moved in behind me and placed his hand over ours.

"My beautiful children...." Mother's voice was barely audible, and I understood the simple act of speaking was requiring what little energy she had left. I wanted to tell her to stop, to conserve her strength, but for what purpose? A moment longer in this state hardly seemed beneficial to her. Her voice caught, and pain consumed her beautiful features. She managed a shallow breath. "What a privilege it has been to be your mother."

The tears finally escaped and made their way down my

cheeks, but I refused to let go of her hand to wipe them. "Don't leave us, Mother," I pleaded. "We need you. I need you."

Father's hand came to my shoulder and I wasn't sure whether it was meant as support or a gentle correction. I hadn't intended to make Mother feel guilty for leaving us; I just couldn't bear to think of life without her.

"I'm afraid that is not my choice." Mother paused and let out another arduous breath. "Do not doubt yourself, Abigail. You are infinitely more capable than you know."

I nodded, though I did not truly believe her.

Her eyes flickered between our three grief-stricken faces. "Take care of each other. Trust in love, trust in the good, and trust that God has a plan for each of you." We all nodded in unison as her voice weakened and her eyes closed. "I love you more than you know." Her voice faded, "I will send your love to Grace and the others—"

I watched in horror as her heavy, labored breaths slowed then stopped. Despite the expression of peace that had over-taken the pain in her features, emptiness consumed me. I crumpled onto the bed next to her, my body shaking uncon-trollably. "I still need you," I wept. "I still need you."

"What shall we be without you, my dear?" A loud sob followed Father's question and I watched as he bent his head low and cried as I had never heard a grown man cry before. Laurence rose to his feet and they wrapped their arms around each other in a heart-wrenching embrace. I wanted to join them, but I couldn't. I couldn't leave Mother's side, not when the warmth in her body would soon grow cold.

I placed her lifeless hand against my wet cheek, soaking in the feel of her warm touch one last time. How could the blessed life I had been handed change so quickly? So drasti-cally? Without her here I would never be the same. I was once again broken.

CHAPTER 1

I scanned the corridor. Satisfied there were no servants present to witness my unladylike act, I squatted down and pressed my ear to the keyhole. Eavesdropping wasn't a talent I was proud of, but it had always served its purpose well enough.

Muffled voices clarified as I positioned myself.

"Father, I believe it is crucial we accept."

"She has made it quite clear she isn't ready. I don't want to force her before she is ready."

"Yet you wished to discuss the invitation again?"

Silence.

"She is a fine young lady, but—"

"Fine lady? Laurence, she is exceptional!" Father's voice grew louder. Little impassioned him more than the subject of his family, and I never tired of it.

"Father, you know I did not mean to imply otherwise, as I wholeheartedly agree. But Abigail needs to prove to herself that she is capable. She has delayed her first Season, and we can't allow her to miss the next. You must realize, the only way she will be prepared is by interacting with others of our social standing."

A thoughtful hum met my ear. "Then shall we invite a small party here? Perhaps her cousins when their obligations are through?"

"Our cousins are likely engaged for the entirety of the summer. And gentlemen? What gentlemen would make your list? We know nothing of entertaining. If Mother were here, it would be different..." Laurence's voice grew quiet. I slowed my breathing to make sure I could hear his words over the reverberating thud of my heart. "But she isn't. So, we must prevail on the good judgment of other notable women to arrange such opportunities."

"I am not even acquainted with the Stantons. Abigail will detest being sent to the home of strangers." Stanton? The name sounded familiar, but I couldn't recall where or who had mentioned it.

"The invitation surely comes at the request of Aunt Marianne. Helena and Hannah will be there as companions." I inwardly groaned at the realization of where I had come across the name Stanton. Hannah had written throughout the Season to convince me of what I had been missing. The name Stanton was among her ramblings though I couldn't recall what had been said. I would be sure to reference my letters later. "Besides, as I have already assured you, the Stantons are a reputable family. I was introduced to their eldest son, Mr. Edwin Stanton, at Oxford and, though I did not know him well, I believe him to be a distinguished gentleman. The kind who has acquaintances we hope for Abigail to engage with."

"I realize the necessity," Father said reluctantly. "But she will not like it."

"She will like nothing that takes her from the safety of Easton Manor, but how much of life she will miss if we continue to allow it."

"Sometimes I believe she has seen enough of what life can be—"

"There is so much good she has not seen."

Father released an audible exhale.

"We have given her all we can Father—she needs more."

It was quiet for too long and an unsettling feeling crept its way through me.

"I suppose you are right," Father said confirming my fear. "Would you bring her to me?"

"Of course." Laurence's footsteps moved toward the door. I straightened, hoping to remove myself to a less incriminating distance. "One last thing," Laurence's voice was near enough it reached me, muted but distinguishable. I couldn't resist and drew close again, returning my ear to the keyhole. "You must resist her charms, Father, she needs to recognize you are quite set on your decision."

Father's laugh reached my ear as the doorknob turned. I straightened just in time for the door to swing past me, revealing the surprised face of my brother staring back at me.

"Eaves-dropping is a vexing habit, Abee," Laurence said, attempting to not appear startled.

My cheeks warmed. "I will be certain to take more care in the future."

Laurence's eyebrows lifted. "To not listen in on others' private conversations?"

"To not get caught doing so," I said with a mischievous smile as I stepped past him.

Laurence's chuckle followed me into the room as he shut the door behind us.

Father stood behind his large desk watching the playful exchange with a look of satisfaction on his face.

"Hello, Father. I heard you wished to speak with me?"

"I daresay you have, and I should correct you for it or you'll never learn your lesson." He shook his head with an amused smile on his lips before stepping out from behind his

7

desk and reaching for my hands. For a moment he didn't speak but lifted my hands nearer his face, rubbing the faded lines on my skin with his thumb. "I'm glad you are aware what I wish to discuss—sometimes certain topics are easier to address when we are eased into them, are they not?" I nodded at the rhetorical question and he looked back down at my hands. He hesitated, looked at Laurence and back to me. "Your brother believes it is time for you to venture away from your over-bearing father."

"But I don't wish to leave you."

"And I don't wish you to be gone, my dear, but your brother is correct." I sent Laurence a pointed glare that made him shift uneasily. "It is time you venture out beyond the gates of Easton Manor—"

"Perhaps if we wait—"

"I fear we cannot wait if we desire to have you ready for next Season. Remember the agreement we made, my child; I let you delay your first Season but only if you willingly undertook preparations to ensure your readiness for the next."

I dropped my eyes to the floor. I had made that promise in desperation to stay at Easton Manor, not be sent away from it. If it were my choice, I would postpone my introduction to the heartless *ton* of London indefinitely.

I nodded. "I remember."

He lifted my chin and smiled down at me. "You are a brave girl, Abigail." His eyes conveyed the message to my soul, and I was certain a father could not love his daughter more. "I must ask you to trust me."

"Can you not come with me? Or perhaps Laurence?" I looked pleadingly between them. "It would bring me such comfort to have you there."

"The invitation is for you, Abigail," Laurence interjected. "Aunt Marianne will be there with Helena and Hannah—" he stared at me until he realized I took no comfort in the idea.

"But if you hate it as much as you fear, perhaps I shall break propriety and demand to join you."

Father chuckled. "And he believes I'm easily swayed—"

"But give it a chance, Abee," Laurence continued. "To your dismay, you may prove to yourself how capable you are."

Laurence's hopeful expression pulled at my heart and I realized there was no use in resisting. "I have recently heard I am an exceptional young lady—though I believe it is quite evident that the sources are biased."

Both men laughed heartily though I understood it was more with relief of my acceptance than the humor in my words.

Kissing me on my forehead, Father walked back to the chair behind his desk. "You two may go. I shall write to Lady Eliza directly and accept her invitation."

As we walked out, Laurence moved to my side, wrapping his arm around my shoulder in a form of brotherly apology.

"Abigail," Father called out, causing us to stop and look toward him.

"Yes?"

"Promise me you will let what is in the past stay there."

"I promise," I responded, causing the corner of his lips to pull up in a smile. His mouth opened, as though he had something else he wished to say, but quickly closed again. "Father?" I questioned, wondering what else he could possibly say.

Father paused. "Have Lydia begin preparations for your departure to Timpton House."

"And when should I inform her our departure will be?"

"Tomorrow."

"Tomorrow?" The shock in my voice caused a brief flash of guilt to tug at the corners of his mouth.

His gaze flitted from me to Laurence and back again. With reaffirmed conviction, he smiled apologetically and nodded. "Tomorrow."

"Very well," I said as confidently as I could muster, my

racing heart attempting to take the breath from my lungs. Laurence grabbed my arm and escorted me out of the study.

"Brave girl," Father muttered to himself before Laurence closed the door behind us. For him, I would be brave.

∾

"TOMORROW?"

I nodded. "I'm sorry, Lydia. I can help with the packing if that eases some of your burden."

"And shall you prefer to fold the gowns or choose which ones you shall bring?"

I pressed my lips together in contemplation though I could hear the humor in her tone. "You well know I trust your opinion more than mine when it comes to fashion." Lydia's face beamed at the compliment. "So I suppose, if you make the selections, I can fold them?"

Lydia scoffed playfully. "It would take me twice as long to teach you how to pack a trunk correctly. Truly, it isn't any trouble. I only was surprised at the news of leaving tomorrow. Laurence had not mentioned—" she stopped, apparently thinking better of what she was about to say. "Really, it is no trouble."

I watched her, hoping to discern what she had thought unfit to tell me before willing myself to leave it alone. I was already causing her an undue amount of distress asking her to have us both ready to leave in the morning. I didn't care to upset her and risk having to pack myself. I would remember to venture on the subject at a less consequential moment.

"I fear we might be in danger of arriving before the Stantons receive our acceptance," I said, smiling to lighten my concern about the idea.

The suddenness of the intended departure had surprised me, and I wondered how long Father had known of the invitation and put off a decision. Since Mother's death, his ability to accomplish things had greatly diminished. Laurence, realizing the need, had begun to run the ins and outs of Easton Manor. Although fitting as the heir, I worried at Father's general lack of motivation since losing Mother. A zealous man renowned for taking up grand causes, he now spent most of his days locked away in his study. He still maintained his strong affection for me and Laurence, but his spark for life and his sense of accomplishment died with Mother.

"I am just thankful your father allowed us to update your wardrobe before the start of this Season. You can't get dresses made in a day." Lydia's round eyes lit with excitement. "I am excited to see you finally wear some of these gowns." She pulled several out and placed them on my bed. "This one is a must." Lydia held a gown of rose-pink muslin with gold embroidery down the skirt and along the neckline. It was one of my favorites, the soft golden shimmer brought out the golden undertones of my skin, making me appear fairer.

I nodded in agreement as my mind went to the wasted money spent on all the gowns I had not yet worn. Father hadn't even mentioned the cost when I asked to delay my Season for a year. Perhaps it was because Laurence had been the one to see to the burden of the expense.

"Stop biting your lip, Abee. Such a dreadful habit. There is no need to feel guilty about your new gowns. Your wardrobe had been neglected since Lady Blakeslee died, and I daresay these gowns will suit the lady you've become more than the juvenile dresses you've been allowed to wear these past two years."

Nearly my same age, Lydia was more a friend than a maid and I wouldn't have been at all surprised to find out my parents had handpicked her for that very purpose. She had beautiful chestnut hair and was lovely with her fair complexion and round eyes that matched the shape of her face. But her best trait was her smile and the way it could light up her face whenever she was happy. Overwhelming gratitude filled me as I watched her deciding what gowns should be included among my things—being accompanied to Timpton House by at least one person I loved would certainly ease my burden.

Leaving Lydia to the packing, I walked to my writing desk and pulled a small stack of letters from the drawer. The majority of my correspondence came from Hannah, though the frequency with which she wrote grew longer the older we became. For years we had planned to have our first Season together, but when I wrote to inform her of my decision to delay, she thankfully took the news surprisingly well. She, of course, promised to keep me updated on what I was missing—when she had time to do so. Yet contrary to her goal, each letter she sent made me thankful I had avoided the endless Society of London and the drama it entailed.

Starting at the first letter after her debut, I looked for references to the Stanton family. I had nearly skimmed through the end of the second letter when I spotted the name.

Helena and I were introduced to acquaintances of Mother's today by the name of Stanton. Mother seems quite fond of the couple and has sung their praises endlessly since our meeting. I felt they were no more superior than other fine couples we have come to know, so I suppose Mother's praise comes more readily because their oldest son, and heir to Timpton House, is not yet married. The Stantons spoke highly of him, and nothing inclines the earnest desire for an introduction as much as parental admiration. That and the understanding that Timpton House is supposedly quite grand, with reportedly some of England's most beautiful gardens.

The next paragraph elaborated on a theatrical performance where Hannah seemed to notice the other patrons more than the play itself, so I skipped ahead to the next letter.

Sure enough, about halfway through, I noticed the name again.

We finally had the opportunity, if I can call it that, of meeting the eldest Stanton, Mr. Edwin Stanton. And though Helena said he is one of the finest gentlemen to make her acquaintance, and I must agree he is very handsome, I fear he leaves much to be desired. I am fortunate to have more freedom in forming opinions of gentlemen than Helena, who is already in her third Season with no substantial marriage prospects. I believe she thinks him more tolerable than he is because she must. Mother says that I am jealous of his attentions for Helena, but he looks as irritated in the presence of Helena as he does in the presence of any lady I have seen him with. It is unfortunate for such wealth to be ruined on an ill-tempered man.

I folded the letter and began reading through the others. An occasional mention of Stanton here and there hardly seemed significant. Perhaps if Helena had written me, I would have more information to decipher, but she hadn't, so I would have to make do with Hannah's vague descriptions. I opened the letter I had just received a few weeks before.

Mother has been seeking an invitation to Timpton House shamelessly for weeks now and Lady Eliza has finally granted her the very thing she desired. We shall leave here in a week's time and spend the first month of summer there, a decision made to ensure Helena will not need another Season. Mother is already planning the nuptials between Helena and Mr. Edwin Stanton, though he has not yet made an official declaration. I may not like him much, but I feel it appropriate to pity him in this regard. Though in the same breath I should perhaps pity myself, for the more I come to know him the more confident I am that I have not met a less amiable man this Season. Indeed, I do fear he will be the most tedious brother-in-law imaginable. My only consolation to the plan is that Sir Wycliffe will also join the party.

Just as I had thought, the letters held little information of consequence regarding my hosts besides the upcoming engagement of my cousin Helena to their son. Returning the letters to my drawer I pondered how I would occupy my time at Timpton House. Hannah's brief description of the Stantons made me far from excited for the company I would be expected to endure, but she had mentioned the beautiful gardens. I turned to Lydia. "Can you be sure to pack several pairs of gloves and a few bonnets? I plan to spend as much time outside as I can get away with."

"I already have them packed," she said with a wink.

Maybe my visit to Timpton House would have some redeeming moments after all.

CHAPTER 2

I watched the passing scenery with growing apprehension. The nearer the carriage got to Timpton House the more my stomach churned.

"You look very poor, Abee. Do you need to stop for some fresh air?" Lydia watched me nervously as though she was readying to catch me, should I collapse.

"It is nerves more than anything." I shifted my eyes back out the window. "Besides, stopping would only delay the inevitable. We are almost there, I think I will make it."

Lydia did not withdraw her attentive gaze. "Are you certain you do not feel unwell? I've never seen you so drained of color."

"Thank you," I responded with a weak grin. "I'm sure there is nothing more comforting than knowing how ill one looks before meeting new people. But perhaps we shall count it a blessing. I can never hope to be considered fair but drained of color is a promising development."

My sarcastic remark lessened the worry in Lydia's eyes.

"Timpton House!"

Both of us startled at the voice booming from above as the driver caught sight of our destination.

"Well, it's too late to stop now," Lydia said looking toward the house that had just entered into view. "House? That isn't a house! Timpton is nearly as grand as Easton Manor."

I smiled at her assumption and hearing the name of my dear home. "Nearly as grand, but I am positive nothing can ever truly compare to Easton Manor."

The house sat stark against the blue sky, its light stone reflecting brilliantly in the sunlight. Centered in the grass that led up to the house was a large pond where birds drifted around the water's edge hiding among the heavy foliage. "It is lovely," I finally conceded as the grounds surrounded us and I looked eagerly out the windows on both sides. "I'm sure it will offer adequate distractions until I'm free to return home."

"First things first," Lydia said with a flick of her head toward the house. I had assumed it was to be a small party, but I was obviously mistaken as a group of people flooded out the entrance.

"Oh, drats!"

Lydia giggled. "I believe that phrase would be included in your father's admonition to watch your tongue and your temper."

I wanted to respond but I couldn't seem to gather the words, at least not effectively enough to make a coherent rebuttal. I closed my eyes and took a deep breath before feeling a sudden sting on my cheek. My eyes flung open in time to see Lydia's hand moving to my other cheek.

"A little pinch will help with the color."

I smiled weakly as the carriage came to a stop.

A footman opened the door, and I gave Lydia one last pitiful glance.

"They shall be enchanted by you."

I accepted the footman's hand and stepped out of the carriage into the bright, afternoon sun.

"My darling girl!" Aunt Marianne threw her arms around me making me tense under the unexpected gesture. "How fortunate we are that your father has accepted Lady Eliza's invitation—even if he did so quite last minute." Her voice seemed unusually loud, and I was certain her words, though spoken to me, were intended for others to hear. "I never thought it possible. Yet here you stand." Aunt Marianne pulled back and briefly examined me with her discontented gaze before putting on a smile again and tucking her arm beneath mine to urge me forward.

She was an elegant-looking woman with light hair just beginning to show the color of aging. Though she and Mother were sisters, and had many similarities between their looks, their countenances differed drastically—being with my aunt always made me long for the warmth of Mother. Walking past the bowing, curtsying servants, Aunt Marianne led me to a handsome couple.

"Mr. Stanton. Lady Eliza Stanton. May I present my niece, Miss Blakeslee, daughter of Lord Blakeslee of Easton Manor?"

I curtsied. "Thank you for the invitation to join my aunt and cousins with you here at Timpton House." My voice quivered, but I continued, "I look forward to my visit and becoming better acquainted with your family." I tried to make my rehearsed words sound genuine.

"It is an honor to have you here, Miss Blakeslee," Mr. Stanton said with a bow and a welcoming smile that eased me slightly.

I turned to Lady Eliza, surprised to find her attentively inspecting me. She did not speak.

Feeling somewhat self-conscious, I looked back to Mr. Stanton expectantly.

"My dear, are we not thrilled to have Miss Blakeslee here with us?" Mr. Stanton prompted, aware that his wife had still not bestowed her welcome.

"Yes. Of course." She looked at her husband briefly before

looking back to me, forcing a smile as genuine as Aunt Marianne's. "Thrilled," she repeated his borrowed phrase as though trying to convince herself.

"Cousin!" The relief Hannah's voice brought was instantaneous, followed by my surprise at how tall she had grown since her last visit. She was now several inches taller than me and I found myself looking at our feet to be sure we stood on the same level. She wasn't as beautiful as her sister, but she had a certain beauty in her own right, which made me happy for her. "How exciting you should actually come. When Mother told me Lady Eliza had received your father's acceptance, I was utterly shocked and thought you would surely find a way to change his mind. But here you are. And how well you look. Helena," she said, glancing sideways, "don't you agree the years have been good to our dear Abigail? She would have been quite a hit in London I daresay!"

A perceptible tension between the sisters forced my gaze from them to the safety of my own hands. My introduction was turning out to be more tedious than I imagined as Helena begrudgingly stepped forward to greet me, displaying the same fixed smile her mother wore. She somehow looked more stunning than she had two years ago, though less approachable. Her blue eyes dazzled in the daylight and the sun on her hair gave the impression of a halo placed on her head. I smiled at the ridiculousness of the idea.

"How right you are, Hannah." Like her mother, Helena's trained tone provided any eager onlooker little difficulty in deciphering what was being said. "I had hoped the years would be kind to you, *cousin*. Without a female influence to guide you, I must confess I fretted unceasingly about your predicament, but I am pleased to see the worry I suffered was in vain."

"Thank you," I said, unsure if that was an appropriate response. In the silence that followed I knew I needed to deflect or risk her delving into the particulars of her unceasing worry, something I had no desire to hear, let alone have an audience present for. "And how beautiful you are, Helena. And you, Hannah." Both girls smiled tightly and tilted their heads almost in unison.

"We should proceed with the introductions," Aunt Marianne said, tightening her grip on my arm and pulling me sideways.

"How exhausted she looks, Mother! The poor thing." Helena's face held a false sympathy that nearly convinced me of her concern. "Can we not make the rest of the introductions to the party before dinner? Surely Abigail needs time to freshen up before she feels—presentable."

Aunt Marianne's eyes scanned me again needing no further prompting. "Of course, my dear. Such a compassionate girl, Helena—always thinking of others. Of course, we shall let her freshen up." She looked around to the group. "Pay no heed. We shall get her cleaned up and brought down forthwith to meet the rest of you. As long as our guest's needs are in line with our hostess', that is?" Aunt Marianne gave an imploring nod to Lady Eliza.

"Certainly, she may rest," Lady Eliza said. I dropped my gaze to avoid the watchful stares of so many strangers. Lydia had mentioned I looked ill, perhaps my presentation was something to be embarrassed about. "I will take her to her room myself, Mrs. Hanford."

"Such a gracious hostess. Follow Lady Eliza, Abigail, and we shall all be anxiously waiting to introduce you once you are put to rights."

As I followed Lady Eliza up the stairs to the front entrance, I refused to glance at the parting crowd of faces I did not know, relieved my bonnet covered the unmistakable shame on my face.

"Are we not to be introduced?" The voice sounded like an older gentleman who made no attempt to disguise his disappointment. "What was the point of gathering the party to meet her if we aren't to be introduced? Senseless game to be sure."

A woman's voice shushed the older man in quiet whispers and I hurriedly walked into Timpton House. What a welcome indeed!

THE ENTRANCE HALL displayed a set of elegant stone stairs along each side. I followed Lady Eliza up the right staircase and down a spacious corridor with high-arched ceilings. We walked in silence to the end before stopping at the last door. "Your cousins are just across from you, should you need them."

"Thank you, Lady Eliza," was all I could muster as she opened the door to let me inside. The room was bright, with three windows along the outer wall. The curtains were drawn back, and an alluring view of the lush grass and pond drew me to the window.

"How splendid!" I said, taking in the picturesque scene before me. "I have heard of the exquisite grounds here at Timpton House and I confess I am eagerly awaiting the pleasure of exploring them." I looked back at Lady Eliza to find her watchful eyes on me. She didn't look away, but she didn't respond to my declaration either. I forced myself to ignore her odd behavior and self-consciously removed my bonnet. Walking to lay it on the bed, I thought better of the careless act and resorted to holding it awkwardly in my hands. "I truly am thankful for your invitation and for such lovely accommodations," I said, glancing around the room again hoping to change the object of her focus. "I hope it wasn't too much trouble adding another guest to your party at such late notice."

Finally, seeming to register what I was saying Lady Eliza's

face softened. "As my husband said, it is an honor to have you here. If you shall need anything during your stay, don't hesitate to seek my assistance."

"Thank you."

She turned to leave but paused and gave me one last curious glance. "I shall send up your maid at once."

I curtsied, and she was gone.

CHAPTER 3

*A*s Lydia finished weaving a lace ribbon through my hair, a knock echoed through the room.

Before I had time to react, Hannah strode in.

"How beautiful you look, cousin!" Hannah's face was beaming with a mischievous grin, but she sounded sincere.

"I at least hope it is an improvement from my appearance earlier," I answered sheepishly. Lydia had picked a simple champagne-colored dress with an intricate white lace overlay on the bodice for me to wear to dinner. I disliked the lighter colors fashionable for unmarried women to wear, as they contrasted my olive skin and made me appear even darker than I was, but I had to admit the dress was so very elegant that I hardly felt self-conscious of my coloring at the moment. Lydia had also managed to place my obstinate hair in an elegant loose knot at the base of my neck, using the lace ribbon to help keep it in place.

"I hope you took no offense at Helena's welcome," Hannah said, watching me. "You know how she can be." The truth was I hardly did, I had only seen my cousins a few times throughout the last several years and it had been nearly two years since their last visit to Easton Manor for Mother's funeral. If it hadn't been for Hannah's letters, I felt I would hardly know either girl at all.

I stood up and faced her. "I'm certain any tension is just a matter of unfamiliarity; once we are reacquainted, we shall get on well enough."

Hannah scrunched up her nose and shook her head. "I don't think so. But let's not let that affect *our* friendship."

"Of course not," I said awkwardly, searching for a change of subject. "And look at you. I hardly knew you when I first saw you. How tall and elegant you've become."

Hannah beamed, held her gown out and twirled. "Mother says I am growing into myself and may not be a disappointment after all."

I cringed. "I'm sure you will not be."

"Abigail, you are too droll." Hannah giggled. "Shall we go down?"

I looked back to Lydia, willing her to make an excuse to postpone the inevitable introduction even a moment longer. Instead, she gave Hannah an enthusiastic nod of approval. Hannah needed no more convincing and eagerly led me from the safety of my room and Lydia's self-congratulating smile.

My heart quickened as we descended the stairs. By the time we neared the open drawing room doors, I had involuntarily stopped walking. I heard voices inside, but I made certain I remained just out of view.

"Are you unwell?" Hannah's eyes scanned my face.

"I..." I couldn't get a deep breath in. "I need a moment to catch my breath."

Hannah nodded as she drew near. "Forgive me. I'm still learning to shorten my lengthened stride."

In my breathlessness, I lacked the ability to explain that my episode had nothing to do with her walking pace. My heartbeat reverberated through me and I pressed my palm against my spinning head.

"Shall I fetch you refreshment?"

I shook my head, inwardly cursing my nervous tendencies. "I don't mean to delay you. Please, go on ahead and I shall be along soon."

Hannah glanced toward the door and back toward me. "I cannot abandon you, Abigail. Besides, I'm eager to see the others' reactions when you enter."

I inhaled slowly, attempting to regain some sort of composure when the sound of voices approaching nearly undid me. I straightened in my panic, like a doe before flight.

"Dreadfully inconvenient to be sure, but let's not fret just yet. We have ways to make things work to our advantage." A flash of relief rushed over me as Aunt Marianne and Helena stepped into view.

Both women paused when they realized they were not alone. Helena sent her mother an apprehensive glance, but Aunt Marianne had already taken a step toward me, an arm outstretched. "And here you are. What fortunate timing. I had hoped, when Hannah had said she wanted to see if you were ready to walk down, she would have had the sense to inform us of your answer." Out of the corner of my eye, Hannah glared at the rebuke. "But, seeing as we have overtaken you before your introduction, I shall overlook her error. Come, Abigail. The others have waited long enough."

Without a hesitation, she grabbed my arm and pulled me through the open doors of the drawing room. My chest tightened as the gaze of the room shifted in our direction. I did not care for strangers' eyes upon me, especially being dragged and pushed around at every occasion like a prodded child. Aunt

Marianne only dropped my arm when we approached Mr. Stanton and Lady Eliza on the far side of the room.

"I hope you were able to spend your afternoon resting, Miss Blakeslee," said Mr. Stanton cheerfully.

Though my head spun, and I had spent the last several hours worrying about my upcoming introduction, his kindness made me want to accommodate him. "I did, Mr. Stanton. Thank you."

"Well then, if you feel up to the task, I'm sure my wife would greatly enjoy introducing you to the rest of the party."

Lady Eliza stepped out from beside her husband. As I joined her, her eyes flashed over me and I became keenly aware she found no enjoyment in her obligation to present me to her guests. Despite our shared apprehension, one by one I met the guests of Timpton House. Mr. and Mrs. Hawkins with their youngest, and only unmarried daughter Miss Hawkins; Mr. and Mrs. Dowding with their two daughters Miss Dowding and Miss Emma Dowding; Sir Giles Wycliffe, both a neighbor and a gentleman; Mr. and Mrs. Ellis, the newly married daughter of Mr. Stanton and Lady Eliza and her husband; and another Mr. Stanton, dearly referred to as Uncle Stanton who resided at Timpton with the family. I smiled at each person dutifully and offered rehearsed greetings, struggling against the unrelenting desire to cross my arms safely around myself.

"And lastly, Miss Blakeslee, this is our eldest son, Mr. Edwin Stanton."

His light eyes lifted from his brief bow with such intensity it forced my gaze to the floor. Although a handsome man, Mr. Edwin Stanton's serious demeanor diluted his admirable features and left me feeling unsettled.

I gave a quick curtsy. "Mr. Stanton."

Lady Eliza looked between her son, Helena, who had claimed a place at his side, and me. "I shall leave you young people to get better acquainted. But, Edwin dear, perhaps you could escort Miss Blakeslee into dinner as well as Miss Hanford? I fear until your friends arrive tomorrow from London, the gentlemen are quite outnumbered." Without waiting for a response, she turned and walked back to her husband's side.

"I do not recall seeing you this Season in London, Miss Blakeslee," Mr. Edwin Stanton's tone erred on the verge of disinterested small talk, which I abhorred almost as much as the topic of conversation he had chosen.

"I did not attend," I answered.

"Were you not yet old enough?"

Helena giggled. "Mr. Stanton! Do not tease her so, she is certainly old enough, a year older than my own sister, Hannah. How cruel you are to jest about her age. You well know, I'm sure, no lady wants to be assumed older than her age; but the same should be said of a lady being assumed younger. Cousin, count it a blessing to look so young. I daresay one day someone will confuse you as a debutante when you have children of your own. Cruel Mr. Stanton, teasing my dear Abigail."

"I assure you I did not say it in jest." He spoke to Helena, but his eyes remained on me. The similarity between his mother's attentive behavior and his own was instantaneously unnerving.

"What a thing to admit!" Helena chirped, before I had a moment to respond. "And after I tried to alleviate the insult. Surely, Mr. Stanton, you must learn to accept my social cues without question. I shall never lead you astray."

I forced back a laugh at Helena's blatant suggestion. Nothing, including the overt hint of my cousin's marital hopes, could tempt a smile from me while I was under the critical gaze of Mr. Edwin Stanton.

His attention did not shift. "What kept you from attending then, if not age, Miss Blakeslee? Desire? Family matters?"

My eyes widened at the impertinence. What kind of man

asks such direct questions to a lady he just met? An unladylike word came to my mind, but I did not betray Father's admonition by using it.

"Do not press her so, Mr. Stanton." Helena was once again quicker to respond. "Look at her shock. Can't you see she has no desire to tell you? Poor dear." Helena giggled and touched his arm. "Besides, what care is it to you what her reasons were?"

"I'm assessing her character, Miss Hanford. Is that not what is supposed to transpire when a gentleman first meets a lady?"

"I daresay! What a notion! Abigail, do excuse Mr. Stanton, his manners are quite abrupt tonight. How droll you are indeed, Mr. Stanton." Helena looked giddy with excitement as her blue eyes flashed back and forth between us. "Do you truly know nothing about winning the good impressions of a lady?"

"I am only trying to weigh in on whether Miss Blakeslee's good impression is worth obtaining."

My irritation at this disagreeable exchange heightened, and I could no longer hold my tongue. "I assure you, Mr. Stanton," I said, matching his fervent gaze, "you should not waste your time on such unnecessary deliberations; especially when whatever conclusion you may come to has been rendered obsolete."

Mr. Stanton's brow lifted though his eyes narrowed. "Obsolete?"

"Surely you are capable of understanding first impressions are reached by both parties, allowing each an opportunity to decide whether they desire to further an acquaintance." I kept my voice light, as though I suffered no hurt at his insult. "Consequently, while you have been wasting your time determining the worth of obtaining my good impression, I have effortlessly come to my own opinion of you."

"Is that so?"

"Indeed, Mr. Stanton. And I must say I am impressed."

His gaze bore into me. "And why is that, Miss Blakeslee?"

I felt unusually bold as my response clarified within. "It is no easy feat for a gentleman to fail at achieving my good opinion—yet you have accomplished it skillfully in one brief conversation. And, as your quick intellect may now perceive, there is no need to think on it further—my opinion is set and has deemed your opinion obsolete."

A muscle in his jaw flexed, but the rushing sensation in my head left little room to relish in my triumph. "I see I have made quite the impression on you," he said curtly.

I offered an affirmative nod. "I fear you have."

His intense eyes held mine, searching. Before he pulled any of the secrets from my soul, I willed myself to look away, past the gaping mouth of Helena and across the room to the friendly eyes of Hannah on Sir Wycliffe. My head spun, and I could hardly believe I had spoken so boldly to a gentleman, let alone one to whom I had only just been introduced. But surely, he and his ill temper had entirely deserved it.

I allowed my thoughts to drown out the endless giggles of Helena that had flooded into the silence. It wasn't until Mr. Edwin Stanton put out his arm for me to take that I realized dinner had been announced. Glaring ahead I placed my hand as lightly as possible in the crease of his elbow as we followed Mr. Stanton and Lady Eliza into the dining room.

Mr. Edwin Stanton didn't speak, but I felt him watching me out of the corner of his eyes as he escorted me to my place at the large, rectangular table. I was relieved to find my seat a comfortable distance from him and breathed easier with his removal. He had been seated between Helena and one of the Miss Dowdings toward the other side of the table, and I was safely positioned between Miss Hawkins and Uncle Stanton. Across from me sat Sir Wycliffe and next to him sat Hannah. She smiled at me, and I was grateful to be near enough to talk with her when the occasion permitted.

It was several minutes into the first course that Uncle Stanton leaned toward me. "By whom do I have the privilege of sitting this evening?"

"Miss Blakeslee, sir." I offered, perplexed how he had forgotten our introduction already. "We met just now in the drawing room."

"Of course. Miss Blakeslee. Such a pretty sounding girl. And I have heard you are quite exquisite though I wish I could see you for myself."

It was only then I noticed the cloudiness of his eyes. "Forgive me, sir. I did not realize you—" the words to finish seemed too harsh to speak.

"That I am blind?" He chuckled. "I'm flattered you took so long to realize. Was it my handsome face that made you overlook the defect or the confident way I hold myself?"

I was convinced it was the darkness of the drawing room, but I had no intention of saying so. "I believe it was both, sir."

He chuckled again and reached a hand toward me. Placing my hand atop his, I gave it a gentle squeeze which he affectionately returned.

After some general small talk around the table, a few failed attempts to entreat Miss Hawkins into conversation, and seeing the focused regard Sir Wycliffe paid to Hannah, I gladly directed my attention to Uncle Stanton. There was something about his openness that endeared him to me immediately.

"And, if you don't mind me asking, Mr. Stanton—"

"My friends and relations call me Uncle, and, if you find no offense in being placed amongst that group, I must insist you do also."

"I would be honored, Uncle."

"And I suppose by how you began to phrase your question, you were curious how I lost my eyesight?"

Now that he said it aloud it sounded alarmingly impolite, and I felt relieved he couldn't witness the color that filled my cheeks. I still needed to learn to not let my curiosity take precedence to propriety. "I—well, I—" I stumbled over my words, endeavoring to think of another question to propose.

"Truly, I don't mind," he said, sensing my hesitation. "But I fear there is little to tell. A few years ago, I began having problems with my vision. Things grew dark at the edges and gradually expanded toward the center until all I now have is a general sense of light and dark. I sought the best physician in London, who assured me there was nothing to be done. So, I have resigned myself to enjoying the world through my other senses."

I smiled. "That is a commendable outlook on such a hardship."

"As I see it, I only had two choices—to be bitter or to not. I simply chose the more enjoyable of the two. Though I will admit, I often wish I could create a more romantic story surrounding it all. You see, I have a very dull imagination—" he hesitated, "not that I care to mislead anyone, but the truth is hardly worthy of attention."

"I don't credit myself with much creativity, but perhaps both our minds together might come to a tale worth sharing —or, in the least, to entertain ourselves?"

"Miss Blakeslee, that is a capital idea!"

"Well then, let us think. The grandest stories are always believable," I paused, trying to determine an appropriate setting. "You were just telling me of your time in the British Fleet." He nodded. "It would be fitting, and perfectly romantic, if your tale occurred at sea. Perhaps a heroic rescue?"

One side of his mouth lifted. "I daresay I prefer to play the hero."

"And nothing is as heroic as rescuing a damsel in distress, do you not agree?"

"I most certainly do."

I couldn't resist grinning as a story surfaced in my mind. "I believe it must occur at night, for the mystery of things is always greater at night. You are walking the deck as Captains do, on watch for pirates or smugglers, when you hear the cry of a woman. You follow the sound to the starboard side of the ship and search the water, wondering who could be in such a state of anguish. The water is dark, with only an occasional reflection of light from the moon dancing off the waves. It would be impossible for someone to be out there, but then—" I nearly giggled at the intensity of Uncle Stanton's concentration.

"Well, what was it I saw?" he asked eagerly.

"A woman, of course."

"In the sea?"

"In the sea! And the most beautiful woman you have ever laid eyes on. But what was most peculiar was how her cry transformed to a song—an entrancing melody that wrapped around you, pulling you toward her."

"But she is in the water? How is she rescued?"

"You are a hero, Uncle. You must jump in to save her!" He lifted his eyebrows in surprise, and I covered my mouth stifling a laugh. "Don't look so startled at the notion, I daresay if it were a real occurrence you wouldn't hesitate a moment. And our story must be accurate—that is why I came to this conclusion."

His face beamed with pride. "I've always had a propensity for acting brashly around beautiful women."

"And so, this is no different. And after you jump into the freezing water, as extremes make the account more exciting, you swim to where you expect her to be but find nothing. You search frantically, diving under the water and yelling for her —for now that you have seen her you will save her or die in the attempt. But you grow tired and, just as your strength is exhausted and you begin to sink, you are pulled from the sea."

"And how should I be saved?"

"A shipmate would be a reasonable rescuer. Possibly a fellow watchman or someone who heard your distress as you searched?" I received a reassuring nod. "When they got you on deck, although you had taken in much water, your only concern was for the woman. 'Woman?' they'd say, 'There was no woman in the water.' Had they not heard the cry or the mesmerizing song? Were they not lucky enough to behold the enchanting face? They'd surely blame it on your longing imagination—though we know how dull it is—or likely a bad meal. And I fear she would forever be a mystery to you, plaguing your very existence— the image of this siren etched in your mind and her song on your heart. And your eyes would ultimately grow dim because nothing in this world could compare with the splendor you once beheld."

A satisfied smile lit his face and my own expression soon mirrored his.

"You have given me quite a story, Miss Blakeslee; yet I am certain I shall never tell it as well. I'd ask you to transcribe it, so I might memorize it," he chuckled, "but that would do little good as I'm no longer able to read."

His laugh was contagious, and I easily joined him. Glancing around to make sure no one had observed my casual behavior, my eyes locked with Mr. Edwin Stanton. His stern look took the smile from my lips and drove my gaze to my plate.

"What is it, Miss Blakeslee?" Uncle Stanton asked gently.

I marveled at his discernment, most people with perfect eyesight would fail to perceive what he did. "I believe I have offended your great nephew with my behavior."

"And how did you come to that conclusion?"

"The intensity of his stare—as though he is condemning me from across the table."

"Many emotions can cause intensity, Miss Blakeslee. But, if he is displeased, let me ease your mind—you can hardly be the cause. These last few years he has had no difficulty finding things to aggravate him. Perhaps it is his way of being hospitable—ensuring he treats us all equally."

"Perhaps," I said, taking comfort in the idea his ill temper hadn't began with my arrival. Looking back toward the other side of the table our eyes met again, but this time he redirected his attention to the smiling face of Helena.

~

AFTER DINNER HAD FINISHED, the exhaustion from the day's travels and emotions overwhelmed me. I found Aunt Marianne to ask if she thought it acceptable for me to retire early.

"It is your first night here. Surely you do not wish the others to think you impolite? Particularly when the men do not stay long taking port."

"Mother, look at the poor dear." Helena approached, apparently having overheard our conversation and feeling inclined to aid me in my request, though I doubted her reasoning was my best interest. "She needs her rest. We would not want Uncle Miles to think us negligent of Abigail's wishes."

Aunt Marianne seemed hesitant to accept Helena's reasoning, her gaze flickering to where Lady Eliza stood talking with several ladies. "I do not wish her to be regarded as unsociable, it will reflect poorly on us," she whispered to Helena, as though I was not present.

"Mother, tomorrow shall be a full day with Mr. Stanton's friends arriving and I'd hate for her to appear as haggard from exhaustion as she did today. We need her to be rested and more amiable, for someone must hold the interest of the new gentlemen, and I daresay," she brought her voice to a low whisper I could barely overhear, "the other ladies are left wanting in their abilities to do so." Aunt Marianne nodded in agreement. "You know how I hope to keep Mr. Stanton's attention for myself, to ensure our courtship continues to progress as intended." Helena's last words dragged as her bottom lip rose in a perfected pout.

"It is decided, Abigail." Aunt Marianne grabbed my arm and began pulling me to where the other women stood. "We shall appeal to Lady Eliza and send you to bed directly upon her approval."

"Thank you," I said sincerely.

~

IT WASN'T long before I was in my room, relieved to be alone in Lydia's company. "Was it truly as terrible as you feared?" she asked, unpinning my hair.

"I admit it was not, though I would have found little enjoyment without Uncle Stanton. I'm certain you would be extremely fond of him, Lydia."

"And what of the heir, Mr. Stanton? I hear he is most handsome."

"Mr. Stanton?" I scoffed. "Where did you hear such a thing?"

"It seems quite the consensus below stairs."

"Perhaps it's one of the job requirements—to believe such nonsense," I said wryly.

"So, he is not?"

I thought about his large stature, strong jaw and the intensity in his light eyes. "Striking perhaps, but handsome seems too pleasant a description."

"Well, I suppose it's no matter, considering he is spoken for. Perhaps the two gentlemen arriving tomorrow will be worth knowing."

"If they are friends with Mr. Edwin Stanton, I doubt they will be worth knowing."

Lydia shot me a look of disbelief but said nothing.

"You would not scold me if you had met him, he is prideful and judgmental—"

"I did not scold you," she corrected as she helped me out of my gown.

Perhaps she had not verbally scolded me, but her face showed her disappointment. "He truly is horrible, Lydia," I said, frustrated that she judged me without ever meeting the man she had chosen to defend.

She stopped and looked at me, the way I supposed an older sister would, with equal amounts of love and correction. "There's more to a person than what one first sees. You understand that better than anyone. It seems—" she paused choosing her next words carefully, "unusual for you to so quickly judge someone, to sum up their character on one brief encounter."

I wanted to defend myself, to make her see why he had lost my good opinion, but I couldn't when I knew how it felt to be judged unfairly. I suddenly had an overwhelming desire to be home with Father and Laurence.

Lydia curled a piece of my hair around her finger. "I know this is hard for you and I'm sure you ache for home, but don't close your heart to everyone outside Easton Manor." She spoke tenderly, discerning my thoughts perfectly. "There's always good, sometimes you just need to search a little harder for it."

Tears welled up in my eyes and I nodded, knowing that if I tried to speak, I would no longer be able to control them.

"I will leave you to get some rest." Lydia turned from me but hesitated before looking back with her reassuring smile. "Don't fret, Abee, tomorrow is a new day."

I listened to the door shut and her footsteps disappear down the corridor until silence surrounded me. I pushed the thought of home from my mind, knowing it would do me no good, and I climbed into bed.

CHAPTER 4

A rapping noise startled me awake. The sunlight crept in through the sides of the curtains illuminating the vaguely familiar room. I sat up and looked around, reorienting myself to where I was. Timpton House. A heavy sigh escaped as a second knock beckoned me. I threw the covers off my legs and walked toward the door. "Who is it?" I whispered through the crack.

"Helena."

I groaned inwardly before opening the door a slit to glance out. There stood Helena, looking perfect in her white day dress; her shiny blond hair already up with ringlets framing her face. Her eyes shifted over my disheveled appearance. "Surely you are not just waking?"

"Indeed, I am." I answered, wondering if my tone sounded sufficiently contrite.

She huffed. "Well, never mind. Have your maid attend to you at once. Mr. Stanton's friends are expected to arrive by ten. We need to be fit to greet them."

"What is the time?"

"Nearly eight!"

"Nearly eight?" My surprise came at how long I had slept, not the hour. I had plenty of time to be ready, eat breakfast, and hopefully enjoy a quick stroll through the gardens. "I will be down shortly."

"And please remember to be civil today. We must make a favorable impression on Mr. Stanton's friends. I hate to be the one to remind you, but your behavior is reflected on to us—whether for good or *ill*."

I narrowed my eyes. "Have I done something to make you question my behavior?"

"You do realize how unkindly you treated poor Mr. Stanton at your introduction."

My jaw dropped at her declaration. "My treatment of him was poor?"

"Telling him he had lost your good opinion—then proceeding to ignore him the remainder of our conversation! You put him in quite a bothersome mood for the rest of the night. I had to keep making apologies for your lack of manners. Though I do believe it was helpful to my general scheme," she said, more to herself than me. "An opportunity to reassure him what an exceptional gentleman he is—and in that I will forgive you your folly. But," her eyes refocused on mine with intensity, "you shall have to endeavor to be more pleasant from now on."

I didn't know how to react. How could anyone find fault with my conduct when it was weighed against Edwin Stanton's? "I—" I repressed all the things I wanted to say in defense of myself, knowing she would not be persuaded otherwise. "I will try harder to not embarrass you, Helena."

A hint of pity accompanied her smirk. "It must be hard learning the expectations of the upper echelon, particularly in the absence of my aunt. Therefore, I hope you do not take offense when I let you know when you err. I act solely out of compassion for your plight." Her smirk lifted into a self-satis-

37

fied smile before she shooed me dismissively. "Now, hurry along."

Before I had time to express my insincere gratitude, she had gone. I shut the door and rested my forehead on it, feeling no desire to 'hurry along' to the events of the day. How pitiful I must be. Aunt Marianne's constant prodding, Lady Eliza's watchful gaze, Edwin Stanton's snide comments, and now Helena's accusations and pity. I was not cut out to be a lady; it simply wasn't in my blood.

I PROLONGED LEAVING my room until Lydia practically pushed me from it. As I neared the dining room, I heard the giggling voice of Helena and decided fresh air seemed more appealing than breakfast. Putting on the bonnet I had brought, I slipped through the front door, not knowing how else to access the grounds. I walked around to the back of the house, overcome with excitement as the gardens came into view. I knew the people at Timpton House would never be as dear to me as those at Easton Manor, but I could not deny the gardens here were superior to our own, though I had no intention of saying so.

A large stretch of grass flowed into a central garden of manicured bushes and roses dispersed with Romanesque statues. However, it wasn't this that caught my eye, but the distinguishable paths that emerged among the bordering hedge. Each path looked unique, and I deliberated which I should choose. Deciding to start with the closest, I took the first path on the right.

The plants were intentionally overgrown, leaving only a small part of the cobblestones beneath my feet visible. Flowers of different varieties and sizes were as pleasing to my senses as the fragrance that hung in the air. Trees shot up from behind, offering periodic shade and producing an embracing effect. A sense of wonder consumed me. It was as though I had entered a well-manicured, enchanted woodland. I closed my eyes, allowing the sunshine on my body to penetrate through me.

"Good morning, Miss Blakeslee."

I startled at the voice and opened my eyes to find the watchful gaze of Mr. Edwin Stanton on me.

"Good morning, Mr. Stanton," I said, trying to remove the sound of displeasure from my voice. He stood so near that the path no longer embraced me, but closed around me uncomfortably, pushing me toward him. How had I not heard his approach? I stepped backwards, but it achieved little as I stared up at his intense, penetrating eyes.

Neither of us spoke and I questioned how long we would stand in silence when Lydia's admonition pressed upon me. It seemed no easy feat to discover goodness in this vexing man, but the attempt, regardless if he deserved it, would at least disrupt our impasse. "The gardens are lovely here at Timpton," I said, attempting to sound amenable. "I don't believe I have seen anything to compare." It wasn't until I spoke the words that I realized I had given the very compliment I had intended to withhold, and I scolded myself silently for the lapse in judgment.

"And are you much traveled to offer such a comparison?"

"I am not," I answered, taken aback at his discourteous question. "I have hardly been ten miles outside Easton Manor in years."

He nodded at my acknowledgment, and I took another step back, planning to make a hasty escape. But something inside me refused to retreat, and instead I moved two steps forward. "I only meant to be civil in bestowing such an unfounded compliment, I urge you to not take offense at something offered in kindness."

"Kindness?" he scoffed. The brief glint of amusement in his eyes did little to lessen the intensity of his scowl.

I exhaled, steadying my trembling hands by interlocking them behind my back. "I had thought since—." I couldn't continue. I couldn't pretend. Contrary to what Lydia thought, there was no good in this unreceptive man, at least not any he would allow me to find. "Never mind, Mr. Stanton. I believe it was a vain notion and I will not make such a mistake again. Please excuse me." Turning, I began my swift retreat toward the house.

Footsteps pursued me, and I hesitantly spun and looked toward him expectantly.

He stopped a few steps before reaching me. "Miss Blakeslee, I planned to seek you out last night, but you retired far too early to render that a possibility." Despite the subtle correction he offered, the tinge of contrition in his tone piqued my interest. Perhaps he intended to offer an apology after all.

"I wanted to ask—" He hesitated.

Suddenly out of patience with his antics and his pride, I decided to aid him with the unmanageable task. "For my forgiveness?"

His eyebrow lifted. "Forgiveness?"

My face flushed with color. "Were you not going to apologize for your poor behavior at our introduction?"

"My poor behavior?" He glowered at me. "I was trying to entreat you in polite conversation, Miss Blakeslee. It was you who gave offense at our introduction, first by your words and then by your manners."

"Insufferable man!" I exclaimed before I found the discipline to stop myself.

"And now a third offense," he said with the same stern look upon his face, though the amusement returned to his eyes more forcibly than before.

I didn't know what to say and resorted to staring at him in disbelief.

"I was trying to ask if you would be riding with us during

your stay at Timpton. We ride in the morning before break-fast. I am aware you did not bring a horse, so you are welcome to one of our mares if you desire." His invitation was one of formal duty and I had no desire to go where I was not wanted, especially if he would be there.

"I thank you, but I do not ride."

"You do not ride?"

I shook my head. "That is what I have just now told you. Is it not?"

"Such an unusual lady you are, Miss Blakeslee: forgoing the Season, giving offense to gentlemen you hardly know, and claiming you do not ride. I'd not be astonished to discover you are disinclined musically, you despise both painting and embroidery, and you dread the idea of a ball."

I lifted my chin to meet his questioning glare. "You are wrong, Mr. Stanton. I do enjoy painting."

His eyes narrowed as he held my gaze, and I was confident he couldn't decide what to make of me.

Determining he would have to analyze on his own, I gave a brief curtsy. "It is time I headed back to the house." I turned quickly from him and hurried away, relieved I didn't hear the thud of footsteps pursuing me.

I MADE my way to the central garden. I had intended to head back to the house directly, but my hands still shook from the encounter with Edwin Stanton and I needed time to calm myself before rejoining the others. I quickly selected another path and welcomed the instantaneous refuge it provided. It wasn't long before I found myself once again basking in the loveliness of my surroundings, my frustrations dissolving into the beauty.

Large trellises engulfed in wisteria enclosed the pathway and I wondered if the garden truly was enchanted. I longed to stay hidden away among the flowers until I could return to Easton Manor, but I had already delayed too long, and propriety called me to return. Reassuring myself I would be back for another visit soon, I headed for the house.

As I turned the corner from the gardens, I froze mid-step. Edwin Stanton and three gentlemen were headed from the stables to the house.

"Drats!" I whispered.

The men were engrossed in conversation and I was hopeful I would go unnoticed if I remained still. I held my breath and stood as motionless as I could on an unbalanced foot placement. My weight shifted sideways under the fluctuating gravel and I carefully corrected my footing to prevent myself from falling.

The movement drew the attention of one of the gentlemen and he motioned for the others to stop. I exhaled in exasperation. It was too late to turn around, so I walked toward the group of gentlemen as any trained lady would have done— had she allowed herself into such a predicament in the first place.

As I neared, the three friends of Edwin Stanton removed their hats. Looking at Mr. Stanton for an introduction I noticed the tightness of his jaw and wondered what news his friends had brought that irked him so.

"Miss Blakeslee, let me introduce you. These are my friends: Mr. Ross Gale and Mr. Luke Kingman, and this is Mr. Kingman's cousin, Lord Ramsby. Gentlemen this is one of my mother's guests, Miss Blakeslee… daughter of Lord Blakeslee of Easton Manor."

Amused at his desire to separate himself so fully from me, I gave the strangers a curtsy as they returned it with a bow.

Lord Ramsby stepped forward and offered me his arm. "May I have the pleasure of escorting you inside, Miss Blakeslee? The ground looks somewhat precarious, and I'd never forgive myself if you were to trip."

I don't know why my instinct was to look at Edwin Stanton for approval, for his face showed no sign of it. Turning my attention back to the handsome newcomer I reached out and placed my gloved hand on the crease of his elbow. "Thank you, Lord Ramsby. That is most generous of you."

As we preceded the others to the front of the house, Lord Ramsby and I spoke of the lovely gardens at Timpton and I encouraged him to not delay his discovery of them.

"It sounds as though you are already familiar with them—"

"Only just, you found me on my way back to the house from my first encounter, but I will admit it was most satisfying."

"Well, as I have not seen them, you are quite the expert between us, so I must insist you show me all they have to offer —the best paths and secret places you have no doubt discovered."

I blushed at his mention of secret places. "Unfortunately, I have found no such places and have only walked down two paths. There are several more to explore."

"Then we shall explore together."

Looking up to find him smiling roguishly at me, I hastily looked back in the direction we were walking. He chuckled, apparently amused at my reaction.

"Come, Miss Blakeslee, you act as though I am the first man to hint at such a thing."

"Perhaps you are." I said, without looking at him.

I worried at my admission as we walked in silence. Certainly, a well-trained lady wouldn't offer such an acknowledgment. Would he suppose there was something wrong with me? Why I had been hidden away at Easton Manor?

We had almost reached the stairs of the front entrance when Lord Ramsby stopped and looked at me. "I find it nearly impossible to believe other men have not desired to know you better; but, if that is the case, I shall do my best to show you how a proper gentleman behaves." He grabbed my hand from his arm and brought it to his lips, studying me with his dark eyes.

My heart reverberated through me as I took my hand back from his perfect, smiling lips. Mr. Stanton and his friends walked up behind us and I felt my face warm, knowing what they had just observed. The two gentlemen hardly seemed to notice the exchange, but Mr. Stanton looked at me with an accusing glare.

"Let's not delay," his voice was harsh. "The other guests are waiting for us in the drawing room."

Edwin Stanton abruptly stepped between Lord Ramsby and me as he made his way to the stairs. His action did not go unnoticed, and I glimpsed the other two gentlemen share a questioning glance before following him up the stairs. Shooting me a sideways smirk, Lord Ramsby extended his arm to escort me inside. Grateful for at least one man who knew how to act a gentleman, we ascended the stairs and made our way to the others.

Not wanting to draw any more attention to myself than was necessary, I dropped my hand from Lord Ramsby's arm before we entered the room. He sent me a curious glance, but I focused my gaze straight ahead and walked in before him. I was pleased at how confidently I managed it, having been petrified yesterday of accomplishing the very same task.

Edwin Stanton had approached his mother and father to present his friends, allowing me to slip in unnoticed.

"It is delightful to see you again, Mr. Gale, Mr. Kingman." Lady Eliza looked between the two men and I thought how beautiful she was without her analytical gaze. "And it is very kind of you to join our party. I fear until your arrival the ladies quite outnumbered the gentlemen."

"It is our pleasure to come to your aid," Mr. Kingman said enthusiastically. "And on that topic, I have a request of you, though I fear I am being rather impertinent." Mr. Stanton gave a nod of permission for Mr. Kingman to continue. "I have brought my cousin along, Lord Ramsby of Handsbury Castle. He came to London straight off his tour, just as I was getting ready to depart for Timpton House. Not wanting to delay my trip, but having a great desire to keep his company, I requested he should come along. I regret I did not even have time to send word. Please forgive me, I do hope I wasn't too much in error extending the invitation to include him."

Lady Eliza leaned sideways glancing in our direction. Her eyes narrowed momentarily before she shifted her attention to her son's rigid stance.

"Of course, he is welcome," the voice of Mr. Stanton was loud enough for Lord Ramsby to hear. "I'm certain he shall add much excitement to our party. Welcome to Timpton, Lord Ramsby." Lady Eliza nodded to him in acceptance of her husband's welcome, though her eyes were full of apprehension. But it was Edwin Stanton's reaction that puzzled me most. Not once had he turned to acknowledge his guest during his parents' welcome. He kept his back to Lord Ramsby, and I wondered why he had chosen to amplify his mother's less hospitable example rather than follow the kindheartedness of his father.

A movement behind me forced my attention from the Stantons and I turned my head to find Lord Ramsby stepping sideways to offer a courteous bow to his obliging hosts. I hadn't realized how closely he had been standing and I felt unsettled at how others would view our proximity.

"My cousin assured me you were people of great hospitality," he said. I discreetly took a few steps from him, feigning interest in a nearby flower arrangement. "And I very much look forward to becoming better acquainted with your family and *guests.*"

I glanced back toward him, alarmed to find him staring at me, a knowing smile on his lips. I promptly returned my gaze to the Stantons, finding little success in commanding the warmth in my face to not color my cheeks.

The group's attention shifted again to the Stantons as mine had, allowing Lord Ramsby the opportunity to take a few unnoticed steps toward me. "And where is Easton Manor located, Miss Blakeslee?"

"Only a few hours by carriage from here, right outside Burrowsly."

"I have heard that is a lovely area of the country," Lord Ramsby responded. "Handsbury Castle is nearly two days' travel from here. Though I did first go to London so I'm not sure if I took the most direct route."

I nodded as he continued speaking of Handsbury Castle. I endeavored to pay attention, but my gaze kept falling toward the Stantons. Lady Eliza seemed preoccupied as she conversed with Mr. Kingman and Mr. Gale. Her worried expression repeatedly turned to her son, and she once grabbed his hand in motherly affection. I wondered again at what news he must have received and knew his mother longed to ask him the same.

"Do you always invoke such attention?" Lord Ramsby's question brought my eyes back to him.

"I must confess, I do not know your meaning."

"Surely you have noticed how the other guests watch you?"

I hesitantly scanned the room. Though the rest of the party was engaged in conversation, curious glances in our direction made their choice of topic unnervingly obvious.

"It is not me who has drawn their captivation, Lord Ramsby." I hoped I was correct in my assessment as I turned toward him. "I am certain it is you that has captured their attention.

There are many hopeful parents and eligible ladies here among the party."

"None as ravishing as you." I forced my eyes from his teasing smile and he chuckled. "Well, I best join the others for introductions to ensure their curiosity will be placated. But I shall find you the instant I am released of my duty."

"Do not rush on my account, Lord Ramsby," I said, looking back toward him.

He gave me another charming smile and bowed before walking toward the Stantons. I allowed my gaze to follow him, analyzing his handsome features. His thick eyebrows added a pleasant framing to his dark eyes. He was nearly as dark as me in coloring, and it made me resent Society's hypocritical stances on beauty. Lord Ramsby could easily be viewed as the most attractive man in the room, his tanned skin and dark features only adding to the conclusion. But for me, my dark skin would never be viewed as a compliment to my looks, especially when it was accompanied by dark hair and brown eyes. Father always told me I was a rare beauty, but I had come to realize 'rare' simply meant unusual, and I was certain no one in Society desired unusual when they were surrounded by ladies who defined societal perfection, like Helena.

Suddenly aware how my watchful behavior of Lord Ramsby could be interpreted, I scanned the room to locate Uncle Stanton. I located him sitting in a chair on the other side of the room. I made my way to him, leaning down and placing my hand on his. Before I made my greetings, his face brightened. "Miss Blakeslee, I have been longing for your company."

I smiled at his recognition and his desire for my company. "And I yours, Uncle."

"Tell me about the gentlemen. I do recall Mr. Ross Gale, an old school mate of Edwin's, but I don't recollect a Mr. Kingman or his cousin Lord Ramsby."

"To be honest, I know little of them."

"Of course," he said, sounding disappointed.

I hated to see him disheartened, even slightly, so I leaned in closer. "I'd be happy to describe the scene for you, if you wish."

Smiling again, Uncle Stanton nodded his head.

I squatted next to his chair, ensuring I was near enough to prevent my voice from carrying. "Mr. Ross Gale looks young, though if he is Mr. Stanton's school friend as you say, he must be older than I assumed. He is a head shorter than your great nephew and not nearly as broad, but he has a kind face. He seems quieter than his friends, apart from Mr. Stanton that is, and has an amusing tendency to bow at odd times." I laughed as I watched him make several small bowing motions to the Dowdings. "Mr. Luke Kingman is taller and thin. He has light hair, light eyes and a ruddy complexion. He is quite pleased with everything around him and as you heard, speaks quite excitedly."

"Is he a handsome fellow?"

"I fear he is rather plain, but I don't count it against him. My father is plain in appearance but he's the best man I know."

"I have heard of your father, Lord Blakeslee, and only the best I assure you. No wonder his daughter is such an extraordinary young woman. But you must take after your mother in appearance then, for I have been told you are an exceptional beauty."

I desired to ask him who had said such a thing, but I did not betray my better judgment by appeasing my curiosity. "I believe people find little resemblance between us." I instantly realized it wasn't a topic I wished to discuss, and I needed to redirect the conversation. "Mr. Kingman seems pleased to see your great niece, perhaps they know each other?"

"Perhaps. Though I can't seem to keep all the young people straight." His brow wrinkled. "But I will not be hard on myself, for they are simply names I overhear in passing conversations. Seldom am I granted such a pleasant companion who will relay what is happening before me."

I looked at Uncle Stanton and my heart swelled for the dear man and the hardship he was called to bear.

He patted my hand reassuringly. "Don't suppose I consider myself neglected by any means, Miss Blakeslee. The Stantons willingly play narrator for their aged uncle when their hosting responsibilities allow it."

"I'm glad of it," I said, squeezing his hand.

"And what of the last gentleman? Lord Ramsby was it?" Uncle Stanton went rigid, as though he had more interest in this guest than the others.

"You are correct. He, I'd venture, would be called handsome."

"Do *you* not think him so?"

"I suppose." Heat flushed over me at my admission. "But I'm certain he will quickly be riveted with one of the other ladies once he is introduced, if he is free to do so at all, so I need not concern myself with what I think of him."

"You must absolutely decide what you think of him. It is dangerous to be caught unprepared. You see, it's difficult to betray yourself if you have considered possible outcomes and determined a plan of action." I grinned at his strategic advice from his life as a Naval Officer. "Besides, you are unquestionably the superior choice."

I smiled at the realization that my biggest admirer was a blind-gentleman decades older than me. "I do believe you are trying to flatter me with your nonsensical conclusions, Uncle," I said lightheartedly.

"Humble too."

I laughed. "Honest."

I had been too involved in our conversation to notice the group of new comers, as well as Lady Eliza and Edwin Stanton, standing in front of us. I quickly realized that squatting near Uncle Stanton's chair was not the most ladylike position, so I released his hand and rose to my feet. Mr. Edwin Stanton looked at me with a furrowed brow and I dropped my gaze.

Lady Eliza cleared her throat. "You mentioned you have already met Lady Blakeslee." I lifted my eyes to smiling faces and nods. "Uncle, this is Mr. Ross Gale, Mr. Luke Kingman, and Lord Ramsby. Gentlemen this is Uncle Stanton—though I believe you are already acquainted with him, Ross?" She turned toward the men as Ross bowed again in the direction of Uncle Stanton.

"Certainly, Lady Eliza. How do you do, Uncle Stanton?" Ross bowed again.

Mr. Stanton looked at his mother as though questioning whether he should explain the extent of his Uncle's vision loss, but the subtle shake of her head told him to approach the topic later, in private.

"I'm well," Uncle Stanton replied. "Quite well, in fact. Thank you."

"I wouldn't doubt it, Uncle Stanton." The term of endearment sounded strange on Lord Ramsby's lips. "With Miss Blakeslee as company, who could not be well?"

"Great point, sir, and I must compliment you on your exceptional judgment," Uncle Stanton said, looking in my direction as though he hoped to witness my response.

After a thorough blushing, I regained my ability for rational speech. "Be assured, Lord Ramsby, it is I who am fortunate for the delightful company of Uncle Stanton." My eyes moved from Lord Ramsby to Edwin Stanton as I spoke. "He is a most amiable gentleman and a pleasure to be with." Edwin winced at my words as though I had deliberately insulted him. Had that been my purpose?

As if to dissipate the awkwardness, Lady Eliza turned from us and cleared her throat again. "Now that our entire party is here and introduced," her voice carried through the drawing room like a melody, "feel free to become better acquainted. It is a lovely day to be outside but do what pleases you. I will have tea announced when it is ready, for those desiring it." She nodded to our group and walked back to the side of her husband, the location she seemed most to prefer.

Helena joined our group immediately. "Mr. Stanton, I'm eager to take a walk to the village. It is a most beautiful day. Shall we collect a group of adventurers?"

"I have been to Chadsmead several times, Miss Hanford, and I am sorry to disappoint you, but it is far from an adventure."

She gave a most genuine pout, and I determined it my duty to defend her. As tiresome as she could be, she was family. Besides, if I convinced the group to go to Chadsmead, I might spend the afternoon alone wandering the gardens.

"The adventure happens along the way, Mr. Stanton," I began timidly. "Surely you have read the great adventure stories. It is never the destination that is written of in the book, but the mishaps of the journey that captivate the reader."

He met my gaze with a quizzical look. "You desire mishaps?"

"I was not talking of myself, but there is wisdom in Helena's words. Adventures can happen anywhere, not just in distant places or on the pages of books. So why not on the way to Chadsmead, or within the uneventful town of Chadsmead itself? And I assure you, mishaps are often the greatest of adventures; though they aren't always a good experience, they lead us to where we are meant to be." I glanced at Helena hoping she was pleased at my willingness to come to her defense but the scowl that pulled at her features informed me otherwise.

No one standing in our small group affirmed either side. They sat looking between us as if they had no desire to do anything but observe the amusing exchange.

"Life is full of mishaps, Miss Blakeslee. And I've found no romantic ideals of adventure in the disappointments."

He seemed to be drawing near me as he spoke, but I once again refused to cower. I squared my shoulders and lifted my chin. "Perhaps you are ignorant to what life offers you then, Mr. Stanton."

Out of the corner of my eye I saw Helena's mouth part in apparent disbelief and I knew I would receive a scolding for my strong words, but could no one see that he was the cause of it all? Someone needed to stand up to him and his ill temper.

His eyes narrowed, and I once again had the strange impression he was staring into my soul. This time I didn't remove my gaze. Let him find what he searched for. Maybe once he discovered it, he would finally leave me be.

"Well," came the excited voice of Luke Kingman drawing Mr. Stanton's eyes from me, "the easiest way to settle the matter is to walk out and see if we find adventure."

The group muttered their agreements and Helena set off to see which other guests cared to join them. She must have realized the necessity to bring along well-mannered ladies, to ensure a better impression than the one I had managed thus far.

"I assume you will accompany us then?" The voice was quiet, but rigid in my ear.

I could not hide the shock on my face at his nearness, even with my best attempt. "No, I did not intend to join the party, Mr. Stanton."

"Such a lively defense of adventure to shun the opportunity? Unusual indeed." His eyebrows lifted, and a corner of his mouth twitched as though he was forcing back a smile.

"I intend to have my own adventure walking the gardens here at Timpton," I said candidly.

"You are not going to join us?" Lord Ramsby said with concern, overhearing my last comment.

"It was not my intention," I answered apologetically.

"Then I shall stay and keep you company. It is too fine a day to spend it in solitude."

My heart raced at the suggestion and I felt a rush of heat settle on my neck. Intuitively I knew the proper course of action. "I had not realized the absence of my company would alter your plans, Lord Ramsby. I shall be happy to walk out with the group."

A smile lit his face. "Then may I seek your specific company during the walk?"

I looked at Mr. Stanton who had fire in his eyes. Surely the kind, handsome face of a Lord was better companionship than Mr. Stanton. Not that I would walk out with my cousin's suitor, regardless.

Before I could accept his offer, Helena appeared at my side. "Abigail would be happy to provide her company, Lord Ramsby. Though I do hope you will spend some time becoming acquainted with the other ladies I have gathered for our outing."

He directed his charming smile at her and I was relieved to see I wasn't the only one who blushed under his attentions. "I should look forward to that, Miss Hanford." He looked back at me and offered his arm. "Shall we head out?"

Bidding farewell to Uncle Stanton, and whispering my wish that he could accompany us, I placed my arm on Lord Ramsby's.

CHAPTER 5

The walk into Chadsmead was uneventful, and I began to think the consensus of the group would fall with Mr. Stanton in his assertion of it lacking adventure. I was at least glad that Lord Ramsby did most of the talking, with only an occasional question regarding Easton Manor or my family. He had a delightful personality, but my thoughts drifted as he spoke of his land holdings and houses.

"They make a lovely pair, do they not?" Lord Ramsby asked, catching my attention.

"Of whom do you refer?"

"Miss Hanford and Mr. Stanton, of course."

I glanced at the couple and nodded. "I suppose they do."

His head tilted sideways, his eyes studying me. "Have you not been analyzing their interactions the entirety of our walk, Miss Blakeslee? Calculating if he should soon offer for your cousin?"

I looked at him, taken aback by his accusation. "I assure you, I have been doing no such thing. Though I do acknowledge the arrangement would be entirely welcome on her part."

"Then I must wonder at the reasons behind your persistent gaze in their direction," he said, a mischievous grin on his face.

I lowered my eyes to the ground, unable to find a suitable answer.

"Since you seem hesitant to share your reasonings, I will venture a guess." He paused. "I can think of only two explanations for such attentiveness, if not in contemplating the match. Either you are studying your cousin's example, whether to emulate or criticize is inconsequential, or..." his eyes narrowed, and his grin disappeared, "I fear you are infatuated with Mr. Stanton." I could feel him interpreting my reaction and I tried to hide my irritation. "But that seems quite impossible from what I've seen."

Had I been watching them? I couldn't remember doing so. I kept my focus straight ahead attempting to keep my gaze from falling on Helena and Mr. Stanton as we entered the cobblestone streets of Chadsmead. "Let me offer a third reason."

He observed me with attentive eyes.

"As looking ahead is vital when one walks, they were inconveniently positioned."

He laughed and took a step nearer. "I am delighted to hear it."

I gave a small nod, glad to have reached our destination and abandon the topic.

THE GROUP GATHERED TOGETHER to determine what each person desired to do. It was decided that Hannah, Lord Wycliffe, Mr. Luke Kingman, Mrs. Dowding, and the Misses Dowdings would visit the shops. Mr. and Mrs. Ellis, Miss Hawkins, and Mr. Ross Gale, who were already familiar with the town, wished to continue their walk through the countryside. The remainder of the group—Mr. Stanton, Lord Ramsby, Helena and myself would tour the parish before meeting back with the others at the shops.

Chadsmead reminded me of Burrowsly, the village near Easton Manor, and the similarities sent an aching through me. How had it only been days since I left when it felt so much longer?

As we began our walk along the main road, Helena asked Lord Ramsby about the continent and he put out his arm, eager to escort a willing ear down the cobblestone street to the church. I stepped in behind them as Mr. Stanton did the same. He clasped his hands behind his back and kept his gaze ahead.

The tension was too unpleasant to neglect. "I'm sorry for the misunderstanding earlier." I inwardly cursed myself for my tendency to apologize when I held no fault. Why must I always be the one to try to add a bit of civility to our awkward interactions?

"Which misunderstanding?"

How could he be so brash? "I had no intention of coming to Chadsmead when you first asked."

"Yet you easily changed your mind at the request of Lord Ramsby?" His tone was accusing, not questioning.

"I thought it a wise decision when weighing it against my alternative."

His eyes flickered to me, but he said nothing.

"How is it you can find something to criticize in everything I do? I was trying to avoid a situation I am certain you would have considered improper, only to be censured for doing it. I have never met a man so ready to judge without reason. You are unbearable!" My voice quickened in my frustration though I was careful to keep my volume low to escape the disapproving notice of my cousin.

I meant to avoid his stern glare but when he did not respond I glanced in his direction. I stopped mid-step in astonishment at the amusement that lit his face. His brows were not brought down but had lifted, allowing the unusual color of his eyes to reflect the daylight; but most astonishing was the smile that had come to his lips. It wasn't a full smile, but it did wonders to his looks. I found myself staring at him, amazed at the transformation of countenance one simple change could bring to a person. This must be the handsome man his servants had spoken of.

I willed myself to say something—anything. "I was not aware you were capable of smiling, Mr. Stanton."

He apparently took my remark in jest, though I had not intended it to be, and let out a deep, rumbling chuckle. My exasperated expression must have confirmed my continued state of shock.

"And I laugh also."

I nodded dumbly. "But why this momentary lapse of character?"

He overlooked the criticism in my question. "Perhaps I am liberated, if only for a moment."

I didn't know what to make of his strange comment, but I hated to say anything that would bring back his harsh demeanor. Instead, I walked in silence periodically glancing at the man I hardly recognized.

"What is it?" he asked, catching me in one of my glances.

"It suits you—smiling I mean."

"Well don't get accustomed to it, I don't need to lose my reputation on account of one smile."

"And a laugh," I said, still astonished at the friendly tone of our conversation.

We reached the gate of the parish and he held it open for me. So, he did know how to act a gentleman.

"Thank you, Mr. Stanton," I said in awe.

He gave me another dashing smile. "You were correct in the ease of earning your good opinion, Miss Blakeslee."

My mind was reeling, trying to make sense of the contradiction of whom I supposed Mr. Stanton to be and his current behavior. "Or perhaps it was always your intention to force my expectations so low any half-decent action on your part would seem quite promising."

He stopped walking and abruptly turned toward me. "I apologize for allowing the standard to be set so low. Please—"

"Mr. Stanton, how slow you are." My eyes followed Helena's voice to the door of the church. "Come and tell us about your parish before I catch a chill. Make haste!"

I hadn't noticed the chill in the air and shivered at the sudden realization. When I returned my attention back to Mr. Stanton, disappointment filled me at the severity once again etched in his features.

WE WANDERED through the parish listening to Helena ramble on about how she would be content to spend the rest of her days in a small country congregation, and yet how she would greatly miss the sermons of the great churches in London and the socializing afterwards with similarly stationed people. Lord Ramsby seemed keen to acknowledge her thoughts, but the way her voice echoed off the walls made my head throb.

"I'm going to walk around the outside," I said, and without waiting for an offer of an escort, I left. The day had unexpectedly turned cold and the dark clouds in the distance hinted at an evening rain.

I glanced around, deciding where I should explore. The parish yard was big but landscaped with the intention of large social gatherings—lots of open grass but little to admire. I moved toward the back of the church, catching a glimpse of the parish cemetery. It was picturesque, with a wood fence around the outside, and as I drew near I had a strong desire to discover the lives of those who laid to rest within its protection.

I pushed open the gate and began to survey the tomb-stones. One section was set apart and the familiar name of Stanton marked several graves—the family plot. I scanned the names and dates engraved in stone.

A grand tombstone in fine white marble caught my attention. It was shaped as an obelisk as though it pointed to heaven and I traced my finger along the name. "Mr. Thomas Stanton," I read aloud. The date of death was fifteen years ago, and I wondered if this was the grave of Edwin Stanton's grandfather. An odd yearning overcame me to ask Edwin about the lives of his relatives buried here. I shook my head and forced the absurd thought away.

As I left the Stanton side of the cemetery, a curious noise caught my notice. I glanced around, certain I was alone, but something inside me compelled me to investigate. I began to walk through the other graves, searching for the source of the sound. As I turned down another row, I glimpsed a small boy prostrated on the ground. There was no tombstone, and the realization hit me as I noticed the freshly-colored soil he laid on—there must not have been time to create a marker for the grave yet.

I took a step closer but questioned if I should leave him to mourn privately. I stood, deciding whether I should retreat, when I heard his small voice shudder as if he had cried so long his body was now trying to purge his despair. His distress compelled me toward him. His eyes were closed, and his face looked filthy with streaks of mud where the dirt and his tears had combined.

I bent low and gently touched his back. "Are you well?"

His eyes shot open in surprise and he quickly sat up. His large, brown eyes blinked at me in a way that pulled at my soul. He wiped at his tears, smearing the trails of mud across his face. "It's Papa," he said, motioning to the grave under him.

"I'm so sorry. I lost a parent not long ago though mine was my mother." I offered it so he'd take comfort in our common hardship, but seeing the raw emotion tormenting him brought my own too near the surface. I had to keep talking to prevent myself from dwelling on my own grief.

"And how old are you?"

"Eight. But Papa died 'afore my birthday."

"And where is your mother?"

"'ome with my sisters."

"And how many sisters do you have?"

"Four."

"Are you the oldest?" I desperately hoped his answer would be no and that his poor mother hadn't been left with five young children to care for without a husband.

He lifted his chin. "Yes, miss. Mum says I'm the man of the 'ouse now."

My heart ached for this little boy and his family. "Well, they are lucky to have you," I said with a reassuring smile.

His muddy face brightened at my confidence in him.

"And where might you live?" I asked, inwardly wondering why I had even inquired.

"You can see our 'ouse from here." Standing up he pointed to a small, thatched roof tucked between several large trees.

"It's lovely," I said with a smile and my instincts pressed me to continue. "Would you mind if I visited soon?"

His eyes grew large. "For true?"

"Perhaps tomorrow?"

He nodded vigorously.

"Wonderful, tomorrow it is..." I paused realizing I hadn't asked his name.

"Silas," he said with an endearing grin that proudly displayed his missing front tooth.

"Silas, I am Abigail Blakeslee."

"Nice to meet you, Miss Abigail," he said politely, and my heart felt overwhelmed at my immediate fondness for this dimple-faced boy.

I stood and dusted off my day dress. "Well, Silas, I shall see you tomorrow. And if you should need me for anything, I am here visiting Timpton House."

His eyes flickered behind me. "See you t'morrow, Miss Abigail." He sprinted from the cemetery before I could say my goodbyes. But as I watched him disappear into the distance, a surge of excitement rushed through me—a sensation I hadn't felt since before Mother's death and one I hadn't realized I missed until now.

"Who was that filthy creature you were talking with, Abigail?"

I turned to find Helena looking disgruntled with a perplexed gentleman on each side.

"Silas," I said, offering no other explanation as I joined them.

"Surely you do not know him?" she asked in irritation, though I was unsure if it was at my shortness or Silas's company.

"I do now. He was here visiting his father's grave when I had the pleasure of introducing myself." I was unwilling to divulge the details of my chance encounter, it seemed too special to rattle on about. "Shall we walk to meet the others?" I asked with feigned innocence. "I'm sure they are anxious to start back before the storm arrives."

We walked from the cemetery and I found myself disap-pointed that Helena's interest with Lord Ramsby did not continue for the remainder of our walk. She seemed to hang on Edwin Stanton's arm over the unsteady cobblestone street, and I had to look away at her ridiculous antics. Lord Ramsby had not lost his willingness to talk. Grateful he did not need much coaxing to continue the one-sided conversation, I tried to listen as I watched the storm clouds draw nearer in the distance.

By the time we reached the group, the consensus was to send for carriages to come retrieve the stranded party.

"Surely we have time to get home before the rain arrives," I suggested, having no desire to spend an hour or two crammed into one of the small shops or the crowded inn we stood in front of. "It was such a quick walk here from Timpton House."

Helena scrunched her nose in disgust at the suggestion. "And risk getting muddy if the cursed rain should come?"

I gave her a playful smile. "I thought you wanted an adventure?"

She scoffed at the reminder and turned toward the others.

The gentlemen left to see about sending for the carriages and to find a place for our group to convene while we waited. I took the opportunity of their absence to declare my intentions of walking.

"Go ahead," Helena said wryly. "But don't think for a moment you are going to convince me to indulge in your nonsensical ideas."

I shot a hopeful look at Hannah who lowered her gaze as did the other ladies in the group.

Helena's reproach did little to discourage me, and I began to relish the idea of this unanticipated alone time. "Very well, I shall see you at the house." If I walked quickly, I would be sure to make it back before them, and hopefully before the rain began.

CHAPTER 6

I was nearly halfway back when I stopped atop a hill, closed my eyes, and permitted my senses to embrace the beauty of the moment. The smells were intoxicating—scents of blossoms and grass—distant rain. The frigid air wrapped around me, blowing my dress tightly against my body. I reached up, untied my bonnet and let the wind flow through my hair. The trees nearby danced to the rhythm, creating a low howling song that resonated within me.

After a moment, I opened my eyes and scanned the clouds again. The thick layer of darkened sky was nearly overhead now, and I realized I needed to make haste before the rain began. I urged myself to take a step, but my body refused the command. The air bit into my skin and the wind beat against me without ceasing. It reminded me of life and the bitterness it brought. But I knew after the storm the sunshine would return, making what it left behind stronger, fuller, and more beautiful. I hoped one day strength and beauty would emerge from the storms I had faced, that my life would once again be full.

A movement in my periphery drew my gaze back in the direction I had just come.

The approaching figure of Mr. Edwin Stanton climbing the hill toward me sent a peculiar sensation rushing through me. He wore the familiar, stern expression on his face, and I questioned if he was cross at my decision to walk. "Miss Blakeslee."

"Mr. Stanton," I returned, not knowing what words should follow.

"Did you assume I would allow a lady to walk home unattended while in my charge?"

"Yes," I said honestly.

He was breathing hard as he neared me. "Well, I fear Lady Eliza would not approve of such a notion. I had little choice in the matter but to set out after you and offer my escort." His declaration felt rehearsed, as though he was still trying to convince himself of it.

"I am capable of walking unaccompanied," I said curtly, turning toward my destination.

"Are you upset by my chivalrous undertaking, Miss Blakeslee?"

I stopped mid-step and spun back toward him. "You have just admitted you had 'little choice' in the matter, but now you wish to take credit for your chivalry?" His mouth parted at my accusation, and I knew he wished to offer his defense, but I had no desire to allow it. "I detest that you felt compelled to be in my company, Mr. Stanton."

"Compelled?" he asked, a mock laugh in his throat. "You accuse me of judgment, yet how readily you can turn and judge another."

There was no one around to dispel our disagreement and though our voices did not rise, my hands trembled at the confrontation. "And how have I judged you? By showing you the truth in your own words?" He took a step closer and the warmth of his body seeped into me. I tried to repress the subsequent shiver.

"There is no truth in your conclusion."

I didn't know what to say, I didn't even quite understand what he meant, but I met his look with all the intensity I could muster. The loose strands of my hair whipped around my face and I was certain it was making a mess of itself, but I hardly cared. My stubborn side refused to retreat. Then a droplet hit my face.

The rain came quickly, and it took only a moment before it poured from the sky. I covered my head with the hand that held my bonnet as I ran toward Timpton House. We were not yet half way, and I regretted my decision to walk with each sodden step. The downpour didn't let up and Mr. Stanton's hand found mine, pulling me off the path.

Water flowed down my face and clouded my vision as I willingly followed Mr. Stanton through the torrent. After several minutes I felt the rain stop. He released his grip on me, and I wiped the water from my eyes to find we were standing under a stone bridge.

I sighed, looking at the newly flowing stream a few paces from where we stood. "How long will it come down like this?"

"I cannot predict weather, Miss Blakeslee." The chill in the air couldn't rival the ice in Mr. Stanton's voice and I eagerly turned from him to observe the storm.

How foolish I was, and how foolish Mr. Stanton must think me, though I wasn't certain I cared about the latter. I felt numb, but my body shivered, and I wrapped my arms around myself.

"You are cold," Mr. Stanton said, watching me in his unnerving way.

"How attentive you are, Mr. Stanton," I said dryly.

He started to unbutton his waistcoat and I considered refusing the gesture, until I scanned the thick, woolen material. When he held it toward me, I reluctantly accepted it. A satisfying heat engulfed me first, followed by the pleasant scent of Mr. Stanton that lingered on the fabric. Unpleasant scent, I corrected myself—utterly unpleasant and smug.

Mr. Stanton looked up at the sky and shook his head. "It would have been wise to listen to Helena's council and await the carriages," he said as though it was a new idea I had not considered. A spiteful remark began forming on my tongue when he cleared his throat. "But I suppose this might fit into the mishap category you spoke of earlier?" He kept his gaze on the horizon.

I stared at his profile, unsure where me meant to lead the conversation. "I suppose."

"And if it isn't a grand enough adventure, perhaps you can still weave it into an acceptable story—just as you did for Uncle Stanton."

I peeked at him, curious what emotion would be displayed in his countenance, but his rigid profile gave no insights.

"He told you our story?"

"I believe he accepted no credit for your creation. He also mentioned it was better from your lips." Mr. Stanton glanced toward me and his gaze went to my lips before he looked away in irritation.

I swallowed. "I'm sure his retelling was more than suitable."

Mr. Stanton didn't answer but folded his arms over his broad chest. Guilt pricked me as I realized he was now cold in only his shirtsleeves.

"I'm sorry I walked," I offered.

He examined me for a moment, as though he were judging the level of my sincerity, but quickly returned his gaze to the spot he preferred on the horizon.

I wondered how long I'd be trapped under this bridge with such a disagreeable companion when a shiver sent my shoulders shaking. I moved to tighten the oversized coat around me, only to realize I could scarcely move my frozen fingers. I removed the drenched gloves and began to rub my hands together.

"May I?" Mr. Stanton asked, stepping to my side and reaching toward me, severity still present in his features.

Cautiously I placed my hands, palms up, in his. The warmth of his touch sent another shiver through me, and I watched as he rubbed my hands in his. It seemed a strange thing, his ability to be simultaneously gentle and distressingly stern. As he moved to the tips of my fingers and back down to my palms, I became too aware of the strength of my beating heart and the shallowness of my breaths that filled the frigid air. I was relieved when a tingling sensation began moving up my fingers and I rotated my hands in his to test my returning dexterity.

The cold had turned the tops of my hands a dark red, and the white scars contrasted harshly against it. I immediately realized my mistake and looked to see if Mr. Stanton had noticed. He was already examining the marks, and I tried to pull my hands from his. His grip tightened, refusing to let go. His thumb brushed across the top of one of my hands and he met my gaze with a look of concern. Mr. Stanton's eyes appeared softer than I had seen them, and I wanted to say something but knew I shouldn't. Unwilling to answer the questions in his eyes I pulled back again. He willingly released them this time, and I wrapped them around me beneath the safety of his coat.

I needed a distraction. "You have seemed troubled today," I said, though I left out the comparison he only seemed more troubled than yesterday. "Did you receive poor news this morning when your friends arrived?"

"What led you to draw such a conclusion?" He looked irritated at the question, but I was thankful he did not press me on the topic of my scars.

"You do not attempt to hide your contempt, so why act

cross when I inquire about emotions you are unwilling to conceal?"

"Do not concern yourself with my emotions, it's not worth the trouble," he said, his eyes bordering on coldness again. "You shall be gone from Timpton House soon enough, and my foul moods will be but a thing to gossip about."

My mouth parted in disbelief. What right did he have to deal such an insult? Insinuating people mattered so little to me—their troubles not worth caring for and their weaknesses to be used for something as trivial as gossip. "I assure you, I am not so fickle as you think me." My voice trembled, but my tone was intended to cut. "Though right now I wish I was far from Timpton House and your irritating ways!"

He looked at me again and an exasperating lift came to one side of his mouth. "Miss Blakeslee, I believe you find my behavior so bothersome because it's a weakness in yourself."

I scoffed, unable to form a rebuttal at his odd conclusion.

My inability to respond pulled at the other corner of his mouth until a handsome, infuriating smile adorned his lips. "Concealing your discontent hardly seems a strength of yours. Though I must admit, you handle it more charmingly than I am capable."

"You are maddening!" I exclaimed at the comparison and he threw back his head and laughed a genuine and hearty laugh.

Anger flooded over me. Overwhelmed again by this strange man and the confusion he created, I flung his coat at him and turned to walk into the storm and away from him, his poor moods, and his mocking ways. His strong hand grabbed my arm and before I had a chance to escape, he pulled me to him. He no longer laughed but his light eyes reflected that same look from earlier I could not place. I stood inches from him, stiff and unmoving, my wet gown clinging to my shaking body. He brought his face near mine and my breath caught.

"You are the one who is maddening, Miss Blakeslee," he said in a low whisper. His words were insulting but the way he spoke them made it sound as though he was pleased with the conclusion.

I dared not move, trying to decide what his eyes were yearning to say. I hadn't found the answer when he released my arm and took a step away. He rubbed his hands over his mouth and then through his hair in agitation. I saw his countenance transform into the rigidness I knew best, the one I was apparently more comfortable with, and I pushed aside the odd sensation of disappointment that overcame me.

He handed me back his coat. "You should wait for the rain to stop, it shouldn't be long now." Not a weather predictor indeed. What a strange man Edwin Stanton was.

WE DIDN'T HAVE to wait long in strained silence before the rain turned to a drizzle and we began our walk back to Timpton. Several times I grudgingly allowed Mr. Stanton's escort to avoid sliding through the mud. His steadying grasp and silent attentiveness pricked my conscience and my pride. What sort of lady finds herself, and worse—her host with her —trudging through the muddy countryside?

As we neared the house, I unwrapped Mr. Stanton's coat from around me and handed it back to him. "Thank you," I muttered, wondering if we had arrived before the others.

He sent me a sideways glance. "Such gratitude."

I was too worried to be bothered by his pointed remark. "Should we go in through the servants' entrance?" I asked, hoping to draw as little attention to our muddied attire as possible. "Or perhaps we could walk in separately?"

"And give the impression we are trying to hide something?" The tightness in his jaw confirmed there would be no

convincing him otherwise. "No, we must go through the front
—together."

I gave an exasperated huff but followed him up the staircase to the main entryway. As we neared the door I looked
down at my disheveled appearance and the mud coating the
bottom of my dress and boots.

Mr. Stanton's lip twitched. "You look well…all things
considered."

Laughter burst from me and I promptly covered my
mouth, as surprised at my reaction as Edwin Stanton
appeared to be. "All things considered," I repeated, still laughing. "I doubt your servants will consider anything besides
their vexation when they discover the trail of mud leading to
my room."

I felt Mr. Stanton's gaze shift to my feet, a look of uncertainty evident in his features. "Here," he said, dropping to his
knee and reaching out for my foot. "Let me help you clear
some of the mud from your shoes."

"You needn't do that." I reached down to pull him up,
embarrassed anew that my folly should have him cleaning
mud from my boots.

A rare, full smile came to his lips. "Consider it a gesture of
friendship. And if that is not reason enough, regard it as an
obligatory attempt to pacify my staff."

Dazed at the reminder of how handsome he was when he
smiled, I dumbly nodded my agreement. Careful to make sure
my dress did not lift high enough to expose my ankle, I placed
my foot in his hands.

He began at the back, pulling large clumps of condensed
mud from around my heel and then making his way toward
the toe. When he completed the first boot, he lowered it and
held out his muddied hand for the other. I lifted the second
one, convincing myself my racing heart was a consequence of
my concern at returning to Timpton too late to go unnoticed.

When he managed to remove most of the mud, he lowered

my foot and turned his attention to his own boots. He made quick work of it and when he finished, he collected the largest clumps, stood, and tossed them off the side of the stairs.

I was still watching him when his gaze met mine. "I hope that will be adequate enough to keep my servants from believing you a vexation on our household."

"Thank you." I grinned, looking down to examine my dingy boots. "They are much improved." My eyes moved to the soiled hem of my day dress and I sighed. "Now if only there was something to be done for my dress—Lydia will be rightly cross at the state of it."

"That, I regret, I cannot help you with."

A wave of heat flushed through me. "Of course not! I did not mean to imply… well, I would never…." I couldn't seem to construct a coherent statement in my embarrassment, let alone find the ability to speak it.

One side of Mr. Stanton's mouth lifted. "Forgive me, Miss Blakeslee. I am confident you implied no such thing."

"I'm glad to know it," I said, searching for a diversion from the uncomfortable topic. My gaze dropped to his muddied hands. "Now look at your hands." I reached out to inspect them, and my breath caught when I touched his skin. The pounding in my chest intensified as I brushed at the dirt.

He unexpectedly caught my hands in his. "You are freezing." Edwin Stanton's voice had turned as severe as his glare. "It's time we go inside."

I pulled my hands from his grasp and nodded, cursing my foolishness as he turned to open the door.

WHEN I FOLLOWED Mr. Stanton through the door and into view of the alarmed butler, I scanned the entry hall for spectators. Relief filled me to find the three of us alone.

"Baldwin, please send up Miss Blakeslee's maid and have a

bath drawn for her at once," Mr. Stanton said. "I fear we have met with unforeseen weather on our walk from Chadsmead."

"Very well," the butler said, offering a bow before he left.

I turned to walk up the stairs when approaching footsteps echoed off the marble floors. I glanced toward the corridor and then to Mr. Stanton, debating if I had enough time to remove myself from view before being seen. Edwin stood firm, staring ahead indifferently, as though he cared little we were to be discovered in our current state. I looked back toward the stairs with longing but realized there was no chance of fleeing without being seen. Reluctantly I returned to Mr. Stanton's side, trying to imitate his confidence with only moderate success.

Lady Eliza sauntered into the hall and stopped when she spotted us, her lips parting in apparent shock. Her eyes shot from her son to me and then slowly down my soaked, muddy dress that clung to my figure.

"We encountered poor weather on the walk from Chadsmead," Mr. Stanton repeated unceremoniously.

"And where are the others?" The relief that came from realizing we had arrived before the rest of the group was fleeting.

"They will return by carriages," Mr. Stanton offered.

"And whose foolish idea was it to walk, just the two of you, from Chadsmead?"

My skin prickled with guilt and I knew I must speak up before Mr. Stanton laid the blame upon me. "It was mine, Lady Eliza." I spoke the words with a shaking voice, whether from cold or humiliation I could not be sure. "I had supposed I could make it home before the storm. I was obviously mistaken."

Her eyes flicked to her son. "And you went along with such a notion?"

He shifted under his mother's unyielding glare and I felt wretched he should receive blame for my mistake.

"He had been arranging for carriages when I set out, so he had no opportunity to convince me how foolish the idea was. I began walking on my own. He didn't even catch up with me until I was half way back to Timpton." I looked at him. "I am sorry—" and then back to Lady Eliza, "to both of you."

Lady Eliza's face softened, and she drew closer to us. "No significant harm done, as long as we can get you to your rooms before the others return or someone ventures out of the drawing room and sees the likes of you two." She grabbed my arm to lead me up the stairs and her brow creased with concern. "You are soaked through, Miss Blakeslee." She paused and looked over her shoulder. "Edwin, have Miss Blakeslee's maid sent up and see that the servants draw up a bath for her straightaway. I will come speak with you shortly."

I didn't have the courage to tell Lady Eliza that her son had already taken the initiative to do as she asked, but I expected him to tout his foresight. Instead he gave a bow. "I will see to it directly."

Lady Eliza escorted me to my room and helped me out of my wet gown and petticoat. I felt self-conscience in only my damp chemise and stay and wrapped my arms around myself, waiting as she retrieved a wool blanket.

Stepping up behind me, she moved pieces of my fallen hair to the side. When the warmth of the blanket didn't come, I peeked over my shoulder. Lady Eliza's eyes were fixed on my upper back. Her hand lifted and gently touched my skin. I blushed realizing what had caught her attention.

"It is a birthmark," I said awkwardly. It would be easy to confuse the dark spot for mud, and I did not blame her for trying to wipe it away. My birthmark was nearly the size of a small coin, but usually remained hidden under the sleeve of my gown. She forced a smile and placed the blanket across my shoulders.

"Come sit by the fire until your bath is ready," she said in a whisper, gesturing to a chair.

"Thank you, Lady Eliza," I said, hoping she recognized I was grateful for the help, but even more so for her willingness to not make a spectacle of the incident.

"You are welcome," she said with a small nod in my direction. Her eyes did not move from my face and I was certain she had more she wanted to say of my foolish behavior. "I shall go see about your bath."

"Thank you," I said again, this time in gratitude she had withheld her rebuke.

I warmed my hands near the fire when the door opened, and Lydia led several maids with hot buckets of water into the room. Her eyes brimmed with questions, but she turned her attention to stationing the bathtub that was being laboriously pulled inside.

Once the bath was full and the other servants left, I removed the last of my soaked underclothing and entered the hot water. My skin stung in protest and I winced.

Lydia reached out to offer her support. "Abee, you are cold as ice!"

"Then why do I feel as though I am on fire?" I asked, looking down at my throbbing toes.

"You poor thing."

I suppressed an unexpected wave of emotion and shook my head dismissively. "I do not deserve your sympathy, Lydia."

Lydia studied my face, and I sensed the questions in her eyes intensify, but she nodded her understanding.

Gradually my body grew accustomed to the temperature, and I began to thaw. Lydia washed my hair; she didn't speak but repeatedly poured warm water over my head and back. I stayed in the bath until the water became tepid and I could finally convince myself it was necessary to get dressed and join the others downstairs to confront their questioning remarks.

"Are you feeling better?"

"Yes, thank you," I said with an appeasing smile. I stood, and she wrapped a blanket around me.

"As much as you don't want to offer one, Abee, I believe I deserve an explanation. Look at the state of your dress. It is no easy task cleaning mud from white muslin."

"We encountered poor weather on our walk from Chadsmead," I said, borrowing the very description Mr. Stanton had given the butler and his mother.

She looked dissatisfied with my answer. "Who is 'we'?"

"Mr. Stanton and myself," I answered casually.

"Mr. Edwin Stanton?"

"Yes."

"And you?"

"Yes."

"Walking alone together from Chadsmead—in the rain?" I couldn't tell if my admission disappointed her until I saw a smile touch her lips. "I thought you said he was a horrible man."

"He is," I answered. "At least most of the time." I didn't wish to go into my current, confusing analysis of Edwin Stanton so I changed the subject. "I met a boy today at the parish cemetery. I hope to visit him and his family tomorrow. Will you come with me?"

"Shouldn't you be asking a proper companion?" she asked, graciously allowing me to leave the topic of Mr. Stanton.

"Besides the fact that you *are* a proper companion, I fear none of the ladies would care to join me."

"Perhaps a gentleman then?" She sent me a teasing smirk. "I heard Lord Ramsby is exceptionally dashing and has been quite attentive toward you."

I lifted my eyebrow at her suggestive tone, unwilling to ask where she had heard such senseless gossip. "I doubt he'd find helping a poor family a worthwhile diversion." I immediately realized the judgment in my comment and knew I must correct it or risk a rebuke. "Though perhaps I am mistaken. Regardless, I would prefer you to come."

Lydia appraised me with apprehension and I clasped my hands together beseechingly.

"Very well, I will agree to go on the condition no one from your own rank desires to accompany you." I nodded enthusiastically. "Though I don't know how I shall find the time with the new task you have set me about."

"What task is that?" I asked, unsure of her meaning.

She pointed to the muddied gown draped over the open door of the wardrobe. "Trying to salvage one of your best day dresses."

I once again felt guilty that the consequences of my foolish behavior had burdened others. "I will gladly help you in the morning, perhaps speed up the process with extra hands?"

Lydia laughed as she handed me a fresh chemise. "Such a generous offer, but I am certain you are supposed to be enjoying your needlework and taking tea with the other ladies tomorrow morning. I'd hate to pull you from your most enjoyable duties."

I sent her a scowl. "How well you know me."

Her laugh rang through the room and I couldn't help but smile, grateful for my dearest friend and her ability to bring a touch of home to Timpton House.

I HOPED to make it to the drawing room before everyone gathered for dinner, but with drying my hair, having it styled, and getting dressed, I walked down just before the allotted time. As I approached the bottom of the staircase, I looked up to find Edwin Stanton descending the other set. My heart fluttered, and I sharply reprimanded it.

I considered pretending I didn't see him, but our eyes met, and he nodded his greeting. Regardless of my mistake, seeing him again reminded me of how desperate I was to know how the conversation with his mother had gone.

"How are you, Miss Blakeslee?" he asked, as we began our slow walk to the drawing room together.

"Very well. And you?"

He gave a subtle nod, staring ahead. "Well enough."

I hesitated. "I hope I didn't get you into trouble with Lady Eliza."

His expression was unreadable. "I assure you, she finds little fault with you."

I scanned his profile again. "And certainly not with you?"

He let out a weighty breath but gave no answer.

"I can speak to her, reassure her again you acted solely out of duty."

He finally looked at me, his brow set low over his eyes. "She would call the bluff, Miss Blakeslee."

My face scrunched in confusion, not understanding his meaning.

As we neared the open door, he stopped and faced me. "I should have brought another gentleman along. Forgive me."

Startled by his apology, I stood and watched as he walked through the doors of the drawing room. Fragmented thoughts ran through my head and I took a step backwards, placing my hand on the wall for support. Did Lady Eliza believe her son acted improperly by offering his companionship? He'd been a gentleman—and that was being generous—and I hadn't felt compromised by his presence.

If another gentleman had offered an escort in Mr. Stanton's stead, I was confident I would have felt no different in their company. My thoughts involuntarily turned to Lord Ramsby and his offer to walk the gardens with me. The hypocrisy of my actions was difficult to overlook—I had gone to Chadsmead solely to avoid walking alone with Lord

Ramsby, yet exhibited no concern at scampering across the countryside in the rain with Edwin Stanton. Why the double standard?

I searched my mind for an acceptable explanation for my ambivalence. Lord Ramsby showed an interest in seeking out my company, Mr. Edwin Stanton did not. I nodded to myself, satisfied with my conclusion. The acceptability of an escort must be a matter of the gentleman's interest. I hadn't considered the situation unsuitable because Edwin's interest was with Helena, not with me. "It is Helena he wants," I whispered to myself, unsure why I needed reminding.

I SLIPPED into the drawing room without anyone noticing and kept near the wall. I surveyed the different groups of people talking, trying to listen for my name on their lips. Only one displeased glance from my aunt caused me to stiffen; but my worry absolved when her attention turned from me, and I convinced myself her expression had been no more poignant than the other seemingly undeserved scowls I had received since my arrival at Timpton.

"Abigail!" Hannah stood with Sir Wycliffe and motioned me to join them. "How was your afternoon? I haven't seen you since you walked from Chadsmead. I assume you beat the ghastly storm? I worried we'd be stranded for hours by the intensity of the rain and several times thought of how we should have followed your advice and walked."

She didn't know? I was uncertain what I should say, wondering what others had been told of the incident. "In truth, I did not entirely beat the rain." Her eyes flashed with curiosity. "I believe you made the correct decision waiting for the carriages. I would have felt responsible if the beautiful dress you wore today ended up looking as muddy as mine was by the time I reached Timpton."

"It was a beautiful dress, Miss Hannah," Sir Wycliffe said, his complexion turning ruddy at his compliment. "Though this one is somehow even more ravishing on you."

Hannah smiled beautifully, and I wondered how much this couple preferred each other. It would be a good match for Hannah and come with a title. I smiled, shifting my gaze between the two profiles that seemed to have forgotten I was there.

"If you will pardon me," I said quietly. "I must speak with —" they hadn't looked at me since I had begun my excuse, so I determined it suitable to walk away without having to decide whose company I should feign to desire. As I searched the room, Lord Ramsby caught my eye with a handsome grin. I hesitated walking to the group where Helena also stood, but I figured I'd prefer to receive her socially acceptable half correction now than her private rebuke later.

"How lovely you look, Miss Blakeslee," Lord Ramsby said as I approached. "I have missed your company these last few hours." He reached for my hand and when I placed it in his, he raised my fingers to his lips and placed a gentle kiss on my knuckles.

"Where were you this afternoon anyhow?" Helena said, forcing her way into the greeting.

"In my room," I answered simply.

"And did you enjoy your walk back to Timpton?"

"Yes, thank you." I knew I had to ask something or she'd require more explanation, and I hardly wanted to mention Mr. Stanton and our rainy adventure in her current state of discord. "And how was the carriage ride from Chadsmead?"

"Quite pleasant," she said, looking at Lord Ramsby for confirmation. "I did fear we'd get stuck in mud the entirety of the trip. Did I not fret irrationally, Lord Ramsby?" She reached out and touched his arm and he nodded in agreement before returning his gaze to me. "My worry was in vain," she continued with a sudden edge of discord in her voice. "The rain stopped, and the mud gave us little difficulty. My only qualm was the lost companionship of Mr. Stanton, who appeared to fly to your rescue." Her eyes narrowed as she looked at me. "Did he ever catch up with you?"

"Only just," seemed an adequate response.

"I told him such. I said, 'Surely Abigail will be nearly back by now' but he insisted it would deem him inhospitable to allow you to walk unattended, regardless how flawed you were in your judgment. Then, when Lord Ramsby insisted he go along, Mr. Stanton said he needed him to fulfill his own obligation of escorting me to Timpton and hurried away before objections could be made." She gave an audible huff. "You are both exasperatingly obstinate when you determine to be."

That was twice I had been compared to Mr. Stanton today, and both in a most irksome manner.

"Are you speaking of me, Miss Hanford?"

Her blush met mine as Mr. Stanton stepped to her side. "Indeed I was, and I do not think myself wrong in doing so. I was relaying your attempted rescue of my cousin and how tiresome the pair of you are with your obscure notions. Surely you cannot fault me for conveying such ideas?"

"Not in the least. I appreciate being called tiresome and having my failed abilities shared publicly as I'm sure does Miss Blakeslee." He did not relax his expression when he looked toward me, but I recognized a playful flicker in his eyes.

Helena gave me no time to respond. "I much prefer being the center of conversation as opposed to being overlooked, even if one's intentions are to tease. As I'm certain Abigail will agree—being a proper lady." She sent me a forceful glare and, deciding against foiling her petty attempt to redeem herself, I nodded my agreement.

"I will keep that in mind," Mr. Stanton said, lifting his arm to Helena. "Shall we go in, Miss Hanford?"

Realizing dinner had been announced, I watched as she smugly grabbed his arm as though I cared. Lord Ramsby offered me his escort, and we made our way into the dining room behind the irksome couple.

I TRIED NOT to be disappointed when I realized I was not placed near Uncle Stanton at the table. The young people were arranged together, and I found myself seated between Lord Ramsby and Sir Wycliffe, with Helena across from me and Edwin Stanton by her side. Mr. Ross sat on the other side of Helena and the other ladies, as well as Mr. Kingman, were filled in around them. I looked longingly toward the other end of the table where Uncle Stanton was seated, knowing he couldn't see me but hoping he felt my desire to have him as a companion.

As we ate, I lacked all motivation in adding to the small talk around me; feigning interest was exhausting enough. At least my mishap today seemed to have been overlooked.

"Miss Blakeslee?"

I looked up to find Mr. Ross Gale looking at me.

"You are the sister of Sir Laurence Blakeslee, I gather?"

"I am," I said, happy to speak of my family.

"I knew him at Oxford. He is a superior man." I recalled Laurence telling Father he had been at Oxford the same time as Mr. Stanton, but I hadn't thought of the fact again, even when I heard Mr. Ross was a friend of Edwin Stanton's from school.

"Indeed, he is," I said proudly.

"I am sorry it took me so long to make the connection. When I finally realized the relation, I could scarcely believe it was true. You two look nothing alike."

My face colored as I perceived those nearby, including Mr. Stanton, turn their gaze toward me. Laurence had golden-red hair like Father, was short with a thick build, and had a reddish complexion. There was hardly a similarity between us. "It is a common mistake, Mr. Ross," I said with an understanding smile. "He is a near replica of my father—I am not."

I saw Helena roll her eyes, and my face flushed again.

"Well if you don't mind me saying, as exceptional a fellow as he is, you are much more pleasant to look at."

Several people laughed, and I pushed a piece of fish around my plate until I felt the heat dissipate from my cheeks.

"Your mother must have been lovely." Mr. Ross's tone turned respectful, and I wondered how he knew Mother had passed.

I glanced up at him. "She was, thank you."

His expression was full of compassion and he gave me a thoughtful nod before turning his attention to Miss Dowding. I was relieved to resume my silent attentiveness, praying I wouldn't be the subject of any more conversations this evening. The more they pried, the more they'd discover. And I doubted anyone would be pleased with what they would find.

As the women reentered the drawing room, I sought out a chair away from the group. Guilt pricked at my conscience knowing Father had not sent me here to sit in seclusion. I scanned the faces of the ladies in the room, trying to motivate myself to join them. Their wide eyes and hushed whispers did little to inspire me and I turned my attention back to the fire. I was hopeless.

"How was your walk home today?"

I gave a start as Mrs. Ellis took the chair next to me. I regarded her knowing grin, uncertain what she had discovered. "Wet," I finally offered. She laughed, and I was glad she did not appear to be angry at me.

"It sounded like quite the *adventure*."

I studied her, wondering who her source had been and if it was coincidental that she'd used the word adventure. Her eyes were the same color as her brother's, but her features were soft and feminine. "I fear it was simply a lack of good judgment, with the fault somehow landing on your brother. I feel terrible."

"Oh, stop!" she said, flipping her hand dismissively. "A lecture from Mother is hardly something out of the ordinary. Edwin and I have been taught to be very—" she paused and tilted her head in contemplation, "*cautious* in our interactions. I fear Edwin didn't act according to his training today when it would have been simple to bring along another gentleman and not risk your reputation."

"Risk my reputation? I assure you, your brother was a proper gentleman."

"Of course, he was. Edwin is the absolute paradigm of a gentleman; but gentlemen, as well as ladies, can make foolish mistakes if they disregard the boundaries put in place to protect their virtue." An inescapable blush filled my cheeks and Mrs. Ellis laughed, revealing an irksome similarity between the siblings. "I shouldn't speak to you in such a forward manner yet; besides, you are still unmarried, and I can see the subject is distressing you. Do forgive me?"

Although she asked forgiveness, I could sense she was much amused by our conversation. "Of course, Mrs. Ellis."

"Please call me Diana," she said insistently. "I feel so old with everyone calling me Mrs. Ellis."

I smiled at her exaggerated pout. "I'd be happy to call you Diana, if you will call me Abigail."

"I had planned on doing so anyway, but I'm glad to have received your permission before I began. Now I can prevent you thinking me ill-mannered in my disregard for formality."

All I could offer was a weak smile as I tried to make sense of this peculiar family: Lady Eliza and her reserved watchfulness; Mr. Edwin Stanton and all the confusion he entailed;

and now Diana with her unreserved familiarity toward a new acquaintance.

"Are you enjoying your stay at Timpton House?" Diana asked, filling in the silence I'd caused during my quandary.

I forced a smile. "I am, thank you." She considered me for an uncomfortable moment, assessing the truthfulness of my answer.

"I heard you met one of the village boys this afternoon in the parish cemetery."

My heart quickened at the realization that Edwin must be the source of her information. Who else would have recounted such an insignificant fact? "I did," I said, unsure how much I should say. "His name is Silas. I found him lying on his father's grave. I—" I hesitated, "I felt drawn to speak with him."

She nodded her head solemnly. "He is the son of Levi Bragg, one of our former tenants. Such a tragedy. Mr. Bragg left behind his wife and five children."

"Do you know what happened to him?"

"He took ill suddenly—a pain in his stomach and a high fever, I believe. He died within a day or two though I don't recall the determined cause."

My heart sank anew. "How awful!"

"It was obviously unexpected, and I have heard Mrs. Bragg has no relatives to call upon for help. I fear they will end up in a workhouse and the youngest children placed in a nearby parish orphanage."

Panic overcame me as I pictured the sweet little boy and his young sisters being sent to such a dreadful place. "Certainly, something can be done?"

She shrugged her shoulders in uncertainty and I instantly felt I had come to Timpton House for a purpose. The confirmation surged through me and a dim flame, that had nearly extinguished with Mother's death, ignited.

Diana watched me cautiously as though she sensed the blaze growing within me.

"After I visit, I will write my father and give him a full account of their needs." I spoke now to myself.

Her eyes widened. "You are truly planning to visit the family then?"

"I am," I said, refocusing my attention. "I plan to go tomorrow."

Her smile broadened, and her eyes lit with excitement. "What a wonderful notion. May I accompany you?"

I tried not to show my astonishment at her suggestion. "Of course, you may come along," I said, only a little disappointed that Lydia would surely refuse to come along now. "But, if you don't mind, I'd prefer to keep our party small; I do not wish to overwhelm Mrs. Bragg."

"Rightfully so," she agreed as her gaze moved to the men filing into the drawing room. Mr. Edwin Stanton stepped in and I watched him search the room until his eyes fell upon his sister, then me. His brows lowered as he walked toward us, his narrowed gaze aimed at Diana. She giggled and put her hand on mine to get my attention. "I do believe Edwin suspects me of betraying him. He will be vexed indeed. Luckily, I did no such thing. I never mentioned he was my source, did I, Abigail?" He stood next to her, his presence putting out as much heat as the fire.

"I hardly suspected him," I replied, grinning at Diana's lack of concern for her brother's scowl.

She smiled up at Mr. Stanton with a wicked smile, and I was certain he was trying to fight off being pleasant.

"I don't believe I will trust to tell you anything again."

She giggled. "You'd go mad without someone to divulge all your secrets to, dear brother. Besides, I did not betray you more than was necessary."

He held her gaze, and I feared she would cower in the severity of it. Instead she stood up and placed her hand tenderly on his cheek. "Have you not learned your sour expressions do little for your cause? You are more persuasive, not to mention more handsome, when you smile—or at least when you remove your scowl. Do you not agree, Abigail?"

I had been enjoying their interaction so much I hadn't expected to become part of it, especially to verify if I believed Edwin very handsome when he smiled. When she did not remove her expectant stare, I reluctantly shifted my gaze to Mr. Stanton. "I am forced to agree with your sister though I admit I have only had the privilege of witnessing it a handful of times."

Diana's mouth opened in feigned shock. "A handful of times? That is a commendable feat in just the short time you have been with us. I can hardly claim to have seen as many in the last several months."

The corner of Edwin's lip twitched at the acknowledgment, but he refused us his handsome smile.

As my gaze shifted between the siblings, the watchful eyes of Helena and Aunt Marianne caught my attention. I stood. "I think I will go ask my aunt if I may retire. I fear our *grand adventure* today has quite exhausted me." I gave Mr. Stanton a knowing glance as Diana looked excitedly between us. Her apparent delight unsettled me, and I hoped she didn't expect to discover something more significant than a few playful remarks. "I will see you both tomorrow," I said, leaving them with a curtsy.

When the softness of my bed engulfed me, I closed my eyes realizing how exhausted I truly was. In my last few thoughts before I drifted into sleep, I recalled the strange look in Edwin Stanton's eyes as he called me maddening. Would I see it again? Probably, though it would most likely be directed at Helena. I didn't wish to think of Helena as I drifted off to sleep, for I feared my dreams would be filled with rattling, giggling angels, but often sleep comes without permission.

CHAPTER 7

"*A*bigail?"

"Hmmm?" My weight shifted sideways, and I impulsively repositioned my pillow to adjust for it.

"Abigail!"

My eyes fluttered open to find Hannah seated next to me on the bed. I blinked again and rubbed the sleep from my vision. It wasn't a dream; she was here, grinning down at me as though she was about to burst from excitement. "What is it, Hannah?" I asked, pushing myself to a sitting position.

A loud squeal echoed through the room. "He has asked for my hand!"

"Sir Wycliffe?" I said, already knowing the answer.

"Yes! And I am beyond myself with joy!"

I grabbed her hand. "Watching the two of you I supposed a proposal must come soon. How thrilled I am for you both."

"We will announce our engagement to the party at breakfast; but, being family, I thought you should be told before the others."

I felt an overwhelming sense of gratitude at her thoughtfulness. "Well, tell me all about it," I insisted.

She began relaying the story of how they had met in London and how he had practically forced an invitation to Timpton House to be with her even though his own estate is not five miles north. As she finished, she grinned. "And the marriage comes with a future title, although I wouldn't care if it didn't, but I shall one day be a baroness—Lady Wycliffe! Does that not sound most elegant?"

"It does," I smiled. "And it fits you perfectly."

She beamed at my acknowledgment and leapt from the bed. "Get ready, I want you to be there when it's announced!"

Proving my eagerness, I threw the covers off and went to ring the bell for Lydia. "I will be down as soon as Lydia can tame my hair."

With one last giddy smile she flew from the room in anticipation.

A CASUAL CHATTER filled the dining room, and I breathed a sigh of relief that I had made it in time for the announcement. My stomach rumbled at the delicious smells and I hurried to the sideboard to fill my plate with food.

"A lady does not gorge herself in public." I turned to find the smug scowl of Helena scrutinizing me. She looked exceptionally cross, and I thought of what a handsome couple her and Edwin Stanton would make in their unwavering moodiness. Defiantly I grabbed another muffin.

"I'm thrilled for Hannah," I offered trying to ease the glower my added pastry had caused.

"It is most exciting," she said with no emotion in her voice. "My sister, The Baroness." A brief rage engulfed her countenance. Hannah, her younger sister, had outmatched her in rank and much more speedily than she could have expected. I scarcely had a moment to feel sorry for her before she huffed. "She can have the rattle and his title. I wouldn't put up with such a distasteful companion for all the titles in the Empire."

"Sir Wycliffe seems tolerable enough, and I believe he will be a suitable match for Hannah."

She waived her hand dismissively in the air. "I'll concern myself with it no longer. I have my own gentleman to snare." She turned her glare toward the food. "I refuse to let my sister beat me to the altar."

I didn't know how to respond. "I better go find a seat before the announcement."

Helena gave a distinct nod of dismissal. Turning to find a place at the table, I met Aunt Marianne's inquisitive gaze.

"Hello, Aunt," I said, walking toward her. "How are you this morning?"

Her eyes lingered on my overloaded plate before refocusing on me. "Very well, thank you."

"I am overjoyed with the news," I offered, hoping to lessen the censure in her eyes.

"News?" Mrs. Hawkins asked from across the table, her gaze shifting to Aunt Marianne. "What news is there to be had?"

My hand impulsively shot up to cover my mouth. "I did not mean...I—" I glanced between Mrs. Hawkins's unyielding stare and the disapproving glare of Aunt Marianne.

Aunt Marianne released a subtle exhale before turning to her friend, an amiable expression altering her agitated appearance. "Do forgive me for not saying anything, but I promised to refrain from telling anyone until the happy couple could share it themselves. However, now that it has been *mentioned*, I feel obliged to divulge that the matter we spoke of yesterday has come to fruition."

Mrs. Hawkins's round eyes grew larger. "Mr. Stanton has proposed?"

"Not yet," Aunt Marianne said, lifting her chin. "I refer to the conversation we had regarding my daughter Hannah."

"Hannah?" Mrs. Hawkins repeated with a whisper, leaning in as much as she was able from across the table. "Hannah is to be married then?"

Aunt Marianne glanced around warily before bestowing an affirmative nod.

"Did Sir Wycliffe not consider the timing of such an offer?" Mrs. Hawkins scoffed. "Decorum would have him wait until after Mr. Stanton's forthcoming proposal—both as a guest here at Timpton and as the suitor for a *younger* daughter." Mrs. Hawkins shook her head with dissatisfaction. "How vexed Helena must be to have her younger sister best her in securing a match."

Aunt Marianne stiffened. "I assure you, Helena could not be more pleased for her sister." I bit at my lips, thankful Mrs. Hawkins's discerning gaze did not stray from Aunt Marianne. "Unlike Hannah, Helena is thoughtful and precise, so the pace of her courtship is exactly as she intends it to be."

Mrs. Hawkins gave an attentive nod to Aunt Marianne, and I suddenly became aware I was no longer a part of the conversation. I took a step backwards, preparing to remove myself.

"And, just between us," Aunt Marianne whispered, compelling me to linger. "Helena shared that Mr. Stanton was unashamedly bold in affirming his feelings for her last night. Apparently, he hinted that a proposal will come very soon."

An odd sensation flowed through my body and seeped into my limbs, causing my plate to grow heavy in my hands. I gazed at an empty chair near the far side of the table.

"Dear girl," Mrs. Hawkins said, though it took me a moment to realize she spoke to me. "How pale you've turned."

I lifted my lowered plate before giving a weak smile. "I must admit I am quite famished. I believe a bite to eat will have me feeling myself again."

The corners of the woman's mouth curved wryly. "How

fortunate for you there are plenty of options for sustenance well within your reach."

I drew a shaky inhale, glancing toward Aunt Marianne whose hand was positioned to hide her amused smile. "Yes, fortunate indeed," I said, dipping into a quick curtsy. "Please, if you will excuse me." I didn't even offer an explanation as I made haste toward the back end of the table.

As I sat, the two Miss Dowdings rose from their places next to me. I was too preoccupied to take offense at their timely departure and was instead grateful for a moment of solitude. Absentmindedly I grabbed a muffin from my plate and took a bite. I was still eating and contemplating my strange reaction to Aunt Marianne's whisperings, when Sir Wycliffe stood to give the happy announcement.

As the congratulations began, I watched the beaming couple welcome the well wishes of their friends and acquaintances. Even Helena put on a false smile and greeted the radiant couple as an adoring sister. Surely, they were precisely what a newly engaged couple should look like. Regardless of what had been said about him, I was confident they were well suited.

My thoughts involuntarily shifted to Helena and Mr. Stanton. Would he appear as thrilled as Sir Wycliffe did when they announced their engagement? Would she exhibit a similar glow as Hannah? I forced the analysis from my mind. For now, I'd simply choose to find amusement in Helena's increased efforts at snaring a gentleman, even if it was Edwin Stanton where she set her aim.

LORD RAMSBY APPROACHED me as I entered the drawing room. "What joyful news," he said, seemingly delighted with the announcement of my cousin's engagement.

"It certainly is," I said smiling, unable to resist his contagious enthusiasm.

"Mr. Stanton and Lady Eliza must be pleased with such an agreeable match being made among their party."

I nodded. "I am sure they are."

His deep brown eyes held mine, endeavoring to convey something I wasn't proficient at deciphering.

He took a step closer. "I hope it isn't the last to be made among the group." I thought of Mr. Edwin Stanton and Helena, but questioned if he was implying a different match, one more pertinent to him. Searching his gaze, I finally perceived his meaning—he spoke of us! A deep blush heated my cheeks at the newfound understanding.

"Abigail." Diana's arm linked through mine and I sought to appear unaffected by Lord Ramsby's suggestion. "I have been most eager to find you. I was hoping to depart at once for our outing, I do not trust the afternoon weather since yesterday and will find great comfort in returning before it has the chance to rain."

Her gaze followed mine to Lord Ramsby.

"Lord Ramsby!" she exclaimed in apparent disbelief. "I did not notice you standing there. How dull-witted I can be. I must beg your forgiveness."

"Mrs. Ellis, please do not—"

"It is just the timing for our outing is pressing on me," she interrupted. "So, as much as I hate to be an irritation, I must insist on stealing dear Abigail from you."

Lord Ramsby's eyebrows lifted in confusion before he gave a stiff nod. "Of course, Mrs. Ellis," he said, ineffectively hiding his disappointment. "And where is it the two of you are off to in such a hurry?"

"It is a secret," Diana asserted with a teasing grin. "But do not think of it again. Perhaps you could find amusement with the other ladies until our return."

The questioning gaze he shot me compelled me to oblige

him. "Shall we walk together in the garden this afternoon?" His charming smile lightened my heart though I refused to reflect on the hope he had just conveyed, knowing how it would jitter my nerves.

"I will look forward to it, Miss Blakeslee."

Before I could respond, Diana pulled me from his side and through the drawing room, pausing only to give her brother a deliberate glance before we exited.

AFTER FETCHING my bonnet and reticule, we assured the butler that despite the potential mud we intended to walk to Chadsmead on such a beautiful morning. The ground was damp, but the large puddles from yesterday's storm were easy to avoid and I found myself enjoying the walk immensely without Lord Ramsby and the rain to divert my attention.

Diana was very amiable, and conversation came easily. She told me how she had caught Mr. Ellis's notice by tripping down the stairs at the theater. In her embarrassment, she had clambered to her feet to find she couldn't support her own weight just as Mr. Ellis reached her and offered his assistance. It had taken little for him to fall madly in love, and I didn't have to wonder what he saw in her. Beautiful, kind, refined, but with a liveliness about her, she seemed a perfect lady to claim one's affections.

"How long did you and Mr. Ellis court?"

"We were acquainted no more than a fortnight before he offered for my hand." I must have done a poor job at hiding my astonishment because she giggled and grabbed my arm affectionately. "Does that seem too hasty, Abigail?"

"I doubt my opinion is worth obtaining. I claim to under-stand little about such things."

"Yet my interest is piqued."

I hesitated until her determined silence became intolerable. "I suppose—if it were me—I'd question my ability to make such a crucial decision in such a short time." I shrugged. "I assume the longer you are familiar with someone, the easier it is to discern if they act in earnest or if they are simply practiced at hiding their true character." Guilt pricked my conscience, and I quickly rationalized it away.

Diana pursed her lips and nodded. "Your concern is valid. I've heard of ladies marrying men who pretend to be one way in courtship only to act quite another way in marriage." Her face turned thoughtful as she continued. "I suppose there was that risk for me, but I somehow knew Mr. Ellis was the best of men. I admit I had been blinded by wealth and title at one time but with him it was different. There was a goodness about him that reached deeper than his generous acts and kind appearance—it seemed to emulate from his soul." She laughed and squeezed my arm. "Now that I say it aloud, I am certain you must find me insufferably hairbrained."

"Not at all," I said, comparing her description of Mr. Ellis to the unmistakable goodness in both my parents and Laurence. "In fact, I will concede that your judgment is likely superior to mine in matters of the heart, for Mr. Ellis seems an exceptional husband."

"He most certainly is! And I must say, I'm pleased to attain your confidence in my *superior* judgment." A mischievous smile spread across her face. "I do believe I have determined another purpose for it." My brow creased in uncertainty as I scanned her profile, but she only laughed again. "And what of you, Abigail? Tell me of your family."

Eager to speak of my family, I permitted the shift in conversation. I told her of Father and Laurence and how much I missed them. Diana and I were both fortunate to be raised by such affectionate fathers, but I tried not to feel guilty as I spoke of Laurence and the ideal way he fulfilled his role of doting older brother.

"And what of your mother? Was she truly as amazing as they say?"

"She was the most selfless person I have known," I said, blinking back the tears that blurred my vision. "It will be two years this summer since her passing and I miss her as intensely as I did the moment she left us." A tear strayed down my cheek and I hurried to wipe it away. "She was the foundation of our family and her death toppled us. I fear we are still trying to put the pieces back together." I thought of how the makeshift version we had been rebuilding scarcely resembled what we had once been.

"Well I can see the same goodness in you. A mother bestows more than her physical attributes to her children, and you are fortunate to have received both from her." Her eyes shifted to my profile, but I would not return her gaze.

"There it is," I said, pointing to the small cottage that had just come into view, grateful at its opportune appearance.

"Surely seven people could not have shared such a small cottage?"

"I've seen more living in smaller quarters than these."

Diana's eyes widened in disbelief.

"Miss Abigail!" Silas came running toward us waving his arms excitedly. "I knew you'd come."

I reached out my hand to the dirty-faced boy and he eagerly grabbed it.

"Mum is feelin' outa' sorts today," he said, nearly dragging me to the cottage. "She's not left 'er bed since yesterday."

Diana and I shared a worried glance as we followed the impatient boy.

As we neared the entrance to the cottage, the noticeable pounding in my chest accelerated. I'd never aided someone without Mother directing me and I suddenly doubted my abilities.

"Hurry," Silas urged as he pulled me through the lopsided door into a musty room of crying children.

I exhaled and stepped through the threshold. The slender frame of Mrs. Bragg lay in a small bed next to the table, a baby lying near her, arms flailing, and screaming in distress. Without hesitating, I walked toward the woman. "Mrs. Bragg?" I asked, leaning over to glimpse the woman's face. "I am Abigail Blakeslee. I hope you don't mind our intrusion but my friend, Diana Stanton, and I have come to offer our assistance this morning."

Mrs. Bragg's eyes fluttered open, focused on me, and closed again before giving a brief nod. She remained motionless and I glanced toward the others.

Five sets of eyes watched me with curiosity. "Silas," I said, coaxing myself to take charge. "Would you mind introducing myself and Miss Diana to your sweet sisters?"

"Mary, Patience, and Rose," he said, pointing to each of the dirty-faced girls one by one before gesturing to the bed. "The baby is Juliet."

"Hello, darlings. I am Miss Abigail." I pulled Diana forward. "And this is Miss Diana. We have come to help your mother for a few hours." I grabbed Juliet, wrapping her coverings more tightly around her, before handing her to a reluctant Diana. "Are you girls hungry?" The three girls nodded their heads in unison.

I walked to the shelf where I suspected food or ingredients for cooking would most likely be kept. But, apart from a few withered root vegetables I found in a large bucket, every container was empty. I scanned the area again—surely there had to be more than this. "Silas dear, what has your family been eating?"

He moved to my side, his shoulders rounded and his gaze on the floor. "Not much." My eyes flickered to Diana, whose face conveyed the alarm I was struggling to repress. "We ran outta flour a few days ago. I was ask'n Papa 'bout it when you found me."

He hadn't been at the cemetery merely to mourn the loss of his father, but to plead for his help. What if I had rationalized away my desire to talk to him? My heart winced at the possible consequences. "Well then," I said, hoping I sounded fairly cheerful as I reached for my reticule, "I'll need you to run to the shops and grab a few items for me. Could you do that?"

He didn't lift his head. "Miss Abigail," he whispered, "we 'ave no money."

I took several coins and placed them in his palm—his eyes widened at the sight. "This should be enough for everything," I said. He nodded, his gaze still locked on the perceived fortune I had entrusted to him. "I will need two loaves of bread, a cooked chicken, salted meat, butter, fresh milk, and..." I watched as he concentrated on memorizing the list, "and a little treat for each of you." His large eyes met mine for only a moment before he darted from my side and disappeared out the door.

The joy I felt at his excitement lingered as I stoked the fire in the hearth. I retrieved the vegetables I had found and examined them. It wasn't much, but I was hopeful I could make an edible soup with what I had. I turned toward Diana whose bewildered gaze greeted me—Juliet red with anger in her arms. "I'm going to make soup."

She looked down at the wailing child and back at me, blinking vacantly. "Did you just say you are making soup?"

"I did," I said loud enough for her to hear me over the baby's screams. "But how about I attempt to calm Juliet before I set myself to the task?" I reached out and she gladly handed me the crying child. I had no intention of allowing Diana to feel incompetent when she'd been so kind to offer her assistance. "There is water in the wash basin," I said, motioning to the table. "Perhaps you could find a cloth and clean up the girls?"

Glad for a directive, she grabbed the basin and a cloth, and headed toward the watchful audience. She sat next to Mary, the oldest girl of about six years. "Hello darling. May I help you wash up?"

Mary tucked her chin and looked up at Diana with an apprehensive expression before giving a timid nod. Diana dampened the cloth and began to rub it gently over the girl's dirtied face.

It didn't take long for Diana to become comfortable with the task and she cheerfully scrubbed the girls' faces and hands, complimenting their beautiful features. She was a natural, and I was grateful she'd asked to come along. I rocked Juliet until she calmed and placed her next to her mother on the bed before going outside to fetch water.

By the time Silas returned, the soup was nearly finished, the soiled laundry gathered, extra water boiled, and I was tidying up the cottage. Diana had the three girls lined up and was working on braiding their tangled hair while Juliet squirmed on the bed next to her mother.

Silas laid the items on the table, thrilled he had not forgotten even one, and then handed me the change. I added more coins from my reticule to the extra and placed them in a pile on a nearby shelf. "If you require anything before I return, please use this money." His sincere relief at the gesture filled me with such happiness I could scarcely wait to see his reaction to the aid Father would surely offer this sweet family.

I poured fresh milk for Juliet and she eagerly lapped at the cup when I lifted her and put it to her lips. "I'll begin the wash as soon as we get the children fed."

Diana drew near. "Surely you are not going to do the washing yourself?"

"And who else will do it?" I asked, shooting her a teasing smile. "Unless that is your way of volunteering."

Her eyes widened, and I had to laugh at her horrified expression.

"Don't look so alarmed, Diana, I was only jesting. Besides, I'm more than proficient at laundering and will gladly see to the task." Her brow creased but before she had a chance to inquire, I walked away to serve up the children's food.

As Diana spoke with the eating children, I saw to Mrs. Bragg. She looked sallow lying there, hardly moving as I raised her head to make her drink. She took a sip and opened her eyes, appearing as though she must be dreaming the whole thing. "How are you, Mrs. Bragg?" I asked.

"I fear I'm not well." Her voice was raspy and scarcely audible.

"Well, we shall try to help," I said, knowing the darkness and grief that filled a person at the loss of a loved one. How much deeper her own anxiety must be losing the man who had provided for herself and her children. "We shall help!" I amended resolutely.

I took to the yard and filled the wash bucket with the remainder of the boiling water, adding well water until the temperature was tolerable for my hands. I had only found a small piece of lye and knew between that and my time restraint I would do a mediocre job of the task, at best; but what more could be done?

My thoughts drifted to Mother while I worked. I smiled at the image my mind conjured of her elbow deep in murky water, humming as she scrubbed the dirt off someone else's laundry. How I had admired her then—how I venerated her now. I wanted to be like her. I wanted to be the lady she intended me to be. The sting of lye on my hands told me I was once again moving along the correct course.

The sound of horses approaching pulled my gaze from my work.

I couldn't move as I sat, hands dirty in washing water, staring at Mr. Edwin Stanton alighting from his horse. He had brought an extra mare and he tied both to a nearby tree before starting toward me.

"What are you doing here?" I asked, still in shock at his sudden appearance.

"I have come to offer my assistance," he said, as though it was common to appear at the doorstep of a widow's cottage.

"But how did you know we were here?"

"I told him." Diana exited the house, an expression of satisfaction lighting her face. "But I only implied he should join us. How fortunate he is more astute than I thought him."

I was uncertain if I'd agree on his arrival being fortunate until the beaming face of Silas settled my opinion. He stared with wide eyes at the horses Mr. Stanton had brought with him.

Silas's gaze skirted in Mr. Stanton's direction before returning to the magnificent creatures. "Are those your 'orses, sir?"

"They are. Would you care to meet them?"

"Would I ever!" Silas yelped as he darted toward Mr. Stanton.

Silas chattered breathlessly as Mr. Stanton led him to the horses. The darker of the two horses was stunning, almost a black but glimmered in the sunlight with a sheen of golden brown. The other was a smaller mare, gray in coloring. It was a lovely horse as well, but anything would appear inferior next to the striking horse Mr. Stanton had rode in on.

Mr. Stanton lifted Silas onto the saddle of his horse, and I smiled to myself at his kind gesture.

"He isn't as fierce as he pretends to be," Diana said, eyeing me as I watched her brother.

My face flushed at being caught in my observation, yet I

couldn't resist looking back to where he stood, a content boy waving wildly at me from the saddle. I returned his wave as Mr. Stanton grinned in our direction.

"Such a handsome smile," Diana said admiringly. "I only wish he might find more reasons to display it."

I continued to watch as he led his horse away from us, Silas hooting excitedly. "I agree."

Diana leaned against the cottage. "He has always been a serious spirit, but the last few years have greatly changed him. I fear if he isn't careful, every remaining bit of life will be wrung from him." I remembered Helena's scowl earlier and wondered if Diana considered my cousin a poor match for her brother.

"Is it not up to him? Perhaps he does not mind the man he has become."

"He won't say it, but I'm certain he still hopes someone will see him for who he truly is, for what he once believed he had to offer." I was curious why she shared her concerns with me. Surely, I had no influence in dissuading my cousin from pursuing him.

I pushed aside my concern for the moment. "What did he once have to offer that he no longer does? Surely he has not lost his fortune?" I tried not to relish in how dissatisfied Helena would be to receive such news.

"No, not his fortune. I can hardly explain what it is he has lost." She hesitated. "I suppose I would say he has lost faith in love— 'a vicious and heartless emotion' he calls it."

"His faith in love?" I repeated, trying to make sense of her disclosure. I turned my gaze back toward the road as Mr. Stanton and Silas reappeared. "Love is the only thing that is real, the only thing that is dependable and constant."

"Though I agree with you, he no longer would. He has accepted the tainted lie that he has nothing to offer but Timpton and his fortune."

I didn't respond. I had nothing to say as I wondered if he

did have more to offer than being an heir. I'd seen small glimpses of something hidden below his stern demeanor, but was it enough for anyone to develop an unwavering attachment?

He helped Silas down, and I turned my attention back to the washing, suddenly aware how improper it must appear to have a lady scrubbing the dirty washing of a poor family. But this was who I was, who I had forgotten to be since Mother's death; and now that I remembered, I had no desire to pretend otherwise. My parents' earliest lessons were centered on serving the less fortunate, on easing the burdens of others. Surely Mother had felt no shame at being covered in mucky water when helping another.

Wringing out the last of the clothing, I took the basket to the line and began hanging the newly washed linen. I turned to grab the next item, startled to find Mr. Stanton holding the basket under one arm and reaching a damp cloth toward me.

"Thank you," I said, taking it and hanging it on the line. He nodded but said nothing as he held out another one.

After the basket was empty, I turned to take it. My hand brushed his, and I felt that familiar warm sensation pulse through me. I tugged at the basket, forcing him to relinquish his grip. "I need to check on Juliet."

"Yes, of course," he said, following me to the cottage door. "And how can I be of assistance?"

I looked at him suspiciously. "You truly want to help?"

"I believe that is why I came."

His response made me pause, and I wondered if he questioned his own intentions. "Well, if you believe it is why you came," I said, pointing to the ax stuck in the chopping block, "more wood is needed for the hearth."

He turned toward the woodpile before removing his waistcoat; without waiting for his verbal acceptance of the task, I hurried to the house.

Diana sat on a wooden chair with Rose on her lap, the

others gathered near her, captivated. She was telling the story of a troll and I laughed at the deep voice she used when the troll in her story spoke. Even Silas seemed completely enthralled.

I set myself to work grabbing the wooden bowls from the table to wash and storing the remaining food. Juliet let out a whimper, and I rushed to grab her to prevent her waking Mrs. Bragg. She seemed irritable, and I decided I best take her outside to distract her.

As we walked into the sunshine, she stopped fussing, her round blue eyes reflecting the color of the sky above her. She was a beautiful child, with a strawberry colored curl coming down her forehead. I wondered what life she would have, and I hoped hers would be as blessed as mine. I grabbed a flower from a nearby bush and held it in front of her. "This is a flower," I said as she looked at it and smiled a most adorable dimpled smile.

The sound of the ax on wood brought my eyes to Mr. Stanton. He stood in just his shirtsleeves, hair amiss and sweat glistening on his brow. The wood seemed to split with little effort as the ax came down, and I disregarded the way his damp shirt clung to the muscles on his back. He stopped and wiped his forehead with his forearm.

I watched him a moment longer before realizing he must be thirsty. I forced my gaze from him and went inside to see about getting him a drink. I had used all the cups for the children and Mrs. Bragg at lunch, and I didn't have the ability to wash them while holding Juliet. I spotted the soup ladle I had already cleaned and grabbed it, dipping it in the newly filled basin.

I waited until he brought the ax down before approaching him. "Mr. Stanton, would you care for some water?"

His bewildered gaze shot in my direction as though he had forgotten why he was here and the purpose for his chopping. "Yes. Thank you," he said, taking the outstretched ladle and draining it. I diverted my eyes to Juliet. He looked extremely handsome out chopping wood, and I had no desire for him to discover I thought such a thing.

"And who is this?" Mr. Stanton asked, touching Juliet's chubby hand resting on my forearm.

I smiled at the sweet face watching Mr. Stanton. "Juliet. And she is quite the cherub with her rosy cheeks and dimples."

"And those blue eyes," he said. "Nearly the same color as the sky."

And nearly the same blue as Helena's eyes, no wonder he mentioned the color.

"Yes," I said a little stiffer than I intended.

He looked at me in his analyzing way, but I swiftly tucked away my discontent. "Your sister is a natural with children. I believe they enjoyed her impression of a troll as much as I did."

His eyes glinted, and a faint grin came to his lips. "She has many hidden talents, some I am rather fond of, others I am not yet certain I support." He paused a moment. "And how is Mrs. Bragg?"

I tried not to show my irritation at his change of subject. "I'm afraid she is not well. She is taking the death of her husband exceedingly hard. And rightfully so, I can't imagine what she must be feeling—the worry of caring for five children without the help of a husband must be debilitating."

"Does she have no family to help?"

"Diana had heard she has no relatives to call on, but I am not certain. She has hardly spoken since we arrived. She seems to be in a state of despair."

"Well, I'm sure she is grateful for what you are doing."

I smiled, distractedly playing with Juliet's hand. "I am not the only one here helping. Besides," I shrugged. "I'm grateful to be here."

I heard giggling behind me and turned to find Diana on the porch with the rest of the children.

Mr. Stanton stepped toward them. "And who are these charming ladies?"

Diana smirked and started the introductions, "This is Lady Mary, Lady Patience, and Lady Rose."

Mr. Stanton bowed to each one with his hands behind his back, sending the girls into mad giggles and my heart stuttered. Perhaps there was more to him, though I doubted Helena would find his ability to bring smiles to the faces of poor children much of an accomplishment.

"I was thinking we might play a game I used to play as a child," he said, directing a hopeful glance in my direction. The children cheered at the idea and I was obliged to accommodate the request.

"My father invented it," Mr. Stanton explained. "It's called Meaches Peaches."

"Meaches Peaches?" I echoed with a lift of my brow.

Diana laughed as I repeated the peculiar name. "I have not thought of that game in years."

"Yes." His brow relaxed, and he grinned at me. "It's quite simple," he said, looking back at the children. "I am a baker and I desire to make a peach crumble. You are the peaches and don't want to be cooked. You must run or hide from me for if I catch you, I will place you there," he said, pointing to a spot under a tree, "and you will remain there until I get all my peaches and bake you into a delightful crumble."

The girls' eyes brightened in excitement, and Silas glanced around for a suitable place to hide.

"I shall count to sixty, with my eyes closed, and then I will search for peaches."

I could scarcely control the intensity of my smile, envisioning Mr. Stanton running around pretending to be a baker and searching for children was more than I could handle.

"1, 2, 3…"

Silas darted away from us as Mary and Patience ran in different directions. I glanced down at Rose, who looked apprehensively from us to Mr. Stanton. She was only two, and most likely too young to understand how to play.

"Do you wish to hide?" I asked Rose.

She nodded her head, and I looked at Diana. "Perhaps you could hide with her?"

"I think you should play," she said, grabbing Juliet from me.

"15, 16, 17..."

"I'm not playing a child's game—with your brother!" I whispered, astounded she would encourage such a thing.

Diana looked down at Rose. "Miss Abigail is not very good at this game. Can you help her find a good place to hide?"

Rose grabbed my hand and pulled me away from the group as I shot Diana a look of betrayal. She was covering her mouth, trying not to startle Juliet with the laugh emanating from her.

"31, 32, 33..."

Realizing Rose still did not quite understand what we were to do, I looked around for an acceptable place to hide and decided behind the wood pile would have to work in our limited time. Rose stood by me, brow furrowed in confusion, as I peered around the edge just in time to glimpse Mr. Stanton say "60" and open his eyes. He walked near the cottage, searching in bushes.

A loud squeal sent me ducking next to Rose. "He has found one of your sisters," I whispered as the sound of giggling burst through the air.

I peeked again and saw he was actually carrying one girl over each shoulder. "They must have hidden together for he has caught both Mary and Patience," I relayed as Rose eyed me with a vacant expression. What an absurd situation I found myself in, yet my heart was pounding in my chest with excitement. I was too nervous Mr. Stanton would spot me if I peeked, so I sat listening, squatted next to Rose.

In the silence Rose turned to walk away. "Rose, we must stay hidden." I gestured for her to return to my side. "Just a little longer now."

She walked back toward me and I grabbed her outstretched hand.

A few minutes later I heard another laugh and couldn't resist looking again. Silas had managed to climb a tree where he had just been discovered. There was nowhere for him to go and he jumped from the branches with a thud. "I almost didn't see you up there," Mr. Stanton said, and Silas beamed at him with pride.

Silas walked to where his sisters sat, and I realized Rose was the last one. Turning back toward her, I was startled to find her gone.

"Rose," Mr. Stanton said as his voice neared the other side of the pile of logs. "How kind of you to save me the trouble. But did you not hide with Miss Blakesl—Miss Abigail," he corrected.

I recognized how silly it would be to continue hiding and stepped out from behind the log pile. I saw Rose running to her beckoning siblings as Mr. Stanton met my gaze with a playful glint in his eyes.

"And now you make crumble with them?" I asked.

"I believe I have one more peach to catch."

"Surely you are not serious?" I asked, taking a step back.

When he moved toward me, I turned to run. I ducked back behind the wood pile, knowing I wasn't fast enough to outrun him. My only option was to continue circling it, changing my direction each time he would attempt to thwart me. I managed fairly well when Mr. Stanton ruined my scheme by clambering over the pile of wood. A childish squeal burst from me as I took off running. Diana laughed, and the children cheered as I made for the back of the cottage. I glanced back to find Mr. Stanton getting closer, my uncontrollable laughter thwarting my efforts for escape. His hand wrapped around my wrist and before I knew what happened he had scooped me over his shoulder.

"Put me down!" I demanded, laughing without restraint.

"And allow you to out maneuver me again? Never."

By the time we got to the front of the house, Diana was laughing so hard she was leaning against the wall of the cottage for support.

"You caught her! You caught her!" the girls exclaimed in utter excitement.

"I have. And now I shall make you all into the most delicious peach crumble."

He placed me gently down next to the others and I smoothed my gown, hot with embarrassment at my girlish reaction.

"Unfortunately, I will need an assistant to make the crumble, and seeing as Miss Diana is occupied, I must call on Miss Abigail." Grateful he had not intended to include me in the remainder of the game I stepped to his side. "Now, I must wash you, peel you, mash you, and then wrap you in dough to cook."

I was unaware who laughed more, myself or the children, as Mr. Stanton pretended to make them into a grand crumble, occasionally requesting help with fetching the pretend water or kneading the ticklish children. By the end of the game, after he had eaten his fill, the happy children hung on him pleading for more.

"Unfortunately, we must leave soon," I said, not wanting him to be the bearer of bad news. "And I need help with a few things before we go."

All the children moaned in unison. "When'll you be back?" Patience asked.

"Soon," I said, though I wasn't certain when that would be. "Silas, why don't you go grab the special treat you bought today," I said, hoping to distract them from the idea of us leaving. Silas jumped to his feet, his sisters trailing behind him in anticipation.

Mr. Stanton stood and dusted the dirt from his pants as I turned to follow the children. Diana handed me Juliet who I nestled close, escaping the accusing smirk Diana was directing toward me. "I will show Silas what he can give the children for dinner and see if Mrs. Bragg will eat or drink anything before we leave," I called over my shoulder. "Diana, would you pull down any dry laundry?" I asked, hoping to prevent her from following me inside.

"Of course," she laughed as she joined her brother in the yard. I peeked behind me to find her still grinning wildly. How relieved she must be at seeing her brother in a more amiable mood because of the children, no wonder she had invited him today. I had to admit, I was also pleased to encounter a side of him I had not before seen and quite enjoyed.

I WAS able to get Mrs. Bragg to swallow a few bites of bread and sip at some water. Her body trembled, and I placed a blanket over her. "Silas, try to give your mother a few sips of water each hour or two and continue to ask her if she desires to eat." He nodded but I could tell it was taking every bit of bravery in him to not break down in tears. My heart wrenched. "If you should need anything, you know where I am."

"Yes, Miss Abigail."

As we walked from the house, I was all too aware of how much responsibility I was placing on this eight-year-old boy. "Brave child," I said, and Father's voice echoed in my mind.

I looked between the three wide-eyed girls, questioning if

I could find the strength to leave them. "Be good helpers to your brother. We will be back soon enough."

Mr. Stanton walked to my side, and I wondered where he had been the last little while. "Mr. Silas," he said. "I hope you don't mind, but I've taken the liberty of speaking with Mrs. Hill. She will be here shortly to keep you company until bedtime."

Relief engulfed me at Mr. Stanton's gesture and I noticed Silas's expression reflecting my own.

"Thank you, sir."

Silas herded the children back inside, and we walked toward the horses.

I glanced at Mr. Stanton's profile. "That was very thoughtful of you."

"Mrs. Hill is a good Christian woman, and I believe she is well acquainted with the Bragg family, so it seemed a natural invitation."

"Nevertheless, it was kind of you to arrange it."

He nodded a subtle acceptance of my compliment, unable to verbally acknowledge his foresight.

As we reached the horses, I realized I had no idea of the time, but I was certain we had stayed later than I'd intended.

"I'm glad you brought the horses," Diana said as she walked to the gray mare and rubbed her neck affectionately. "If we do not hurry, we shall be late for dinner."

The black horse lifted his head and whinnied. I took a step back, noticing how large he looked up close. "Certainly we can get back before dinner by walking?"

"I fear we cannot," she said with a false innocence. "We must ride."

"But there are only two horses," I responded, as though an extra horse would have made a difference in my willingness to ride.

I didn't miss the mischievous smile Diana sent her brother. "Diana feared the weather might turn poor and asked for me to supply a faster means of transportation, if the need arose. I informed her you don't ride, so she told me to bring only two horses if I came—one for her," the corner of his mouth twitched in his moment of hesitation, "and one for us."

"For us?" I glanced between the siblings. "Surely you jest?"

Diana's smile broadened. "You can't ride a horse without first learning how and, at the moment, we have no time for such things. You must let Edwin ride you back to Timpton or we shall be late."

My mouth widened as my gaze shifted from Mr. Stanton to his sister. "You planned this!"

Her brother aided her in mounting her horse and she looked down at me. "What a thing to accuse me of! As if I could predict our late departure and need to ride." She shook her head. "Besides, Abigail, what purpose do I have at meddling in your affairs?"

"I—" my face flushed as I thought how to phrase it with Mr. Stanton standing near, fussing with the adjustments of his saddle. "I can't say what you are up to, but I'm not getting on that horse."

"Oh, Abigail, why must you be so stubborn?"

"And why must you be so—irritating!"

She feigned an insulted expression and backed her horse from us. "Unless you intend to explain to my mother why you are late, and why you were alone with my brother again, I'd get on the horse."

The nerve! Instantly the insufferable similarities between the two siblings became apparent. I sent Mr. Stanton a beseeching glance, but he only shrugged his shoulders. "I fear you have discovered one of the hidden talents I spoke of earlier—she is a capable schemer." His tone made me wonder if it was one of the talents he was fond of.

"Cursed creature," I muttered, causing Mr. Stanton to chuckle.

He took a step closer and my breath caught. "I promise to be a gentleman."

I exhaled a shallow breath and nodded my forced acceptance.

Placing his hands on my waist he easily lifted me to the saddle and mounted behind me.

I was intent on keeping my distance, as much as was possible on a saddle made for one, but found myself feeling insecure with the combination of the horse's movements and the height. Grudgingly I settled back into the safety of Mr. Stanton's arms, promising I would never forgive Diana.

CHAPTER 8

*W*e followed Diana's horse, and I tried not to think of the last time I was on a horse so many years ago. After what I had experienced, I never thought I would ride again; yet here I sat, in the security of a man's arms so unlike the one who had last forced me to share his saddle. I concentrated on the feeling of safety Mr. Stanton's arms provided.

"Feeling better?" Mr. Stanton asked, apparently noticing my rigid posture soften.

I nodded. "It is not quite as terrifying as I remember it, perhaps it is because I'm older and the height is not quite so overwhelming."

"So, you have ridden before?"

"I have been transported on a horse before; I'm not sure that would count as riding."

He sat silently, leaving me the opportunity to finish but I didn't continue. I felt his chest rise against me. "There are few things I can do to feel myself anymore, but riding is one of them."

I thought of his morning rides with Helena and

wondered if those were the moments he spoke of, the moments he felt most himself. I was oddly disappointed I had not been able to observe it, and she had. There was something about seeing a person as they truly were, when they stepped outside the walls they placed around themselves for protection. I knew all about protecting what you wished to hide, what others wished to hide about you; it made things easier even if it felt deceptive and arduous at times.

"Outside of Easton Manor, I fear I can never fully be myself." I didn't know why I had said it, why I hinted at what I could not share. Maybe it was a form of protection, so he would know there was something wrong with me, allow him to keep his distance and tell others to do the same. But as I sat in his embrace, it felt like a hollow excuse. Besides, I didn't need to protect myself against him—he was Helena's and would keep his distance without my efforts.

DIANA KEPT a good distance in front of us until we neared Timpton House. "Perhaps you should walk her in, Edwin," she encouraged with a pointed glance.

Obviously agreeing with her, he moved one hand to my waist. "Hold on tight while I dismount."

I grasped the saddle horn and held on, feeling unbalanced without Mr. Stanton for support.

"Now I am forced to sit on a horse unassisted?" I directed my comment to Diana, remembering why I was in this predicament. "I hope you do not have to explain to your mother why you allowed an untrained rider to fall from your brother's horse."

I caught Mr. Stanton glance in his sister's direction but couldn't see the expression on his face.

"You will not fall, Abigail, Edwin won't let you," her confidence eased me slightly. "But I do think it a more appropriate gesture, if he were to lead you in."

I narrowed my eyes. "Appropriate? Am I to assume riding with him would appear inappropriate then?"

Diana released an exasperated sigh. "I only said it would appear more appropriate if he walked you in. Truly, it is you I am thinking of."

I might as well keep the look of puzzlement on my face for the remainder of our conversation. "Me?"

"I am sure your doting cousin is going to be eagerly awaiting our return. I figured you would rather not explain why you were sitting on a horse with the man she is pining for. Am I misled in my reasoning?"

I could tell by the tightness in Mr. Stanton's jaw he did not appreciate his sister's comment, but she willingly overlooked it. I fixed my eyes forward and silently stewed in my irritation, unwilling to acknowledge she had a valid point.

As Mr. Stanton led us past Timpton House, I intentionally kept my gaze from the windows, not wanting to see if Diana was correct in her assumption.

Diana drew her horse near, but I refused to look at her. "Don't be vexed with me, Abigail." The sincerity in her voice was apparent but I didn't feel like wavering in my irritation. "I didn't mean to upset you, I just wanted..." her voice trailed off. "I'm sorry."

"It is nothing," I said unconvincingly as we reached the stable. Mr. Stanton walked to the side of the horse and grabbed my waist, slowly lowering me to the ground.

"I'm sorry I went along with it," he whispered. "We didn't intend to upset you."

I ignored the sensation his nearness caused, allowing anger to take its place. I knew he had been a co-conspirator, after all he had brought the two horses, but his admission confirmed his guilt and I felt an overwhelming exasperation with him. Confounded man! "Thank you for your assistance,"

I said coldly as I turned from him and began a brisk-paced walk toward the house.

~

As I WALKED from the stables, a familiar laugh sent me searching the scene to my left. Sure enough, Helena came into view escorted by Lord Ramsby. Apparently, she had not been anxious enough about our absence to forego a walk through the gardens with such a charming companion. Both looked pleasantly engaged in conversation, when Lord Ramsby noticed me and my startled expression.

"Miss Blakeslee," he said less amiably than I was accustomed. Had Helena said something to him?

"Helena. Lord Ramsby." I nodded a greeting, but their close proximity and intertwined arms only added to my irritated state. She should not be walking with another man when she desired Mr. Stanton, especially not with Lord Ramsby.

Helena considered me a moment with an apprehensive expression. "Where are Mrs. Ellis and Mr. Stanton?"

I shrugged. "I suppose they are in the stables with their horses."

"And where have the three of you been all day?"

"I had arranged to meet with the little boy from the cemetery yesterday. His father has recently passed, and I thought I might be of assistance to his mother." They watched me as though they were individually calculating the truthfulness of my story. I displayed little emotion in my retelling. "Diana had discovered my intention and asked to join me. Mr. Stanton followed later with horses at his sister's request, though I did not know of it until his arrival."

Helena forced out a smile. "Diana, is it?"

"Yes. Diana," I asserted unable to conjure any patience.

Helena directed her smile at Lord Ramsby. "Such an unusual lady, *Mrs. Ellis.*"

I didn't agree verbally, though I wanted to.

"Well," she said, looking back toward me, "Lord Ramsby and I are returning from taking a walk through the gardens since you were not here to oblige him, as you had promised."

I must have looked quite ridiculous as I remembered my failed commitment, for I could see the pleasurable look Helena displayed at my discomfort.

My eyes fell on a waiting Lord Ramsby, and I hoped that was why he seemed agitated with me. "Please forgive me, Lord Ramsby. There was much to be done and we left as soon as we could." My explanation had left out the matter of me completely forgetting him, but a smile brightened his expression and I knew he would not hold too much of a grudge.

"All is well, Miss Blakeslee," he offered kindly. "It seems a justifiable reason for your delay, perhaps we could plan on walking tomorrow?"

"I would like that very much and thank you for your understanding."

Helena looked less than pleased with how willingly Lord Ramsby overlooked my folly, and I rebuked myself for relishing in her displeasure.

Hearing Diana and Mr. Stanton's voices coming from behind I made my excuses and continued toward the house.

LYDIA PRESSED me on the day's events, and I eagerly told her of the Braggs while leaving out most of the redeeming contributions of the Stanton siblings. I had no intention of recalling how much I had enjoyed their company when I was still furious with them both.

She fussed with a strand of my hair that was unwilling to conform to the style she was attempting. "I overheard the stable hand say you had arrived on Mr. Stanton's horse?" Her eyes flit to my face.

"I did, but it was not by choice."

She stopped styling and waited for me to continue.

I was obliged to explain how the scheming Diana had compelled me to ride with Mr. Stanton or risk rebuke at being late to dinner or being left in his company unchaperoned.

Lydia shot me a look of disbelief, covering her amused shock with her hand.

"Traitor!"

"I'm sorry," she said as a laugh burst from her. "I can't believe they got you on a horse. Mrs. Ellis is most effective at accomplishing her purposes."

"Yes, and at my expense," I said with an exaggerated pout on my face.

Lydia's smiling eyes turned contemplative. "Why would she bother with such a scheme? Surely she knows Mr. Stanton and Helena are soon to be engaged."

"Where did you hear that?" I asked, startled at how confidently she mentioned it.

"The staff," she said, looking perplexed. "And you have made mention of their upcoming engagement yourself."

I suddenly felt out of sorts. "Yes, of course—I, I wanted to be sure, for Helena's sake, if something more official had been decided."

Lydia's eyes searched mine, endeavoring to discern why I had rambled through my excuses. "What is Mrs. Ellis's purpose in bringing the two of you together?" she repeated, concern apparent in her voice.

I gave a subtle shrug. "Perhaps she's intending to draw a wedge between her brother and Helena."

"That seems dreadfully heartless. Helena and Mr. Stanton make a very handsome couple."

I turned toward Lydia. "There is more to being a well-suited match than appearance alone," I said, slightly surprised at how quickly I came to Diana's defense. "Diana loves her brother and wants to see him happy."

Lydia did not remove her appraising gaze. "And you are the chosen wedge?"

I blushed as I fixed my eyes on my lap. "Perhaps not the only one, but likely the most practical."

"Helena is your cousin—" Lydia's disappointed tone rebuked me.

"I know. I intend to have no part in Diana's scheming," I said, wondering if Helena would be as loyal if the roles were reversed.

She returned her attention to the fallen curl and tucked it back into place. "I'm confident you will manage the situation admirably."

I nodded in agreement though I was certain she knew, as well as I did, that handling social situations capably had never been a talent of mine. In fact, there were few things I could claim to be accomplished in, but my trip to the Bragg's had been a much-needed reminder of at least one thing I was capable of doing.

"I must write Father before I go down; I fear the Bragg family is in quite an unfortunate position. Will you have it posted?"

Agreeing to do so, Lydia grabbed a book and took a seat next to the fireplace. As I began writing, I allowed myself to hope that my letter might appeal to Father's former self, a man I longed to see again.

I WAS MUCH IMPROVED by the time I walked down to dinner and even smiled at Diana when I found her staring in my direction from the other end of the table. I had been seated by Lord Ramsby but felt fortunate I was near enough Uncle

Stanton to overhear him relaying the story of how he had lost his sight.

"Did you never find the lady in the water?" Lord Ramsby asked, concern in his brown eyes as he glanced at me, assuring I had heard the unfortunate tale.

"Never. But her song is etched on my heart and her beauty in my darkened eyes."

I was glad Lord Ramsby returned his gaze to Uncle Stanton for I needed to push back a laugh with my hand.

"What was she like?" Lord Ramsby asked. "I would very much like to hear a description."

I glanced toward Uncle Stanton wondering what he would say; I had not given him a portrayal of the woman to recite.

He only hesitated a moment. "Though my words could never do her beauty justice, I will attempt to appease you, Lord Ramsby." He shifted his body toward us, his voice now low, "Her eyes were dark, and beckoning, drawing you to gaze into her soul, yet hiding what you wished to discover when you searched. Her long, dark hair had a glint of brilliant light that fell around her shoulders, floating through the darkened water endlessly.

"Her skin was also dark, not too dark to hide the pink in her cheeks and lips, but dark enough that its contrast brought light to all her other features as though a golden sun shone from within her. And her voice," he paused as though he were trying to recall the sound, "her voice was intoxicating, and you knew you would do anything to partake of it one more time...." His voice drifted before continuing, "I fear you never have beheld the likeness of such beauty in this world, Lord Ramsby."

Lord Ramsby glanced at me and then back to Uncle Stanton. "I do believe you just described Miss Blakeslee." He looked more bewildered than intentional in his compliment and Uncle Stanton released a jovial laugh, drawing the attention of those nearest him.

"I may have borrowed a few ideas from a description I received of her," he said beaming. "My memory is not what it used to be."

Warmth spread all the way to my ears, and I knew my dark skin must look quite pink as he had just described. "And where, might I ask, did you hear such an untrue description, Uncle?" I asked, trying to keep my tone light.

"Abigail, you know, as well as anyone, how I enjoy the world through my other senses. Listening to the descriptions I have collected of you these past few days has given me much joy though not as much joy as your company has brought."

"It is obvious to us all, Uncle, that it is your company that brings so much joy."

Uncle Stanton waved his hand dismissively. "Lord Ramsby, I hope you consider yourself a lucky man to behold such a beautiful... and humble lady."

Lord Ramsby appeared to have regained his composure. "I know myself to be the luckiest of men, Uncle Stanton." His charming smile and purposeful gaze in my direction ensured the color did not leave my face for the remainder of the course.

CHAPTER 9

*A*fter dinner finished, the whole group assembled in the music room. The room had been arranged so the pianoforte sat centered against the central wall, two rows of chairs slanting out on each side from the center aisle. Lord Ramsby took a chair next to me as Lady Eliza introduced the first piece. One of the Dowding girls moved to the pianoforte and began playing Beethoven's first movement of Moonlight Sonata. It was obvious she had meticulously practiced the piece, and I found myself captivated by her precision.

A few minutes into the performance, the heat of Lord Ramsby's leg reached my skin through my gown. The notes of Miss Dowding's sonata began to blur as my concentration turned to how closely he sat. As I attempted to shift myself inconspicuously to a more tolerable distance, my thoughts raced ahead of the music. Why did Lord Ramsby's nearness make me uneasy? It seemed an odd reaction when I was still uncertain whether I disliked the idea of him desiring me or yearned to embrace it.

"Are you performing tonight?" he whispered in my ear, causing the skin on my arms to prickle.

"If I had talent enough to share, I'd not hesitate, but I fear I sing and play very poorly." It was an excuse I was practiced at making though I had always wished it were not true.

"Perhaps I shall request a private concert at some point. No matter how poorly your accomplishments, I would hardly take notice. I have no great ear for music though I do claim an expert eye for beauty."

I blushed as I looked toward Miss Dowding who had just finished her piece, applauding loudly to distract myself from the watchful observation of Lord Ramsby. As I scanned the room for the next performer, my eyes stopped on Mr. Stanton seated across the aisle, glaring in our direction. I nodded stiffly to acknowledge his impolite behavior and turned back to Lord Ramsby. "Do you intend to perform tonight?"

"Miss Hanford was attempting to convince me to sing a duet with her, but I doubt it would be beneficial." He looked at me, awaiting a response.

"I cannot think of why it would not be, particularly if you have the desire and abilities to do so."

"And you'd not mind if I performed with your cousin?"

"Of course not." Why should I care if he sang a duet with Helena?

He must have given her a signal of sorts because Helena and Lord Ramsby stood in unison. He looked down at me contritely, and I smiled my encouragement. As I watched him move to the center of the room, the absurdity of my indecisive attitude consumed me. Most of the time I wanted him to leave me be—until he did, and then I wanted nothing more than his attentions; other times I was quite happy in his company and thought him very tolerable. I pushed the perplexing conflict from my mind as I glimpsed someone slip into Lord Ramsby's seat. I glanced sideways, not surprised to find Diana studying me.

"What are you up to now?" I asked suspiciously.

"Absolutely nothing. I have been yearning to apologize

since you left us in the stables. I counted your directed smiles at dinner as a hopeful sign I'd been forgiven?"

I listened to Helena's angelic voice trilling through the notes, keeping my eyes fixed on her to avoid having to look at Diana. "I will not play a part in your scheme."

"A part in my scheme?" her inquiring tone brought my gaze to hers. "I do not intend to use you as a playing piece in a game, Abigail."

I leaned close to her, ensuring no one would overhear. "If you hope to separate your brother from my cousin, I will take no part in it. My loyalty must be to my family."

Sympathy filled her features. "I understand that."

I returned my attention forward and listened as Lord Ramsby began singing. His voice was pleasant though noticeably untrained. Lord Ramsby winked at me, and I bowed my head to regain my composure. When I was certain I had managed to suppress the laugh that had attempted to escape, I looked up, my eyes falling to Mr. Stanton. If he had noticed Lord Ramsby's blatant flirtation, it didn't evidence in his features nor did his attention stray from Helena. I chastised myself before following his example.

When the duet concluded, I was eager for Lord Ramsby to return to my side. I looked to Diana, expecting her to relinquish her seat. She didn't budge. "Well done, Lord Ramsby," she said, as he approached. "Such a nice quality in your voice."

"Thank you," he said with a small bow, pausing next to her. He waited a moment longer before his eyes drifted to me and back to Diana. Realizing Diana had no intention of removing herself, Lord Ramsby bowed again and took a seat on the last row. I gave him an apologetic smile which he returned with a less-enthusiastic, half-smile. Did he think I'd invited Diana to take the seat in his absence? I'd have to explain the situation to him, assure him I'd been an innocent party to Diana's maneuver.

After a few others played the pianoforte or sang, Lady

Eliza stood to thank everyone who had shared their talents. "Is there anyone who had hoped to perform who hasn't?" she asked, glancing around the room. I kept my gaze on the floor, trying to make my desire obvious.

"I would love to hear you play, Mother." Diana said from the seat next to me. "Perhaps you could accompany Edwin for the finale?" Diana's face beamed with that familiar mischievous grin.

"Very well," Lady Eliza said turning to her son. "Will you join me, dear?"

He stood, glaring at Diana, before stepping toward his mother. "Of course."

She positioned herself at the pianoforte and looked up at him expectantly. He murmured something to her, and she nodded. Without sheet music she began playing a captivating tune I had not heard before. The notes were dark and brooding and Lady Eliza played it as though the music came from within her. The pianoforte suddenly grew soft and Mr. Stanton began singing. I could not move, I could scarcely breathe as a tingling sensation crept up my back.

The words were in another language, but his melodic voice told a familiar story—a story of loss and misery. The deep, pure sound swirled around me, and I felt as though I was intruding on a private moment of shared sorrow, a sorrow I somehow understood.

"What is it?" Diana whispered.

I shook my head, unable to explain why I felt so affected—her brother sang of a story too much like my own. A tear slipped down my cheek. I wiped it away, and another took its place. I could feel Diana's eyes on me and I bit at my lip to quell the quivering when her hand grasped mine. More tears welled in my eyes and I squeezed her fingers appreciatively, instantly forgiving her.

We sat motionless, listening. Edwin kept his gaze on the keys as he sang, and I oddly wished he'd look up—allow us a glimpse of the emotions hidden in his light eyes. What sorrow would I find there? Would it reflect some of my own?

As the song ended, my heart was heavy, and I longed for more—for a happier conclusion. Applause resounded through the room, and I quickly dried my eyes.

When I was composed enough to speak, I leaned near Diana. "You did not tell me your brother sang so well."

"It is one thing to tell of great talent, it is another thing to experience it."

I nodded, recalling Edwin's captivating voice. "And your mother is likewise accomplished," I said, needing a subject change. "Do you take after her in that regard?" My gaze shifted back to the performers as Mr. Stanton kissed his mother's cheek before returning to a beaming Helena.

"Of course not!" she exclaimed, commanding my attention. "Though she has influenced my appreciation for music." Her eyes moved to her mother. "I am not an exceptional talent myself, but I am always a willing audience whenever either desires it."

The room filled with conversation as people stood and began to move around. Mr. Ellis stepped to Diana's side. "That was quite an ending, was it not?" he asked with a smile directed toward me followed by a head-shaking chuckle directed toward his wife and her self-congratulating grin.

"Indeed," I said, curious whether he had seen my humiliating reaction.

"And well done, Lord Ramsby," Mr. Ellis said, reaching out to shake his hand as he approached. "Not every man can hold his own next to Miss Hanford, and you did a fine job of it."

"Thank you. I do not claim to have as fine a voice as your brother-in-law, but a man must do what he can to impress a lady."

Diana looked from Lord Ramsby to myself, and I was confident she had witnessed the reddening of my cheeks at his comment.

"Tell me, Lord Ramsby, have you decided how long you will privilege us with your company here at Timpton?" She wore a bright smile, but the kindness did not reach her eyes.

His gaze returned to me. "I'm not yet certain. It depends on a few things."

I stiffened at his inference. I should be flattered, and perhaps a part of me was, but I couldn't overlook the sense of misgiving that unsettled me. We had just met and had hardly spent more than a few moments together, it was too soon to form any real attachment. Helena and Mr. Stanton had known each other months now, and he had not even offered for her yet, and Hannah and Sir Wycliffe had certainly courted longer.

"Darling?" Diana looked toward her husband. "Don't Miss Hanford and Edwin make a lovely pair?" The sudden shift in topic sent my gaze to the couple across the room who stood talking to Lady Eliza and Mrs. Hanford.

Mr. Ellis appeared confused as he met Diana's glare but cautiously nodded in agreement. "Yes?"

"I am still in awe wondering how Edwin was fortunate enough to attract her attentions. I hope Miss Hanford does not come to realize how entirely beneath her a match to my brother is, even with his great wealth. Such a noble family—the Hanfords. Abigail, was not your uncle a relation of the Prince Regent himself?"

I studied Diana suspiciously. "I have heard it said, though I'm unaware of the particulars."

"The Prince himself?" Lord Ramsby asked with a lifted brow. "I don't believe I was acquainted with the name Hanford until I arrived at Timpton."

"Is that so?" Mr. Ellis asked. "I am surprised—the House of Hanford is well known and of noble heritage."

"Abigail," Diana interrupted, her eyes lighting with excitement. "Tell us truly, are the Hanfords as wealthy as they say?"

I tried to cover my disbelief at Diana's petty question.

"I'm not certain what wealth my uncle had, though their London house is quite exquisite." Diana nodded in encouragement as I continued, "Their country estate was also grand, but I believe my uncle's nephew inherited it on his passing."

"Well I've heard Miss Hanford will bring a remarkable dowry to a marriage; Edwin is indeed lucky to have found her." Diana looked again in their direction, a thoughtful smile on her lips. Our group followed Diana's example, as Mr. Stanton turned to discover us in our observation. With a raised eyebrow he started in our direction, pausing to see if Helena would accompany him.

Mr. Ellis's smile widened mischievously as the handsome couple moved toward us. "And what I can't understand is why a lady as breathtaking as Miss Hanford should return your brother's affections. How I envy him."

"Perhaps your enthusiasm is a tad excessive, Mr. Ellis." Diana's pointed glare only increased the intensity of his smile. "Edwin," she said, shifting her attention as Edwin arrived with Helena on his arm. "I know you are likely vexed with me, but in defense of my request, I do believe your performance was most advantageous."

"I daresay it was!" Helena was still beaming with pride at her nearly betrothed. "I had no idea your brother had such a heavenly voice. He never even told me he was musical. But now that I'm aware we shall make quite the pair in future performances, for I must insist on arranging regular duets."

He looked at Diana cynically. "Most advantageous. Thank you, Diana."

Diana covered her mouth attempting to hide the laugh building inside her.

"I must say," Helena continued, "Lord Ramsby was a most affable partner, and I should very much like to sing another duet with him as well."

Lord Ramsby nodded toward Helena at her acknowledgment. "I find singing a most enjoyable pastime and would happily join you again."

"Let us not procrastinate then, shall the three of us meet in the music room tomorrow after breakfast to prepare a few ensembles?" Her eyes stopped on me and her smile dimmed slightly. "I suppose you may join us, Abigail."

"How kind of you to include me, cousin," I said, as though her invitation was not one of social obligation. "But I'd much prefer to hear the finished result at your next performance." I rarely minded being the encouraging spectator, but I had no desire to watch Helena mesmerize both men with her angelic talent.

Helena looked pleased with my excuse and shifted her gaze to Mr. Stanton.

"I must also decline the invitation," Mr. Stanton said firmly. "I have business to attend to in the morning. You two go ahead without me."

"If you are certain you'd not be put out, Mr. Stanton," Lord Ramsby said, glancing back at Helena with a sultry smile that caused her face to color in a most flattering way.

"Not in the least," Mr. Stanton said confidently.

I gazed at the faces around our small group, feeling like a spectator of a peculiar dramatic performance. They deserved applause for their exasperating acting skills, but I was too intrigued to end it.

"How parched I am," Diana said with a pout, apparently continuing the charade. "Why don't you gentlemen fetch some refreshment."

Mr. Ellis did not hesitate but patted Lord Ramsby on the shoulder. "Lord Ramsby, I have not yet heard...." His voice trailed off as the two men made their way to the refreshment table, but Mr. Stanton did not move.

"Surely Helena could use refreshment after her lovely *duet*," Diana encouraged.

Mr. Stanton analyzed his sister before ultimately accepting

what I had also discovered—it was best not to know what she was up to.

"What charming men," Diana said when Mr. Stanton was far enough to not overhear her. "And though I do dearly love Mr. Ellis and my brother, how can either compare to Lord Ramsby's charms? Abigail, you are fortunate he favors you."

Stunned that she considered Lord Ramsby superior to either man and keenly aware of Helena's scrutinizing glare, I shook my head dismissively. "He doesn't favor me."

"Miss Hanford, what a ninny your cousin must be to think Lord Ramsby does not prefer her. I assure you, he is most adamant in his desire to snare you." Before Helena or I could make a reply, she continued, "And if you should marry him, you will not only gain a fortune but a title—you and Miss Hannah both rising in society!"

Helena's eyes narrowed.

"I care nothing for titles, Diana," I said, suddenly annoyed at this odd game she was playing.

"None of us care for such things." She heaved a heavy sigh. "Until we realize we have settled that is…." Her voice grew quiet and her eyes drifted toward her husband. "*Missus* Ellis," she said reflectively. Helena and I followed her gaze toward the men returning with our drinks. Surely the theatrics were part of her scheme, she didn't truly regret marrying Mr. Ellis? I suddenly felt very confused at what she was trying to accomplish.

Lord Ramsby brought me back a drink, and I found myself glad he once again focused his attentions on me. "Mr. Ellis told me your father is a well-known philanthropist?"

I looked over at Mr. Ellis, grateful for his kind words regarding Father. He stood near Diana whispering something in her ear. She laughed and motioned for her brother to join them.

"He is," I confirmed, looking back toward Lord Ramsby.

"He said your father obtains individuals at workhouses,

has them trained for household duties at Easton Manor, and then finds them new employment among his wealthy connections when they are ready?"

I tried not to show my surprise at Mr. Ellis's knowledge of such things. "It was my mother's idea, but Father helped her in her endeavors and has continued with the practice since her death." I didn't mention that Laurence has been the one seeing to the task the last few years.

"What an unusual initiative. Does he not fear he is letting thieves and troublemakers into his home? I understand workhouses have the vilest of people; and then to send those with such backgrounds to reputable homes." He shook his head. "I am certain I could not take on a servant without qualified references and a thorough training in their duties. Servants should be bred for the task."

I scarcely knew what to say, or at least what to say I'd not later regret. "I assure you, they are good people who have fallen on difficult times. Take Mrs. Bragg for example, she has done no wrong but has lost her husband and is now threatened with being sent to such a place. My father gives people like her a way to have another chance, and most are grateful and work hard."

"Most of them?" His head quirked sideways. "So, there were some who are unfit for the position?"

"As is the case amongst every class," I said, trying not to let my annoyance make the comment sound too pointed. "But if they did not demonstrate a good work ethic at Easton Manor, my father would not allow them to find employment among his connections; they typically obtain their own and many times will be found amongst the workhouses again."

"But surely your personal servants did not come from among such circumstances?"

"They did." His shock at my acknowledgment pressed me to clarify. "My maid, Lydia, has been with me since she arrived at Easton from a workhouse, and she has been of great value as a companion and a friend."

He narrowed his eyes. "And your father sees no risk in allowing someone like that to be an influence on you?"

Someone like that? The words dominated every crevice of my being until I shook with the excess. I exhaled slowly, convincing myself he had not intended to insult my dearest friend. My throat felt tight. "If you ever had the privilege of meeting Lydia, you'd not question the quality of person she is. Any influence she has had on me has been for my improvement."

His face brightened though it was unclear whether he now understood or simply desired to leave the topic. "Perhaps you are right. I'm sure there must be a few good people among the poor. And it is decent of your father to do it though I don't believe I would be willing to figure out who is worthy of a second chance."

"Indeed, it takes a certain type of person to undertake such a task." A forced smile crossed my lips as we came to an unspoken agreement—this was not a topic worth debating at present.

"Do you speak of my aunt and uncle's philanthropic work?" Helena chimed in with a hushed voice, overlooking our decision to let it alone.

"We had been," I said, hoping she'd recognize my desire to move on.

"Such blessed people. Though I could never understand why they needlessly exhausted themselves with the daily concerns of others. I can't help but think the stress of it took a toll on my dear aunt—what a saint she was." I wondered how she could so casually speak of my parents in front of me as though I was one of her gossiping friends who had never met them. "But as I have pondered the situation of so many needing assistance, I've come to realize it is best to leave them where God has placed them and let it be." She refused to make eye contact with me as she spoke, though I was confident her message was intended for me.

"Them?" An irrational urge to slap the smug look from her face shot through me as she met my glare. "Helena, they are people with lives and concerns more extreme than you can imagine. To act as though they are wholly separate, just because of circumstance, harms us both."

Helena scoffed. "I wonder why you are so adamant about the topic, *cousin*."

I slowed my breathing, realizing the need to calm my anger before I revealed something I shouldn't. I glanced toward an uncomfortable Lord Ramsby who silently watched our exchange.

"Your solution then, Miss Hanford," Edwin Stanton said stepping up to the triangle we had formed, "would be to do nothing?" I did not realize Mr. Stanton had been listening in on our dispute and I was convinced, by the shocked expression on Helena's face, she also had not been aware.

"How unfair of you, Mr. Stanton. Do not make me out to be the villain. I do not suggest that nothing should be done; there are facilities put in place to help those who fall on hard times. But I take the stance we should trust they are adequate, or we'd not have them. Besides, we help pay for such places, so in actuality we are helping those who find their way there."

Regaining her composure, she lifted her chin. "And I must add, I don't consider it unsuitable to find a good cause to support *financially*. But there are people to run charities and it's best if we allow them to handle the details of such work. I don't see a need for individuals to waste their time and resources to help a few lost souls in a sea of them when others are more fit for the task."

My thought to stay silent was promptly repressed. "But it's the very act of helping—the obligation we have to those less fortunate—that awakens the reality of others in us while making us more authentic in return. Can you perceive it as clearly with a slight inconvenience of a monetary donation, as noble and necessary as that is, or—"

"Or is it more evident as you scrub the dirt from another's laundry?" Mr. Stanton watched me with that peculiar look in his eye.

"Laundry?" Helena said, scrunching her nose in disgust. "Why would I ever handle another person's soiled laundry? This discussion has quite gone off course. As though a distinguished lady would do such a thing."

"Forgive me for mentioning something so distasteful," Mr. Stanton said, turning his full attention to Helena. "A lady, like yourself, would never take part in such a lowly task and should not be made to think on it."

My stomach twisted at his criticism. Could he so easily differentiate Helena's breeding from mine? I could feel the rage boiling to the surface. Perhaps, if it had simply been me he had offended, I could leave it alone, but I was not the only one condemned under his disparaging judgment.

Helena batted her eyelashes at Mr. Stanton. "I'm glad you recognize—"

"My mother was willing to lower herself to any task that needed done," I said ignoring Helena's displeasure at my interruption and focusing my glare on Mr. Stanton. "Yet she was one of the finest ladies in all of England. She knew others, no matter their condition, were worthy of our help." I was alarmed by the sharpness in my voice with so many onlookers, but the blame should be Mr. Stanton's for siding against me after I thought his intent was to affirm my stance.

"Worthy?" Mr. Stanton looked disconcerted at my word choice, his stern brow set low over his analytical eyes and his jaw fixed.

"That is what I said."

He rubbed at his tightened jawline as though I had just slapped him across the face. "Please excuse me," he said abruptly before turning and walking from our group.

Helena's icy glare was enough to silence me, but she quickly turned her refined attentions to Lord Ramsby. Wisely choosing to leave the subject, she commented on the desirable diversions of London and how much she longed for them. I didn't care for false pleasantries, so excused myself to go find a more tolerable companion—Uncle Stanton.

~

I LOCATED Uncle Stanton speaking with Edwin's father on a nearby settee. Not wanting to interrupt, I turned to examine a painting while I waited for the two to finish. The painting was a portrait of a striking woman with eyes much like Edwin's and I wondered if she was related.

"Uncle, Edwin has requested an audience with me," I glanced over my shoulder to see Mr. Stanton standing up, "but I shall leave you in good company. Miss Blakeslee, would you care to take my seat?"

"Only if you are finished with your conversation," I said, inwardly cursing my impatience.

"We are, though I thank you for your consideration." Mr. Stanton gestured for me to take his seat and I once again experienced a fondness for this man I scarcely knew.

"Even if we were not finished," Uncle Stanton interjected, "my nephew is aware his place is below you in my hierarchy of desired companions. I have also advised him of the protocol if someone above him should desire my company and he has done exactly right. Now go fulfill your contrived excuse, Ernest, so I may speak to my favorite guest."

Both men were grinning generously, and I soon wore a similar expression.

"Should you need assistance in taming this old sailor, Miss Blakeslee, do not hesitate to ask."

"He does appear a little sprightlier tonight, so I will keep your offer in the forefront of my mind. Thank you, Mr. Stanton."

With a small bow, Mr. Stanton left us.

"And how are you this evening, Miss Blakeslee?"

"I am in need of a diversion."

"Is that so?"

I nodded before remembering he needed me to answer vocally. "Yes. I fear I have contradicted Lord Ramsby, quarreled with my cousin, and somehow offended your great nephew in a single conversation."

"Three birds with one stone, huh?"

"Something like that though I did not intend to cause distress. I simply get overexcited discussing... certain topics."

"I assume you mean the lively conversation you had on aiding the less fortunate?"

I was mortified anew at my inability to hold my tongue. "That is the one," I admitted reluctantly.

"No need to be embarrassed, I found it a most interesting diversion in contrast to the tiresome news Ernest was relaying on the estate. Besides, I wholeheartedly agree with you."

I smiled, validated that Uncle would side with me and finding relief that Edwin's father hadn't overheard my passionate exchange with his son.

"What I can't seem to figure out was the intensity, both in your belief and in the question your cousin asked you—why you are so adamant regarding the subject. Surely, it's not uncommon for first-rate parents to instill good morals in their offspring, but your case was well thought out and powerful."

I glanced around making sure no one was close enough to overhear Uncle Stanton's uncanny assessment. Why had I sought out his company? I should have recognized his ability to dissect truth from the vaguest of statements. I needed to appease him without revealing more. "I know many people who have been helped in their suffering."

"As do I. But my conviction is not near what yours is."

"Then we shall have to attribute it to foolish ignorance of youth." I forced a small laugh. "That, and an inability to hold my tongue when propriety demands it."

His expression did not reflect my attempted cheeriness. "It is clear you can speak your mind, but you are not ignorant, Miss Blakeslee. If I had to venture a guess, I would propose it's quite the opposite."

I didn't answer him, not certain exactly what he implied, and what I'd betray about myself if I continued.

"I believe that is a conversation for another time," Uncle said, waving his hand dismissively. "Did you enjoy my retelling of your story earlier? It was my first public attempt and, though I experienced a few rough spots, I felt the rendition was adequate."

My posture relaxed at his chosen topic. "I very much agree, though we must figure out a more promising description you could give of the lady in the water. I found that part most unsatisfactory."

We both laughed, and I was once again glad I had joined him.

CHAPTER 10

I awoke the next morning refreshed and sat up in bed. A dim glow lightened the night sky and a sudden eagerness pressed on me to start my day. I left the warmth of my covers and the brisk air wrapped around me, alighting my spirit in anticipation. It was finally my chance to walk the grounds.

I questioned if Lydia might be awake to help me dress, but decided I would prefer to hurry out and return before others in the household woke. I moved cautiously in the darkness toward the wardrobe and rummaged through it until I found a day dress I was certain I could get into myself. After I haphazardly succeeded in dressing myself and tying on my boots, I grabbed for a bonnet. No one would see me, but if they did, the bonnet would hide the fact I wore my hair down and not styled.

Walking into the brisk morning air sent a shiver through me and I glanced at the sky expecting to see rain clouds. Thankfully, in the soft pre-dawn glow, the clouds appeared friendly, and I was confident it would be a pleasant day. I walked carefully down the front steps deciding where I should venture. I knew I couldn't be gone long if I wanted to slip back in unnoticed, so I started toward the pond instead of the spellbinding gardens.

A light fog hung near the ground, dispersing in my wake as I moved along the pond. I spotted a few sleeping birds tucked around the foliage, and I stepped lightly in an attempt not to startle them as I passed. As the plants became too thick to continue, I took a narrow, dirt trail leading away from the water's edge and between the large trees that surrounded most of the bank. The thickness hid Timpton House from view, something I hadn't realized looking out my window, and I felt oddly liberated by the knowledge.

The path coiled through the trees, occasionally meeting the water's edge before it bent back into the foliage again. I allowed myself to get lost in the moment, in the beauty of this place, when a sound caught my attention. I stopped walking, trying to determine what I had heard and where it was coming from. Voices?

Silently I moved along the path until I saw the shapes of two men in the dim light. I was not close enough to see them clearly or hear what was being said, but knowing I had no desire to be discovered in my current state, I turned to begin my walk back the way I'd come. I took a few steps when something pressed me to return. I nearly resisted the temptation, but eaves-dropping had always been the most enjoyable of my vexing habits.

Cautiously I drew nearer the men, thinking ahead of places to hide if they started toward me. I smiled to myself at the idea of making a plan, recalling Uncle Stanton and his admonition—this was a situation where a premeditated escape might actually be necessary.

"I don't think it would be too difficult, though we may need to hire a few local men for labor. There is a well-known tradesman by the name of Smith who might be just the man to approach with a job like this."

The voice carried clearly in the morning hours and I was disappointed to discover I had only happened upon the grounds keeper. I took a cautious step back.

"Reach out and see if he would consider such a project."

I froze when I heard the other voice, finding myself needing to concentrate to hear what Mr. Edwin Stanton was saying over the sudden drumming in my chest.

"And please don't mention it to anyone else until the project is complete. I intend to surprise her." Her? Was he planning on a surprise for Helena? Perhaps something to do with their engagement? I found myself moving forward, almost involuntarily, until their shadowed figures emerged. A tree near the path offered satisfactory coverage at this distance and I quickly ducked behind it.

"Of course, Mr. Stanton. And was there anything else?"

I peeked around the trunk in time to see Mr. Stanton shake his head.

"Very well, I'll let you know what I find out." The grounds keeper left in a direction that would not require me to duck into the large bush to my left, and the tension in my body eased slightly.

Mr. Stanton stood near the water's edge, unmoving. I realized I should leave, but my resolve was not sufficient enough to act. It had always been a weakness of mine, watching someone when their guard was down—an opportunity to glimpse another's soul.

His gaze was set toward where the grounds keeper had gone, and I yearned for him to change the focus of it. As I willed it, he turned and looked to the side of the pond just opposite me. His jaw was tense, and his eyes brimmed with emotion. My legs weakened beneath me and I knew I had invaded too far into his moment, seen too vividly into his sorrow. The desire to withdraw overwhelmed me and I took a shaky step backwards, followed by another, until Mr. Stanton disappeared from view.

As I turned to make my way back down the path, a stone under my boot set me off balance. I shifted my weight, desperately attempting to remedy the misstep; but the uneven ground in the dim light only exacerbated my predicament, and I tumbled sideways with a shriek. The impact was softer than I expected, and I was at least grateful I had landed on an ivy plant and not in the water a few steps from where I had fallen.

My initial shock of falling dispersed, and in its absence the possible consequence of my folly clarified. I drew in a breath and listened, praying I had been far enough away from Mr. Stanton to remain undetected.

Heavy footsteps filled the stillness and before I managed to remove myself off the ground and into a more ladylike position, Mr. Stanton came into view.

His eyes widened when he caught sight of me sprawled on the ground and he hurried toward me. "Miss Blakeslee?"

I pushed myself to a more proper sitting position. "Mr. Stanton," I said coolly, as though it was not unusual to be half prostrated on a plant in the early hours of morning, near where he had just been standing.

He offered me his hand and the warmth of his touch penetrated through me as he helped me to my feet.

"Were you spying on me?" His eyes narrowed, but he sounded amused.

"I would hardly call it spying," I responded, examining the damage to my gown and brushing off some loose dirt. Lydia would certainly reprimand me for the green stains I had added to the color.

"What would you call it then?"

I sighed. "Coincidence?"

"Coincidence?" he repeated.

"I was taking a morning walk around the pond when I came upon you, and whom I assume was your grounds keeper, talking. I didn't want to interrupt, so I backed away."

One side of his mouth lifted. "You are terribly inefficient at walking backwards."

"How very astute of you," I said. "Though if your foliage could talk, I believe it would have easily come to the same conclusion."

"I was not referring to your fall," he said with a chuckle. "Though that would stand as evidence against you as well. I'm referring to how long you took to walk such a small distance." He looked from where we now stood toward the place he had just been. "If you happened upon me when I was speaking to my gardener and began your removal immediately—"

"I—" my face flushed, and I decided a confession would be most appropriate to avoid further humiliation. "I hadn't intended to encroach on your privacy, but you looked so..." I couldn't decide what emotion I had seen, let alone verbalize it.

"Tormented?"

"Yes—tormented," I said with a reflective nod, realizing that is exactly what I had seen in his gaze.

His expression was pensive as he studied me, and I wondered if he would be angry at my intrusion.

"I should have left directly." I lowered my head. "Forgive me." Why did I always make such a fool of myself around him?

I felt the warmth of his hand on the front of my neck as he gently raised my chin. "Perhaps next time you would do better to walk forward."

I nodded, uncertain if I understood his meaning.

"Your hair is down," he said, moving his hand from my chin, down my neck to where a strand of my hair laid against my shoulder. My heart pounded in my chest at his touch and I questioned whether he could hear it as my hair slid through his fingers.

"I didn't want to wake Lydia," I said with a small quiver in my voice. "Besides, I plan to return to the house before I'm seen in such a state."

He lowered my hair back down. "You have already been seen," he said with a smile. "And I assure you, you look lovely."

I needed to think of something else, anything else to talk about. I once again felt tormented by this strange man and the feelings he could invoke within me. Torment. "Why are you tormented?" The question came out forceful and sounded unfeeling, but it was all I could do in my current state of mind.

He studied me a moment and then shrugged. "Obligation, I suppose." His words stopped but I could see that his mind had not, and I yearned to be allowed into his confidence. "When I feel as though I'm finally free to choose, circumstances remind me my life is not my own. I wish to live free of the constraints that bind me."

"What constraints are you bound by?"

His head tilted, and his lips lifted into a gentle smile. "I have no intention of burdening you with my troubles, Miss Blakeslee. I should not have mentioned it." He gave a brief bow. "Please excuse me."

"I suppose you feel a slave of obligation as intensely as I feel a slave of my past," I exclaimed to keep him from leaving. His gaze returned to me, shifting from reflection to curiosity and I immediately regretted my reckless impulse.

"What is in your past that oppresses you?"

"I—" I couldn't tell him. "I need to get back," I said, turning from him.

He grabbed my hand. "Miss Blakeslee, please."

I tried to free myself from his grip, but he held my hand firmly in his. My eyes brimmed with tears I did not want him to see. Cautiously, he moved his grip up my arm before turning me to face him. I ducked my head, allowing my bonnet to obscure the view of my face until a small tug on the ribbon sent my bonnet sliding into his hand.

"Miss Blakeslee." His voice was soft and close. "I cannot

allow you to leave until you give me some indication of what distresses you."

I looked up as a tear slid down my cheek. "I truly cannot say." He searched my soul for the answer, but I had hidden it so deep inside, even he couldn't pull it from me.

He wiped my tear so tenderly that for the first time I wanted to tell someone—I wanted to tell *him*.

"Surely nothing you've done could cause such suffering."

"It is not something I have done, it is who I am." His brow creased in confusion at the partial pieces I gave him to the puzzle of who I was. I had promised Father I would not tell, and I would not break a promise to him even if it meant disappointing Edwin Stanton.

He wiped another tear from my face and pulled me into an embrace. His arms encircled me and for a moment I felt wanted and safe. I could hear his heart beating in his chest, synced with the rapid rhythm of my own. When he finally released me, I stood like a weeping child before him. He looked down at me with an expression of distress, or perhaps pity, before pulling me forward and tenderly kissing my forehead.

As he pulled back the light reflected in his eyes, allowing the full spectrum of colors to be seen—such beautiful eyes.

The light.

"I need to go!" I said, realizing how light it now was. This time he nodded his agreement. I moved from him at a very unladylike speed, wiping the remainder of the tears from my face as I went.

"Abigail!"

Surprised to hear my Christian name, I turned to find him jogging toward me.

"I mean, Miss Blakeslee," he corrected himself with a delightfully embarrassed look on his face and a hint of color in his cheeks.

"Yes?" I asked with a curious smile.

"I thought you might appreciate your bonnet."

I placed my hand on my head, having forgotten my hair hung freely. "Thank you," I said as I grabbed it from him and tied it into place. "That could have been disastrous."

He gave a mock bow. "I'm honored to be of service." He paused. "And thanks for spying on me today," he said sincerely.

"It was my pleasure."

I MADE it back into Timpton with little consequence besides a disconcerted expression from the butler who stood in the entry hall. "What a beautiful morning for a walk," I said casually, as I turned to go up the stairs. His eyes followed me, but he said nothing.

I had nearly reached my door when I heard a doorknob turn. Knowing I wouldn't make it to my room in time, I shifted my body sideways to hide the stained part of my gown as Helena came walking out. She closed the door behind her, inspected her riding habit, and nodded to herself in approval before her eyes fell on me.

Her initial surprise quickly changed to cynicism. "What are you doing up so early?" she asked, scanning me. "Surely you are not thinking of riding out with us in a day dress and your hair loose?"

"I am not."

"Then what are you doing sneaking about at this hour?"

"I am not sneaking, I have just returned from a morning walk."

She sneered. "Looking like that?"

"I hadn't planned on seeing anyone."

Her eyes narrowed. "And did you?"

"The butler," I said dismissively. "But I assure you, he was not nearly as distressed by my appearance as you seem to be."

She scoffed, and I realized my current manner was not helping my situation. "But I understand your concern and appreciate your interest on my behalf, cousin, you are always so—" I tried to make my voice sound sincere, knowing Helena had a weakness for praise, "helpful."

I wasn't sure it worked but then her eyes regained their normal shape and her face appeared pulled but no longer hostile. "I suppose, if no one saw you, little harm has been done. But even you must realize any gentleman of sensibility would not consider courting a lady who runs unkempt outdoors like a country brat." Her gaze shifted to the large green stain I'd attempted to position out of her notice. "Particularly when evidence of your troublesome habit is frequently obvious."

I fussed with the skirt of my gown, covering how much her words stung. "I will be more careful."

"That would be sensible of you—" she said, and I took a step toward my room hoping she was finished. "As would subduing your temper and bridling your tongue."

I swallowed back a spiteful defense and returned my attention to her.

"My only lament shall be Uncle Miles's disappointment when you return to Easton Manor scarcely improved." She tilted her head and blinked at me with increasing pity. "At least my conscience will be clear, knowing how I have sought to advise you."

I repressed a scowl. "Perhaps there is hope for me yet, with such a superior tutor to aid me."

Her eyes brightened, overlooking the cynicism in my comment. "What a wonderful idea. I recognize you speak of me but, seeing as I'll soon have little time for anything other than wedding preparations, I will have Mother write Uncle Miles and suggest a social tutor be hired for your return. With persistent direction, there yet may be a chance for you to appear a proper lady by your debut… or at least make significant headway toward that ideal."

"Inspired," I managed through a forced smile, wondering if a social tutor is where Helena had learned to place the perfect insult while appearing thoughtful. I'd rather be considered a country brat than be under the instruction of someone who'd educate me in the art of deception and callousness.

Helena let out a satisfied exhale. "I will see to it when I return. But now I must hurry along, I'd hate to infringe on my time riding with Mr. Stanton." Helena grabbed a handful of her skirts and hurried past me.

I ignored the tinge of jealousy and focused on the relief I felt at her absence, quickly making haste toward my room before Aunt Marianne had the opportunity to come upon me and add her words of displeasure to Helena's.

As I stepped inside, Lydia stood near the window, an odd expression on her face.

"Good morning," I said, turning my attention to the closing door.

"I'd ask where you've been, and in such a state, but I've seen you come from the pond."

The Butler, Helena, and now Lydia; I was drained by the cross-examination and returned my gaze to her apathetically. "Since you already know where I've been, I don't see why you are looking at me as though there is anything to tell."

She looked at me in disbelief. "Would you care to offer details on your walk or should I share with you how I saw Mr. Stanton exit the same path you left from before you even reached the entrance to Timpton?"

"I had not meant to meet Edwin there if that is what you are implying," I said defensively, increasing the seriousness of Lydia's expression.

"I implied nothing, though I'm concerned by what we spoke of yesterday. You are not developing any sort of attachment to Mr. Stanton, are you?" She said his name slowly, deliberately.

"Of course not! I haven't explored the grounds yet but for the few minutes I spent in the garden the first morning, and you know how I have desired it." She nodded for me to continue. "I assumed I'd be the only one awake and out at dawn, so I walked around the pond and I happened upon Edwin and his grounds keeper. We spoke briefly, and that is all."

"I must say, for so much imagination, that was a very poor retelling. Besides, Abee, you've called Mr. Stanton by his Christian name twice now. Are you on such familiar terms with one another?"

I realized my folly and my cheeks heated. "No, I simply—" Why had I used his Christian name? Surely, his slip of using mine did not give me permission to use his. "I'm not sure," I admitted, feeling as though our relationship had somehow evolved during our last encounter but unable to explain how.

Lydia was disappointed though I couldn't decide if it was in me or in how guarded I'd become since our arrival. I'd always shared everything with her so why did I wish to hide the truth from her now? Perhaps it was because I hardly understood it. "I nearly told him," I said with a blatant confession, awaiting her response.

She eyed me, and I shifted beneath her examination. "For what purpose?"

"I'm not certain; I can barely understand my own feelings."

"What benefit could come of it?"

I was certain no good would come of sharing who I was, at least not for me, but perhaps I merely wanted to stop hiding the truth. "None, but to strengthen Mr. Stanton's resolve for Helena," I said, noticing how his formal title felt unexpectedly strange on my lips.

"Does his resolve need to be strengthened?"

I didn't think so; besides an occasional moment, where I

may have misinterpreted his feelings in my naivety, he always favored Helena. Between his stern glances, rebukes, his childish game, and the last few moments we spoke by the pond where he'd embraced me and kissed my forehead to comfort me—as Laurence would have done. My heart sank at the conclusion. "I believe he views me like a little sister." And who could blame him? I run around like a country brat, spitting out my opinions and emotions, repeatedly proving I am far from the well-trained ladies he is accustomed to admiring.

"And does your resolve need to be strengthened?" she asked, concern in her eyes.

I didn't respond as I sat down in front of the mirror, tears blurring my vision. I wasn't sure what I was feeling, and why I was so upset by what I'd discovered. He had been spoken for before I came to Timpton, and by my cousin, nonetheless. Why did I care anyway? He was harsh and critical, confusing and prideful, and aggravating beyond comprehension. So why did I feel like sobbing? Lydia wrapped her arms around me and I closed my eyes, convincing my tears not to betray me again.

As I walked out from the dining hall after breakfast, Diana caught my arm.

"I have just been thinking how everyone received a tour of Timpton House before you arrived. Has anyone given you one?"

"No, but I have found my way around well enough, and I hate to be an inconvenience."

"Nonsense. I've already told Mother I am giving you a personal tour of the house—and getting myself out of a morning spent in the drawing room doing needlework." She winked at me as we passed the room where the other ladies gathered.

"I must admit I am grateful for the escape."

"Edwin did mention your dislike for needlework."

"He did?" I asked, searching my memory.

"He said you hinted at it your first morning here, when he found you walking in the gardens. And I will openly confess, only to you of course, I also detest it most ardently."

I grinned though I couldn't stop my mind from pondering Edwin's intention in relaying such a bizarre detail. After spending too much time on the notion, I concluded that regardless of his reasoning I'd simply be grateful it saved me from a morning of the monotonous task.

As we wandered through the house, every room appeared to link to another; by looking at its symmetrical shape from the outside, you would not realize what a labyrinth it was inside. I compared it to Easton Manor's intentional corridors and room locations, wondering what the architect had been trying to accomplish when building Timpton.

After walking through the billiard room, we exited to a sizable corridor with wood archways. "This is where my father's study is," Diana said, pausing to knock on a large door.

"Should we disturb him in his work?" I whispered.

"My father is out today," she said with a smile. "But Edwin should be here."

The door opened, and Edwin stood glancing tentatively between us.

"She hasn't received a tour yet," Diana said, answering his unspoken question. "You will show us the study?" Somehow, her request sounded more like a demand.

He opened the door wider. "You may come in, though I'm obliged to mention I have an appointment shortly."

Diana sent him a pout. "What dreadful timing. Had I remembered we would have ventured here sooner. Oh well, Edwin, do take over for me until your appointment arrives. I am dreadfully tired from all this walking."

"It's a study, Diana," Edwin said with a raise of his brow. "There is little here of interest."

"Perhaps give her a tour of the library then, we hadn't made it that far yet."

They stared at each other in a silent battle of wills. I shifted awkwardly, deliberating how long it would last, when Edwin finally conceded. "Would you care to see the library, Miss Blakeslee?"

I glanced at Diana who nodded her head in encouragement. I'd said I'd have no part in her scheming, but I was now confident whatever her goal was in bringing Edwin and me together, it wouldn't work. He saw me as a child, a little sister much like herself—though less demanding, I was sure. "Of course," I said, and he opened the adjoining door that led into the next room, gesturing me inside.

The library was filled with books, and it reminded me of the one at Easton Manor with overstuffed shelves, large windows, and numerous seats for reading. I grabbed a thin book off a nearby shelf and held it in my hand. I traced my finger over the title, *The Tempest.* It had been some time since I'd picked up a book. Mother taught me to read and had given me the joy of new worlds and unforgettable stories. I'd spent countless afternoons tucked in a chair in our library, unable to stop reading; but when Mother died, I found little delight in anything, including the things she'd taught me to love.

"Have you read it?" Edwin asked, peering over my shoulder.

"Of course," I answered, placing it back on the shelf.

"And I presume you enjoyed it?"

"Very much. I admit I am easily satisfied by a happy ending." I kept my eyes searching the books, having little desire to receive the look of censure awaiting me. "The Shakespeare writings I enjoy most are those that end well—Twelfth Night, Midsummer Night's Dream, The Taming of the Shrew—the ones where love is victorious."

"A common *ideal* among ladies, I believe, and the reason his comedies are so popular."

I turned toward him. "Life has enough of tragedy and grief, is there something wrong with finding satisfaction in love and happy endings?"

"There is," he said. "The harm is believing in something that isn't real, Miss Blakeslee." He stepped closer, and my feet faltered. "Love only brings misery. To think otherwise is foolish. You just declared life is full of tragedy—"

"And that is why love is needed!"

"And that is what *love* causes."

Neither of us moved and I could feel his warm breath on me. It was only then I realized how close we stood, my neck craning to look up at him, but I had no desire to move away.

"You do not understand love then," I whispered.

The resentment in his gaze caught me by surprise. "And you do?"

"Love has saved me." His eyes searched mine. "The love I know has the power to lift and to heal, to see past weakness and turn it to strength."

"Love is fickle and will fail you."

"Never." I said, shaking my head as tears stung my vision. "I do not know what counterfeit you describe but the love I have found is faithful and unconditional."

He said nothing, and his eyes drifted from mine in contemplation. After taking a deep breath he looked down at me again. He wore the stern expression I knew so well and took a step back. "I hope you are correct in your judgment," he said with a brisk nod.

As he turned from me, I wanted to call out to him, but I was too confused to contrive a response. I followed him to the study in a daze. Edwin positioned himself near the desk with his eyes cast to the floor as Diana glanced between us bewildered.

"How is it you've found something to quarrel about

already? You were in there less than five minutes. Perhaps I should take on the role of mediator instead of chaperon for the two of you."

Neither Edwin nor I smiled.

"This will not do. What was the disagreement this time?"

"There was not a disagreement," Edwin said. "Well, at least that is not what caused the discontent."

Curious what the cause had been I glanced in his direction, anxious for him to finish. A knock interrupted his revelation.

Diana shot to her feet and reached out her arm toward me. "We will go out the library."

Edwin blocked our retreat. "You are fine to leave out the study door." He shifted his gaze at the repeated knock. "Come in."

The butler opened the door, his eyes gliding over Diana and me. "The Slytons are here to see you, Mr. Stanton."

"Show them in."

The Slytons? I was familiar with the name, but surely they were not the same as I had known. My heart picked up pace regardless of what I told myself. The door opened again, and a tall, wiry lady accompanied by a shorter, burly man stepped through the door. They were older and somehow uglier, but it was them. My knees nearly gave out, and I tightened my hold on Diana's arm for support.

"Mr. and Mrs. Slyton, I am pleased you finally agreed to make the trip to Timpton. This is my sister, Mrs. Ellis, and our friend, Miss Abigail Blakeslee."

Mrs. Slyton nodded in our direction but abruptly turned her attention back to Edwin. "With such a gracious offer, how could we resist?" Her scratchy voice brought a slew of memories that made my body tremble.

I cautiously turned to find Mr. Slyton inspecting me through squinted eyes. Did he recognize me? I hadn't seen him since I was a little girl, and I hoped the years had done their job adequately enough to disguise me. I lifted my chin, attempting to appear unaffected by his presence and was relieved when Mr. Slyton turned toward Diana, appraising her with the same disgusting grimace he'd given me. I looked to Edwin and found him returning my gaze, a peculiar expression on his features.

Edwin moved to my side and placed a firm hand around my waist, guiding me to the door. My ears were ringing, and I was confident he said something to me, but I couldn't be sure. As we walked from the study, his touch retracted, and Diana took his place, directing me back down the corridor.

I was uncertain where I was being led and soon found myself seated in a distantly familiar room. "Bring refreshment at once!" Diana's voice echoed through my mind. My head was spinning, and I rested it against the chair as my vision faded into blackness.

CHAPTER 11

J opened my eyes to find Diana and Lady Eliza staring at me, smelling salts in hand. I sat up, but my head spun so I rested it back again.

"How are you feeling, Miss Blakeslee?" Lady Eliza held up a cup of lemon tea and I took a sip. Her eyes flitted about my face, her brow creased in concern.

"I... I'm simply feeling out of sorts."

"Out of sorts?" Diana repeated looking alarmed. "You fainted! How fortunate I got you to this chair first. What happened? One minute you were fine and the next you looked rigid and pale. Surely it wasn't because of your argument with Edwin?"

Lady Eliza's look of concern shifted to Diana.

"No," I said. "I merely encountered a dizzy spell."

Diana seemed unconvinced. "Perhaps it was that vile way Mr. Slyton looked at you. Despicable man, how unfortunate the likes of someone like him should be at Timpton House today—"

"Who is Mr. Slyton?" Lady Eliza interrupted.

Diana looked as though she had revealed something she

shouldn't have. "A man whom Edwin wished to speak to, regarding the estate I'm sure. He just arrived and has brought his wife along. She doesn't look friendly by any means, but Mr. Slyton appears to be quite the rogue."

"Why your brother would bring such people to Timpton…" She didn't finish but returned her attention to me. "I'm sorry if this visitor has caused you grief."

Grief was an understatement. She would never know what pain that couple had caused me, and it was no concern of hers. "It was only a dizzy spell." I smiled as authentically as I was capable. "Please don't stay on my account. I realize you have plenty requiring your attention."

Lady Eliza searched my face. "If you are certain you are well?"

"I am," I answered, impatient to be alone. "Thank you."

"Diana, stay with Miss Blakeslee until she is recovered."

"Of course, Mother."

Lady Eliza pushed a piece of hair from my face then brought her hand to hold my chin momentarily, as Mother used to do, before she stood up and walked briskly away.

Diana sat by my side for several minutes until my head stopped spinning and I was able to sit up straight. I was drained from the incident, but fresh air sounded more appealing than resting under Diana's watchful gaze. "I think I will take a turn in the garden." I needed to be alone and the garden seemed the perfect place to recuperate.

"I'd be happy to attend you."

"You have already spent the entirety of your morning with me, I could not think of asking any more of you. Besides, I'm sure Mr. Ellis will be missing you terribly."

Diana studied me, clearly assessing whether I desired her company. "I suppose you are right," she said astutely, "though I worry about you having another spell while you are alone."

"I shall be fine. The tea has worked wonders and I feel myself again."

She shook her head. "I'm still hesitant...." Suddenly her eyes brightened. "But I suppose it could be advantageous. Yes, go walk, it will do you good to take fresh air."

I recognized her calculating expression, but I was too eager to get outside to question her motives. "I will check in with you later—assure you I survived my saunter outdoors."

"So considerate of you," she said sarcastically as I turned to leave.

I stopped before reaching the door and looked over my shoulder. "Thank you, Diana, for everything."

"You are welcome, my dear friend."

I wasn't certain if it was her words or the sincerity behind them that impacted me most, but as I left a sense of belonging bloomed within me.

DIANA HAD SHOWN me the back way to the gardens, but the rooms were such a maze I wasn't sure I'd be able to find it again in my current state. As I went to leave the house from the main door, the Stanton's butler approached me hesitantly.

"Miss Blakeslee, there is a young Mr. Silas here requesting an audience with you. I told him to wait outside. I understand you are not feeling well, if you would like I can send him away."

"I would be happy to speak with him," I said, attempting to overlook my embarrassment at the butler knowing my ordeal. Surely seeing this boy with so many troubles would put my own into perspective.

I followed the butler out the front entrance when the same tear-stained boy I had first met came into view.

"Silas, what is it?" I said, rushing to him and crouching down so I could see his face more clearly.

"Mum's ill, and Juliet won't stop cry'n. I went to Mrs. Hill's and she's not there. I don't know what to do, and you said...."

"I said if you should need anything to come find me, and you have done exactly right. Let me inform Baldwin that I am leaving, and we will depart immediately."

I turned to find the curious gaze of the butler still on me.

"I will be going to the Braggs' home if anyone should need me."

"Very well, Miss Blakeslee, would you like the carriage brought around?"

I was certain we could get there nearly as fast by crossing through the fields without causing a fuss. "We will walk, but thank you, Baldwin."

He offered me a cautious smile and bowed before stepping back in the house, shutting the door behind him.

I grabbed Silas's hand and we hurried down the steps and across the drive.

AS WE NEARED THE COTTAGE, the distinct screaming of Juliet cut through the stagnant air like a heralded warning of what I would encounter. My heart quickened. I had attended to the sick before, but never on my own. Tending children and doing laundry was one thing, relieving sickness without direction was another.

Silas did not allow me a moment's pause as he pulled me along and finally through the threshold of the cottage door. The large room was unchanged, including Mrs. Bragg who laid in the same spot I had left her, though her breathing was now shallow and quick.

"How long has she been like this?" I asked, hurrying to the bed.

He stepped up next to me and shrugged his drooping shoulders. "Juliet cried al'night. I had to keep 'oldin her so Mum could sleep. I was so tired... I fell asleep." His voice trailed off and his eyes brimmed with tears. "When I woke, she was like that."

I scanned her, deliberating what to do. "Silas," I said, leaning down and taking a hold of his shoulders, "you have done amazingly. And I know you must be exhausted, but we need a doctor. Do you think you can send for one on your own?"

He gave his mother a lingering glance, before nodding and darting from my grasp.

I leaned over Mrs. Bragg placing my hand on her forehead —the heat of her skin penetrated through me. Juliet's cry rang in my ears, but my instincts told me I needed to cool Mrs. Bragg and slow her breathing before attending to the others.

I promptly removed the blankets from on top of her and began to undress her down to her chemise and stays. "Mary dear, can you fetch me some water?" I asked, trying to keep my voice calm as I hurried to remove Mrs. Bragg's dress.

She scurried to her feet and grabbed the wash basin, carefully walking it to where I stood.

I reached for a clean cloth, grateful I had attended to the laundry yesterday, and took the basin from Mary. I saturated the cloth and brought it to Mrs. Bragg's mouth, squeezing it gently to allow the water to moisten her dry lips. She swallowed and winced. I dipped the rag in the water again, rubbing the cool fabric over areas of her exposed skin and across her forehead. As I dabbed at her chest, she let out a distressing moan. I examined the area and noticed a hard lump beneath her chemise. I looked to Juliet still screaming on the bed, realizing what the trouble might be. Uncertain how to proceed, I picked up Juliet and brought her to her mother's side.

"Mrs. Bragg," I said, not sure she could hear me. "I'm going to help Juliet feed. I think it will help relieve some of your discomfort." I fumbled awkwardly with her stays and chemise, unsure how to help an infant breastfeed, and rolled Mrs.

Bragg onto her side. Cautiously I pressed Juliet to her mother's breast and was glad to see little effort was needed on my part as Juliet latched on and began drinking eagerly.

Mrs. Bragg let out another low moan and her body went rigid. I worried I had done something wrong but before I had time to react the stiffness eased. Juliet's content suckling filled the cabin as I continued to dab my cloth over Mrs. Bragg's forehead.

Silas opened the door and rushed inside. "I have sent for the doctor," he said, and I was certain he'd have been proud of himself had he not been so worried for his mother. His gaze moved to Juliet feeding contentedly, and he grinned at me, as though I had accomplished some great feat.

"I'm not around infants much, and I'm afraid yesterday I overlooked that your mother was probably accustomed to feeding Juliet. I hope it will relieve a little of both of their discomfort."

Silas sat next to me, helping to prop his mother's body onto her side. My eyes flitted around the cabin, falling on the wide-eyed girls watching me tentatively. I smiled reassuringly at the two oldest girls when I noticed Rose curled up on Patience's lap shivering. Panic filled me. Just yesterday her cheeks had been full of color, today her complexion was pale and sallow.

Ensuring Silas could support his mother's position without me, I hurried to Rose's side and placed my hand on her forehead. She was also feverish, and I quickly grabbed another clean cloth to dab over her forehead and along her legs and arms. I lifted the hair from her neck, allowing the wetness of the cloth to penetrate her heated skin. Her body shivered wildly, and she began to cry.

"I know it is cold, Rose, but I must cool you."

I continued cooling her as she clung to Patience, a heartbreaking whimper making me feel as though I was torturing the poor thing. The cottage was silent as I worked, only the suckling sounds of Juliet filled the heavy air.

Looking back toward Mrs. Bragg I realized I needed to switch Juliet sides before she was satisfied and unwilling to relieve the other breast. I handed Mary a cup of water and directed her to her sister.

"Rose, Mary has water for you. I need you to drink while I help your Mama."

She nodded her head and took a sip obediently as Mary lifted the cup to her lips.

"Silas, we need to turn your mother to her other side," I was torn at asking such a thing of him; but I was hopeful, being the oldest, he was accustomed to his mother nursing his sisters. He stood up and his mother's body shifted to her back, causing Juliet to unlatch and begin screaming again.

I grabbed Juliet, placed her on the other bed, and slowly rolled Mrs. Bragg across the small bed until she faced us. The wall now supported her back, which prevented her from turning any further. Satisfied with her position I grabbed Juliet and placed her near her mother's other breast; she at once stopped crying and began suckling contentedly. I rubbed my hand along Mrs. Bragg's collar bone and was glad to see the lump had decreased on the side from which Juliet had just fed.

I moved Rose next to her mother and alternated dabbing wet cloths across their exposed skin. Silas saw to getting Mary and Patience something to eat before I insisted he rest. Complying in exhaustion, he instantly fell asleep as both of the older girls curled up to him, following his example. By the time the doctor arrived, Juliet slept contentedly on the edge of the children's bed with her sleeping siblings.

The doctor was younger than I expected, only a few years older than myself, and after a quick introduction he asked me questions as he assessed Mrs. Bragg and Rose. I told him how I had tried to slow their breathing and keep their temperatures down by exposing the skin and keeping it cool, and how I had fed Juliet to relieve Mrs. Bragg, who seemed to flinch in pain when touched. I only blushed once in my retelling, but I was certain he hadn't noticed, as his focus was on Mrs. Bragg and checking her pulse.

"Well—" the doctor said, turning toward me, "I am quite impressed with your knowledge of treatment, Miss Blakeslee, especially in your conclusion to have the baby feed. It isn't often you see a lady, such as yourself, so accomplished in tending ill patients. They were lucky to have you here," he paused, a look of concern filling his kind eyes, "though I do fear for your health. I believe they have contracted influenza, which is highly contagious. I have seen several cases throughout Chadsmead and in nearby towns." He glanced back to Mrs. Bragg and Rose. "An odd thing, being so late in the year."

I nodded, though I felt little concern at his conclusion. I'd been around countless sicknesses and yet I couldn't recall the last time I contracted one.

The sound of an approaching horse caught my attention and I moved to the doorway. Edwin had dismounted and was walking hastily toward the cottage.

"Mr. Stanton, what is it?" I asked, taking a few steps toward him. The rage overwhelming his features made me feel faint again. Had the Slytons said something? Did he know what I had hidden from him? From everyone?

"I came searching for you after my meeting—."

"I informed your butler I was coming to see the Braggs," I interrupted defensively. "But regardless if you were not told immediately, there is no need to worry so—"

"Is there no need, Miss Blakeslee?"

Panic consumed me at hearing the accusation in his voice, but I refused to let him see it. "Not enough of one that would require you to act so presumptuously." My body tensed as I returned his glare, preparing myself for the allegation he was about to place against me.

The doctor stepped in the doorway next to me. "Is anything the matter, Miss Blakeslee?" he asked, looking at me before turning his questioning gaze to Edwin. "Oh, Mr. Stanton," he said, recognizing who it was I was arguing with.

"Doctor Walter," Edwin said stiffly, without removing his eyes from me. "I have come to fetch Miss Blakeslee," his unyielding eyes dared me to refuse.

I willingly accepted his challenge. "I cannot leave! There is no one here to care for Mrs. Bragg and her children."

His jaw clenched but his gaze finally shifted from me. "Doctor Walter, surely you know of a woman who can care for this family? You may assure them the pay will be generous."

Doctor Walter nodded. "Yes, I'm sure I can have someone here within the hour, Mr. Stanton."

"Thank you. If you will inform them to send regular updates as to the family's condition, we would be most grateful. Have the correspondence on such matters directed to Miss Blakeslee at Timpton House."

"Of course."

"An allowance has been set up at several of the shops in Mrs. Bragg's name, so there should be no difficulty in obtaining anything the family should need. If there are any additional costs or fees, please direct those to me."

"Very well, Mr. Stanton."

Father could not have already received my letter petitioning for his help, let alone offered his aid. Had Edwin taken an initiative to see to the needs of the Braggs before he even knew they were ill? The anger permeating from him gave little indication that he truly cared for the Braggs and their distress.

"I shall wait for you by the horse," Edwin said to me before turning his back on us.

I followed Doctor Walter back into the house, acknowledging I'd have to say my goodbyes. All the children slept, and I did not have the heart to wake them. I kissed each on the head and gave one last sympathetic look to Mrs. Bragg.

"I will enlist an able caretaker, Miss Blakeslee," Doctor Walter said kindly. "They will be well looked after."

"Thank you. And if you are here when the children wake, tell them I will return soon."

"I will." He paused, glanced toward the door and back at me. "And take care of yourself, Miss Blakeslee."

Certain he spoke of my health, I offered a reassuring nod; but as I walked out the door to a brooding Edwin Stanton, I wondered if he had meant something different entirely.

EDWIN SAID nothing as he lifted me onto the horse. I looked at his low set brow and wondered what he knew. He mounted behind me and wrapped his arms around my waist, taking the reins in both hands. We sat silently as the horse began to move, and I watched as the muscles in his hands contracted as he gripped the leather strap tightly in a repetitive rhythm.

As we crossed into the path that led back to Timpton, I debated whether I more angry with Edwin's brashness or intrigued by his generosity. Knowing my temper had found more opportunity to find satisfaction than my curiosity as of late and, having no desire to speak of what had brought him seeking me in such a mood, I decided to end the silence. "Did you set up the allowance for the Bragg family?"

"Yes." His voice held little emotion. "With my father's agreement, I sent our steward to town this morning to arrange it."

"Why?" I asked, looking back toward him, hoping to discover more than just words.

"Why did I feel obligated to help?" He paused. "I am not as heartless as you think me."

"Are you not?" I asked, searching his eyes. I sincerely desired to understand who this confusing gentleman was— the playful man who entertained the Bragg children with a silly child's game or the seemingly uncompassionate man who had sided with Helena against the poor being worthy of our aid.

I felt his arms tighten around me as he pulled on the reins and his horse stopped obediently.

He met my gaze with one of equal fervor and I refused the strange urge to look at his lips.

"Why are you so angry at me?" I finally managed to ask when he refused to speak. "Surely I have done nothing that you are not also guilty of."

"I did not run off and risk my health for a family I hardly know."

I stared at him in disbelief. "And what concern is it to you what risks I take?"

He looked affronted by my question. "Your welfare is a great concern of mine, you are my guest and..." I watched as he tried to think of a term for who I was to him, apparently unrelated sister would be considered inappropriate, so he continued without finishing. "I have heard reports of influenza nearby, so when Baldwin told me you had gone to help Mrs. Bragg who had fallen ill..." His eyes held an emotion I understood, one of loss and grief. "I just wanted to make sure you were safe."

"Doctor Walter thinks Mrs. Bragg and Rose have influenza," I offered hesitantly.

His nostrils flared, and he closed his eyes. I could see his chest rise and fall, the slowness of the motion intentional. He opened his eyes and I was taken aback at the depth of worry in his features. "So you could contract it?"

"I suppose, though I don't think I will."

"I can't imagine you have had much exposure growing up at Easton Manor."

"I assure you, I have." I decided to give him a partial answer. "My mother and I would often tend the sick. She was not quite as fortunate as myself, sometimes contracting one of the illnesses we encountered; but when she recovered, she would go right out again and bring me along." I smiled at the memory of Mother assuring Father she would be more cautious only to find ourselves a few hours later amid a sea of sick faces. "She always told me God had blessed me with a good constitution, so I'd feel ungrateful if I didn't use it to help others."

Edwin looked at me with an odd expression and I was certain he was somehow contented by my answer. His gaze turned forward and he nudged his heel against the horse's side. Unprepared for the motion of the moving horse, I lurched backwards. Edwin's strong arm quickly wrapped around me, pulling me to the safety of his body.

"Thank you," I whispered.

He didn't respond as he loosened his grip, but his arm stayed protectively around me. It was a beautiful day, but I hardly noticed anything besides the stiff way I rested my arm on his and the warmth of his hand on my waist. The horse walked so slowly I was certain we would be able to arrive at Timpton faster if we walked, but I found myself glad we were riding.

"And how are you feeling?" he asked.

"Well, thank you."

"This morning you seemed quite...unsettled."

I realized he spoke about my reaction to the Slyton's visit and I once again wondered what he had been told. "I encountered a slight dizzy spell is all," I said, keeping my eyes ahead as Timpton House came into view.

"Diana said you fainted?"

"Only for a moment," I answered, as though that was somehow reassuring.

"You looked panicked when Baldwin mentioned the name Slyton, and when you saw them…" he paused. "Surely you did not know them?"

I hesitated, unsure how to answer. "Surely they did not claim to know me?" My tone bordered on insulted to cover my unease.

"Of course not. But I'm sorry if their visit did in any way cause you distress. They are not the typical sort of people who visit Timpton, I assure you."

So, they hadn't recognized me? He hadn't discovered my secret? I inhaled deeply at the thought, unaware I had been holding my breath. "So why did they come?" I asked casually, hiding my desperation to know.

"A personal matter," Edwin answered, most unhelpfully. "It wasn't a very useful meeting in the end and I regret having brought them here. I just didn't want to leave Timpton right now."

My heart fumbled at the reminder of Helena and I berated myself for my persistent stupidity. Why did I keep finding myself with my cousin's suitor? I awkwardly pushed off his leg to sit up.

"Did Diana send you to find me?" I asked, already knowing the answer.

"Yes. She was quite worried about you."

I nodded, confused why I found myself disappointed at his admission. Of course she had. I knew she was up to something when I left her—Edwin wouldn't search me out on his own initiative. I needed to find a time to talk to her, tell her to stop meddling. It would be easy to realize Edwin didn't care for me, if Diana would stop pushing us together and sending him on these calculated assignments. Not that I truly cared, it would just be simpler without having to question.

~

As we neared Timpton, Edwin dismounted his horse and walked us in. He guided the horse by placing his hand firmly on top of its neck, walking close enough to catch me if I fell. I appreciated the gentlemanly behavior though I found I was not as unbalanced as I had been when I sat alone before. As we approached the house, the guests were gathered out by the pond, blankets spread across the grass. I heard laughter and spotted a group standing in a circle with Helena blindfolded in the center.

"They must be playing Blind Man's Bluff," I exclaimed. I had never played the game but had overheard it being described.

"It seems they are," Edwin sounded unimpressed. "Would you like me to let you off, so you can join them?"

"If you wouldn't mind," I said, twisting my upper body to get a better view. "I understand it is quite entertaining to watch."

"It sounds as though it is," he said as Helena's laughter floated toward us. He reached up and gripped my waist before lowering me down. I blushed at our proximity and was thankful the horse hid us from the view of others.

"Will you come play?" I asked, with an inviting smile.

He lifted an eyebrow. "I don't play games, Miss Blakeslee."

"Surely you cannot make such a claim, for you played one just yesterday."

His mouth pulled up at one corner. "That was an exception."

"And could you not make another?"

He seized the reins of the horse and led it away, answering my question.

I hurried to join the group as a blindfolded Helena grabbed at a teasing Lord Ramsby. She caught the lapel of his jacket and smiled victoriously as he stilled like a statue.

"Now to figure out who you are." She brought her hands to his shoulders, as though she was measuring his height, and traced the top of them inward to his neck. "A good build," she exclaimed to herself. "Thick hair," she continued, smiling as she moved her fingers through his hair and down his forehead. She clasped his face in her hands and ran her thumbs over his eyebrows, around his eyes, and down the bridge of his nose. "A fine nose!" She was giggling in delight as she touched his lips.

The gesture forced me to divert my eyes. My gaze fell on Diana who wore an amused grin on her face. I looked back toward Helena who stroked Lord Ramsby's lips once more. "These lips." Helena's smile lessened, and she bit her own lip thoughtfully. "This has to be Lord Ramsby!" She removed her blindfold to the cheers of the group. When she confirmed it was him, she clapped excitedly looking very pleased with herself. She offered him her hand and he willingly bestowed a congratulatory kiss.

"Who is next?" Diana asked, and Miss Hawkins stepped forward. Poor Miss Hawkins did not have the same luck at catching a gentleman but handled it more graciously than I would have given her credit. She inspected Hannah's gown with her hands. "It must be Miss Hannah, for her gown is the only one that buttoned this high in the back today and has a lace trim around both the sleeves as well as on the collar." She received recognition from an impressed audience as Diana came to the center again.

"I believe most everyone has had a turn," she said, smiling as her eyes scanned the group. "Except you, Abigail."

I stiffened under the shifting glances in my direction. "I do not intend to play."

"I must insist—either you or Edwin." She shifted her gaze from me and I followed it to where Edwin had just joined the group.

"I'll pass," Edwin said curtly.

A wicked smile crossed her face. "Well, it is either you or Abigail."

I looked toward him and found him mirroring my expression of expectation. I shook my head and pointed at him imploringly. Grudgingly he walked to the circle and stood in front of Diana.

"I promise you will find pleasure in our silly game, dear brother," I heard her whisper before tying the blindfold in place and spinning him.

He looked quite absurd walking with his outstretched arms swinging around unenthusiastically. The gentlemen had backed away from him and all the ladies giggled wildly as they circled him, attempting to be the one he captured without making their desire too obvious. Helena let out a shrill laugh he was certain to recognize as she neared him. He made an attempt in her direction before he turned and staggered the opposite way. Diana came toward me and grabbed my hand, pulling me nearer the group.

"I only intend to watch," I whispered, planting my feet.

"I know," she whispered back, "but you might as well have a good view. It isn't often you get to witness Edwin looking so utterly ridiculous."

I conceded and allowed her to pull me a little closer before stopping again.

"Abigail," she said in a loud whisper. "Come on!"

I shook my head seeing Edwin moving toward Diana, arms outstretched. I let out a small giggle as his hand nearly grabbed the skirt of her gown. Edwin must have realized there was someone close because he reached again in our direction. I tried to loosen my hand from Diana's, but she held me tightly. I looked at her just in time to glimpse her mischievous grin turning away from me, the force of the rotation throwing me right into Edwin's opened arms.

He fastened his arms tightly around me, and I barely restrained a laugh.

"Let's see," he said, allowing me to take a step back but keeping his hands on my waist. He held his hands there for a moment and I sensed the strength of them as he lifted one hand to my shoulder followed by the other. My heart raced as he moved to my neck and then my hair.

This game, that had been so entertaining to observe, instantly became very disagreeable. I felt the heat rising to my ears as he touched them gently, and I closed my eyes hoping if I couldn't see him, I wouldn't feel as exposed. The sensation of his hands as he caressed my cheeks and ran his finger over my nose was gentle and warm, and I opened my eyes to realize neither of us were smiling or laughing as the others had done. I wanted to pull away, to escape the impression he cared when it was all for the sake of a game. What a fool I was, he hadn't even discovered who I was yet.

I stiffened as he ran his fingers over my lips making my breath catch. He took a step back, moving his hands from my shoulders down the length of my arms.

"Any conjectures?" Ross said with a laugh. "Surely you have had ample time to contrive one."

I glanced in Ross's direction and found the glaring eyes of Helena on me. I pulled my hands from Edwin's.

"I would know my sister anywhere," he said as he began to remove his blindfold. The whole crowd laughed as his gaze settled on me. "Miss Blakeslee," he said, grabbing my hand and kissing it as though offering an apology.

I smiled feebly, still too shaken by the experience to brush it off as effortlessly as he was capable. I took a few steps back.

"Such an entertaining way to end," Diana said to the group, and I willingly turned my attention to her. "Shall we get some refreshment?"

I walked amidst the crowd toward the shore of the pond where several of the parents sat on blankets enjoying lemonade.

Someone looped their arm through mine and there was no

need to confirm who it was in my agitation. "I can't believe you did that, Diana. Helena looked very vexed."

"Do you think?" Diana asked innocently. "It looked to me as though she thoroughly enjoyed the game. Perhaps not that Edwin happened to run into you, but her finding Lord Ramsby was most fitting."

"Happened to run into me?" I kept my voice as quiet as I could in my exasperation. "You threw me at him!"

"You are rather dramatic, Abigail. I was trying to dodge him and didn't realize how vulnerable it would leave you."

"You are the worst sort of liar."

"Darling?" Diana asked over her shoulder and I looked over to find Mr. Ellis closely trailing us. "Do you hear the accusations Abigail is placing against me?"

"I believe she thinks you are literally tossing her into your brother's path," he said chuckling.

I blushed, realizing he had overheard our entire conversation.

"Can you imagine such a foolish notion? What reason would I possibly have for it?"

I narrowed my eyes at her. "Whatever you are trying to accomplish, you need to stop. Your brother is in love with my cousin."

"He is not," she said defiantly, fixing her gaze forward.

"Well, he certainly prefers her, and rightfully so," I looked to where the two of them sat talking in the shade of a large willow tree with Mr. Kingman and Lord Ramsby. "She is everything I'm not," I whispered to myself.

I FOUND a spot on the blanket near Hannah and Sir Wycliffe, glad to finally spend time talking with my more amiable cousin. I hadn't expected her to be so quickly swept up and inaccessible during my visit. Sir Wycliffe was a nice man, though I could see why Helena had referred to him as a rattle, doting on Hannah in every moment in an exaggerated but perhaps endearing way. Though I would find such attention irksome, I was happy to see Hannah never seemed to tire of it —blushing appropriately and batting her long eyelashes at him constantly.

"I am quite parched," I said, realizing my thirst. "Would either of you like a refill of your drinks?"

"We are fine for now. In fact, I feel a need to stretch my legs a bit," she looked imploringly at Sir Wycliffe who hurried to his feet and offered his assistance in helping her stand. "Find us later, Abigail, I need assistance deciding the style of my gown for our wedding."

"Of course," I agreed, thrilled she would seek my opinion but reluctant to explain my uselessness with such a task. As I neared the refreshment table where the drinks and sandwiches had been set out, the false smile of my aunt greeted me.

"What a lovely day. Is it not, Abigail?"

"Certainly," I said, trying not to echo the same insincere tone I heard in her voice.

"I must admit, I was surprised to see you participate in Blind Man's Bluff—during Mr. Stanton's turn nonetheless."

Glad no one else was around to see the accusation in her eyes, I shifted awkwardly. "It was not my intention to play."

"Of course not." Her eyes narrowed as she continued, "Yet I do believe intentions hold little credence when our actions contradict them."

I looked down at the refreshments and began to fill a cup of lemonade, refusing to meet her piercing glare.

"Helena told me you and Mrs. Ellis have become fast friends. I wonder what her purposes are in seeking you out?"

I hesitantly lifted my eyes. "I believe her intention is to be friendly."

Aunt Marianne scoffed. "Whatever she is scheming, it won't work. I don't think she realizes who she is up against."

"You mean her future sister-in-law?" I said, trying to help my aunt see the irony in her words.

"Precisely," she confirmed. "And you would be wise to keep your distance. Do we understand each other?"

"Miss Blakeslee?"

Before I had an opportunity to clarify who she wished me to keep my distance from, Lord Ramsby walked to my side, a generous smile on his face.

"Did you need something, Lord Ramsby?" I asked with a smile, attempting to hide my distress.

"You promised me a walk today," he answered with a hint of disappointment.

I had not only managed to forget the obligation once, but twice. I nodded stiffly to my aunt as I turned gratefully toward him, accepting his outstretched arm. "I certainly did."

Mr. Ross and Miss Hawkins waited for us by the path that followed the pond.

"I hope you don't mind I invited another couple to accompany us?"

"Not at all," I said, relieved at his foresight. I offered a polite greeting to the patient faces as we approached.

The other couple fell an appropriate distance behind, allowing for myself and Lord Ramsby to converse privately. Still shaken from the confrontation with my aunt, I tried to listen as Lord Ramsby began talking of singing duets this morning and how he wished I could have joined him and Helena in the music room.

As he spoke, I studied his handsome face and dark features. I considered him very attractive, charming, and kind —so why did I find myself recalling my encounter with Edwin here earlier this morning? I shook the thought from my mind but as we neared the same place where I had seen

Edwin standing at dawn, I evoked the tormented look on his face. I yearned to know more of Edwin's troubles.

"Do you not agree, Miss Blakeslee?"

I glanced toward Lord Ramsby. "Perhaps?" I answered, thinking it the most generic response I could offer without giving a definite yes to an unknown statement.

He regarded me, searching my face for some sort of revelation. "Forgive me," he said suddenly. "It is probably not a desirable topic. Let us leave it immediately."

"Truly, I don't mind," I said, suddenly curious what subject he had been discussing that he now seemed so eager to leave.

"No, this is a rare opportunity to become better acquainted; we need not talk of others."

I stifled a sigh. "Very well, what do you prefer to discuss?"

"Tell me about yourself, Miss Blakeslee. I wish to know everything about you."

Suppressing the urge to turn my back on him and run, I focused on his good intention—he desired to know me without anyone forcing his interest. Perhaps I should give him a fair chance.

Refusing to let the pitting sensation in my stomach control me, I began contriving an answer. "I don't believe there is much to tell," or at least that I was able to tell. "I miss Easton Manor dearly, as well as my father and my older brother. My mother passed away nearly two years ago, and I wonder if I will ever be able to think of her, or speak of her, without the desire to weep." I swallowed back my emotion and continued, "I used to be an avid reader but find little joy in it since her passing."

I looked to see if he was satisfied with my answer so far and his intent gaze told me he was.

"I enjoy drawing and painting but am not fond of many of the talents ladies are supposed to be accomplished in. I don't ride horses. I don't like large groups. I will do anything to avoid gossiping in the drawing room. And I would spend every day out of doors if I could." I inhaled deeply, reminding myself of the beauty surrounding us. "I have a quick temper, which my father says I must learn to control before a gentleman will consider marrying me."

Realizing I had just spoken of marriage in front of Lord Ramsby made me blush, and I hastened on, "I'm never full, my maid picks out my gowns for me because I know little of fashion, and I have no desire to be a debutante next Season, or any Season for that matter. Anything else you wish to know?" I asked, glancing toward him from the corner of my eye.

"How you manage it?" He said with a devilishly handsome smile as he stopped and turned toward me.

"Manage what?" I asked, facing him.

"How you manage to be so peculiar yet captivating." His dark eyes lit up. "I find it refreshing that you do not pretend to be what you are not, no matter what is said about you or your abilities." I suppressed scoffing at the unintended insult as he continued, "You hold odd views, unlike any lady I have met, but you don't shy away from them. You spend your days helping others, which seems entirely strange, but with you it just adds to this compilation I've been creating of you since I first saw you outside Timpton House. I am desperate to know more, to hear your obscure opinions, to be fully enveloped in your enchantments."

I was certain he meant his words to be a compliment, and in some ways, I was genuinely pleased with his assessment of me; but I wondered if he would find me as captivating if I disclosed to him parts of my past that had influenced me in becoming the person he surprisingly enjoyed. It would be easier to keep talking than dwell on such ideas. "I believe you have already been forced to listen to several of my strange opinions," I said with a smile, "and I must apologize for it. Two of my greatest faults are an inability to hold my tongue and my stubbornness."

"I must say I enjoy watching both thoroughly. There are

not many ladies who could set a full-grown man in his place." I gave him a puzzled look and he obliged me, "I have now seen you surprise the younger Mr. Stanton twice with your abilities. The first time with your debate on adventure and your second on charity. Though I must say I found it quite peculiar how agitated he got when you spoke of the less fortunate being worthy of our aid, for he had used the exact term earlier that morning when he spoke to Mr. Dowding and my cousin on rendering assistance to the Bragg family."

My lips parted in disbelief before I clenched them shut. Why had Edwin seemed so upset by my choice of word when he had used the very same in his own reasoning? I decided a diversion was in order to keep my thoughts focused on Lord Ramsby. "Well, I believe it is your turn," I said as I began walking again.

He spoke about his mother and how he adored her even with the pressure she placed on him to find a wife. He told me of how he had found it difficult to rise to his responsibilities when his father had died and that he still felt ill-prepared for all he was expected to accomplish. He had been to London during the Season twice before; but he opted for six months abroad when he realized it could be his last chance to visit the Continent before *settling down*. He arrived home not long before he traveled to London and immediately here.

"You must also long for home," I said.

"At times. Though I find my thoughts have been occupied with other things of late."

I blushed and lowered my gaze, refusing him the chance to expound if he cared to take it. A rustling sound piqued my interest and I glanced up as Lord Ramsby held a lovely purple flower out toward me.

"Thank you," I said, bringing it close to smell.

"It does not compare to you in beauty, but what could?"

I laughed at his sentiment before realizing my reaction might not be the desired one. "I do believe Uncle Stanton's story of the lady in the water has influenced your opinion most abominably."

"I assure you, as much as I enjoyed his story, I have held that opinion since our first acquaintance." He reached out his arm to me, an unnervingly handsome smile on his lips.

I gladly accepted his escort, feeling surprisingly delighted with Lord Ramsby's compliment. Perhaps there was potential for something more than friendship with him after all.

~

WHEN WE FINISHED OUR WALK, Lord Ramsby led me back to the refreshment table.

"Thank you," I said, surprised at how sincere my gratitude was. "I very much enjoyed our time together."

"As did I," he said, turning to me with a cup of lemonade. "Perhaps we might find another occasion to get better *acquainted?*"

I giggled. "You have promised to be a gentleman." The words slipped from my lips in a flirtatious tone, and I wasn't sure who was more surprised, Lord Ramsby or myself.

"You should expect nothing less from me," he said, reaching for my hand.

I willingly placed it in his and watched as he brought it to his lips before bestowing a gentle kiss on my glove.

"Miss Blakeslee."

At hearing Edwin's voice, I dropped my hand and spun toward him.

He didn't acknowledge Lord Ramsby as he stepped to my side. "You have received an update on the Bragg family," he said, holding it out to me.

Eagerly I grabbed the note and gave Lord Ramsby an apologetic glance.

He looked to Edwin and back to me before nodding his understanding. "I will let you read your correspondence in private. Find me later and we shall continue our conversation."

"I would like that," I said with a smile before turning my attention to the letter.

MISS BLAKESLEE,

MY NAME IS MRS. REED. Doctor Walter has asked me to aid the Bragg family in their illness. I shall send regular updates as requested. Patience has also developed a fever, but both she and Rose seem to be doing well enough, so far. I regret to inform you, Mrs. Bragg's condition is very poor, and I am uncertain if she will remain with us much longer. She is unresponsive, except for an occasional murmuring. I'm doing all I can for her. She sleeps now, as do the children. Pray she may find the strength to recover.

SINCERELY,
    Mrs. Reed

MY HEAD SPUN as I glanced up. Edwin stood studying me, my worried expression increasing the intensity of his brow.

"A caretaker has been hired, a Mrs. Reed," I offered, and he nodded as though he recognized the name. "She says Patience has now taken ill and though she and Rose are doing well enough, Mrs. Reed does not know if Mrs. Bragg will survive." My voice quivered, "What will the children do with their father and mother being taken from them so suddenly?" I thought of their sweet faces and the hardships being sent to a parish orphanage would have on them. Tears welled in my eyes. "I should have recognized yesterday she suffered more than just grief, I should have sought help."

"You did not know."

The guilt hung heavy over me and I shifted my feet to compensate for the weight of it.

"You must rest, Miss Blakeslee," he said, offering me his arm. "You have had a taxing day. Let me escort you to your room."

I nodded despondently and placed my arm on his. Perhaps I did need time to rest, to ponder, and to plead to God for Mrs. Bragg and her children.

"Baldwin, will you have Miss Blakeslee's maid sent up to assist her?" Edwin asked as we passed him on the lawn.

"Of course," he said, motioning for a servant carrying refreshments to come speak with him.

We walked into the entry hall and started up the staircase to my room. Each step we took in silence seemed to make me more aware of the childish weakness I had once again displayed in his presence.

"It is a beautiful day," I said awkwardly. "I am sorry to take you from it."

"Don't be sorry," Edwin affirmed, glancing at me out of the corner of his eye. "Was your stroll around the pond refreshing?" I saw his gaze move to the purple flower I still clutched in my hand.

"It was, thank you," I said, removing my arm from his to shift the flower to my other hand.

He nodded but said nothing.

"Lord Ramsby did mention something I wished to ask you about."

"That's promising," Edwin retorted.

I took his remark as consent to proceed. "Do you recall our discussion last night and how vexed you became at my word choice?"

He kept his gaze forward as we ambled down the corridor.

"Worthy?" I offered when he didn't respond.

"It was not the choice of word that irked me," he said, still looking ahead as we neared my room. We stopped, his eyes still fixed on our destination. "It was an inward revelation I was not ready to address."

"That must be quite a revelation to induce such a response —especially when I was told you used that exact phrase describing the very same situation."

He glanced at me before turning to finish the walk to my room. "It certainly was," he said over his shoulder.

I hurried to catch up to him. "You will offer no defense or further explanation?"

A sideways smile came to his mouth. "I will not."

"Very well," I said, trying to hide how disagreeable I found him in his secrecy, knowing it would only add to his pleasure. "I also meant to thank you for making a second exception to your strict no game policy." My cheeks reddened as I thought of his warm hands on my face, and I rebuked myself for my senseless reaction. "I hope you realize I had no intention of playing, and I certainly did not mean for you to pick me... it was Diana, she...." I fumbled over how to phrase his sister's role without bringing up another humiliating topic. "Well she—"

His rare, full smile captivated me. "I meant to pick you."

"You did not!" My look of disbelief sent a rumbling laugh echoing down the corridor.

"I did. I figured your first game of Blind Man's Bluff should be memorable."

"But you thought I was your sister."

"I was convincing in my deception then?" I nodded suspiciously as he continued, "I'm glad to hear it. I thought it the best option for us both."

I narrowed my eyes at him as we reached my room. "You are incorrigible!" I said, and I made sure my voice sounded appalled though I couldn't hide my smile.

"And you are maddening," he whispered, leaning close to brush a wisp of hair from my forehead.

I couldn't pull my gaze away from the intensity in his eyes. The entirety of my being wanted him to caress my face as he had in the game, but this time I wanted him to mean it. His hand grazed my shoulder as he lowered it, coming to rest so close to my own I felt the heat of it through my glove.

"Edwin darling." Lady Eliza's voice caused us both to startle, and he straightened though he didn't take a step away from me.

As Lady Eliza approached us, she smiled apologetically at me before her eyes darted back to Edwin. "I was hoping you might help me with something, dear."

He sighed and ran his hand through his hair. "What is it?"

"I don't wish to bore Miss Blakeslee with such trivial matter. Will you escort me downstairs and I can discuss it with you in private?"

Edwin let out a deep, audible breath. "Of course." He offered his arm to Lady Eliza. "Please rest, Miss Blakeslee," he said in his usual tone as the two of them turned to walk back down the corridor.

My face burned long after they had left my view. I entered my room, already pleading with God for Mrs. Bragg's life and for the return of my ability to think rationally.

CHAPTER 12

I spent the remainder of my afternoon resting, praying, and pondering and I was certain it had been beneficial to my soul as I entered the drawing room before dinner.

Diana smiled at me invitingly, and I eagerly joined her.

"Edwin told me you received a message about the Bragg family, such sad news. I hope Mrs. Bragg soon recovers." She looked worried. "How are you? It has been an unusual day for you, I'm sure."

"I've had much harder days," I said, suddenly aware my answer was not as reassuring as I had intended.

"I'm certain you have," she said, reaching out to give my hand a squeeze.

"Have you heard the exciting news, Abigail?" Helena exclaimed nearly bouncing into me.

My chest tightened, and my breath grew heavy as I exhaled. The inevitable proposal had come. "I have not heard it was official," I choked out, almost inaudibly, trying to conceal my shock. I glanced at Diana. Why had she not told me? Not prepared me? Is this why Lady Eliza had come in search of Edwin?

Helena placed her hand on my arm. "Well it is, and I couldn't be more thrilled! Though I'm sure it will be simpler in style than I am accustomed, it shall be quite an affair." My legs felt weak beneath me as she continued, "It will take place two weeks from Friday."

"So soon?" I managed.

"I thought the same thing," she said, as though she meant to reassure me. "In London, it's proper to have at least a month's notice for a ball, but unfortunately we are not in London and I must grow accustomed to the strange manners of country life."

"A ball?" I echoed in dismay.

Helena looked toward Diana before offering me a thin smile. "Did I not just relay the very thing?"

I choked on the mix of my words and my thoughts. "Yes, of course. How wonderful." Relief flooded over me and a genuine smile formed on my lips.

Helena giggled in our apparent shared excitement. "I must go find Mother for we will have much to discuss. I'm certain it will prove to be a momentous occasion." I watched as she glided across the drawing room, and the realization struck me —when Helena's engagement did come, there would be no reprieve.

"That was eye-opening." Diana said, commanding my attention.

"What?" I asked innocently. Surely my surprise was not a betrayal of the deeper feelings I concealed.

"Did you assume Edwin had proposed to Miss Hanford?"

"I didn't think such a level of excitement could come from a ball being announced."

Diana smiled, eyebrows raised in accusation.

"Stop looking at me like that."

"Abigail, you are blushing in a most guilty manner."

My mouth opened in disbelief. "Anyone who must come under such an implicating smirk as you are capable of giving would do the same."

Her laughter was immediate, and I couldn't help but smile at her inability to stop. She wiped tears from her eyes as she finally composed herself. "Mr. Ellis will greatly appreciate the description you have just given, what did you call it again—implicating smirk? For lack of a better name he refers to it as 'my vexing ability.' He shall be quite grateful to you, I am sure."

"What is so humorous?" Edwin asked, stepping next to his sister, his light eyes moving between us curiously.

"Abigail," Diana answered.

His eyebrows lifted, imploring one of us to continue.

"Apparently I have just described a vexing habit of Diana's in a way she found most enlightening."

"I found it entertaining," she corrected. "Mr. Ellis will find it enlightening."

"What will I find enlightening?" Mr. Ellis asked as he walked to Diana's other side.

"Abigail has just described my vexing ability in a way I believe you will find most satisfying."

Now it was Mr. Ellis's turn to appraise me with raised eyebrows.

"I called it an implicating smirk," I said in an unimpressed tone.

His expression turned thoughtful, and he nodded enthusiastically. "That is quite a perfect description. Though I am sorry if she made you endure one. I was under the impression she reserved that talent for me alone." He looked at Diana with such an expression of endearment it brought another smile to my face.

"I typically do darling," she assured him, resting her hand on his arm. "Well, you and Edwin. But it was entirely necessary, I assure you." Edwin and Mr. Ellis sent each other a curious glance, but Diana shook her head. "I cannot tell you the reason, I'd hate to implicate poor Abigail twice, and in front of gentlemen, she'd never forgive me."

I was far from eased by her current resolve for discretion. What if she were to inform Mr. Ellis later—or worse, her brother—of what she assumed she'd seen in my reaction?

"Besides, Edwin," Diana continued, "I've been meaning to ask if you've met with Mr. Stimpson about the filly he is selling."

Edwin shook his head. "I have not yet made an inquiry."

"You said you were contemplating the purchase of another horse and she would be the perfect addition to Timpton's stables." Diana gave a little pout. "Perhaps we might set up a time to go see her early next week?"

Edwin considered his sister for a moment. "I suppose it would do no harm to write Mr. Stimpson and see if he is ready to show her." Diana squealed, and Edwin pointed his finger at his sister. "But, if I agree to bring you, you must agree to not fall in love with the creature before I can verify its pedigree. I will not risk such a large investment on a horse of poor breeding."

My heart faltered at his declaration.

"Agreed," Diana said, grinning triumphantly. "And you must come along, Abigail." She turned to me. "I can't be expected to keep my word without adequate support."

I nodded absently, and her eyes narrowed; but before she could question me, the butler announced dinner. Edwin's attention slid from me to Helena and back again.

"It is fine," I said, not wanting him to choose Helena over me. "Your obligation is to my cousin; besides, I was hoping to walk in with Uncle Stanton tonight." I scanned the room until I located Uncle and hurried toward him, without looking back.

～

"UNCLE, would you be willing to escort me into dinner?"

"Surely the gentlemen present are not so harebrained to allow such a thing," he said, disappointment in his voice.

"I had to fight off the suitors to get to you, but now that they have been confounded you must not deny me the pleasure."

He reached out his hand and I helped pull him to his feet. "It would be my greatest delight," he said with a grin.

Leading Uncle Stanton from the room, I noticed Lord Ramsby watching me. In my rush to flee the situation with Edwin I had forgotten I should probably seek out his escort. I sent him an apologetic smile, and he generously accepted with a nod before turning to offer his arm to a delighted Miss Emma Dowding.

Once Uncle Stanton was situated at his place, I found my seat next to a beaming Diana.

"How fortunate we should finally be close enough to converse during dinner."

"Most fortunate," I answered, before noticing the familiar gleam in her eye. Curious, I looked down the table to find Lord Ramsby placed in the middle of nearly every eligible lady present. "You didn't by chance have anything to do with tonight's seating arrangements?" I whispered, placing my napkin on my lap.

"What would be my purpose in taking on such a tedious task?"

Just on the other side of Diana, Mr. Ellis pressed his lips together.

"What purpose indeed?" I retorted.

"What do you speak of?" Helena asked from across the table, looking between me and Diana affably.

"I was just asking Diana how they come up with the seating arrangements each night," I said, skimming over Edwin who sat across from Diana on Helena's left. I could tell his gaze was on Helena as we spoke, and I tried not to care.

Helena tilted her head. "It's the responsibility of the lady of the house to see to the task. A hostess must consider many things when seating her guests: which guests tolerate one another's company, and which do not; which guests seated near one another will achieve the most advantageous conversations; and which guests might need special accommodations." Helena spoke as though she was reciting a textual passage she'd memorized on the topic. "Not to mention she must always consider rank, age, the sexes, and marital status. Does that answer your question, Abigail?"

I feigned interest in realigning the silverware to avoid her pointed expression. "Perfectly. Thank you, Helena."

I sensed Diana's gaze on me and wondered if Edwin displayed a similar look of pity. I glanced in his direction, but his head was down and when he looked up, his eyes once again shifted to a victorious Helena.

"It is fortunate I am not yet responsible for such a task." Diana smiled at me. "I'm certain I'd make quite a mess of it all —sitting the drunkard next to the abstainer, the Torie next to the Whig, and the tempted across from the tempter." As she finished speaking Diana's eyes shifted from me to Edwin causing my neck to prickle with heat.

Edwin's jaw clenched, and he fixed his glare on Diana. Helena glanced from him back to his sister. Her eyes narrowed briefly before offering a forced smile.

"Miss Hanford," Edwin said, still glowering at Diana. "Perhaps I could convince you to offer lessons to my sister regarding the proper decorum of a hostess? Instruction on placing your guests' needs over those of your own would be most timely."

Diana returned his glare with one of equal intensity. "That sounds most enlightening, dear brother, but perhaps you should consider joining me. I'm positive Miss Hanford has ample material she'd be eager to share with you on being an amiable gentleman."

I dipped my spoon in my soup and glanced to the left. How regrettable I had been placed beside Mr. Dowding who seemed fully engaged in discussion with the group next to him.

"Tell me, Mrs. Ellis," Helena began, finally interrupting the deafening clang of silverware, "how often do you and Mr. Ellis visit Timpton House?"

Diana lifted her chin and met Helena's gaze. "As often as we are able."

"How fortunate," Helena responded with a pulled smile. "Though I'd assume a couple so newly married would desire time apart from their family. It seems difficult to learn to rely on your spouse when they are still attached so earnestly to others. But perhaps I am mistaken?" Helena glanced between Mr. Ellis and Diana, expectantly.

"It is quite the contrary," Mr. Ellis answered. "Diana's family is my family now and I am as willing to spend time here as she is. It has become clear to me when you learn to embrace the people your spouse loves, in time you become part of that love—which in turn only adds to the love between you as a couple."

Diana smiled at Mr. Ellis, and I glimpsed her reaching toward him beneath the table. He welcomed the gesture and intertwined his fingers through hers. It was such a simple display of affection, but I felt strangely moved by it. Diana was strong and independent, yet his steadfast support strengthened her.

"Well I simply cannot disagree with such a picturesque argument, Mr. Ellis," Helena said, nodding in his direction with an endearing grin. "I hope, when I marry, my husband will be as sympathetic regarding my feelings as you are to Mrs. Ellis's."

At her inference, my gaze fell to Edwin, who sat staring at the plate the servant had just placed before him. He lifted his gaze to her expectant eyes. "Miss Hanford, I hope the same."

Helena offered him a beautiful smile and gazed at him from under her long lashes. I forced my attention back to my food, jabbing at a stray vegetable so forcefully it rolled across my plate. I could detect Diana watching me again but refused her my civility, looking past her to the other side of the table.

Lord Ramsby seemed to be entirely entertained amidst the doting females surrounding him and I silently cursed Diana for interfering with the seating arrangements. I may not always prefer Lord Ramsby's company but sitting near him would be more pleasant than being forced to watch Edwin and Helena interact.

By the time the last course was brought in, I hardly glanced up from my plate. Diana had apparently taken her brother's rebuke to heart and let Helena dominate the conversation throughout dinner without as much as a sarcastic reply. The other three commented just enough to encourage Helena along and she now prattled on about the time she had met the Prince Regent and how he had called her a timeless beauty.

I had not said a word since the first conversation and I ached to be free of this dining room, the people in it, and Edwin and his observable devotion to Helena.

"Abigail," Diana whispered, and I reluctantly looked toward her. "Are you well?"

I nearly scoffed at the look of concern on her face; after all, she had been the one to cause my foul mood with her endless tampering. "I'm just tired," I said, more cordially than her behavior merited.

"I—" she paused, looking unsure what to say. "I'm sorry."

There was something about the sincerity in her eyes that softened me. "I know."

She reached out and grabbed my hand beneath the table. A sudden urge to weep overwhelmed me and I pushed my lips together to prevent it. A single tear slipped down my cheek, and I quickly wiped it away, chastising myself and how irrational I had become since coming to Timpton House.

~

"DID YOU ENJOY DINNER?" Lord Ramsby asked, finding me standing alone by the fire when the gentlemen rejoined the ladies after port.

"I must admit I was feeling out of sorts," I answered.

"Have you quarreled with someone?" he asked with a frown, and I immediately regretted answering honestly.

I mustered a convincing smile, preferring to hide away my feelings instead of explaining my irrational state of mind. "Not at all, I am guilty of being homesick. But I have just stepped outside to take some air and am feeling much improved. How are you this evening?" I asked, hoping to change the topic. "You looked to be enjoying yourself at dinner."

"You were watching me?" His handsome smile and sultry tone lightened my foul mood.

"I may have glanced in your direction once or twice." I was once again surprised at how easily I had flirted.

"I'm pleased to hear it," Lord Ramsby said, taking a step closer and lowering his voice. "And as content as I appeared to be, I was far from it. I could hardly keep my eyes from you—I still cannot."

My cheeks grew warm, but I did not shy away as I typically did. Regardless of his sincerity, I was grateful to be noticed. I craved for him to continue, to feel worthy of attention.

"You must be the most beautiful woman I have ever beheld," he said, apparently realizing my desire.

"Perhaps you are blinded by what you believe I am," I whispered, momentarily wishing it was not true.

"How could I not be? You are intoxicating. I somehow lose grasp of my senses when I'm near you." His eyes searched mine before he lifted his hand to the side of my face and tucked a piece of hair behind my ear. His touch felt strange on my skin and I stiffened, cursing myself for encouraging his flirtation. I glanced away briefly, wondering where Diana and her meddling instincts were now that I needed her.

His hand grazed mine as he lowered it and the air seemed heavy as I inhaled. He smiled down at me, intertwining his fingers with mine. I froze, unable to think, as I took in Lord Ramsby's handsome face too near my own.

"Miss Blakeslee."

I startled as Edwin stepped to my side.

"Are you well?"

I looked at my rescuer, unsure of whether I was pleased or agitated it would be him.

"Yes, Mr. Stanton. Thank you," I said, untangling my fingers from Lord Ramsby's before Edwin noticed. I took a step back. The increased distance between myself and both gentlemen eased my breathing.

"Diana has requested an audience with you, Miss Blakeslee. She said it was urgent." Only after he was finished speaking did he let his piercing gaze shift from Lord Ramsby to me.

Lord Ramsby shook his head in disbelief but stilled when Edwin took a warning step toward him.

I instinctually placed my hand on Edwin's arm, stopping any further advance on his part.

"I'm sorry, Lord Ramsby, please forgive the interruption." I offered a timid smile to pacify the disappointment on Lord Ramsby's face before turning toward Edwin, who waited with his arm extended toward me. Hesitantly I grabbed it and he led me across the sitting room.

"Are you certain you are well, Miss Blakeslee? You look pale."

"It is nothing to trouble yourself with."

I sensed his eyes on me as we neared Diana, but he said nothing.

"Thank you for your escort," I said, dropping his arm when

we had reached her. I couldn't explain why I was overwhelmingly cross and embarrassed, but I was confident it was his fault. "I did not intend to inconvenience you again, please make my apologies to Helena."

His eyes remained locked on me, the dim light and his low set brow intensifying the severity beneath them. He looked as though he wished to speak but closed his mouth and clenched his jaw before turning and walking away.

"There you are, Abigail," Diana whispered, grabbing my arm and pulling me into a circle where Mr. Ross Gale enchanted a small group with a story. I listened to the animated retelling of a school prank he once instigated before leaning close to Diana.

"Did you wish to discuss something with me?" I whispered.

She looked at me, a vacant expression on her face.

"Your brother," I said, pointing where he had just been. "He told me you wished to speak with me. He mentioned it was urgent."

"How strange," she said with an innocent shrug. "But I am glad he brought you to me. In fact, I was about to search you out. We had previously discussed playing cards and as much as I love Mr. Ellis, he is an abominable card player. Do say you'll partner with me and forestall my typical thrashing?"

I nodded absently, my thoughts turning to Edwin. Did Diana truly not send him to find me? If not, why had he sought me out? I glanced behind me, scanning the group of people. Perhaps the answers to my questions would be evident in his features. My eyes locked with his, and the intensity of his scowl forced my gaze back to the safety of Diana's smile. Whatever his reasoning had been, it simply couldn't matter.

CHAPTER 13

*A*s soon as I was dressed for the day, I made my way downstairs and to the dining room. I heard no voices from inside and hoped that Lydia's information—that most of the guests preferred their Sabbath morning meals to be taken in their rooms—was correct. Slowly I pushed the door open.

The room was empty, and the sideboard was filled with fish, pastries, eggs, and ham. I eagerly grabbed a plate and began serving myself—I needed to make haste if I wanted to spend ample time walking the gardens before leaving for the parish.

A sound outside the door sent my heart racing and I watched as the door swung open. A young servant walked inside, carrying a pitcher. Relief filled me, and I smiled at him as I moved to take a seat at the table. "Good morning."

"Mornin', miss," he answered stiffly, setting down the pitcher next to the glasses. He did not look back toward me but stationed himself next to the sideboard and set his gaze to the far corner of the room. I turned my attention back to my plate, strategizing what part of the garden I should first explore.

The door opened again, and my eyes drifted to the doorway. Edwin entered the room and I instantly regretted my lack of foresight in not asking Lydia to have a tray brought up. He looked around the large empty room, his eyes locking with mine momentarily, before nodding an unenthusiastic greeting.

He moved to the sideboard and I took a few quick bites, hoping to make my plate appear empty enough that my leaving would not seem tied to his arrival. As I looked down at the uneaten food, I scolded myself for my unladylike portions that thwarted my hasty retreat. Surely, I was hopeless. I took an elongated breath in, resigning myself to act politely if the need arose.

Edwin took the seat across from me and began eating without looking up.

I followed his example, picking at one of my pastries. The room was unnervingly quiet, only the clanking of silverware on china filled the silence. I glanced at the servant whose eyes remained fixed on the other side of the room, overlooking the tension between us.

I forced myself to take another bite.

Eventually I peeked at Edwin who ate without pause, eyes fixed on his plate. Surely he was not angry at me for last night? If anyone had a right to be cross it was me with the inconsistent way he acted toward me. Besides, if he was so upset, why had he chosen the seat across from me? Irksome man! I took another bite, refusing to end the silence.

The door opened again, and Mr. Dowding stepped into the room. He looked apprehensively between us, nodded, and walked briskly to the sideboard.

"Surely you are not going to ignore me the remainder of your stay?" Edwin asked quietly, causing me to pause mid-bite.

My gaze met his. "Me?" I asked confounded, keeping my volume at a similar level. "Surely I am not the guilty party."

A side of Mr. Stanton's mouth twitched. "How do you justify such a thing?" he asked. "You have not said a word since I entered."

"And what words have you spoken?" I scoffed, my voice rising in volume.

Mr. Stanton's eyes moved to Mr. Dowding. When the gentleman's attention did not shift from the pastry selection, Mr. Stanton continued, "I offered you a greeting when I first entered, which you did not return."

I considered whether or not I had given his curt nod a response before realizing he might be correct. "Well, inform me, Mr. Stanton, how should one respond to such an inhospitable welcome in the future? Does a severe glance and unwilling nod warrant a false smile? Perhaps I should bat my eyelashes at your severity as Helena does? You obviously take well to such nonsense."

Mr. Edwin Stanton pushed his lips together before covering his mouth with his fist, his light eyes watching me thoughtfully. He finally nodded. "Yes, that is what I would advise. Why don't you try both and I will tell you which I prefer?"

My mouth dropped open in disbelief and I narrowed my eyes at him. "You cannot be serious?"

"And if I were?"

"If you were, I believe you would find yourself amply disappointed, as would I."

He lowered his chin and cleared his throat, and I was positive I had glimpsed a smile on his lips. As I watched him, Mr. Dowding crossed behind his chair carrying a plate full of food and a newspaper tucked under his arm. Instantly I lowered my gaze. Had Mr. Dowding caught me observing Edwin? I heard a chair move several places down from us and I ate another piece of ham without looking up.

"Anything of interest in the publication, Mr. Dowding?" Edwin asked.

"Depends if you are a Whig or a Torie," Mr. Dowding responded shaking his head. "I would let you have it when I am finished but I made the mistake of taking it with me on my morning walk." I looked up with interest as he held up the crinkled paper as evidence. "I fear it did not take well to the rain."

"It is raining again?" I interrupted, disappointment filling me at the realization of another walk in the garden thwarted.

"Just started," Mr. Dowding answered. "It isn't a heavy rain, just enough to bring me inside and wreck my newspaper." Mr. Dowding tilted his head, examining my disheartened countenance. "Don't allow it to distress you, Miss Blakeslee, I do believe it should clear before we take the carriages to church."

I smiled as kindly as I could before turning my attention grudgingly back to my food, allowing the men to continue their discussion on current events. I feigned disinterest as they discussed Parliament and the latest worker strikes. When I finished my breakfast, I stood and excused myself.

"Miss Blakeslee," Edwin said, rising. "May I have a word with you?"

I looked at Mr. Dowding who eagerly looked back to his tattered newspaper, before offering a hesitant nod. Edwin met me at the door and opened it, placing his hand on my back as he ushered me through. I ignored the sensation it caused and paused just outside, waiting for the door to close.

"What do you wish to discuss?"

He glanced down the corridor and hesitantly back at me. "Perhaps you would join me in the library?"

I thought of the rain and how I now had nowhere else to be until we left for church. "Very well."

We walked in silence until we reached the large wooden door next to the study and he gestured me inside.

I complied and stepped through the door as he followed behind me.

"Shall we sit?" he asked, and I once again nodded, following him to a small settee near the window.

We sat in silence and I watched him shift as if attempting to find a comfortable position. He ran his hand through his hair, rubbed his chin, and shifted again.

"What is it?" I asked uneasily.

His gaze met mine. "Miss Blakeslee," he began and then paused. "How are you feeling?"

"How am I feeling? Surely you did not have to bring me here for such an inquiry?" I gave a tight smile attempting to ease my own anxiety.

He didn't return it but shifted restlessly again. My stomach dropped, and I had a sickening premonition what he was about to disclose.

"You are right," he said, taking a deep breath in but refusing to look at me. "I need to discuss a rather sensitive topic with you," his eyes finally met mine. "I'm hesitant because I'm not certain how you will receive it."

The ringing in my head disoriented me. "I believe I already know what you wish to discuss," I said, dropping my gaze to my lap, preparing myself to hear him say the words aloud. I thought of Father and how he had claimed certain topics were often easier to address when we were eased into them; this must be one of the exceptions.

"I have your best interest in mind, Miss Blakeslee. I don't want to see you get hurt."

I nodded, looked up at him, and smiled in what I was certain was an absolutely pitiful attempt. "I believe you." My lip quivered, and I quickly dropped my gaze again, feeling foolish he should feel obligated to prepare me. This announcement had been fixed since before my visit, yet I had grown to dread it with my whole being.

"I have already upset you and I haven't even begun." I felt him shift again and I was certain he had moved closer.

"Please," I said, just wanting it to be over. "Go on."

Edwin rested his hand softly on my back and I wanted to tell him he was only making it more difficult by trying to comfort me, but the truth was I didn't want him to move; I loved the strength and pleasure his touch gave me. Even as he was about to confirm his feelings for someone else, I strangely wanted him here, with his arm around me.

"Very well," he sighed. "I must caution you."

I looked up, my brow furrowing in confusion. "Caution me?" I repeated.

He nodded. "I understand you have a strong regard for Lord Ramsby, but I feel it my duty to warn you against him."

"Warn me against Lord Ramsby?" I asked, still confused. "That is what you wished to discuss with me?"

His brows drew together. "I watched the two of you together last night in the drawing room—your familiarity with each other, not to mention your proximity, was quite alarming."

Relief and anger filled me simultaneously and I laughed out loud at the insanity of it all. "I'm sorry you were alarmed by his desire to be with me, though I am surprised you took notice of me at all with Helena by your side."

Edwin tipped back his head and ran his hands through his hair, looking as though he wished to yank it from his head. "I knew it would be this way, here I thought you were being penitent for your behavior."

"My behavior?" I scoffed. "I did nothing to be ashamed of beyond reciprocating a harmless flirtation."

"Harmless...Lord Ramsby is a scoundrel," Edwin's voice grew louder. "He is attempting to find a willing bride he can put on display at Handsbury Castle. I thought of all the ladies present you would be above such a hasty, superficial attempt —apparently, I was mistaken in your character."

I stared at him in disbelief. Moments ago, I had dreaded losing Edwin to Helena, now I wished nothing more than to be rid of him and his foul temper. "You are a presumptuous, arrogant man and apparently know nothing of my character," I snapped, standing up to retreat.

"Miss Blakeslee," his voice was soft, and I stopped but did not look at him. "I spoke brashly, I did not mean to…" his voice trailed off.

I didn't move.

"Why can nothing be easy with you?"

I turned toward him, his light eyes full of a sorrow that dissipated the anger I was trying so hard to hold onto.

He dropped his gaze and leaned forward, resting both elbows on his knees. "Forgive me, I just don't want to see you hurt."

I sighed, my conscience pricking at me to forgive him for his poorly executed, good intentions. I sat back down and leaned close to him. "I can understand that."

We sat without speaking for several minutes, the silence between us no longer feeling strained. Edwin moved toward me and his knee pressed against my leg. My heart went into a frenzy at his touch and I attempted to convince myself it meant nothing.

"Promise me you'll be careful," he finally said, looking down at me.

"I promise," I said.

"Lord Ramsby is a very charming suitor and apparently quite capable—"

"He is merely infatuated with me," I said, making Edwin's eyebrows raise disapprovingly. I laughed. "I only meant he likes the idea of me, at least the person he has created me to be in his mind."

"And is his creation so very different from who you are?"

I thought a moment. "Not so very different, I suppose, though I do believe Uncle Stanton's retelling of the lady in the water may have prejudiced him to how beautiful he now thinks me." Edwin chuckled, and I questioned if I should continue. "The disparity comes from his inability to account for the past that has formed me into who I am."

"Oh yes, the mysterious past you have eluded to," Edwin said with a sideways grin. "It still remains a mystery to Lord Ramsby as well then?"

I nodded.

Edwin's smile brightened. "Perhaps one day I shall find myself fortunate enough to be placed within your confidence."

I studied his hopeful face, suddenly doubting if even he could overlook such a tainted history. "And alter the way you look at me?" I teased. "Never!"

"I doubt that would be the consequence," he answered solemnly.

"I'm not certain if it is a risk worth taking," I whispered, strangely desiring for him to disagree.

He stared at me until my skin began to pink under his attentive gaze. "Until you trust me it is difficult to know," he said, lifting his hand to my face, brushing my cheek with his thumb.

I paused, the fear inside of me parting long enough to attempt to trust him. "I'm not truly—"

"There you two are."

I jumped at the voice and spun in my seat. Diana stood in the doorway appraising us with a smile pulling at her lips. Her eyes shifted back and forth between us. "I'm sorry. Have I interrupted your tête-à-tête?"

"It can hardly be a tête-à-tête when I have left the door open," Edwin said sharply.

"Regardless, it is lucky for you both that it was me who happened upon you," she said, walking toward us. "Your positioning when I first glimpsed you was quite incriminating."

"We were just talking," I said honestly.

Diana scanned us, apparently noticing how close we sat,

and lifted one eyebrow. "And what topic would require such close proximity in an empty room?"

I glanced at Edwin who glared at his sister.

"Oh...do tell!" she laughed. "You cannot look so aggravated without having good cause."

He refused to oblige her.

"I was just relaying the notion that people are often more accepting of a person, the less they know of them," I offered.

Diana's eyes shifted from mine to Edwin's, as if attempting to decipher whether I spoke the truth. "Very well," Diana said, apparently appeased. "And as much as I would love to hear Edwin's convincing rebuttal, Mother has requested an audience with us."

"Perhaps, Mr. Stanton, we can finish our conversation another time?" I asked, giving my unneeded permission.

"I would very much like that," Edwin said standing, the void he left behind causing me to shift.

"We will have the carriages ready to leave in an hour," Diana said, causing me to pull my gaze from Edwin. "I insist you ride with me to Chadsmead."

I looked between the siblings. "I would be delighted."

Edwin bowed and followed his sister from the room.

I walked to the window and looked out at the gray morning with a smile. When my thoughts turned to Edwin, I was no longer disappointed at the unforeseen rain. I had come so close to telling him, to allowing him into my trust. How would he have responded to the truth? A fluttering inside made me hopeful it would be with understanding and kindness.

I turned from the window, looking at the books before me. For the first time since Mother's death, I had a desire to lose myself in a story. I eagerly headed to the shelf where Edwin and I had spoken during my tour. I grabbed *The Tempest* and returned to the settee, opening the cover, and eagerly flipping to my favorite part—when Miranda and Ferdinand meet and fall instantly in love.

∽

Diana rushed to greet me as I walked down the front staircase. "I was about to send Edwin to find you."

I scanned the five carriages lined up down the drive. "I hope I have not caused us to be late," I said, not realizing I had been tardy. "I was reading in the library and lost track of time."

Diana giggled. "Do not worry yourself. You are not the last of the guests, and I have saved you a seat in our carriage. I was just hoping to send Edwin in to find you."

"Diana, you must stop attempting to bring us together. Your brother is nearly engaged to my cousin."

"Me?" She looked around before drawing near. "I hate to contradict you, but I had no hand in the last few times you have met." A mischievous smile lit her face. "Perhaps I'm not the only one who wishes to bring the two of you together?"

I looked at her in disbelief. "Are you accusing me of trying to come between my cousin and your brother?" I asked in a sharp whisper.

"I'm accusing you of nothing, Abigail," she said cautiously, placing her arm through mine and holding tightly. "I know where your loyalty is. I only meant to tease you. Come, let us join the others."

I followed Diana to the lead carriage. Mr. Ellis offered his greetings as we neared, and he held out his hand to help us inside.

"Abigail!" I turned to find my aunt moving toward us. "Were you planning on riding with the Stantons, dear? I was hoping you would ride to town with me. I feel I have hardly had a moment to talk to you since you arrived."

I glanced at Diana, who wore a wary expression.

"I had told Diana I would ride with her—"

"And I would feel awful to force you to break your commitment," she said, her shrill voice easily overtaking. mine, "but I must insist. You are a difficult one to converse with, always engaged elsewhere, and we must make time for family."

I looked back toward Diana regretfully, realizing I could not disregard my aunt's wishes. "Perhaps I shall ride home with you?"

"Of course," she said, releasing my arm so I could make my way to my beckoning aunt.

Aunt Marianne smiled as she wrapped her arm around my shoulder tightly, directing me to the open carriage door. "I'm so pleased you could spare me a moment of your time. I know it is not easy adhering to family obligations when there are so many distractions about."

"I am happy to oblige you, Aunt," I said as convincingly as I was able.

"Hannah and Sir Wycliffe will also be riding to Chadsmead with us, so please be on your best behavior. I do not wish for Sir Wycliffe to think he is marrying into poor connections."

I stood motionless at her criticism, watching numbly as a servant helped her into the carriage. My thick skin had weakened in the last few years and her blatant mistreatment felt disorienting. I took a deep breath, eager to calm my nerves, before stepping in behind her.

"Abigail!" Hannah said excitedly, making room for me on the seat next to her. "I am so delighted you are riding with us."

"As am I," I said, moving in beside her. Once again, the relief her presence brought me was instant. "How beautiful you look today, cousin."

"Isn't she ravishing?" Sir Wycliffe asked, though I wasn't certain his question was directed to me the way he kept his eyes on Hannah.

"Please, Sir Wycliffe," Hannah said with a flirtatious smile. "One cannot always be ravishing."

"I disagree," he said, reaching out his hand for hers. She obliged him, and he kissed it most ardently.

I held back a laugh and looked at my aunt who inconspicuously rolled her eyes before her gaze moved to me. Her eyes narrowed, returning my attentive stare, and I quickly corrected myself and looked back toward the happy couple.

"And how is Lord Ramsby?" Hannah asked with a wicked smile. "I saw the two of you talking by the fire after dinner and I must say you looked to be on quite familiar terms."

My face filled with warmth, shocked she would ask such a thing in front of others. "I assure you, looks can be deceiving."

Hannah's eyes narrowed as she appraised me. "Are you officially courting?"

"No," I said firmly. "We are not."

"But surely he made his intentions known?"

I could feel my aunt's gaze burning into me. "He has not."

Hannah smiled. "Well, it shall be soon, it is evident how much he prefers you. Perhaps there shall be two weddings this summer."

"There will certainly be two weddings this summer," my aunt snapped, looking at Hannah as though she had given a personal offense.

Hannah grinned more spitefully than I had thought her able. "I had not heard Mr. Stanton had officially proposed. Forgive me, Mother."

Aunt Marianne looked as though she hoped her next words could wound. "Foolish girl."

My eyes shot to Sir Wycliffe who seemed only slightly aware of the tension surrounding him. "Well, it will certainly be the most joyous summer of my life," he said carelessly.

Hannah offered him a weak smile before turning her gaze out the window. Following suit, I turned my attention to my hands. We sat in silence until voices outside the carriage drew near. Edwin stepped into view with a giggling Helena on his arm.

As they neared, Aunt Marianne leaned her head out the door. "Helena darling, I'm afraid there is no room for you in our carriage with Abigail taking your seat. Perhaps you could ride with Mr. Stanton and his family?" I looked at her in disbelief, suddenly realizing why I had been invited into this carriage.

"Mother," Helena said with a pout. "Have I not already told you—until things are more official, Mr. Stanton does not think it fit we should be seen arriving at church together?"

"I do recall the conversation," Aunt Marianne said with a rehearsed innocence. "But I was under the impression he meant the two of you alone could not take the carriage— which obviously would be quite improper. I did not think he meant simply riding together in the same carriage as his family, I have never heard of such precautions being taken for a couple who is courting."

"Mother do not pressure him so, I truly do not mind squeezing in," Helena said, looking up at Edwin from beneath her bonnet. I was certain, though I could not see from where I sat, her blue eyes were flashing beneath her lashes. "I will not compromise your wishes, Mr. Stanton, though your carriage seats six and ours only four."

He looked hesitantly toward the front of the carriage line. "Of course you should ride with us, Miss Hanford. I do not wish to see you tightly packed in a carriage for four when we can easily take another."

"Only if you are certain," Helena said, beaming triumphantly at her mother who nodded approvingly.

"We shall see you there my darling girl," Aunt Marianne called out to a retreating Helena before the door closed, blocking her from view. "I expect the announcement any day now," she said shifting her gaze out the window, and I was uncertain whether the declaration was meant for Hannah to hear or for me.

We drove the entirety of our ride to Chadsmead without another word. Even poor Sir Wycliffe seemed to notice the unnerving quiet, his gaze shifting to each of our faces and back out the window repeatedly. He released an audible sigh of relief as we stopped outside the familiar church.

The door opened, and Aunt Marianne gracefully exited the carriage, walking straight ahead without looking back.

"Sir Wycliffe," Hannah said, looking at her fiancé endearingly. "Would you mind giving Abigail and me a moment alone?"

"Of course," Sir Wycliffe responded eagerly. "I would not mind if you desire it!" He bumbled from the carriage and shut the door.

Hesitantly I turned toward Hannah.

"Abigail, I must warn you that my mother believes you are out to steal Mr. Stanton from Helena."

My mouth widened in disbelief, and I covered it with my hand.

"I told her it would be foolish to think you could favor someone as brash as Mr. Stanton when you have the charming Lord Ramsby to distract you, but she will not be convinced otherwise."

"And what evidence does she have against me?" I asked, hoping I didn't seem too anxious in my tone.

"A woman's intuition. Besides that, I can't say. I don't often find myself privy to her scheming as Helena is. She simply told me to stay vigilant to any attempts you might make to secure him."

"Helena is my cousin," I said, ignoring the guilt that pricked at my conscience.

"I told her the very thing," she said with a shrug. "But she views you more formidably, given past events."

My voice caught. "I see."

"Once Mr. Stanton proposes, you will not seem like such a threat," Hannah said, intending to offer me comfort. "You heard Mother, any day now it will be official. Until then, just make sure you are careful in your interactions with both him and Diana. Mother can be quite vicious when she doesn't get her way and I'd hate to see you at the receiving end."

"Thank you," I paused, unsure what should follow, "...for the warning."

"You are most welcome," Hannah said, tilting her head and scanning me with a look of pity. "I'd better get inside before Mother suspects me of divulging her secret."

I watched as she opened the door and exited to the waiting hand of Sir Wycliffe. They sauntered across the lawn as I sat in the quiet of the empty carriage, letting the conversation replay in my mind.

Regardless of what my aunt thought, I had no intention of stealing Edwin from Helena. Perhaps, on occasion, I enjoyed his company and yearned to be near him, but surely that was not evidence of betrayal. Relishing his arm around me as we rode back from the Braggs, or the way his skin felt on mine as he swept a hair from my face, or the way I desired for him to look at me instead of Helena—

I stopped, realizing how self-incriminating the evidence was and a sickening feeling engulfed me. "I'm such a fool," I whispered in disbelief. How had I allowed myself to develop such strong feelings for Edwin when he was courting Helena? I had hidden behind good intentions and excuses that were no longer willing to offer me cover, the motivation behind my efforts becoming clear in front of me—I wanted Edwin to choose me over my own cousin.

The heaviness of my situation overcame me. What would Father say, and Laurence, if Aunt Marianne wrote them concerning the matter? The shame felt paralyzing. If only I had heeded Lydia's warning and separated myself from Edwin before the process became unbearable and the pain of his absence so poignant. But I hadn't listened, and now I would suffer the consequence.

"There you are," Diana said, stepping into the doorway of the carriage, causing me to gasp. "The sermon is going to begin soon, and I saved you a seat." Concern touched her brow when I didn't respond. "How was your ride?"

I sighed, knowing what I had to do. "Eye-opening," I said, offering a pathetic smile as I made my way to the open door.

"As was mine!" Diana exclaimed, reaching out her hand to aid me. "I dearly hope that I did not just endure a glimpse of my future."

I climbed out and began swiftly walking toward the parish with Diana in my wake. "Diana, I have decided it would be best if I avoid any unnecessary interactions with your brother."

"You have decided this?" Diana asked, trying to keep pace.

I stopped and turned toward her. "I have. Your brother intends to marry my cousin. I know we have had this discussion before, but this time I intend to honor it, to honor my family, and truthfully to honor myself and what I know is right. I will not change my mind."

"Abigail—"

"I know you do not wish for Helena to marry Edwin," I said, unwilling to let her speak, "but clearly it is not your choice, it is theirs. Edwin has chosen Helena to court and regardless of what you think, Helena loves him and will make him a suitable wife. Consequently," I paused, hesitant if I should go on, "if you wish to continue our friendship you must realize I will not tolerate any schemes to separate them."

Diana watched me unblinking, then dropped her chin and nodded. "Very well. No more schemes."

"I'm sorry, Diana, I wish I—"

"What diverting topic are you two discussing that missing the beginning of the sermon seems an acceptable alternative?"

Edwin stepped to our side and lifted his brow, a teasing tone behind his stern expression.

"Nothing to worry yourself with, Brother," Diana said curtly. "We are coming."

Edwin's eyes darted to me and I dropped my gaze, knowing I could not find the strength to do what I needed to if I saw the concern on his face. "I think I will go in and find a seat," I said, turning toward the entrance.

Diana said nothing as I walked inside ahead of them.

I scanned the crowded pews, relieved to find Hannah gesturing for me to sit with them. I hurried to her side, eager to appear separate from Diana and Edwin who would soon follow. A movement in my periphery sent me fussing with my gown, and I did my best to ignore the siblings making their way past our bench to the front pew, where an elated Helena sat with the Stanton family.

I tried to concentrate on the words of the hymns as we sang and to the vicar as he gave his sermon, endeavoring not to curse him that he had chosen love as the topic.

By the time church finally ended I needed air and a diversion. "Hannah, how long until the carriages head back to Timpton?"

"On a beautiful day like today, I'd suppose at least an hour."

"Wonderful," I said, glad the rain from that morning had come and gone. "I will try to be back before you leave, but if I don't make it in time go on without me and I will walk."

Hannah quirked her head sideways and pursed her lips. "Should I ask where you are going?"

"I'm not quite certain where I shall go. I just need some time alone."

"Very well," Hannah said with a shrug. "Do be careful."

"I will," I promised, though I realized it was not necessary with the speed which she returned her attentions back to Sir Wycliffe and the others.

Determined to escape unnoticed, I stepped in with a

cluster of parishioners leaving the building. An older woman looked at me oddly when she realized I was not part of her group, but I continued along regardless, offering a timid smile as compensation for my strange behavior.

When I made it outside, I separated myself from the others and hurried out toward the road. I was impatient to escape, glancing back only once to ensure no one had followed me out. Satisfied my speedy departure had been successful, I slowed to a leisurely pace and began my way up the road. The fresh air and sunshine were healing to my soul.

"Miss Abigail!" Silas came bolting toward me from the yard, wrapping his arms around my waist. I hadn't realized where my feet were taking me, but here I stood in front of the Bragg's cottage.

I smiled, enjoying the warm welcome. "I'm relieved to see how well you look. How are the others?"

The smile faded from Silas's mouth. "Mum is not gettin' better." His lip quivered as he spoke. "The doctor said she's gonna join Papa soon." A tear rolled down his cheek, and I pulled him to me as he let out a heart-wrenching sob.

I didn't know what to say to offer comfort, so I just stood there holding him, supporting his trembling body. I hurt for him, knowing how exhausting it was to act strong when you felt so weak and to attempt to bear hardships far beyond your abilities. When he finally straightened, I leaned down and kissed the top of his head. "You are a brave boy, Silas."

He wiped the tears from his face. "I wish I didn't need to be brave."

Tears welled in my own eyes at his lament. "I wish you didn't either."

We stood a moment in shared grief before he grabbed my hand and we started walking toward the cottage.

"I'm glad you came," Silas said, opening the door to lead me inside.

A woman, who I supposed was Mrs. Reed, was hunched over Mrs. Bragg, saturating her skin with a wet cloth.

"How is she?" I asked, immediately regretting my decision to not announce myself directly. The petite gray-haired woman shot up and covered her heart in shock.

"Forgive my reaction, I wasn't expecting anyone. You must be Miss Blakeslee. I'm Mrs. Reed," she said, straightening her skirts and fussing with her disheveled hair. "I had not thought you would stop by today, it being the Sabbath, but it is no bother. As you can see, I was just tending to the Missus. Oh yes, and to answer your question I'm afraid to report she is not much improved since my last letter." Mrs. Reed's gaze fell back on the unmoving body of Mrs. Bragg, and I wondered if the stillness somehow accentuated her rapidly rising and falling chest. "I suppose we should count it a blessing she is still with us."

"I do," I said, pulling my gaze from Mrs. Bragg and remembering my manners. "And please forgive my interruption, I was at church and figured I would drop by to see if I could be of assistance."

Mrs. Reed glanced over my Sunday gown before she cocked her head sideways and pursed her lips as though in thought. "Perhaps you could take the three healthy ones on a walk? I have been non-stop since I arrived, and I do feel as though the poor dears have been neglected of my attentions. I believe fresh air and willing company would be just the thing to lift their spirits." I nodded my acceptance, and she turned toward Mary who sat watching in anticipation. "Would that be agreeable, little dear?"

Mary jumped to her feet excitedly and hurried to my side.

"Come, Juliet," I said, grabbing the blue-eyed baby from the bed with her sleeping sisters. "We are going on an adventure."

"She is all fed and should be no trouble for you," Mrs. Reed said with a smile, but before I could answer Mary grabbed my hand and started leading me out.

"We will not be gone long," I called with a laugh as I was tugged out the door.

"Where do you wanna go?" Silas said with an ear to ear grin as we stepped outside.

I looked around and pointed away from the church. "That way!"

"I was 'oping you'd say that. There is a pond just beyon' that 'ill where I catch frogs," he said over his shoulder, leading the way.

"How exciting," I said with another laugh.

It wasn't too far of a walk and when we reached the small pond Silas sat down and began pulling off his shoes and stockings. "I s'pose you don't 'ope to catch frogs in such a nice dress?" he asked, scrunching up his nose.

"I better not today," I said, repositioning Juliet. "But I shall watch your technique closely. Frog catching has always been a favorite pastime of mine."

The look of surprise on Silas's face was worth the embarrassing admission and I couldn't help but laugh again.

"I thought you looked like someone who knew 'ow to catch frogs, Miss Abigail."

Realizing an eight-year-old boy most likely considered that the ultimate compliment, I smiled proudly. "Well I do not claim to be an exceptional talent by any means, so any tips you can think to give me would be much appreciated."

"Sure," he said confidently as he stepped into the water.

His movements made a frog spring from its hiding place with a splash.

"There, Silas! There!" Mary yelled, pointing her finger and moving around excitedly.

Silas oriented himself to where his sister pointed before going still. "Quiet, Mary, or 'e'll know what we're about."

I covered my mouth to ensure my laughter didn't also startle the frog.

Suddenly Silas sprang forward, cupping the water, and making a large splash.

Juliet squealed in delight and kicked her feet excitedly.

"I got 'im!" Silas exclaimed, lifting his soaked arms in triumph, a large frog dangling from one of his hands, croaking riotously.

"You certainly did," I said, shaking my head with a laugh. "But I'm afraid you moved too quickly for me to take notice of your method."

"That's 'ow I do it," Silas said, wading through the water to the bank where we stood. "I 'ave to be faster than the frog to catch 'im."

"I suppose there lies my problem," I said, still grinning. "I am not capable of moving that swiftly. Now bring him over here and let us see your catch."

Silas hurried toward us and displayed the large frog proudly. "Well 'ee isn't the biggest one I've caught, but 'e'll do."

"I wish we would have thought to grab something to put him in," I said, looking around the banks for anything that would work.

"I'll just put 'im in my pocket," Silas said, maneuvering the unwilling amphibian deep into his pocket.

"The benefit of trousers I suppose," I said with an envious grin.

Silas caught three more frogs before I reluctantly announced it was time to head back. Obediently he climbed from the pond and picked up his shoes to follow me and his sisters.

As we walked back over the hill and started down the path, a low croaking sound caught my attention. I looked toward Silas's pocket just as a large frog jumped from it.

"Silas, you kept the frogs?" I asked, ready to burst into laughter.

"I wanted to show Rose and Patience," he said. "I brought two, one for each of 'em." His hand went to each pocket and his eyes went wide when he found one empty.

I pointed to the hopping creature now a few steps away. "It looks as though they will have to share."

Silas took off after the frog with such determination I felt bad for standing idly by, laughing. "It looks as though it is more difficult to catch a hopping frog than a swimming one," I said to Mary, who nodded in giddy agreement. "Perhaps you could hold Juliet while I assist him in his pursuit?"

Mary quickly kneeled and reached out her hands toward her sister. I carefully put Juliet in her sister's lap and joined Silas on the chase. The task was trickier than I had imagined, and my endless laughter seemed to only make the situation more difficult.

"Perhaps if I come from the other side," I said, walking in a wide circle to where the frog had positioned himself to hop. Silas waited until I was in place and bounded near it, forcing it toward me. Swiftly, I reached down and covered the frog where he landed. "I got him," I called excitedly before carefully moving one hand beneath it and pressing it against my palm as Father had shown me. I stood up to show Silas. "I got him!" I laughed. "I got him!"

Silas ran to my side and I handed him the frog carefully. I couldn't stop smiling. How I had needed this today, a distraction from the task ahead of me.

When we turned back toward Mary and Juliet, my smile faded. Edwin stood near the girls, an intrigued smile on his lips.

"What have you got?" Edwin called out.

I looked at Silas, willing him to not betray me.

"A frog," Silas said, already hurrying toward him with the specimen outstretched. "I was carrin' two back from the pond but one escaped, so Miss Abigail was 'elpin me catch 'im."

"And it looks as though she is quite the skilled frog catcher," Edwin said, his smile broadening in a most irritating manner.

"It is one of my lesser-known talents," I said directly, walking toward where Edwin stood. "Come children, let's get you home."

I reached down and grabbed Juliet from Mary before offering her my hand and helping her to her feet. I walked briskly past Edwin, only slowing when I realized how Mary was jogging to keep up.

"Miss Mary, would you like me to carry you?" Edwin offered stepping up to my side, causing me to stop.

She nodded and reached her arms out to him as he bent low and scooped her up. I refused to notice the way she wrapped her arms around his neck and instead adjusted Juliet in my arms.

We walked in silence, and I cursed Edwin under my breath for ruining the end of our walk. I felt Silas glance from Edwin to me and I thought of how childish I must appear in my sudden moodiness.

"Silas, are you going to name your frogs?" I asked, trying to ease the tension.

"I was gonna let Patience and Rose name 'em," he answered. "But maybe I can talk 'em into namin' one Abigail after you."

Unconsciously I glanced sideways at Edwin, who was attempting to keep himself from smiling most unsuccessfully.

"That would be quite an honor," I said with a laugh that betrayed me. "Perhaps you could persuade them to name the other one Edwin—I did notice a peculiar similarity between the larger frog and Mr. Edwin."

"Is that so?" Edwin said with a raise of his eyebrow.

"I didn't want to point it out," I said. "But now that it has been brought up, you do hold your mouths in a very similar manner."

"Now that it has been brought up?" Edwin asked with a laugh, shaking his head. "Unbelievable."

Silas smiled easily, still glancing between us. "Maybe the frogs 'ill fall in love and give us a 'ole family of frogs to keep as pets."

My heart was called to repentance. Disappointment filled me as I realized how easily I had allowed Edwin right back into my heart. I had to be stronger. "Wait here, Mr. Stanton," I said as we neared the cottage yard. "I do not wish to give another wrong impression today." He looked at me quizzically as I moved to take Mary from him. She wrapped her arms around my neck, and Edwin helped shift her weight onto my free hip. His hand steadied her, then moved to my arm. The sensation of his skin on mine tormented me and I quickly turned from it, knowing I was not strong enough to bear it.

By the time I made it to the door, the weight of both girls seemed barely sustainable and I promptly placed Mary down. I apologized to Mrs. Reed for Silas's wet clothes as well as the frogs, but she assured me it was nothing and thanked me unduly for what I had done. She promised to send an update later that evening and I was grateful for her thoughtfulness.

I gave Juliet and Mary a kiss and hugged Silas, telling him to inform Patience and Rose I would be back soon to visit them and that I would keep praying for them all, especially their mother. He thanked me for the walk and went inside holding a frog in each hand, eager to show his sisters.

I let out a heavy exhale exhorting myself to be stronger as I walked back to Edwin.

As he came into view, his watchful eyes sent my heart beating like the traitor it was. "What are you doing?"

"Waiting obediently where you told me to," he said, and one side of his mouth pulled up in a partial smile.

"I mean what are you doing here?"

He dropped his gaze as if contemplating what to say before his eyes met mine. "I'm not certain."

"And does Helena know where you are?"

He shook his head. "I told her I had to speak with a tenant."

"You lied to her?"

"I did not lie to her, the Braggs are one of our tenants and I spoke with Mr. Silas, the man of the house."

I glared at him unimpressed. "I think it best if you leave."

He stared at me in disbelief. "You are the most infuriating woman I have ever encountered!" His voice grew loud and rigid. "One minute I think you genuinely enjoy my company and the next I'm certain you abhor me."

"I don't abhor you," I said defensively.

"What is it then? You can only tolerate me for so long?"

I huffed my frustration. "I think it will be easiest if we stop meeting. Helena is my cousin and I know she would be disappointed to find out about this—" I said, gesturing between us before realizing what he might think I was implying. "This —friendship."

"Friendship?" Edwin repeated with an exasperated nod.

I swallowed, ignoring his poignant slight on what I felt had been a mutual conclusion. "Helena admires you—"

"And I admire her," Edwin said sharply. "Yet is that reason enough to marry someone?"

"I'm not certain what is reason enough," I said candidly. "What I am certain of is Helena's devotion to you and the fact that she will make a remarkable wife."

"Don't I know it," he said, running his hand through his hair in agitation.

"Then why have you not asked..." I paused, suddenly realizing the internal longing influencing my question. I couldn't ask it of him. He didn't feel for me as I did for him, why was it so difficult to convince myself of it? To convince myself his answer would not be what I desired? He would never confess it was his love for me that prevented him from moving forward with Helena. He couldn't love me, he didn't even know who I was.

Besides, how could I ever face my family again, my own father, if by some miracle it were true, and he'd accept me? I wouldn't do something to make Father think less of me, to make him doubt the way he had chosen to raise me. My resolve strengthened at the thought. If I couldn't do it for myself, I had to do it for Father. "You need to ask Helena to marry you," I finally choked out.

He took a step toward me, closing the distance between us and making me waver in my determination. "That is what you truly want?"

I clasped my hands behind my back so he could not see them shaking and nodded, unable to speak the lie.

Edwin's gaze held mine as he searched my soul for the truth. "I see. Forgive my interruption," he said with a brisk bow. "I should get back."

I stood motionless, watching him walk away. I attempted to congratulate myself on the feat I had accomplished, but the loss felt too great to pretend otherwise. I covered my mouth, muffling a sob, and crumpled to the ground in complete despair.

CHAPTER 14

By the time I returned to the parish I was not surprised to find the carriages gone and the church yard empty. Slowly I made my way back to Timpton House, refusing to think of the last few times I had made the journey, Edwin always with me. The cool breeze swirled around me, but I no longer felt enlivened by it.

As I finally reached Timpton House I felt empty. How I wished I had never been made to come here, that I had never met the Stantons—and Edwin. The day had fittingly turned cloudy, but the soft light only accentuated the beauty around me and I cursed it for its tricks. I cursed all the things that made this place so alluring, the things that had made me start to feel alive again after so long—the pond, the house, the gardens, Diana, Edwin—then Edwin again and again.

The sound of a door shutting interrupted my cursings, and I turned my gaze to see Lord Ramsby walking down the front steps. He was alone, and I quickly ducked behind a nearby tree, desperate to not be seen. I could not pretend right now, I could not be what I was expected to be.

I watched as he made his way toward the pond. He

stopped at the water's edge, looked around and then vanished into the foliage along the path. Once he disappeared, I hurried toward the entrance, hoping he would be long enough occupied I could make it inside unseen. As I approached the stairs I glanced over my shoulder, relieved I did not see him.

My eyes shot up the stairs at the sound of the door opening again. Before I had time to panic, Helena slid out the door and closed it behind her. She donned her bonnet and began tying it into place.

"Hello, Helena," I called, not wanting to startle her.

Her gaze landed on me and then flickered past me before she offered a placid smile. "And where have you come from, Abigail? Surely you are not just now returning from Chadsmead?"

"I am," I said, starting up the steps. "And where are you headed?"

Helena's eyes narrowed. "You are not the only one who prefers Sabbath Day walks."

"Of course not," I replied, surprised by the callousness in her voice. Had she realized where Edwin had gone when he had come to speak with me? "I meant no offense with my question. I was only attempting to be civil. Forgive me."

"It is no matter," Helena said, fixing her gloves and pinching her cheeks. "I do believe Edwin's foul mood has rubbed off on me again. Perhaps I should be the one asking for your pardon."

Apparently, that was her apology, because she did not offer another. "I think I will go in and rest until dinner," I said, quieting the absurd desire to ask about Edwin's foul mood. "Do enjoy your walk."

"I believe I will," she said with a hint of mischief as she turned and glided down the stairs toward the front lawn.

I offered the butler a brief greeting as I stepped inside before starting up to my room. When I opened my door, I was simultaneously disappointed and relieved to find that Lydia was not waiting for me. I did not think I was currently capable of relaying to her my weakness, but I dreaded being alone with my traitorous thoughts.

Reluctantly I climbed onto my bed hoping sleep would provide me a respite from the dilemma that had engulfed me. Even a nightmare seemed more promising than the situation in which I found myself, and I was no stranger to the darkness of nightmares.

WHEN LYDIA finally returned it was time to begin getting ready for dinner. I was relieved to see her; having forgotten I had given her the day off to attend church with the servants as well as a picnic given by some of the parishioners in town. Had I remembered, I might have thought to search her out before walking home on my own; but the way she smiled when she entered made me glad she had not been subject to my sour mood.

"What is wrong?" she asked, the twinkling in her eyes evolving to concern.

"It is nothing," I said, standing and walking toward her. "Tell me all about your day."

Her smile returned, and she instantly began speaking of the picnic, the delicious foods that had been served, and a handsome man who had offered to bring her lemonade and then would not leave her side. She blushed beautifully as she told me how he had asked to see her again and I was grateful for how happy she seemed.

"It all sounds marvelous," I said, sitting in front of the mirror while she restyled my hair.

"I have been missing Easton Manor desperately," she whispered. "But today was a good day."

My eyes went to her reflection as she worked, and more

guilt added itself to my load. "I have not been a very good friend to you since we came to Timpton, have I?"

Her gaze met mine. "You have had your own struggles to deal with. I did not wish to trouble you with more."

My heart hurt anew, and I stood up and wrapped my arms around Lydia. She gasped in surprise. "I am so grateful for you. Forgive my foolishness. I will endeavor to be a friend more deserving of you."

"You can be so dramatic, Abee," she said with a laugh as I released her. "Sit and let me finish, so you won't be late for dinner."

I obediently returned to my seat and watched as she began placing small, white flowers in my hair.

"I found these on my walk home and thought how lovely they would look with your dress for this evening."

"They are beautiful," I said, admiring her placement of them.

"Abee, where did you go after church ended?"

I looked toward her in the reflection. "Aunt Marianne believes I am trying to steal Edwin from Helena."

She nodded, as though she wasn't surprised by what I had said.

"I would never intentionally mean to betray my own family, but I admit I have erred in unconsciously allowing myself to develop feelings for Edwin." I lifted my chin. "I should have listened to you."

"Perhaps, but perhaps not."

I narrowed my eyes in confusion, but she did not offer an explanation. "I have made it clear to both Diana and Edwin that I will not betray Helena. I would never forgive myself for ruining her happiness and distancing our families."

Lydia opened her mouth, as though she wished to speak, before closing it again.

"I told him he must propose."

"Surely you didn't?" Lydia asked in disbelief.

"The sooner he does, the sooner I will be able to regain my sanity."

"What if," Lydia paused looking hesitant to continue. "What if Helena is not the right lady for Mr. Stanton?"

I scoffed. "Of course she is, do not let my injured feelings prejudice you against her. She loves him and will make him an exceptional wife." I had repeated the phrase to myself so many times in the last few hours it almost felt natural coming out of my mouth. "He can be nothing more to me than my cousin's suitor."

Lydia released a heavy sigh. "Very well," she said, stepping back to admire her work. "I am proud of your loyalty, regardless if it is deserved."

A knock at my door sent her hurrying to answer it. Diana entered, walking timidly to my side. "I thought I would see if you were ready to go down to dinner."

"Yes, I suppose I am," I said, glancing toward Lydia, still trying to make sense of her last comment.

"I promise I will be on my best behavior," Diana said, looking between me and Lydia repentantly. "You will not regret forgiving me for my meddlesome ways."

"I'm sure I will not," I said, offering a smile as she tucked her arm through mine. I glanced back before stepping into the corridor. "Lydia, thank you."

"Of course, Abee," she said, giving me a knowing smile and Diana's grip on my arm was the only thing keeping me from running back to ask her what she meant by it all.

"How were the Braggs?" Diana asked, and I knew she must have spoken with Edwin.

"There has been little progress with Mrs. Bragg, but Silas said the doctor expects Rose and Patience to make a full recovery."

"Those poor children," Diana whispered. "How shall they manage if they lose their mother?"

"I don't know," I answered honestly.

As we neared the door to the sitting room I paused, taking a moment to calm myself and ask God for the strength to do what was necessary.

"If you need a moment—"

"I'm ready," I said, holding tightly to her arm.

We stepped through the doors to find most of the guests already conversing among themselves. Diana led me to Mr. Ellis who bowed graciously.

"How was your walk home from Chadsmead, Miss Blakeslee?" he asked, glancing at Diana for apparent approval of his chosen topic.

"Uneventful," I answered with a smile.

"I'm glad to hear it. Edwi—" he paused, and I could see Diana shaking her head subtly in my periphery. "Some of us," he corrected, "were concerned letting you walk home unattended."

"I appreciate the consideration," I said, wondering why, even after our conversation, Edwin should care if I walked alone.

"And did you enjoy your Sabbath?" I asked, glancing between them.

"Very much," they said in unison.

"Wonderful." The conversation felt false and I hated it. I wanted them to talk to me as they always did, but I knew it had been my own condition that warranted the caution.

"There you are, Miss Blakeslee," Lord Ramsby said, stepping to my side. "I feel as though I have hardly seen you since yesterday."

"It has been a busy day," I said feebly.

"And did you rest well?" he asked.

"I did, thank you." I said, wondering how he had known I had been resting. "And how did you spend your afternoon?"

"There's really nothing of note to mention," he answered.

Helena appeared at my other side. "Nothing of note? Surely, Lord Ramsby, you spent your afternoon more pleasantly than you relate?"

Lord Ramsby and Helena exchanged a strained glance before he looked back toward me. "Nothing that Miss Blakeslee would find of interest, I'm sure."

Helena let out a shrill laugh. "I think my cousin finds little interest in most things being said, but that hasn't stopped you before."

I felt too disoriented by her insult to be offended. "Helena, why would you say that?"

"Why? Because the only things worthy of your attention seem to be tending sick people and wandering about the countryside unchaperoned."

My breath caught at the realization—she knew! She must have discovered that Edwin had come to speak with me. It was the only reason she would be so uncharacteristically impertinent in front of others.

"Helena, I can explain."

"Explain what?" she asked with a pointed glower in my direction.

I looked toward Diana hesitantly, who gave a subtle shake of her head.

"What can you explain?" Helena repeated in irritation, and I suddenly questioned if I truly did know why she was so irritated with me.

"What seems to be the commotion?" Edwin asked, walking up to our small group.

"Nothing at all," Helena said, deceitfully sweet. "Abigail was just about to explain something to us. Weren't you, Abigail?"

A tightening in my chest made me feel light headed, and the room spun beneath me. "I think I need to sit down," I said, reaching out my hand to steady myself.

Edwin's hand came to my back as Diana and Lord Ramsby reached for me. My body felt suddenly heavy and weak, but after a moment the support they offered alleviated the strange sensation.

"Do you need to sit, Miss Blakeslee?" Lord Ramsby asked, sounding concerned.

I shook my head. "I believe it was only a dizzy spell."

"At least let me support you until we are certain it has passed."

"Very well," I said, releasing Diana's hand and taking Lord Ramsby's outstretched arm. "That is very kind of you."

I felt Edwin remove his hand from my back and I glanced in his direction. He stood rigid, his eyes fixed forward, his jaw tight.

"I do hope we will still hear your explanation," Helena said with a wicked smile. "I must admit you have truly piqued my interest."

"Perhaps later," I said in an accommodating tone, hoping she would be pacified and leave the subject behind.

"Miss Hanford," Diana interjected. "I was hoping you could recount your story of the Prince Regent again. I was trying to relay it to Mother and I seemed to forget the exact wording of his compliment."

Helena smiled and gave a nod before beginning. I looked at Diana appreciatively and she gave me a brief, understanding glance.

AT DINNER I was beyond pleased to find myself sitting between Diana and Uncle Stanton, with Lord Ramsby across from me and Edwin and Helena at the far end of the table. I knew it must have been Diana's doing and I was grateful that her desire to be my friend hadn't rested solely on her wish for me to separate her brother from Helena.

The gentlemen did not take port but joined the women directly in the sitting room after. When Lord Ramsby asked me to partner with him in a game of cards, I quickly accepted, once again grateful for his attentions. I tried my best to pretend I wasn't hurting, but I knew I was only acting every time I smiled at Lord Ramsby or laughed at a joke being told. By the end of the game I was exhausted and was relieved when the butler walked in with a note from Mrs. Reed.

"Please excuse me," I said, standing up. My eyes scanned the room for a private place to read the letter when they stopped on Edwin, who sat watching me. Regardless of our conversation earlier, I knew he was concerned with the contents of the message. I offered a hesitant smile and he gave a subtle nod of understanding. His eyes remained on me until Aunt Marianne grabbed his arm, demanding his attention. As his gaze shifted away, I turned and walked to a secluded arm chair, trying to convince myself he meant only to show his support for what news I might read from Mrs. Reed.

MISS BLAKESLEE,

LITTLE HAS CHANGED *since your visit. Both girls are continuing to improve and I'm happy to report Rose ate some soup and bread at dinner. Mrs. Bragg is still with us. Her breathing has not improved, but it has not worsened. The girls brightened when they saw the frogs you and Silas caught—they have named them Abigail and Edwin. Rest well and I shall send an update in the morning.*

Mrs. Reed

I FELT the gaze of someone on me and looked up to see if it

was Edwin that awaited the news. My stomach knotted when I realized it was Aunt Marianne watching me with a dour expression.

"Is that news regarding the poor family you have been aiding?" she asked, approaching my chair.

"Yes." I responded, not surprised she had heard of it, but confused at the severity in her tone.

"I don't know why you trouble yourself with such causes. You remind me of my sister. Such romantic notions, always needing to rescue the downtrodden." Her eyes narrowed as she lowered her voice. "But I wonder if it is not a ploy of yours, taking on her noble actions to catch yourself a gentleman—or several perhaps?"

"How can you say that?" I said in disbelief. "I have no desire to trick anyone into thinking I'm someone I'm not." My heart sank as I realized the irony in my words. Aunt Marianne's look of skepticism deepened my shade of red.

"Do you not? Or have you really come to believe you are one of us? That you deserve the same connections and opportunities as my daughters?" Her eyes brimmed with anger. "I should never have mentioned your name to Lady Eliza, allowing her pity to procure you an invitation to Timpton House you did not deserve."

My heart raced, making me feel faint again. "You told Lady Eliza?"

"No. Though I can't help but think I should have." She paused, perhaps wondering if she had said enough. Apparently, she had not. "I had mentioned you in conversation—the socially awkward daughter of my poor deceased sister. The postponement of your first Season after my brother-in-law spent exorbitant funds to procure you the finest gowns, all because you were too scared to leave Easton Manor."

Her eyes skirted across my gown before settling back on my face. "Apparently Lady Eliza felt the need to include you, after all you would soon enough be family, of sorts. I daresay she regretted the decision the moment she laid eyes on you, and rightfully so." Aware there were no listening ears other than mine, the falseness in her voice I was so accustomed to was gone and I found myself longing for its return. "It is obvious you don't belong here. You can never pretend to be what you are not, no matter how fine your appearance and how excessively you attempt to ensnare the gentlemen."

Tears stung my eyes as she spoke. How could anyone feel they had the right to be so brutal with their words? Even if what she said held some truth—she was family.

As if she had read the hurt in my eyes and seen the thoughts behind it, she lifted her chin. "You are not family. You will never be more than an orphaned ward, with a merciful benefactor!"

I could not believe she had just said the truth aloud. Panicked, I stood to flee. As my gaze shifted away from her smug face, my eyes fell on Lord Ramsby, eyes wide and motionless, standing directly behind her. He looked from me to my aunt and then turned and walked out the door. Frantically I followed him.

~

I NEARED the bottom of the stairs and called to him before he reached the top. He stopped but did not turn toward me.

"Is it true?" he asked. "Are you Lord Blakeslee's ward?"

"I am his ward, but my parents have raised me as a daughter."

He looked at me, anger flashing in his eyes. "You lied!"

"I have not," I said, imploring him to believe me. "I have just not been able to tell the whole truth."

"The intention was the same. You meant to deceive me."

"I am sorry," I said quietly, lowering my head as tears flooded my eyes.

"What a fool I am. Thinking you are someone you are not."

"Am I changed somehow?" My voice was desperate. If someone who had admired me as much as Lord Ramsby didn't understand, how would others ever accept me? I glanced up. "Surely my parentage does not change who I am?"

"It changes everything!" he spat. "Do you think my mother would allow me to marry a ward? I am a Lord! I have a responsibility to uphold! Heaven knows where you came from." The look of disgust pierced me, and I was certain he would not have looked on a stray dog with more revulsion than he now looked at me with. "Were you orphaned? Do you even know who your parents were?"

Tears began to flow as I watched my dignity being torn from me. My silence strengthened his resolve and he turned from me, quickly ascending the remainder of the stairs and disappearing down the corridor. I sat unmoving, wiping the tears from my face when I heard a noise behind me. I turned, horrified to discover Diana and Lady Eliza staring apprehensively toward me, lips parted in disbelief.

Defeated, I sank down and began to sob.

DIANA HURRIED to my side and began rubbing my back. She didn't speak and a few minutes later I felt the strong arms of Edwin cradle me as he carried me back down the stairs. I couldn't tell where he was taking me, as I buried my face in his chest. After a few minutes he gently set me down, keeping his arm around me as he sat by my side. I couldn't talk; I could hardly breathe through my sobs.

Diana held my hand and leaned in close. "It will all be well, Abigail. You'll see." Her empty promises did little to calm me and I shook with emotion. Lady Eliza handed Edwin a blanket, and he wrapped it around me. After several minutes my sobs lessened, though tears still ran down my cheeks, and I knew I would have to give an explanation to the patient faces watching me.

"I'm sorry," I said, wiping my hands across my swollen, splotchy face.

"Don't be sorry," Diana said kindly. "Did Lord Ramsby speak the truth? Are you truly a ward of Lord Blakeslee?"

Edwin's eyes narrowed in disbelief as he sent me a questioning glance, and I realized he had not overheard my conversation with Lord Ramsby. Shamefully I nodded my head. "My parents, Lord and Lady Blakeslee," I began, "had a difficult time having children. They lost two children in infancy before my brother Laurence was born and Mother had multiple miscarriages as they tried for another child. They were finally able to have a little girl who was healthy and full of life—they named her Grace."

My voice faltered with my shaking exhale. "When she was nine, she began to get tired all the time and complain of headaches. My parents became worried. The doctors were not certain what ailed her. One day, quite suddenly, she became pale and began vomiting, refusing to eat or drink. My parents put her to bed, thinking her ill...later that night when her nursemaid went to rouse her, she would not wake. She never regained consciousness and passed away a few days later.

"Both of my parents, but my mother especially, felt a deep void with her death. She told me, not long after I had gone to live with them, that seeing me was the first time in years she hadn't felt lost in emptiness. I think I brought a new hope, a healing. Though I could never replace Grace, I was a reminder to them that through loss, goodness can still be found."

When no one said anything I continued, "And whatever I did to help them heal, it was their love that saved me."

Edwin looked confounded. "*Their* love saved you?"

Realizing they all deserved an explanation, and feeling an inability to keep up my deception, I nodded weakly. "I had just been transferred to the orphanage in Burrowsly and found myself in trouble with one of the mistresses for my sharp tongue. Lady Blakeslee, who was on the Board of Governors for the orphanage, walked in as I was receiving the strap across my hands." Diana tightened her grip on my hand. "She told me I hadn't even flinched as the leather strap was brought down, and she wondered how much pain I had endured to cause such numbness. She stopped the Mistress immediately and brought me home to a very surprised Lord Blakeslee.

"After a private meeting, the longest minutes of my life, they had decided they would raise me as their daughter. They renamed me Abigail, saying I reminded them of the Bible story of Abigail—having to bear the burdens of another's transgression. It was as if instantly I had truly become theirs. Their hope was to keep the truth hidden, as much as possible, to allow me the opportunities I would have been given had they truly been my parents. Obviously, some people were aware I was not their actual daughter, but those needing an explanation were told I was a relation that had been orphaned and would now be raised as their own. Only my Aunt Marianne was told the truth, trusting she would not betray their wishes."

I glanced up to find Lady Eliza pale and motionless, both hands over her mouth as though she were about to be ill. I should have known how utterly horrified she would be by my admission and I wasn't surprised when she turned and walked hastily from the room. I returned my gaze to the safety of the flames.

"Abigail." Diana's voice was kind and warm and I cautiously turned to look at her. She searched my eyes and I was relieved when a sympathetic smile came to her lips. "To me you are as much the daughter of Lord and Lady Blakeslee as you have ever been."

"Thank you," I whispered.

"Edwin?" Diana said encouragingly.

Hesitantly I turned toward Edwin, dreading to see the same disappointment in his eyes that I had just witnessed in his mother's. His gaze was locked on the fire. "Do you recall much before the Blakeslees found you?"

"I do," I said, wishing I could forget some of the things I remembered.

"What do you recall?"

I glanced at Diana, who nodded her encouragement.

"I didn't go to a parish orphanage until I was eight— though, in all honesty, I'm not even certain if that was my exact age. The vicar knew nothing about me when I turned up, and I refused to tell him what little I did know." I hesitated, unsure if I had the strength to continue—the strength to risk losing the last bit of dignity I still retained.

Edwin's focus remained forward. "What did you not tell him?"

We sat in silence as I persuaded myself that they deserved to know, that I wished to keep nothing else hidden regardless of the outcome. "I remember being sent from family to family, whoever could spare some food and needed extra help. Some were not so horrible, others—" I swallowed, willing myself to face what I wished to conceal, "others were vicious." The memories flooded into my mind, and I desperately struggled against being consumed by them.

I closed my eyes and took a few deep breaths, attempting to reorient myself. "I am illegitimate," I whispered, determined to continue. "From my earliest memories I was told I was wicked, that my birth mother had sinned, and I would forever be marked by her wrongdoings. A sort of excuse to treat me as they did, I suppose. But nonetheless, it followed me wherever I went. I don't remember my mother, but it was clear she had abandoned me in her shame.

"When I was around eight, I was being transported, by horse, to my next purgatory when I decided I couldn't take it anymore.

I tried to jerk free from the man who held me, but his strong arms refused to let go. Desperate, I turned and began clawing at his face. My only advantage was that we sat on a horse that had become restless under my attempt to get free. The horse startled, and I went flying backwards onto the ground.

"The man got the horse under control and looked at me from his saddle as though..." My voice trailed off as I recalled the fury in his eyes, a look I knew well but was difficult to describe so I shook my head and continued without finishing. "I quickly got up and ran off the road and through the shelter of trees and underbrush. I didn't stop until I could no longer move from exhaustion. I remember finding a stream where I drank and fell asleep.

"A kind man found me, bruised and shaken, but unbroken. Not wanting him to figure out where he should return me, I told him I needed to get to the church. I had been filled with stories of parish orphanages and the horrible places they were, constantly being reminded how the families who sheltered me had saved me from the cruel fate; but I was desperate and felt it couldn't be as terrible as what I had experienced. The man brought me to the nearest parish and after I explained to the vicar I had been orphaned, I was sent to a nearby parish orphanage to live.

"I spent three years there before it closed down. I had overheard the governors talking and, because I was eleven, the intention was to send me to a workhouse. Somehow, I suppose due to how young I looked when the groups got separated, I was placed in a herd of children being transferred to the orphanage in Burrowsly—the place my mother found me."

I saw Edwin's jaw tighten and he finally turned toward me, a look of anger in his eyes. "Did you know the Slytons?" he asked, accusation in his voice.

I nodded my head. "He was the man on the horse."

Edwin's heavy breathing seemed to echo through the silent room.

"Why did you not tell me?" he demanded.

I had deceived him, I had deceived them all. "I wanted to," I muttered as I looked down at my shaking hands.

Edwin swiftly stood, and I could see resentment in his eyes. "I must go," he said, repressing his rage unsuccessfully. "Forgive me."

I returned my eyes to the fire as I listened to his boots retreat down the hallway and out of my life forever.

CHAPTER 15

"*I* should have told you," I said weakly to Diana, as my eyes searched the flames.

"I don't blame you for not telling us," Diana said reassuringly. "Look how we have all reacted. And look at the pain it brings you to tell such horrors!" Tears ran down her cheeks as she wrapped her arms around me. "I'm so sorry, Abigail."

Diana held me in the silence until the fire ran low.

"Let me help you to your room," she said, lifting me by my elbows. "I feel suddenly drained, as I'm certain you do."

I felt as if I were dreaming, as though I were floating just above my body, unwilling to see the reality in what had just occurred.

As Diana opened the door to my room, Lydia's face filled with concern as she hurried to my side and helped seat me on the bed.

The two women passed silent questions back and forth, before Diana turned to me. "I will come check on you first thing in the morning. Things will look brighter tomorrow." She leaned in and gave me a light kiss on the top of my head before leaving Lydia to tend to me.

Lydia hurried to undo my hair as I sat staring off in the distance. I had no emotions left to feel. I sat like a broken vessel, nothing left inside for it had all drained out.

"Shall I help you remove your gown?" Lydia asked quietly.

I shook my head. She removed my shoes and pulled the covers down without another word. I climbed in and closed my eyes. I knew I could not sleep but I could not face the reality of what this world had given me. I tried to fill my thoughts with images of home, but they all turned back into the angry eyes of Edwin, rejecting me and who I really was over and over again.

THE SUN WAS bright in my room when I woke, and I knew it was much later than I usually slept.

"I had breakfast brought up for you," Lydia said as she walked to the side of my bed and sat down next to me. As I sat up, she tenderly wiped the hair from my face. "Looks like your sleep was almost as bad as your night," she said with a half-smile coming to her lips, motioning toward my matted hair.

"They found out I'm a ward," I said soberly.

"I know," she said. "I heard it being whispered among the servants. Apparently, Lord Ramsby is supposed to depart soon, and Mr. Edwin Stanton has already done so."

I swallowed, feeling a tightness in my throat. "Mr. Stanton has left Timpton?"

She nodded. "Early this morning."

I could understand Lord Ramsby leaving, but this was Edwin's home. My stomach churned at my ability to make a man run from his own house. "I'll talk to Lady Eliza and see if we can arrange transportation home; if not, I will write Laurence and tell him to send our coach at once."

She nodded and stood. "Shall we get you ready then?"

As much as I desired to remain hidden in my room, I knew my only way home would be to seek out Lady Eliza. I pushed the covers from my legs and followed Lydia to the mirror. My evening gown was wrinkled and my hair a mess, but it was my swollen face that drew my attention. There would be no doubting how I had spent the night when I returned to the drawing room.

Lydia gently began unsnarling my knotted hair while I pondered what I would say to Lady Eliza. A sharp knock at the door stilled Lydia's hand and my heart.

"Who is it?" I asked, my voice nearly faltering.

"Helena!" A shiver moved up my back at the ice in her voice.

My gaze shifted to Lydia who looked as worried as I felt. "Come in," I called.

As the door opened, Helena's tear-streaked face came into view. "This is all your fault!" she screamed, her finger pointed at me. "Mr. Stanton has left and now Lord Ramsby said he cannot stay! You have come to Timpton to ruin me! I hate you! I hate that my aunt and uncle ever took a dirty orphan into their home! I have always hated you!"

I stood, unable to speak. I glanced at Lydia, her expression cautioning me.

"I have not meant to hurt you," I said calmly. "I am sorry."

"But you have! You have taken Mr. Stanton from me and now you have driven Lord Ramsby away! It is all your fault!"

"Why should you care if Lord Ramsby should leave?" I asked, unwilling to dwell on the truth of being the reason behind Edwin's departure.

Her eyes flickered to Lydia and back to mine, a look of hesitation discernible in them.

"Surely you don't care for Lord Ramsby?" A sudden recollection of Diana's inferences flooded me.

"None of it matters anyway. He leaves within the hour,

and I will never see him again!" A loud sob escaped her mouth.

My eyes narrowed. "What of Mr. Stanton? I thought you loved him?"

"Love? Who has the opportunity to marry for love?" she asked with a look of disgust at my unrealistic ideals. "Of course, I believed we would make an advantageous match, but if there is an opportunity to reach higher, surely I should take it. Who wants to live in the shadow of their younger sister?"

"And the more advantageous match would be Lord Ramsby?" I asked uncertainly.

"Mr. Stanton cannot offer me a title. Lord Ramsby could have, had he not been blinded by your lies."

I did not feel angry at her words, only surprised. "Well he is no longer blinded by them."

Her bitterness slowly turned into a look of confusion.

"He is still here, is he not?" I asked, feeling my final betrayal toward Edwin would be for his own good.

"Yes?" she answered carefully.

"Perhaps you should ask him to stay. Inform him I will be leaving soon, and you desire to make things right."

She looked at me in the same calculating way her mother was so accomplished at. "And what shall happen when Mr. Stanton returns?"

"He left you. In the moment you needed him, he left." I felt the words heavily on my own heart, knowing in actuality the truth was mine.

She contemplated my words and a pulled smile came to her face. "It seems quite presumptuous, begging Lord Ramsby to stay, does it not?"

I returned her smile. "It sounds quite romantic."

Helena looked to Lydia, as though a second opinion was needed, and Lydia nodded her head in agreement.

Bending down to look in the mirror, Helena wiped at her

face and pinched her cheeks, before letting out an audible sigh.

"It will serve you well to look as though you have just finished crying, perhaps make your emotions more genuine," I said with an encouraging smile. "I do believe gentlemen like to know we are more than good manners, witty phrases, and fine accomplishments."

She straightened, and a genuine smile lit her face. She looked stunning, and I believed Lord Ramsby would feel similar. "I better hurry before he is gone," she said as she rushed from the room in a most unladylike fashion.

"She doesn't love him?" I asked rhetorically.

"Forgive me for not saying something yesterday," Lydia said apologetically. "I suspected as much yesterday but wasn't yet certain, so I held my tongue."

"What are you referring to?" I asked, realizing I had never had an opportunity to talk with her last night when I returned.

"When I was walking home yesterday from the picnic, a group of us happened upon Lord Ramsby and Helena locked in an embrace."

"By the pond?" I asked, as I realized Helena must have planned to meet Lord Ramsby there.

Lydia nodded.

How could they act so selfishly when their interests were supposed to be elsewhere? "That must have been why Helena was so upset last night," I said aloud, though I spoke more to myself. "She must have been put off by Lord Ramsby's attentions toward me after their...meeting."

"There have been rumors of such rendezvous taking place between them. But it is hard to know what to believe belowstairs, for I also heard rumors of similar encounters between you and Mr. Stanton that I knew to be untrue—or at least innocently intentioned."

I blushed thinking I had been a subject of discussion amongst the servants, let alone about such a topic.

"I believe you made the right choice in pushing Helena to pursue Lord Ramsby," Lydia said, wrapping her arms around me. "They are a good fit."

"It wasn't a choice," I said, melting into her embrace. "She does not love Edwin, he needs someone who will." Though I already knew that someone would not be me.

I FOUND Lady Eliza in the drawing room with several ladies, each working on their needlework as though nothing had happened. Even Aunt Marianne seemed unaffected by the previous night's events as she gossiped idly with Mrs. Dowding. It was only when I approached Lady Eliza that I felt several of the gazes shift to me, followed by the sound of whispers.

"Lady Eliza," I said quietly when I stood before her. "I was hoping to speak with you for a moment."

She looked up from her stitching, her face slightly swollen and blotchy as though she too had spent the previous night in tears. She probably hated me for the scandal I had brought, for chasing her son away, and now I was certain she would hate me more for encouraging the girl he was supposed to marry to pursue another man. She stood, walked toward the door and exited. Looking around at the judgmental gazes, I timidly followed.

"Perhaps a French whore…she is too dark to be of English blood." Unwilling to look at who had said the spiteful comment, I hurried through the doorway.

Lady Eliza turned, and I dropped my eyes to the floor, not wanting to confront the stinging look of trepidation I had seen in them last night. "I can write to my father and have our coach sent to pick me up immediately, unless you would prefer to offer a means of transportation, allowing our departure to be sooner. I am confident my father would reimburse you for the trouble." My words came out unnaturally fast, just wanting to be home and rid of these feelings of disgrace. I would never leave Easton Manor again.

"Why should you leave?"

The kindness in Lady Eliza's voice startled me and I looked up to find her watching me with a look of concern. "I assumed..." I wasn't quite sure how to phrase it, "that you should all desire my departure after last night's discovery."

"Our desire would be for you to stay." The sincerity in her eyes once again confused me.

"But surely you do not want the good name of Stanton tainted by association?"

"I see no reason to be ashamed of anything you have done, or who you are. I assure you, we all have things in our pasts we wish to keep hidden." She looked as though she wished to be free of her own deceptions as I now was.

Remembering Helena, I shook my head. "I thank you for your understanding, Lady Eliza, but I feel it would be best to be home with my family."

Her eyes held a sadness I was not prepared to encounter. "Very well. I will have the coach prepared. You can depart within the hour."

"Thank you," I said, anxious to go upstairs and inform Lydia to begin packing for our return home. "I should like to say goodbye to Diana before I go. I did not see her in the sitting room." I intentionally didn't mention how she had neglected to check in on me as she had said she would.

"She has not come down yet this morning. Mr. Ellis said she had complained of exhaustion and a headache before bed last night, she is probably still resting."

Surely it was because she had stayed up too late comforting me. "Do you think it would be acceptable if I called upon her before I left?"

"I think she would insist upon it," Lady Eliza said with a reserved smile.

~

I HAD a difficult time recalling which door was hers, having only seen it briefly on our tour of the house, so I knocked quietly on the one I believed most probable. I thought I heard a voice, though I couldn't distinguish what was said. Opening the door slightly, I squinted into the darkness. The curtains were still drawn but seeing the setup of the room I was positive it was hers.

"Diana?" I whispered, quietly moving toward the bed. "I have come to say goodbye."

When she didn't answer I hesitated. I hated to wake her, but I was certain she would be quite put out if I left without a word; besides, I knew she wouldn't feel even a prick of guilt rousing me from slumber. I exhaled, feeling only partially convinced by my reasoning, before trying one more time. Increasing the volume of my voice I called out again, "Diana?"

An indistinguishable murmur drew me closer. My eyes had started adjusting to the darkness and I could see her figure lying curled up under the heavy covers. Quietly I walked to the side of the bed and listened.

"Diana?"

Another low moan sent my heart racing. I reached my hand over and placed it lightly on her forehead. She was burning up! Quickly I pulled the covers off her and she shivered at the change in temperature, moaning again.

"Diana, you are ill! I must get help!" I thought to ring the maid but realized no one should be around Diana to prevent it spreading. I ran all the way down the stairs until I stepped through the drawing room door.

Lady Eliza's wide eyes glimpsed the urgency in mine and she rushed to meet me.

I waited until she stood next to me in the doorway, before leaning in to whisper, "It is Diana, I fear she has contracted influenza."

She nodded her understanding, pushing the fear from her eyes, and evenly turned toward the group who watched with curious stares. "It seems my assistance is needed. Please continue your needlework or feel free to ring for refreshments. I will be back shortly."

We hurried up the stairs and down the corridor to Diana's room.

Her brow creased with worry. "Are you positive it is influenza?"

"Yes," I said without hesitation. "I am nearly certain."

As we entered the room, I quickly pulled one of the curtains back, letting in a small amount of light. Lady Eliza stood next to Diana, a worried expression on her face. "Diana? How are you feeling darling?" Lady Eliza pushed the hair from her feverish forehead. Diana whispered something unintelligible and turned her face away from the light.

I grabbed a water basin and a clean cloth from a nearby table, saturating it to begin cooling her off. "Send for Doctor Walter," I said authoritatively. "I will stay with Diana and keep her temperature down."

Nodding absently, Lady Eliza's eyes scanned Diana one last time before she hurried from the room.

I grabbed a cup of water and gently lifted her head to allow her to drink, but she refused, only groaning at my efforts.

"You must drink, Diana!"

She tossed her head sideways at my next attempt. Deciding I would have to drip water into her mouth, I found another clean cloth, drenched it, and brought it to her lips. I could see Diana struggle to swallow.

"Is your throat raw?" I asked rhetorically, realizing what

the difficulty was. I hastily rang for her maid but locked the door, so she would be forced to knock instead of entering.

Several minutes later a maid came, asking through the door if Mrs. Ellis needed anything.

"Yes, lemons and honey as well as warm water, and please hurry."

Certain she had found the request quite odd, I was glad when she returned quickly. I opened the door just enough to grab the tray, thanked her, and shut it again. Mixing the warm water in a bowl with the lemon and honey, I grabbed a spoon hoping to drip the mixture into Diana's mouth.

As I neared her, she tossed her head violently, causing me to spill the sticky liquid. "Diana, this will help with your pain," I said, as though she was capable of reasoning in her current state. I made a second attempt, but she again refused to comply.

A light knock sounded, and I replaced the spoon before moving toward the door. "Who is it?"

"Lady Eliza."

I unlatched the door and Lady Eliza hurried in. "How is she?"

"She refuses to drink. I believe it is because her throat is raw, but it is imperative we keep her hydrated." I walked toward the bed with Lady Eliza at my side.

"What must we do?"

"I fear we must force her," I said reluctantly.

Lady Eliza nodded, but she looked as uncertain as I felt.

I scanned Lady Eliza's slender frame. "I will restrain her, if you will be ready with the liquid."

She nodded again.

I moved onto Diana's bed and scooted in behind her. Wrapping my arms tightly around her shoulders and chest, I lifted her until we were positioned upright. Diana struggled against the confinement. "Please trust me, Diana," I whispered. "We need you to get better." *I need you to get better.*

When her wriggling finally subsided, I nodded for Lady Eliza to proceed. Cautiously she brought the spoon to Diana's lips. Diana tried to turn away, but I tightened my grip and placed my face next to hers as a barrier. With no other choice, Diana swallowed.

By the time Doctor Walter arrived, we had managed to get Diana to drink several teaspoons of the mixture. I joined Lady Eliza, nervously awaiting his assessment as he counted her pulse.

"It is a bad year for it," he said, walking toward Lady Eliza and myself. "The high temperatures seem to be causing a state of delirium. What is odd is it seems to be harder on the adults." He paused, as though he was taking mental notes of his observations. "Let as few people in this room as possible and perhaps consider re-housing the guests here at Timpton for now. As for treatment, I fear there is little to be done but wait."

"Surely there is something more we can do for her? Perhaps a tonic or tincture?" Lady Eliza looked hopeless, her gaze urging him to reconsider.

"A different doctor might prescribe such remedies, but I have seen little proof they are effective. The only thing I know will help is to continue what Miss Blakeslee has already been doing—keep her hydrated and see to managing her temperature. I can arrange for someone to tend to her if it seems too demanding a task."

"I will tend to her," I said without hesitation.

Lady Eliza looked at me, apparently surprised by my offer. "I thought you were leaving?"

I looked toward Diana. "She would not leave me, and I will not leave her. Besides, I brought her to the Bragg's cottage, so the blame is mine."

"This is not your fault," Lady Eliza grabbed my hand and gave it a gentle squeeze. I appreciated her kindness, but I was not certain I felt the same, nor would Edwin when word reached him.

"Well then," Doctor Walter said, "if you should need anything, or if her condition should worsen, send word immediately."

"Thank you for coming," Lady Eliza said, walking him to the door.

"I can see myself out," he said, offering a brief bow and one last encouraging nod in my direction.

Closing the door behind him, Lady Eliza sighed. "The men left early this morning for a hunt and have not yet returned. I will send a servant to find Mr. Ellis and inform him of Diana's condition." She observed Diana apprehensively. "My poor child."

"And what of your husband and son?"

"Mr. Stanton had business to attend to in London. I will write to him but I am not certain it will do much good, considering we expect him back the day after tomorrow." She paused, and her eyes skirted over my face as if in indecision. "And I hate to admit, but I do not know where Edwin has gone. He left a note saying he needed to attend to a personal matter, though the suddenness of it seems odd."

I felt my face warm and I moved to Diana's side table, busying myself with cleaning up.

"I will go relay our situation to the guests. Sir Wycliffe will most likely be able to host the party without too much inconvenience; and if not, the Hawkins will surely be eager to entertain."

I glanced up at her and a look of distress filled her features; it was most likely out of worry for her daughter, but I didn't blame her for feeling dread at the task ahead.

"I will be back soon," Lady Eliza said, leaving me to my duties.

There was little to do as Diana slept, so I sat on the bed next to her and softly stroked her long hair. "I'm so sorry,

Diana," I said as tears ran down my cheeks. It was a blanket apology. There were so many things I was sorry for. I was sorry that she had become ill and I had not. I was sorry that I had lied to her and brought scandal into her home. I was sorry that I had sent her only brother running when he should be here with her. And I was most sorry I could not be a woman her brother could love.

CHAPTER 16

*W*hen Lady Eliza returned, she informed me the guests would go to Sir Wycliffe's with the exception of Mr. Ellis and Uncle Stanton; though, to his disappointment, Uncle Stanton would be banned from visiting until they were certain Diana was no longer contagious. Lady Eliza mentioned she had been surprised to hear Lord Ramsby, who had given his regrets for an early departure that morning, had now decided to stay. I inwardly smiled at the news, glad Helena's angelic pleadings had worked. They would certainly make a lovely couple.

Lady Eliza then handed me a note from Mrs. Reed, apologizing that it had been placed in my room earlier in hopes I would receive it, and a letter from Father that had just arrived. I opened the note from Mrs. Reed anxious to see how the Braggs were faring. She once again reported there was little change, and I felt my breath come easier.

I then turned my attention to the letter from Father. Surely it was too soon to be a reply regarding aid for the Braggs. My heart swelled seeing the familiar writing and I began reading.

. . .

My Dearest Abigail,

I hope you are enjoying your stay at Timpton House and the company is not as tedious as you had thought it would be. Your absence here is keenly felt and I am not sure which of us, Laurence or myself, misses you more.

I have little to relay since your departure but wanted to make you aware of how proud of you I am. I know this is not easy for you, and I'm not ashamed to admit it has been more difficult on me than I could have foreseen, but I can't help but think much good will come out of it in the end.

I love you my girl. Please write to me soon and ease your father's worried heart.

All my love,
Father

How I missed him. How I longed to be home at Easton Manner where I was loved completely, without exception. But I had Diana to tend to, so I folded the letter and tried not to wonder at the disappointment that Father would share when I wrote to tell him how the truth had come out. He would surely hurt for me, hurt for the disgrace from which he wished to keep me.

Mr. Ellis joined us in the room as soon as he had been informed of Diana's condition. I assured him I would keep a vigilant watch, but he was unwilling to leave Diana's side, holding her hand and stroking her hair as I had just done. I found it fascinating that the same gesture could be rooted in such different types of love. I thought of Edwin and the way he had kissed me on the forehead the morning I saw him at the pond. I had associated it with something Laurence or Father would do to comfort me, but I wondered if it had meant something different to him. I shook the thought away.

∿

DIANA MURMURED IN HER SLEEP, causing all three of us to hurry to the side of her bed. She thrashed her head about, her skin sullen and pale. Lady Eliza and Mr. Ellis looked at me, desperation in their eyes.

"It is the fever," I answered trying to appear composed as I reached out my hand and gently touched her forehead. Her temperature had risen again, and I could see her heart racing under her clammy skin. "We need to cool her down. Mr. Ellis, grab the water basin."

He hurried over, sloshing out water in his haste.

I grabbed the linen in the water, squeezed some out, and began rubbing it across her forehead and cheeks. I dipped the cloth again, and repeated the process moving from Diana's cheeks down her neck. She moaned at the touch of the cloth on her chest, and Mr. Ellis shot me a worried look when her chin shivered uncontrollably.

"She is cold, should we not cover her with more than this thin sheet?"

"I know it seems counterintuitive, but we must cool her down. It is her high temperature that is making her feel cold and covering her will only raise it more."

He nodded hesitantly and watched as I lifted her gently and touched the cool cloth to her back. She let out a whimper that intensified his frown.

"See if you can get her to drink something while I have her sitting up," I said, hoping a meaningful task would help ease his anxiety. "And Lady Eliza, if you wish to grab another linen you can help me until we see an improvement in her temperature."

They both went to work, obviously grateful for a direction in which to place their worry. Mr. Ellis leaned Diana against him, and I was thrilled to see him coax her to take a few sips of water.

Lady Eliza and I worked together cooling her and it wasn't long before we managed to get Diana's temperature to a tolerable level. Her breathing slowed, her heart rate decreased, and I felt relieved at how well her body had responded to our efforts.

"Perhaps we should figure out a schedule between us," I said, looking from Mr. Ellis to Lady Eliza, the dark circles around her eyes deepening in the late afternoon light. "Two on watch while the other rests."

They nodded their agreement.

"You rest first," I said resolutely to Lady Eliza. "When you wake, Mr. Ellis will take a turn and then I will."

She looked as though she wished to protest.

"I will wake you if you are needed," I promised.

She looked reluctant to comply. "I don't know how I shall sleep, but I will try."

She kissed Diana on the head and gave Mr. Ellis a reassuring squeeze of the hand before walking toward me.

"Thank you, Miss Blakeslee," she said, reaching out and grabbing my hand. "Your mother would be so very proud of you."

Tears filled my eyes at the sincerity in her voice and the image of Mother's smiling face she had brought to my mind. "Thank you," I whispered.

She looked back at Diana somberly, exhaled, and walked from the room.

"I will have dinner brought up," I said to Mr. Ellis, attempting to fill the silence. "We need to maintain our strength."

He nodded again, stroking Diana's hair as she slept. "Will she recover?" he whispered.

There was such a depth of anguish in his voice, it caused a knot to form in my stomach. "She will recover," I said unwaveringly. "I will make sure of it."

His eyes finally met mine. "I believe you, Miss Blakeslee."

I offered a weak smile and he turned his gaze back to Diana.

"How is Mrs. Ellis?" Lydia asked as I came walking into my room just after midnight.

"I fear she is quite unwell," I answered, my emotions instantly bubbling to the surface in the presence of my dearest friend.

Lydia reached and pulled me into a tight embrace. "She will be fine, Abee. She has you watching over her."

I allowed myself to find comfort in her embrace as tears streamed down my face. "I should have never brought her to visit the Braggs." I sobbed.

"You didn't know," Lydia said, stroking my back. "You couldn't have known."

Lydia did not rush me, allowing me to rely on her strength until I was ready to once again find my own. I finally straightened, and she gently cupped her hands around my face, brushing the tears aside with her thumbs. "I know this has been hard on you, all of it, but you have managed it with dignity. You have been through more hardship than anyone I know, yet you have not allowed it to harden you. You are so much more than all your disappointments—so much stronger. You will help Mrs. Ellis get through this, as you helped so many before her."

I didn't answer. I wasn't sure if she was right.

She dropped her hands, grabbed mine and led me to the bed, pulling back the covers. I climbed into its comfort, exhausted. I fought the heaviness in my eyes, wanting to thank Lydia for being here for me, for being the support she always was. I opened my mouth to speak and she rubbed my face tenderly.

"Sleep," she said smiling. "I already know how grateful you are."

I smiled at her discernment and allowed my eyes to close.

~

"Miss Blakeslee! Miss Blakeslee!"

My eyes shot open to darkness, a faint outline of a woman above me. I focused my eyes, trying to make sense of the voice, disoriented by the throbbing in my head.

"Miss Blakeslee, please come quickly."

Lady Eliza's panicked plea pulled me from my confusion. I shot up, dread consuming me. "What has happened?"

"Diana's temperature has spiked, and it won't come down. She has begun convulsing."

I threw the covers from my body.

"Have a servant bring up a vile of vinegar," I said, following her out the door. "Tell him to hurry!"

Lady Eliza's footsteps descended the staircase as I ran down the corridor to Diana's room. The door had been left open and when I entered the flickering fire and soft candle-light outlined Mr. Ellis holding Diana firmly in his arms, her body convulsing violently.

"What can be done?" Mr. Ellis pleaded.

"We must cool her," I answered, running the rest of the way to the bed and touching her scorching skin.

"We have tried but it hasn't worked."

"How long has she been convulsing?"

"It seems an eternity," he said, searching his mind. "Maybe five minutes. Lady Eliza ran for you shortly after she began."

I went to Diana whose rigid, seizing frame was hardly recognizable. "Help me undress her."

He hesitated only a moment before gently laying her down to help me pull off her nightgown. I grabbed the water basin and handed him a cloth. "Keep trying," I commanded, hurrying to the windows to let the cool air in. The night breeze was warmer than I had expected, and my thoughts scanned my memories for what else could be done for Diana —for what Mother would do.

If I had thought to have the vinegar brought up earlier, I could have applied it and hoped the evaporation would cool her skin, but without it I felt unsure what to try. I glanced around in desperation. I needed something to cool her quickly. I wrenched the sheet from her bed and dipped it in the basin, soaking it through, before spreading it out and lying it over her midsection and legs.

Mr. Ellis and I frantically dabbed at her exposed skin, rewetting our cloths until we had nearly run out of water.

"Diana, don't you leave us!" My voice sounded distant in my own ears, beseeching. "We need you, Diana! Please!"

"Please, Diana," Mr. Ellis echoed desperately.

As though she had heard our pleas, her body stopped convulsing and an eerie stillness took its place.

"Diana!" Dread filled my entire being. "Diana!" I placed my hand on her limp body, waiting for the stillness to end, pleading for it to end. Her chest lifted then lowered. "She is alive," I cried, looking over to a terrified Mr. Ellis.

He could bear no more, and tears of relief burst from him. "Diana," he whispered as he laid down next to her and pulled her close, kissing her face, again and again. "Thank you, God."

The door opened, and my eyes went to Lady Eliza. She froze, looking from our tear-filled faces to the stillness of her daughter's body.

"She has stopped convulsing," I said quickly, trying to ease the look of anguish in her expression.

Lady Eliza put a hand over her mouth and crumbled to the floor.

I stood and ran to her side. Her whole body trembled as I wrapped my arms around her. "She is fine. She is fine," I repeated to us both.

A bang at the door brought a breathless and disheveled Baldwin inside carrying the vinegar. The butler's eyes scanned the dim room, falling on Lady Eliza's crumpled figure next to where he stood. His eyes shot to the bed.

"How is she?" he asked, distress overtaking his features.

"She is alive," Lady Eliza said shakily, a sob behind her words. "My dear Diana is alive."

The relief in her voice sent a chill through me. How fearful she must have been, thinking her child was dying as she ran to get help. That she might return to find her only daughter gone from this life. The pain would have broken her.

I helped Lady Eliza to her feet and urged her to Diana's bed before retrieving the vinegar from Baldwin.

"Thank you, Baldwin."

"Is there anything else you need?"

"If you could see the doctor is sent for, I think we can handle the rest."

"Very well, Miss Blakeslee," he said with a bow, closing the door behind him.

I walked to the bed, the whispers of Mr. Ellis and Lady Eliza stopping as I neared.

"Why did she convulse?" Lady Eliza asked when I came near.

"I'm not certain," I admitted. "I have heard of children having fever seizures from their temperature rising too quickly. Perhaps this is similar."

"And do the children recover fully? After the seizure, I mean."

"I believe so," I said, hoping I was correct.

Lady Eliza returned her gaze to Diana, concern creasing her brow.

"We should replace the wet sheet with a light blanket," I said, reaching past Lady Eliza to grab the soaked linen. "We don't want to cause a chill now that her temperature is lower." Lady Eliza quickly complied as I moved toward the fireplace and draped the sheet over an armchair to dry. My body ached, and I reached up to feel my own skin, relieved there was no fever. I must simply be exhausted.

I walked back to the bed.

"You must finish resting," Lady Eliza urged, though I could distinguish the worry behind her good intention. "It is only two o'clock, you mustn't have slept long before I woke you."

"I think it best if I stay," I said, hoping not to insult Lady Eliza or Mr. Ellis with my assertion. "Perhaps, if you would not find it improper, I can rest on the settee near the fire to ensure I'm here if needed?"

"I think that would be more than suitable, considering the situation," Lady Eliza said with an appreciative smile. "Let me grab you a pillow and blanket."

I nodded my acceptance of her kind offer and walked to the settee. I allowed the warmth of the fire to penetrate through me before realizing the numbness inside was not due to cold.

When Lady Eliza returned, she placed the pillow on one side and motioned for me to lie down. I quickly complied while she unfolded the blanket and draped it over me. I closed my eyes. A light kiss on my cheek caused me to open them again, and I smiled up at the loving face of Lady Eliza looking down on me. The gesture should have felt strange, but it didn't; or perhaps I was too tired to realize it. Like a child being tucked into bed, the warmth of her kindness surrounded me, and I closed my eyes to sleep.

~

A GENTLE KNOCK startled me awake. The light of early morning seeped through open windows and I sat up, feeling the heat of the newly stoked fire warming my sore body. A door opened, and I looked to find Lady Eliza leading Dr. Walter into the room. I tried not to pay any heed to what I must look like as I stood to greet them.

"I am sorry we have woken you," Lady Eliza said apologetically as I approached.

"It is no matter," I said quickly. "I am anxious to see how Diana has fared the last few hours as I slept."

Lady Eliza gestured us to a sleeping Diana. "She is still warm, but her temperature has not spiked again since her convulsions."

"Fevers tend to be higher at night." Dr. Walter said. "That is most likely what caused the seizure—the sudden rise of temperature; we see it more in children, but it is not unheard of in adults."

"And will she recover from it?" Lady Eliza asked, worry creasing her brow.

"How long did the episode last?"

She glanced at me before answering. "We concluded about seven or eight minutes."

He exhaled and looked at Diana, pausing as though doing a large calculation in his mind.

"That is a fairly long one," he finally said. "But it is promising she hasn't had another. And although it is not always the case, long term effects from a single episode of seizing are rare."

Lady Eliza nodded her understanding, a relieved smile touching her lips.

"May I examine her?" Dr. Walter asked, glancing between Mr. Ellis and Lady Eliza for permission.

"Of course," Mr. Ellis said, rising from his position next to Diana on the bed.

Dr. Walter grabbed Diana's hand and pressed two fingers on her wrist.

"Has she taken drink?"

"Yes," Mr. Ellis answered. "As well as a little broth."

Dr. Walter nodded. "And has she voiced any complaints? Headaches, throat soreness, body aches, nausea?"

Mr. Ellis sent me a worried glance. "She has not spoken since she took ill. A few times she has opened her eyes briefly or moaned but—no, no complaints."

The doctor's steady breathing and slow movements did not betray what he thought of the information, and the quiet became deafening. After a minute he turned toward us, his face more solemn than I cared to see. A heaviness settled in my chest, already knowing what he was about to say.

"As I have said before, it is a bad year for those suffering from influenza. We have already lost several people in neighboring villages, an unusual amount being healthy adults." Dr. Walter shook his head and exhaled. "Diana's temperature is still high, her heart rate too fast, and her breathing too rapid. Her seizure and her unresponsiveness are signs her body is having a difficult time fighting. Though I hope it is in vain, I would prepare yourselves for the worst."

I covered my mouth in disbelief, and a sickening feeling consumed me. My eyes shifted to Mr. Ellis, his head hung down, his hands gripping the frame of the bed tightly. Lady Eliza looked as stunned as I felt, hand over her heart, lips pressed tightly together attempting to hold in her emotions. He must be wrong, we could not lose Diana, not now.

I looked at Diana. Her brow was lowered as though she was still struggling, still battling even as she slept. She looked so much like her brother.

Without permission my thoughts turned to Edwin and I tried to ignore the vivid image in my mind of what he would look like when he returned to find his sister ill, or worse—gone. The tightness in his jaw, the stiffness in his shoulders, the sorrow in his eyes—I could envision it so clearly. How he would hate me, and I would not blame him for it. I could not give him another reason to hate me.

"She will recover," I said firmly, lifting my chin. "I appreciate that you do not wish to give us false hope, Doctor, but I assure you that Diana will live."

Lady Eliza and Mr. Ellis eyed me cautiously, unsure of whether to take hope in my declaration. Dr. Walter did not flinch at my words and I was certain, by the look of pity distinguishable in his features, this was not the first deathbed denial he had heard from his patients' relations. This time however, he was wrong.

"I pray you are right, Miss Blakeslee," he offered kindly.

"I am," I said, eradicating the dread that had been struggling for control within me. If it were simply up to my stubbornness I would waiver in my resolve, but the moment I spoke the words I could feel their truth resonate through me, dissipating any doubt.

"Very well, I shall visit again tomorrow." He bowed to Lady Eliza, nodded at Mr. Ellis and turned to me, stopping before offering his goodbye. He watched me a moment, his gaze firm and confident, and then he smiled. "You know, Miss Blakeslee, if anyone can produce a miracle, I do believe it's you."

I returned his smile. "I cannot take credit for God's doings, but I'm happy to help Him where I can."

He nodded thoughtfully. "Tomorrow then."

"Diana?" I heard Mr. Ellis's alarmed voice pierce through the air and I rushed to the bed, nearly tripping over my feet in my urgency.

I followed Mr. Ellis's gaze to Diana's face. Her eyes were

opened, a faint smile on her lips. "You look so sad," she whispered to her husband, her eyes taking in his face.

"Oh, Diana!" he said, raising her hand to his lips and kissing it. "You are mistaken, I am so very, very happy."

I smiled as relief filled my soul but backed away before she saw me, allowing the couple a much-deserved private moment.

"Where are Mother and Father?" I heard her ask, her voice hoarse and quiet.

"Your father is not yet back from London and your mother is resting. Would you like me to wake her?"

"Not on my account," Diana said. "Let her rest."

"It is probably best, it has been a tedious few days."

"Days?" she questioned, sounding confused. "How odd. Though it does feel as though I have been stuck in a dreadful nightmare for ages."

"Well then, your awakening has brought us both from a nightmare."

I heard Mr. Ellis lean in and kiss her and I busied myself with the linens.

"And Abigail, where is she?"

Mr. Ellis looked at me invitingly. "She is right here."

I walked back over, a lightness in my step at being asked for. "Hello, Diana. How are you feeling?"

"Quite haggard. My body is aching and my head pounding, but I shall live."

"You certainly shall," I said with a laugh of relief, reaching out to squeeze her hand. "And I will be forever grateful for it."

"Of course you shall," Diana said, attempting a mischievous tone. "And where is Edwin?"

Mr. Ellis looked at me hesitantly. Since Diana's illness Mr. Ellis, Lady Eliza, and I had come to an unspoken agreement to remain focused on the task at hand and not discuss things past. "He is not yet home from his trip," he said, trying to manage a tone of indifference.

"Trip?" Diana asked, her brow creasing. "He did not mention to me he was leaving."

"He didn't mention it to anyone. He left a note for your mother with little explanation."

My eyes dropped, not wanting to see the realization in Diana's eyes of where the blame should be placed.

"Well I'm sure it is important if he left in such a hurry," she said affably, and I raised my eyes to meet a soft smile directed at me.

"Well, when he returns, I will be certain to not inform him you asked after Miss Blakeslee before asking after him." Mr. Ellis offered Diana a teasing smile.

Diana looked as though she wished to laugh but couldn't find the strength. "How tired I am," she complained, her eyes closing momentarily, before she forced them open again.

I reached out and touched her skin. "You are still feverish. You need to rest."

Her eyes closed again, as though she had been waiting for permission, and Mr. Ellis held her close, keeping watch over his sleeping wife.

I returned to the settee by the fire. Perhaps I could find a little rest myself.

DOCTOR WALTER TOOK Diana's pulse as she slept and nodded his approval. "I'm not certain, but it seems as though she is over the worst of it. It will still be several days before her fever breaks and several weeks until a full recovery could be expected."

Lady Eliza shot me a pleased smile at Dr. Walter's assessment. Diana had improved much since she had awoken last night. Her fever had remained constant, but with much diligence it had not spiked again, and the few times she spoke she showed no lapses of mind.

"I shall come again in a day or two, but I'm very pleased with her improvement thus far. Well done."

"And how is the Bragg family?" I asked anxiously. I hadn't heard anything since yesterday afternoon and I had let the silence worry me.

"I fear Mrs. Bragg has been hit much harder than even Diana. To be honest, after examining her yesterday, I did not think she would make it through the night; but Mrs. Reed sent word this morning saying she has surprised us yet again. She must know there is still a reason to live." He paused as Lady Eliza and I nodded our agreement. "Rose and Patience are improving slowly but surely. And it seems the other three children are still healthy as can be."

I was relieved. "Well if you see them, tell them I shall come visit them as soon as Miss Diana is well enough."

"I will, and they shall be very pleased to hear it," he said smiling, grabbing his bag to leave.

"Thank you for checking in on us," Lady Eliza said, turning her attention back to Diana. "And if you see Mr. Ellis on your way out, please convince him to rest. The most we could persuade him of was a quick walk to the stables to check on his horse."

I walked Doctor Walter to the bedroom door before rejoining Lady Eliza, who sat brushing Diana's hair as she slept. I sat down next to her and grabbed Diana's hand, watching her breaths, steady and slow, grateful her illness had not gone to her lungs as it had with Mrs. Bragg.

"You have done us a great service, Miss Blakeslee," Lady Eliza said, an appreciative look on her face. She wore her hair half down and the long honey-colored tresses around her face brought a softness to her features that somehow made her more striking, accentuating her youthful beauty.

"Perhaps it will somehow begin to cancel out the disservices I have done during my visit," I said, looking back toward Diana.

"This is not your doing," Lady Eliza responded, clearly overlooking the scandal I had brought with my stay at Timpton.

I wasn't sure she was right, but I nodded graciously.

"You did not know Mrs. Bragg was ill, and what you did for that family was exceptional."

"I did little compared to the assistance your family gave." Her expression wavered as though their role had not been related clearly to her and I felt compelled to explain. "An account set up in the family's name as well as the cost of both Doctor Walter's care and that of Mrs. Reed's."

She nodded, whether in acknowledgment or remembrance I was not sure.

"We should receive little credit for it," she replied. "Edwin was the one who proposed it, as well as carried it out; my husband just gave his approval." She held my gaze. "Edwin is a good man, Miss Blakeslee." The way she said it made me wonder if she thought I doubted it.

"I know he is." And, even with my wounded heart, I did know.

"He may not display his feelings for all to see, but that does not mean he is not deeply affected by them. Edwin has had to overcome some difficult circumstances, and with each one he seems to add a layer to protect himself—who he really is receding further from us."

I watched as her face turned thoughtful, and it struck me just how much I had appreciated her company these last few days. There was an ease about our interactions, something natural and familiar.

"I fear my own influence has not helped the situation. I have frequently instilled in him the need to repress one's feelings, to act wisely and prudently, to always be vigilant and act within the bounds of honor. I thought I would alleviate the grief that comes through forsaking such principles, but now I wonder if I have caused a deeper conflict within him, forced him to betray his feelings for his duties."

A moment of silence passed before I found the courage to voice my curiosity. "Diana mentioned something happened, something that has led him to believe his position as heir to Timpton is his sole contribution to a match."

Lady Eliza hardly hesitated. "It was a few years ago. Edwin was in London for the Season and he fell in love with a young debutante—Miss Madeline. She was everything a young gentleman could think he desired. He doted on her tirelessly, and eventually she gave him permission to court her. Her family was wealthy, but like ours, they did not hold a title. It seemed a well-suited match and Edwin felt the luckiest man in London."

I shifted, trying to appear unaffected at the idea of Edwin being so thoroughly smitten by this Miss Madeline.

"He made a quick trip home mid-Season to help his father, and when he returned rumors of Miss Madeline awaited him. She had been spotted by several close friends interacting with a certain gentleman on very familiar terms. But to Edwin, Miss Madeline could do no wrong. Feeling an urgency to confirm her affections, he offered for her."

Lady Eliza sighed. "She turned him down most cruelly, explaining she never should have entertained the suit of someone with so little to offer, and that her parents had only tolerated his court to allow her experience until a more quali-fied match should come along. The gentleman from the ball, it turned out, was a Baron. He could give Miss Madeline a title and a connection to a noble family that Edwin could not."

She looked me directly in the eye as she spoke. "You see, Edwin's grandfather made the fortune Edwin will inherit, making Stanton little more than an obscure name and new money, a tempting offer to only those who fear they cannot achieve more from a marriage."

I sat processing what I had just been told. "*Achieve* and

marriage seem quite contradictory terms," I finally managed. "Marriage should not be about personal achievement."

Lady Eliza smiled sweetly at me, perhaps it was at my naivety. "Certainly, it should not be, but I fear it often is, as we have seen time and again from debutantes like Miss Madeline."

"But surely Edwin...I mean Mr. Stanton," I sheepishly corrected myself as a fleeting smile touched Lady Eliza's lips, "understands Lady Madeline could not have loved him?"

"She was quite convincing in her affections toward him, even I could not determine the falseness of them in the beginning. And his love for her felt true, which confused him all the more. I fear that his experience has led him to believe a woman is not capable of anything but false love, only seeking for her benefit. And I fear the last two years have done little to show him otherwise." I thought of Helena and how she had also deceived him, deceived us all.

"And he had resigned himself to a life without love..." Diana's words echoed in my mind.

"Yes. That is what we all feared, until recently that is."

My stomach knotted at her words, at what she implied. Would she believe I had just ruined Edwin's chance at love by encouraging my cousin toward Lord Ramsby? Encouraging her to do the very thing Miss Madeline had done to him? I would not have urged Helena had I not discovered her falseness, but I was certain Lady Eliza and Edwin had not yet recognized the deception and may not believe my intentions were to protect him from someone who would not love him.

Lady Eliza watched me, and I realized I had taken too long to answer. "I'm sorry, Lady Eliza..." My heart pounded as I found the words to tell her what I had done. Perhaps if she knew my reasoning, she would realize it was for the best. "I could never—"

A knock at the door stole my courage.

Lady Eliza did not turn her gaze but kept her eyes on me,

seemingly intrigued by the words I was about to speak. But the knock came again, and the opportunity was lost.

"Come in," Lady Eliza said, her voice tinged with regret.

The door opened, and my heart nearly stopped. Edwin had come back to Timpton.

CHAPTER 17

*E*dwin looked beside himself with worry as he walked toward us. I stood, stepping away from the bed to allow a spot for him by Diana's side. He eagerly filled it without a response.

"How is she?" he asked, not turning his attention from her.

"Doctor Walter says she is much improved," Lady Eliza answered, after a quick glance in my direction.

He did not seem comforted by the image of his pale sister lying motionless, and he looked at his mother with a furrowed brow.

"We had a few scares but we are now confident the worst is over. It will take time, but she will be herself again." Lady Eliza walked to his side and placed a reassuring hand on his shoulder.

I could no longer see his face, but I could sense his anguish as he grabbed Diana's hand, kissed it, and put it to his cheek. "I should have been here," he said quietly. "I'm so sorry, Diana, I should have been here."

My heart trembled inside me. I was the reason he had not been here; and now he had returned, thinking I would be gone, only to find more damage I had caused. I slowly backed away, wanting to give them their privacy and needing to be removed from the intense guilt I felt at the sight before me. I slid out the opened door and started down the corridor to my room.

I rebuked myself as I walked. Had I known Edwin was going to return I would have left before his arrival, spared him the awkward need to disregard me at his sister's sickbed —spared myself the torment of seeing him again.

The doorway to my room came into view as I rounded the corner. I would go tell Lydia to pack for our immediate departure. The thought at leaving Diana before she was fully recovered made me feel a sense of abandonment, but what else could I do?

"Miss Blakeslee!"

I stopped at the sound of Edwin's voice and turned cautiously back toward him. "Mr. Stanton," I managed shakily, preparing for the rebuke that would surely come.

He drew close. "Thank you, for taking care of Diana."

"It was the least I could do," I said, penitently lowering my gaze.

"The least you could do? Surely you don't hold yourself responsible for her illness?"

I drew in a shallow breath. "I brought her to the Braggs."

"You allowed her to accompany you and, had you not, she would have shown up without your permission."

"But I should have realized Mrs. Bragg was sick, the signs were in plain view and I missed them."

"You need not carry every burden, Miss Blakeslee. You have had enough to bear; you needn't accept those that do not belong to you."

I appreciated his willingness to overlook my fault, but the contrast of his response was so vastly different than I had expected, I found it difficult to reconcile the two.

"I'm sorry I left in such haste from Timpton," he continued when I didn't answer. "I should have been here."

His remorseful tone confused me further. It was one thing to overlook my responsibility in Diana's sickness and quite another to act as though my scandal had not angered him greatly. I glanced up wondering if I would be able to distinguish the anger in his features that was absent in his voice. To my surprise his eyes were warm, urging me to forgive him for leaving us to care for Diana. Perhaps for that I could forgive him, but not for the reason he truly left.

"How did you hear of Diana's illness?" I asked, needing to understand the truth in what he felt.

"I fear you caught me in my first moments of discovery. I was returning home when I passed Doctor Walter on the road to Chadsmead. He told me he had just come from Timpton to check on Diana. I'm not sure he perceived my shock as he updated me on Diana's condition and how well you had cared for her. Apparently between your care of the Braggs and now Diana, he is quite impressed by your nursing abilities—he called you a miracle worker." His smile made my heart pound and my mind fill with puzzlement.

"Why did you return then?" I asked, narrowing my eyes, continuing my inquiry.

"Why did I return... to my own house?" he asked, looking perplexed by my strange question.

My face warmed. "I just didn't think you would come back while I was still here."

His eyes searched mine, his brow set low. "You thought..." his eyes held a look of grief and he took a step closer grabbing my shoulders and pulling me into his embrace. "You thought I left because I rejected you for what you told me?"

I took a step back, pulling out of his embrace. "But you were so cross when I told you and then—then you just left me."

He winced. "I admit I was angry, but not at you. What fault could I find with you in any of it?"

The bewilderment in his voice brought tears to my eyes. He did not blame me? I pushed any comfort from the realization away; just because he did not blame me did not mean he would accept me.

Before I could respond he grabbed my hand. "You must be curious as to where I have been. Come."

He led me back to Diana's room, his hand grasping mine as though he thought I might flee at the first opportunity. I tried not to notice the way his large, rough fingers engulfed mine protectively. As we entered, I saw Lady Eliza waiting expectantly on a chair by the fire. Edwin walked me to the settee across from her and then stood between us, his eyes lighting with eagerness.

"What are you up to?" Lady Eliza questioned with narrowed eyes and a tone of distrust in her voice.

He looked between us, a tangible excitement exuding from him, though he endeavored to repress it. He cleared his throat. "I have spent the last few days verifying Miss Blakeslee's story."

Lady Eliza looked at me cautiously, evidently perceiving the disbelief I'd feel at his declaration. Had he thought I'd been untruthful in my retelling? That the tragic story I'd relayed was a scheme, a dramatic story like I created for Uncle Stanton? What was I to accomplish through such a tale? Obtaining his pity? Surely I had already had that.

The obstinate grin that came to his face did not help ease my aggravation. I readied myself to leave, having no desire to sit by and be made the fool once more. He quickly walked to my side and placed his hand lightly on my shoulder, apparently sensing my reluctance to hear him out much longer.

"I went and saw the Slytons, who you had admitted to knowing, and the last family with whom you had any interaction before going to the parish orphanage. After several attempted denials, Mr. Slyton finally saw reason in relaying the whole truth and your story was confirmed."

My chest felt tight at his admission, as though a rope had been fastened around my ribs and was being tightened around me. Edwin had met with the Slytons again? And this time about me? And how had he managed to tear the truth from them?

He continued, "I have also made visits to the Humphries, the Meads, the Dykes, the Hills, the Cluetts, the Greys, and the Wares."

Each name he said seemed to add another loop of rope around my chest, inhibiting my ability to breath until my head spun.

Lady Eliza watched him, not seeming to understand the significance of the names.

"Those are all the families Miss Blakeslee had stayed with since birth," he said, looking at her as though it would be significant. "Wares was a name I found on the ledgers at Kempton Hall a year ago, a name that received an annual payment for the previous *seventeen* years."

Edwin stepped toward his mother as her face went pale and her hand covered her mouth, hung open in disbelief. Slowly she looked at me and tears filled her eyes. I glanced between her look of astonishment and Edwin's satisfied smile. Where was Kempton Hall? What tie did they have to the Wares and to me? And how could he possibly have discovered information about me a year ago? Too many questions were trying to form at the same time. "I am afraid I don't understand," was all I could manage, though it felt like a severe understatement.

"Kempton Hall is not three miles from here," Lady Eliza's voice trembled as she spoke. "It is where I grew up." She looked wide eyed at Edwin, who knelt by her and grabbed her hand. "Years ago, I had a child, a little girl, who was taken from me and given to another family to raise without my consent..." tears began to flow down her cheeks and her shoulders shook as she began to weep.

I looked at Edwin, my head reeling, trying to understand.

"A family was paid to care for the child," he continued for his mother, "and that family was the Wares. The family that first cared for you eighteen years ago."

My memories of the family were faded, distant but still there. "You think I am the lost child?" I asked in dismay. "How can that be?" I looked at Lady Eliza, unsure how I should feel and what I should do if his conclusion was true. I had spent my whole life envisioning what it would be like to meet my birth mother. Sometimes those thoughts included running to embrace her, but often it included turning from her and never looking back, doing the same thing she had done to me. Uncertain how I felt and whether I truly believed it, I just sat disconcerted, listening as Edwin spoke.

"A year ago, Lady Eliza's nephew, who had inherited her father's Earldom, desired to sell a few of their less visited estates to free up some assets, including Kempton Hall. I convinced him to let me look through the ledgers before it was sold. Not realizing how adamant his grandfather had been against the idea, or simply not caring, he obliged.

"At first, I could find nothing significant among the books, but then I came across one tucked away and separate from the others. When I opened it, there were several seemingly unconnected expenses, one being an annual payment to a man named Richard Wares. The payment began the same time the child was taken. The large sum paid out each year for the last seventeen years with no stipulations except a stop payment notice to be put in place after the eighteenth year." He watched my face, his hand tenderly rubbing his mother's back as her sobs subsided into a gasping quiver.

"I went to the Wares directly, asking after the child. After some strategic questioning to pierce through their obscure story, I discovered that after four years of no one checking in on them, they decided to sell the child to the Greys, a family who had become enchanted with the child and whom they felt could offer her a better situation." I shuddered when I thought of the Greys and what they had offered me.

"The Wares continued to receive the annual payment, until my visit. I threatened to press charges if they did not give me the information for the Greys, and they immediately complied. I have spent the last year piecing together the whereabouts of the missing child. There were lots of dead ends, misinformation, and difficulties locating each family, but eventually I came to the Slytons. I had written to them and they responded with a familiar story of half-truths and desire for financial gain. Wanting to speak to them, but obligated to stay at Timpton, I set up accommodations for them to visit and offered a tempting monetary incentive."

"And that is when I saw them?" I asked.

Edwin nodded. "Once the Slytons got here and were rewarded with their bribe money, they told me the little girl had run away. I questioned them as to where they thought she had gone, to no avail. I realized they truly didn't know where she had gone. I was livid, unable to accept defeat. Mr. Slyton informed me where he had been when the girl escaped, and my next attempt was going to be to question all the locals, hoping that someone remembered a young girl being found all those years ago. That is until I heard your story. As you spoke, your past matched too closely to what I had constructed of the lost child—switching families, the foul characters that you stayed with, and your escape. Your odd reaction to the Slytons only strengthened my conviction."

"Why didn't you say something?" Lady Eliza asked, wiping her eyes.

"I didn't say anything to you because I know how you have suffered over your child's loss and I did not want to give false hope." He turned his gaze to me. "And I didn't say anything to you that night because I wanted to make sure my conclusion was correct. Watching you tell of your past seemed a most difficult task; I did not want to hurt you by making you discuss it further and more in depth, especially if it would come to nothing.

"I knew how to get the information, and you would never have to be the one to say it. And quite honestly, I wasn't sure if I could handle any more of your story that night. I had never felt so much hatred before, imagining you as a child under the influence of some of the people I had met. I had always felt sympathy when I thought of the poor child that had to endure such circumstances, but when I thought of you as that child I could hardly cope with the rage. I needed to act without delay."

I had so many questions, but one thought filled my mind pushing everything else to the fringes. "If I'm Lady Eliza's daughter," my mouth felt stiff as though my whole being was rebelling against the revelation that would follow my question, "you are my brother?" I didn't know why, during such a momentous revelation, I could think of nothing else.

Edwin looked at me oddly, as did Lady Eliza. "Surely you know Lady Eliza is not my mother," his voice was gentle as my face confirmed otherwise. "At least, not by birth."

How could I have missed something so significant?

"Lady Eliza married my father when Diana and I were children. My mother had died of an illness very similar to what Diana now has." I thought of the look Edwin had given me after finding out the Braggs had contracted influenza, now understanding where his distress had come from. "I suppose I thought it such common knowledge among our associations, I never thought to explain."

I just nodded awkwardly in stunned silence. Edwin Stanton might regard me as a little sister; but thankfully, for my own sake, I was not.

"Edwin and Diana have a strong resemblance to their mother," Lady Eliza offered shakily. "She was very beautiful."

"Is she the woman in the portrait? The one in the drawing room downstairs?"

They both nodded, and my mind flashed to the striking woman with Edwin's eyes. I should have known.

Lady Eliza placed her hand on Edwin's, as if to signal she was ready to explain. "I was seventeen and felt I was ready for my first Season in London, but my father felt I was not yet mature enough. He had little tolerance for nuisances, as he called us, so he left me at Kempton Hall with my two younger sisters. Not trusting my judgment and freedom, my father hired a companion for me, but he had been misled regarding her character. Though I do not blame her, she allowed me any diversion I saw fit to pursue and one of those diversions was a handsome stable hand."

Her lip quivered as she continued, her eyes remaining on her lap as she spoke. "He was kind, and charming, and I was certain I loved him. We quickly became too familiar with each other as my companion turned a blind eye to our growing affection. I didn't realize I had become pregnant until my family returned from London—my older sister engaged to marry. When my parents discovered my situation, they were rightly distraught and my father beyond livid. I was instantly taken from Kempton Hall to a remote country cottage to finish out my pregnancy and have the baby."

"It seemed I had been forgotten for those months, without even a letter regarding my sister's wedding, and when the time came to give birth only my servant and the midwife were there. I felt unprepared and terrified." She stopped, and her eyes met mine. "Until you were born, and they put you in my arms. I knew I loved you instantly."

Tears blurred my vision and I quickly wiped them away.

"I held you for hours, just taking you in." Her smile was tender as her gaze turned distant, and I knew she was momentarily back in that cottage, holding her newborn daughter—holding me! "Your perfect face and thick, dark hair. The small birthmark on your right shoulder." I recalled how Lady Eliza had brushed her thumb across it the day she helped me remove my wet clothes. Had she suspected I was her daughter then?

Her eyes refocused on me. "Exhausted, I was finally persuaded to sleep, reassured you would be well taken care of." Lady Eliza's face flashed an emotion I'd not seen in her before, and the intensity of it sent a shiver through me. "When I woke the midwife was gone and you with her. I jumped from my bed screaming with grief and betrayal, unsure what I should do and only knowing how desperate I was to have you back. By the time I reached the outside gate my strength had failed me, and I crumbled to the ground defeated. You were gone, and I knew it." Her eyes implored me to believe her, to see the pain she had felt at my loss, the pain she had carried all these years. "They hadn't told me. They didn't even let me say goodbye."

Tears now streamed down both of our faces. She stood and came to me, sitting by my side and taking both my hands in hers. "I was distraught, yearning to die if I could not have you. For months I kept to my bedroom, never leaving the cottage where I knew I would spend the rest of my life mourning your loss. Then one day, without warning, a coach came to bring me back to my family. When I arrived, my family, as well as our close associations, acted as though they were unaware of the whole situation—they had been told I had been sent as a companion to my mother's aging aunt."

"And what of the stable hand?" I asked with a trembling voice, unable to bring myself to call him my father.

"Dismissed. As was my companion and several servants in the house. There was no one left to question and I never had the courage to ask my father where he had sent him. When I first returned, he had made his point very clear that I was never to talk about or ask him questions regarding my scandal or I would find myself sent away, working the famous

London brothels where I belonged. I did as he required, but my spirit was broken, and I could not pretend otherwise. My father insisted I attend the next Season, but within a few weeks of arriving in Town, he realized it was a futile endeavor. He sent me back to Kempton Hall vowing one more mistake would cost me everything—I knew the first mistake already had.

"After two years, living with little company besides my servants, father sent word he had arranged for me to meet with Mr. Ernest Stanton, a young widower. I was not fond of the idea, but it seemed better than a life of imprisonment, so I conceded. I was pleased to find at our first acquaintance he was a good man, and I instantly adored his children. Diana, only a little older than you would have been, brought a healing to my heart—the way, I suspect, you did for Lady Blakeslee. When Ernest asked for my hand, I knew I could not deceive him, and I told him of my past. Without a moment's hesitation he embraced me, assuring me our mistakes make us who we are and the suffering I had endured had formed me into the woman he loved."

She smiled, her fondness for her husband evident. "He rescued me. He gave me something to hold on to, to look forward to. He knew I would never be whole without my child, but he accepted me for it and loved me through it. Just before we married, he asked my father for information regarding your whereabouts, though the conversation ended quite poorly, and I lost hope of ever being reunited with you." Her grateful gaze turned to Edwin and I followed it. Edwin stood watching us, his own eyes brimming with tears, and he returned her smile then gave me one of my own.

"I can't believe it is really you! My baby girl," she said, looking lovingly at me. She reached over and touched my cheek, her hand soft and warm against my skin. "Since you first came to Timpton, I have not been able to draw my eyes away from you. You looked so very much like your father and exactly what I had envisioned my daughter would look like, beautiful and dark—you seemed so very familiar.

"Then when I saw the birthmark on your shoulder..." her voice trailed off. "It seemed a ridiculous thought, a self-betraying hope to think my own child could end up at Timpton on her own accord, especially when I knew you had a family of your own, so I pushed it from me. I convinced myself you were a phantom sent to vex me and I placed layers over my heart attempting to remain unaffected by your presence."

She exhaled. "I fear, even the other night when you told of your past, and my whole heart screamed that you were mine, I pushed you from me, unwilling to be disappointed and face more loss—I could bear no more. That night I sat, facing my demons; my head telling me how unlikely it was that an orphan from Burrowsly could be my daughter, while my heart tried convincing me otherwise. But you are mine, and I finally feel whole."

With no more delay I fell into her arms, our embrace over-shadowing years of loss and pain. Tears streamed down my face until there were no more to give. Though I wasn't sure what this all meant, right now I was content. I had been wanted, I had always been wanted.

"Mother? Abigail?" Diana's quiet voice sent us eagerly to her bed.

"What is it, dear?" Lady Eliza said as she sat next to Diana and reached out her hand toward me. Pulling me close, Diana looked back and forth between us. "I thought I heard weeping."

Lady Eliza gave me a brief smile before looking back toward Diana. "You did, but it was for joy we wept. Your brother has discovered Abigail is my missing child."

Diana's eyes grew large, their brightness contrasting against the dark circles and pale skin. "I thought her story sounded too familiar to be a coincidence, though I did not wish to say anything until I could speak to you or Edwin privately." A small grin came to her face. "And that makes you almost like my sister," she said, looking at me. "Though I would still prefer you marry my brother to make it official."

My cheeks grew warm and I refused to look toward Edwin, who I was certain had heard his sister's comment. As Edwin stepped up behind me, and into his sister's view, my fear was confirmed. "You do know that I'm standing right here, Diana?"

"I did not know," she said, looking in his direction with her endearing smile. "Though I was hoping you were."

Obviously relieved for Diana's upbeat spirit, Lady Eliza covered her mouth in an attempt not to laugh, but as Edwin's laugh echoed through the room it was difficult for the rest of us not to join in.

"Looks like you will be back to your scheming in no time," I said with a smile. There were now two people, outside Easton Manor, who I knew loved me, and that seemed entirely enough. Almost.

"I'M GOING to go fetch Mr. Ellis," Lady Eliza said, standing. She squeezed my arm affectionately as she passed to leave the room.

"Can I get you anything, Diana?" I asked, filling the place Lady Eliza had just been.

"I will have my husband attend me when he arrives but thank you," she said. "I'm just going to close my eyes and rest until he gets here."

I knew she must be exhausted; but the way she rolled away, putting her back toward Edwin and me, made me wonder if she was already returning to her mischievous tactics.

I stood motionless, still facing Diana, as I gathered the

strength I needed to confront Edwin. When I finally turned, I found his gaze on me and his face gentle.

"You were born on the twenty-second of January, and will turn 19 next year," he said smiling, reaching out his hand for mine. "I thought you would like to know."

I didn't know what to say as I placed my shaking hand in his. I had never thought I would know the date of my birth. The silence between us urged me to fill it. "Thank you, for…" the words felt so trivial, "for everything."

"It was truly my pleasure." The way he smiled made my heart stutter. "I'm only sorry that I left without an explanation. In my eagerness I did not anticipate how you would perceive my absence. But I hope you realize there is little that would make me think less of you."

My chest tightened as he spoke. There was still one thing he did not realize I had done. He would rightfully think less of me when he heard I had encouraged my cousin to pursue Lord Ramsby, inspiring Helena to do the very thing that Miss Madeline had done to him. The very thing that had made him lose his faith in love. I pulled my eyes from him.

"What is it?" he asked, taking a step closer.

His proximity didn't help my courage as I looked down at his large hand still clasped around mine. "The other guests have moved to Sir Wycliffe's estate…"

"Have they?" Edwin's eyes searched mine.

"I believe Helena will be anxious to speak with you."

He stood near a moment longer, before releasing my hand and taking a step away. "Of course. And I am anxious to speak with her." His eyes shifted to the door.

I tried to persuade myself not to be hurt by his admission. "You should go," I said regretfully.

His jaw tightened as he met my gaze one last time. "Yes, I should. I will send your regards," he said, bowing. As he turned to leave, I wondered if he would ever forgive me for what I had done.

~

I WALKED to the window and looked out at the gardens. It felt an eternity since I first came to Timpton. The view beckoned me, yet it seemed the only way I would ever enjoy it was through the glass of a window. The sound of the door opening made me turn.

Lady Eliza was escorted by her husband, followed by Mr. Ellis.

"Look who I found," she said, smiling up at Mr. Stanton. His eyes first glanced at a sleeping Diana and then at me, a warm smile on his lips.

"We have finally found you!" he said, leading Lady Eliza to my side, softly dropping her arm before wrapping me in an embrace. Although surprised by his gesture, it was easy to welcome it. I could feel his love and acceptance as he kissed the top of my head. The warmth ran through me and I knew another person would be added to my list. "And I hear you have been indispensable in the care of Diana," he said as he pulled back to look at me.

"Truly, it was nothing. Diana would have done the same for me."

"Regardless, you have done a venerable thing my child, and I am eternally grateful." He smiled as his gaze fell on Diana who was now smiling up at Mr. Ellis. "And how are you feeling my darling girl?" he said, walking to her side.

"I have been better," she said with a weak smile. "Though I am certain I shall be well soon enough."

He placed a kiss on her cheek. "I am sorry I was not here for you."

"I assure you I was well taken care of and, to be honest, I hardly would have been aware had you been here."

I watched him stroke her hair softly as Lady Eliza leaned in close to me. "Where did Edwin go?"

"To Sir Wycliffe's," I stated, forcing my voice to sound unaffected.

I could feel her gaze on me.

"I am confident my cousin is anxious to talk to him," I said in explanation, still not looking in her direction.

"I am positive she is," Lady Eliza said, as though she already knew what I implied.

Cautiously shifting my gaze toward her, I encountered a knowing glance.

"Your aunt wrote me yesterday, asking after Diana." I felt the color drain from my face at the incriminating rise in her eyebrows. "She regretted to mention a certain affection she had begun to witness between Miss Hanford and Lord Ramsby, and what it could mean for our families' future alliance."

My guilty conscience forced me to admit my role in the connection. "I fear I was the one who encouraged Helena to pursue Lord Ramsby."

She nodded. "She had mentioned something along those lines."

My eyes widened at her admission as well as the slight look of amusement on her face. "She didn't love him," I said, dropping my gaze. "I thought I was saving him from a loveless marriage, but it turns out I unknowingly replicated the same fate Miss Madeline imparted upon him years ago."

Lady Eliza's arm wrapped around me. "It is through the difficult things we often learn the most about ourselves and what love is capable of."

I nodded again, but the knowledge of causing Edwin pain suddenly overwhelmed me. "If Diana is well cared for, I think I will take a walk through the gardens. I believe I could use a little fresh air."

Lady Eliza leaned in and kissed me on the cheek before walking to Mr. Stanton's side, allowing me to take my leave.

CHAPTER 18

I had not been outside in days, and the fresh air flowed through me, instantly reducing my current apprehension. As I passed through the entry of the garden, I started down a path with large hedges that reached up as high as trees on both sides. The path was wide, with large bushes manicured into different animal shapes along the center. I traced my hand over the shapes as I walked, determining what each had been pruned to represent.

When I had finished admiring a bush in the shape of a peacock, I spotted a wooden bench tucked back into the engulfing hedge. The warmth of the sunlight on it was inviting and it seemed an adequate place to sort through the chaos of my thoughts—what I had recently learned and what I hesitated to discover upon Edwin's return.

When my mind felt a little less muddled and the shadow of the hedge blocked the warmth of the sun, I stood and walked back down the path. The light around me seemed softer, almost magical, and I wondered how long I had been lost in reflection.

Before I left the garden to return to the house, I came

upon a narrow path I had not yet noticed. The flowers that grew along the stone walkway were thick and wild, every shade of color visible among them, and I knew I could not resist its lure. As I entered, the plants grew thicker and higher until I felt engulfed in their beauty. A muted trickle of water enticed me further, until I reached a small opening where the path ended.

My breath caught at the sight before me. A large stone wall with crawling ivy lined the back of the private alcove where a small, flowing waterfall led to a life-size statue at its base. The statue was done in a shimmering marble and displayed a woman holding an infant in her arms. The woman stood, her dress and hair seeming to flow around her in the wind, as she looked on the small bundle she held. I drew closer in astonishment. Her face was solemn, and her expression portrayed an emotion I was not even aware could be captured in stone—worry. Her shoulders were drawn forward as though she meant to shelter the child from a great weight being pressed upon her. I reached my hand out to touch the child and the chill of the stone flowed through me.

"It is a surprise for Lady Eliza."

I startled at the sound of Edwin's voice but refused to turn and meet his gaze.

"I saw the sculpture while in London and knew it had to come to Timpton."

"It is beautiful," I said without moving.

"I will show her once the hired man finishes the waterfall." I looked to the side and only then realized it was not yet finished.

"Was this the project you spoke about to your grounds keeper?" I asked, trying to delay the inevitable accusation that was coming.

"It was. Do you think she will like it?"

"It is perfect," I whispered.

Silence overtook our conversation and I still could not

find the strength to look at him. I heard his footsteps on the stone path as he drew nearer. "Why did you send me to speak with your cousin?"

I thought the answer would be obvious with her declaration of feelings for Lord Ramsby. Had she seen Edwin and changed her mind? The thought sent my heart racing. "I knew Helena wished to speak with you," my tone betrayed my uncertainty.

"So she could tell me she had developed an affection for Lord Ramsby?"

He waited patiently, and I knew he probably wanted me to explain my part in her betrayal before he placed his accusation. I took a deep breath. "I encouraged her."

"Why?" his voice was soft but demanding.

"I know you do not believe in love, but I do, and I could not let you marry someone who did not love you."

I felt the warmth of his hand on mine and he drew me toward him, lifting my chin so my eyes met his tormented gaze.

"Why?" He came nearer, and I could now feel his warmth on me.

"Because I know the loneliness that living without love brings." My words came quickly, as though I had only a moment to make him understand before he forever shut his heart to me. "Because I know the influence love can have if you let it. And because you deserve to be loved for who you are, not for what you can offer."

"Is there no other reason for your interference besides altruism?"

I pulled back. Surely, he could not think my actions selfish? What motivation did I have to separate Edwin from my cousin, other than that I cared about what he had to endure? And suddenly I knew what he was asking me.

My thoughts raced to keep up with the pace of my heart. Was he asking how I felt about him? If I had intervened because I could not bear to have him end up with Helena? I was certain that had not been my motivation. Had I remained unaware that she truly did not care for him, I was prepared to leave without a word. My only concern was to see him happy, or at least satisfied in his choice.

But my reasoning betrayed me, for I knew how exceptionally pleased I had been at Helena's admission, how I had felt a need to justify my actions in encouraging her away from Edwin. My guilt was sufficient evidence of my selfishness. Though I had not intentionally acted in my own self-interest, my heart verified I had done just that. I did not want him to be with Helena because I wanted him to be with me.

My throat suddenly felt tight, and I attempted to hide away the discovery before he could see it within me. The tormented look in his eyes was because of me, because I convinced Helena to change her course. I knew she and Edwin would have been content with each other, and I knew he would not be able to forgive me for doing what I had done.

His eyes still searched mine, aching for my honesty. I could not appease him, but I could not lie so I did not speak.

He brought his hand to my face and gently rubbed his thumb over my lip where I was biting it to keep it from quivering. "Perhaps I'm asking the wrong question." His voice grew soft, "You know I have lost all confidence in love. It has proved itself to not only be useless, but a deceptive emotion. Yet despite my well-contrived reasoning, you have informed me you hold a different opinion?"

"It is not an opinion," I said, my tone resolute. "As well contrived as your reasons may be, you are not considering love but only love's imitations. It is impossible to form an accurate conclusion on misinformation."

A grin lifted one side of his mouth. "I forgot that you are an expert on the subject." I scoffed as he continued, "But I'll count it a good thing, for in my current state I find myself in need of enlightenment."

He gave a rueful smile. "A man once loved a girl. She was beautiful and enlivening and exactly what he believed he wanted. He doted on her and she endlessly flattered him, consuming his thoughts with the next time he could see her, the next time he could gaze into her eyes or take her hand in his." His eyes skirted over my face, but I refused to reveal my irritation at his description of Miss Madeline. "He knew she liked the idea of his wealth and he liked the idea of having her as his wife, a sort of prize to exhibit. Besides, they were a handsome match, and he was certain they could find contentment together." He paused. "Is this not love?"

"To clarify, I never claimed to be an expert. But, if I must render a judgment, I do not believe that is love. Perhaps it has pieces resembling love, but a counterfeit is not convincing if it does not hold some truth, twisted as it might be."

"A counterfeit?" he asked, and I felt as though he was baiting me.

"Yes. Love is not infatuation nor ambition. This girl you speak of was apparently lovely, and it seems evident there was an attraction between you... I mean them," I said purposefully but more harshly than I meant to. Yet, to my dismay, the only effect it had was to widen Edwin's smile. "Although natural desires for closeness are part of love, when it is the only part it becomes infatuation, which is certainly an imitation." He nodded smugly, but I wasn't yet finished, "And ambition is self-serving, making it contrary to the truth that love is unconditional. Therefore, choosing someone based on what they could offer you cannot be love."

His brow lifted in amusement. "A most interesting lecture, Miss Blakeslee."

"It was you who sought my opinion," I countered, uninterested at his apparent enjoyment.

"And will you grant me another analysis?" Before I could deny my consent, he began, "A man has realized he is completely besotted by a woman. He thinks about her constantly, her mesmerizing eyes, about running his fingers through her soft hair, and kissing her perfect lips."

I blushed as he looked at my lips. Insufferable man, surely this would be my punishment for what I had done—receiving his brazen teasing while he expressed his feelings for my cousin.

He laughed in apparent enjoyment at my discomfort. "But he also thinks about her kindness, her endearing personality, and the way she makes him want to be better, so he can be worthy of her. She means the world to him and he would do anything to protect her and honor the woman she is—a woman who is bright, captivating, and enchanting beyond description."

I didn't want to validate him, admitting it was like incriminating myself. Hesitantly I confirmed what he already knew. "That sounds more like love." My heart ached, and I turned my gaze back to the statue. "I didn't realize you felt that way— I am sorry."

"You're sorry?" I could hear the smile leave his voice.

I did not want to, but I looked back into the grief that filled his eyes, wanting him to see how sorry I truly was. "I should not have interfered, I did not realize how strong your affection for Helena was, though I'm certain she did not return nor deserve it."

His brow lowered, and his eyes narrowed. "Surely you know...." A smile once again appeared on his lips. "Let me amend the list I have just given. It turns out although bright, she might not be as astute as I have given her credit; or, a more likely assessment, I very much lack in my abilities to get my point across."

Now I was thoroughly confused. Had he not just described his feelings for Helena? My eyes moved back and forth between his, trying to discern his meaning.

"Let me be more direct. Abigail, you are the most enchanting woman I have ever known. You have found your way into my every thought, my every action, and my every desire. I believe you were correct in your assessment of how I feel, though it may have taken me a while to learn what you have already known about real love."

I brought my hand to my mouth in stunned silence.

"Abigail, you are absolutely maddening, and I love you."

I reached out toward him to steady my legs. "Me?"

He looked ready to laugh. "Of course you."

"But...but you were going to marry Helena! Are you not disappointed I have motivated her to pursue Lord Ramsby?"

"Helena?" He lifted his eyebrow in mock disbelief. "I just confessed my unfathomable love for you, not to mention my renewed belief in it, and you want to talk of another woman? Maddening indeed." He let out a small chuckle but when I continued to watch him, wide-eyed, he gave an understanding smile. "I can see that your curiosity needs to be appeased before mine can be placated."

He paused briefly before continuing, "I always knew Miss Hanford did not love me, and since I did not believe in love, I was fine accepting it. I had no hope to feel differently and when Lady Eliza told me of your aunt's desires to come to Timpton and further the connection between our families, I decided if it wasn't her it would be another like her, so I agreed, tired of putting off the inevitable. The first few days she was at Timpton, I committed myself to the idea and mentioned my intentions to ask for her hand. Then out of nowhere you arrived. From the first moment I saw you I felt bewitched, not simply by your beauty but by the goodness that exudes from you." The way he smiled at me set my heart pounding and I moved both hands to my chest in an attempt to restrain it.

"That first evening, when I was introduced to you with your genuine nature and feisty temper, I began guarding my heart against betraying me, against allowing myself to feel again. Though I wouldn't admit it to myself, I stood no chance; from that first exchange I ached to be with you. Every time I realized how superior you were to any lady I had ever met, I forced myself to push it from my thoughts, and you with it.

"Remember the time you thought I was cross with you for your word selection in our discussion on aiding the poor?"

"Worthy," I offered with a shaky smile.

"Precisely—that the poor are worthy of our help." He chuckled softly as though remembering the confrontation before explaining the humor in it. "My strong response was out of utter frustration. I was in the midst of an internal rebuke for siding with you and not Helena, when you spoke the exact phrase I had given earlier as my reasoning for aiding the Braggs. It instantly drove me to madness—the realization that you were everything I desired, and I could not have you." He shook his head. "I was forced to leave or risked revealing the discontent within me. I was courting Miss Hanford and had as good as promised she should expect an offer; I could not go back on my word simply because my intent had wavered."

"Like Miss Madeline had done to you?"

He nodded, apparently not surprised I knew her name. "That first day when Lord Ramsby unexpectedly showed up with Ross and Luke, I allowed myself to hope he would draw away Miss Hanford's attentions with his title and free me of my obligation. But before we even reached Timpton, who should he see but you in all your perfection—his immediate interest was obvious.

"I was confounded at how enraged I became every time he sought out your company." His jaw clenched reminding me of the first time I'd met Lord Ramsby and how upset Edwin had seemed. "I believe I did a poor job at concealing my irritation."

He paused, waiting to see if I would contradict his admission but when all I offered was a weak smile he nodded. "I wanted nothing more than to be with you, and I found every excuse within limits to do so, yet I felt I was in turmoil—longing to be with you when my obligation to your cousin prevented it. Besides, I was certain I had no chance of procuring your affection even if I managed to free myself from my commitment to Miss Hanford, so I continued along my preconceived path."

"What led you to believe I would not return your affection?" I asked, suddenly realizing there were plenty of reasons he could have come to such a conclusion, most of them having to do with my sharp tongue and hasty temper.

"Certainly, the daughter of someone as highly regarded as Lord Blakeslee would set her hopes for a match higher than a *nouveau riche* with no title. Besides, Lord Ramsby is a seemingly charming fellow, with much to offer..." His voice trailed off. "And that day we spoke in the library I assumed your description of love was intended to declare your feelings for him, a tactful correction of my undesired attention."

"You thought I spoke of Lord Ramsby?" I asked, recalling my confusion at his odd reaction.

His cheeks darkened at his admission and I couldn't help but smile. "I am embarrassed to say, in my irrational state, I did. And it wasn't until you spoke of your parents, the night you told of them taking you in and how their love saved you, that I finally made the connection. It gave me hope. Hope that perhaps you were not yet settled on your feelings."

"It would not have mattered what my feelings were, Lord Ramsby would not have accepted me with my tainted past." Edwin took a step closer, closing the space between us and making my voice catch. "He didn't even know a small portion of what I endured, and he could not accept me." My voice grew quiet and I felt the warmth of Edwin's hand on mine giving me the strength to continue. "Not that I needed it, but it made me wonder if others could accept me when they found out—if you would."

One of his hands came to my waist as the other one

cradled the back of my head, sending a warm sensation through me. "You couldn't tell me anything that would make me love you less. In fact, I am certain, every new thing I learn about you only adds to my admiration and devotion."

Tears spilled down my cheeks. Edwin loved me! He accepted me with all my faults, with all I had been through! I could hardly breathe at the realization, when he pulled me gently to him. "And now, it is your turn."

"My turn?" I managed to ask, staring into his light eyes.

His perfect lips curled into another charming smile. "To placate my curiosity."

Lifting my arms around his neck I leaned even closer to him, our lips nearly touching. "Well, Mr. Stanton—" I said, my voice shaking.

His breath was warm on my face. "Edwin, if you please."

"Edwin..." I whispered readily. But how could I put into words all that I felt, all that he had done for me, and what he meant to me? I looked from his lips back to his eyes that eagerly awaited my confirmation. But the moment and his nearness rendered me speechless, there was no way to adequately tell him.

Without a word I tightened my arms around his neck and pulled him toward me, closing the last bit of space between our lips. I kissed him deeply, allowing every feeling and emotion inside me to flow to him. He welcomed it and ran his hands from my waist to my neck and back again before settling on my back where his arms engulfed me and pulled me tightly against him. I could feel his chest rising and falling beneath mine as I ran my hands through his hair and to his jaw, feeling the motion of his kiss under my hand.

His kiss slowed, and his hands came to my waist. Reluctantly he pushed himself just out of reach, his handsome face smiling with satisfaction. "I do believe, your choice of communication was most—effective."

My face flushed with color as I placed my hands on his

chest, his heart racing nearly in rhythm with my own. "It seemed a more direct way to let you know how I feel." I reached my hand up and gently rubbed his bristled face. I traced his full lips with my finger and couldn't resist lifting my mouth to his and placing a soft kiss on them. He closed his eyes and I watched as he seemed to engrave the feeling in his mind, taking a deep breath before he opened his eyes and looked at me.

"I love you." My voice was quiet but sure.

"And I shall be grateful every day of my life for it," he said, suddenly lifting me in the air and spinning me. I laughed without restraint before he set me down in front of the stone wall, keeping me close in his embrace. "Assuming you will marry me."

"Of course I will!" I said beaming.

"You have saved me," the seriousness in his eyes stilled my heart. "It was no easy task to teach a man as arrogant and misled as me to love, yet you have managed it beautifully."

He looked at me so intently I was certain he was searching my soul, but this time I willingly let him, for I knew he would find nothing that would change his love for me. I held my breath as his hand seemed to mindlessly graze my cheek before his thumb settled on my lips. Edwin's eyes shifted to my mouth, as though he had just been made aware of his caress. He dragged his thumb downward causing my bottom lip to separate and he slowly brought his lips to intertwine mine.

His kiss was slow and restrained and I slid my arms under his waistcoat and around his back, wrapping my fingers in his shirt and drawing him to me. He removed his arms from around me and placed them on the stone wall. I felt an irrational desire as he kissed me and then once again he pulled away, this time putting more space between us.

"I do believe we should return to the house," he said, his chest rising and falling as he spoke. "I now fully understand what Lady Eliza has ingrained in me all these years—even the strongest men can stumble with the right temptation." A small grin came to his mouth, but I knew he meant what he said because I felt it too.

"I think that is a wise choice," I said, taking the arm he had offered me, half-heartedly cursing him at choosing to be a gentleman at the most inopportune moment.

~

As we walked back into Diana's room, Diana and Lady Eliza shared a knowing glance.

"It is official then?" Diana asked without hesitation.

"I still must ask her father's permission, Diana," Edwin answered with a smile. "But I do believe you will have your way." He looked at me with an endearing smile. "Are you positive you can endure having such a meddlesome sister?"

"Somehow I shall manage," I said, giving Diana a grateful smile.

Lady Eliza rushed to us and wrapped her arms around us. "I couldn't be happier for you both."

"Thank you," I said, looking from her to Edwin who wore a mischievous grin.

"Yes, Lady Eliza, and thank you also for teaching me the art of self-restraint. I now see the logic in your years of warnings as well as your particular cautioning against finding myself alone with Abigail."

"Your longing for one another was evident," Lady Eliza said smiling apologetically. "I did not wish to see either of you hurt by the consequences of passion."

"And rightfully so," Edwin said, grabbing my hand. "I have hardly felt such a lack of self-control as when I was kissing Abigail just now in the garden." An exasperating smile lit his face and I froze in shock as he continued, "I do believe a short engagement would be preferable, do you not agree darling?"

The whole room filled with laughter as my mouth opened in disbelief.

Bringing his hand to my chin he steadied his laughter. "I'm sorry," he said, lowering his mouth to mine and kissing me in front of everyone. "I just didn't want them to think I had waited this long to finally kiss you." I looked around cautiously at the smiling faces and felt relief that they seemed unaffected by such a public display. "And I will not embarrass you further by divulging to our parents what a spectacular kisser you are."

"You are insufferable!" I said in dismay.

"And you are utterly maddening, and I love you," he said, bringing his lips to mine again. I thought of refusing him but found that I couldn't as the room once again filled with laughter.

CHAPTER 19

*D*iana took several weeks to recover, and while she did, we filled our days with all sorts of *chaperoned* diversions. We walked often to the Bragg's cottage to play with the children and talk with Mrs. Bragg who was still weak but recovering daily. Dr. Walter called it a miraculous recovery, and I didn't doubt his claim for a moment, though I was certain no one deserved a miracle more than those sweet children.

Mrs. Bragg was most grateful for our assistance, but not as grateful as Silas appeared when Edwin told him he would teach him to ride and offered him a job as an apprentice stable hand. He also offered Mrs. Bragg a job as one of Timpton's launderers when she fully recovered. The clothes would be brought to her and picked up, so she could remain at home with her children. I was surprised to hear the salary of a launderer at Timpton, though I wondered if it may have received a charitable inflation with the way Mrs. Bragg's eyes lit up at the offer.

Edwin set out to help me overcome my past aversion to riding, and I was surprised at how natural it soon felt to sit high above the ground when I was in control of the reins. I found it quite liberating and enjoyable, though I still preferred sharing a saddle with Edwin, his strong arms wrapped around me. These were some of the only moments we had to talk alone, as the groom kept a good distance from us while we were riding. Only once, when we had stopped to picnic one afternoon, did the groom need to clear his throat as a reminder of his presence.

The rest of our time was spent keeping Diana company, having invigorating conversations with Uncle Stanton, or speaking with Lady Eliza of wedding plans. Presuming Father would have little inclination for arranging such things, and feeling it to be her motherly obligation, she gladly took on the responsibility.

Lady Eliza sent a letter to Sir Wycliffe letting him know that, if the group desired it, Doctor Walter had deemed Timpton safe for visitors again. Sir Wycliffe replied insisting he was very much enjoying hosting and, if it would not be too bold, he would very much like to keep the current arrangement. Lady Eliza did not press the issue but sent a response assuring that an invitation for the promised ball would be forthcoming when the date was decided.

Edwin wrote to Father to invite both him and Laurence to Timpton. He stated his hope to announce our engagement at the upcoming ball if Father, upon meeting Edwin, found him worthy of my hand. I was delighted Father accepted the invitation without delay.

～

I LOOKED around at the small group who had gathered to welcome Father and Laurence. I was especially glad Diana was feeling well enough to join us, though Mr. Ellis supported her firmly at the elbow as we waited. We could now see their carriage approaching, and I smiled with excitement; soon all the people I loved most would be in one place. I squeezed Edwin's hand and glanced up at him, surprised to find a distant look in his eyes.

"He is one of the kindest men you will ever meet, and you know Laurence is no different," I said, placing a quick kiss on his cheek. He granted me a small lift of the corners of his mouth. "They shall love you as I do."

"I have little to offer you," his eyes looked heavy with realization. "You could have any man, surely your father will think you are settling."

"Do you not remember how Lord Ramsby reacted when he discovered my past? I am certain there are a limited number of gentlemen willing to overlook such a history. I'm just grateful I fell in love with one who would."

"Lord Ramsby is a fool," he said harshly.

I looked with concern at his tightened jaw.

"I'm sorry," he said, looking down at me and releasing a heavy exhale. "I just don't know what I shall do if your father refuses me."

"He will do no such thing, Edwin. Father cares only for my happiness."

He looked at me with longing despair, as though the bliss we had been living in was about to forever be taken from him with all his hopes of our future.

I felt like making light of his needless worry, but I could not tease him in his grief. I knew that the idea of not being enough had once had a detrimental effect on him. "My father is not Miss Madeline's father. If you are enough for me, you will be enough for him."

As the carriage rolled up, I squeezed his hand and took a step toward it in anticipation. Laurence sprang from the door first and wrapped me in his brotherly embrace. "Oh, how we have missed you, Abee!" he exclaimed pulling back and appraising me fondly. "Though I wonder if you have missed us at all," he said with a laugh.

"You know I have missed you both terribly," I said as Father walked toward me. His arms engulfed me, and he held me longer than I had expected, but I gladly welcomed it.

Finally releasing his grip, he turned to Lady Eliza. "And you are Lady Eliza, I assume?"

When she nodded, he walked to her and grabbed her hands affectionately. "How you must have ached for your child." I knew he would be happy to meet her after I received his response to my letter, but I was thrilled to see the nervous look on Lady Eliza's face dissipate at Father's kindness toward her.

"As I'm certain you understand," she said graciously.

They sat a moment in shared grief before he turned to Mr. Stanton and shook his hand, exchanging greetings.

"Now Abigail, where is this fellow of yours? Let us see if he is worthy of my little girl."

Edwin shifted nervously as we approached. "Father, this is Mr. Edwin Stanton."

Edwin shook his hand firmly. "I'm pleased to finally meet you," he said, his voice stiff and his brow set low.

I hadn't seen him look so stern in weeks and Father sent me a questioning glance. "It is a privilege to be here. Thank you for the invitation."

"It's great to see you again," Laurence said stepping up with an extended hand.

Edwin seemed to ease somewhat as he shook Laurence's hand. "It's been far too long. Had I known you had such an enchanting sister, I would have invited you ages ago."

The group laughed, and my heart lifted as I turned to introduce Father and Laurence to the rest of the group.

As we walked into the house, Laurence spoke of their trip from Easton Manor and reflected on how dull it had been without me there.

"And how has Lydia been getting on?" Laurence smiled

brightly, but I knew him well enough to see the concern beneath his question.

"Very well," I said, reassuring him. "I believe there is a beau from the village pursuing her, though she is hesitant to speak of it."

He nodded thoughtfully. "That does not surprise me."

"Which?" I asked, confused at his melancholy expression.

He raised his eyebrows as though he was unsure of what we spoke of.

"Which is not surprising? That a beau is pursuing Lydia or that she will not speak of it?"

"Oh," he nodded his recognition. "I suppose both."

The disappointment in Laurence's conclusion pulled at my sisterly discernment and I knew I could not leave the subject there.

"You must be tired from your journey." Mr. Stanton's voice stole my attention as he spoke with Father. "Would you care to rest before dinner?"

"I shall find it easier to rest once I have spoken to your son and analyzed every bit of his character." Edwin stiffened at my side as Father turned toward us, a feigned grimace on his face. "Shall we?"

I thought to scold him for his chosen charade of intimidating father, but before I could, Edwin gave a brief nod and stepped from my side. My own heart began to race as they walked in the direction of the study, though I was positive it wasn't because I was nervous of Father refusing the match.

The rest of us made our way to the sitting room where the Stantons engaged Laurence in conversation. I watched the clock on the mantel tick by. The minutes since they had left felt nearly as long as those when I first arrived at Easton Manor—an orphan under consideration. Looking toward the door I wondered if I could find a way to slip out unnoticed, so I could hear what was being said.

As I pondered a plan, Diana neared me. "I always

wondered what Mr. Ellis and my father spoke of when he asked for my hand." She offered a mischievous smile. "I will make your excuses if you long to listen in." I smiled appreciatively and without a second thought I rushed from the room.

I approached the study quietly and pressed my ear to the door. I could hear muted voices inside but couldn't decipher what was being said. Realizing the wood was too thick and the keyhole more secure than ours at Easton Manor, I went to see if the adjoining library door could offer me a more advantageous spot for eaves-dropping.

I peeked into the library, pleased to discover the study door slightly ajar on the far side of the room. I could now discern Father's voice, and I eagerly made my way toward it. In my impatience, I brushed against a table where a small stack of books rested. The stack shifted to the edge as I passed, and I quickly reached out my hand to steady it. The hasty motion sent the top book flying from the stack and I winced as it tumbled to the ground with a thud.

Drats! I held my breath, waiting to see if I would be discovered. After several long moments, I was relieved my folly had gone unnoticed and I more cautiously finished my walk across the room.

"...though you could offer her little more than your devotion? I have an inheritance enough for her as well as my love —she needs more!" My breath seemed to leave me, unwilling to return. Father sounded upset, an emotion I rarely heard unless he was—defending me. But surely, he would not object, not after years of caring only for my security and happiness. "She needs a man who will push her to rise to her full potential in Society. I have raised her for it and I demand it!" I could not understand why he would say such a thing.

"But, sir..." Edwin's voice sounded stiff.

"Do not 'sir' me! You will not marry my daughter and that is final!"

My heart dropped in my chest and I leapt through the

door, not sure of my next action, but positive I had to do something. "Father," I cried, running to him and grabbing his arm. "You cannot mean it!" I glanced up to find an amused expression on his face. I looked to Edwin who wore an apologetic grin.

"You!" I said, taking a step back and pointing to Father accusingly before turning my finger on Edwin. "And you! I shall never forgive either of you. What a foul trick to play!"

Father could hardly get a word out between bursts of laughter. "Don't blame him, Abigail, it was all me. We heard the clatter in the library and I was certain it was my ever-curious daughter, come to make sure her father was being fair to the man she loves. I insisted Edwin go along, and how could he refuse his soon-to-be father-in-law? I am a most intimidating man." It had been a while since I had seen Father laugh so hard and even in my irritation, I felt a smile coming to my lips.

"You are both incorrigible and I hope I'm not seeing a glimpse into my future with the two of you taking sides against me."

I shot Edwin a pointed glare, but it was ineffective as his shoulders now shook with laughter. He walked toward me, with an air of complete contentment. "You best be careful not to appear so charming while you are mad, or I fear I shall make a point of provoking you regularly."

I narrowed my eyes at him. "I believe you have made that point quite regularly since my arrival."

He smiled too endearingly and lifted my hand to his lips. "You must find it a charming quality, if you have fallen in love with me."

"I have fallen in love with you despite it," I said with a teasing smile. "Think how much I should love you if you stopped persistently vexing me."

He lifted a playful brow. "But love is unconditional, Abigail, you said so yourself."

"He's got you there," Father agreed. His face still shone with laughter, but his voice grew sincere. "You have found yourself a most admirable gentleman, Abigail. One with so very much to offer. He is the kind of man your mother and I had hoped you would find, and I feel no reservation in bestowing my consent for your marriage."

I jumped into his arms and hugged him tightly around his neck.

"Though I must demand you do not spend all your time away from me. Easton Manor has been awfully dull with just Laurence as company." He pulled back until he held my hands, rubbing the tops of them as he always did. "You are a lucky man," he said, looking at Edwin. "I don't believe there is a finer woman, or a braver one."

"I am certain there is not," he said, putting his arm around my waist. "And I shall never let her forget it, sir."

"Sir? I insist you call me Father," he said, releasing my hands and bringing his right hand down heavily on Edwin's shoulder. "As I'm sure Abigail must certainly call Lady Eliza 'Mother' and Mr. Stanton 'Father.' The transition will be quite easy, and no one will be the wiser." Hearing his permission to call Lady Eliza 'Mother' caught me off guard but I smiled at the idea and his generosity for offering it. "Now, I'm in need of some refreshment—why don't you two escort me back through this maze, so none of our party gets lost along the way." His wink in our direction made me blush. "I'd hate for Mr. Stanton and Lady Eliza to accuse me of shirking my chaperonial duties."

As we entered the sitting room, everyone stopped talking and looked apprehensively in our direction. The smiles on our faces confirmed the good news and they clapped their hands in excitement.

"I take it by the clapping that all has gone well?" Uncle Stanton asked excitedly. "Has Edwin become the luckiest man in all England?"

"It is official Uncle, I am the luckiest of men the world over." Edwin beamed down at me before looking back to Uncle Stanton. "I suppose you should like to boast of your foresight on the subject and your insight into Abigail's superior character?"

"Is it not ironic that the man without sight could best see the situation?" A self-congratulating smile filled his face. "But let's not dwell on me right now and my exceptional abilities, for there shall be plenty of time for that later. Let us offer our congratulations!"

As though permission had been granted, the Stantons arose from their seats. Lady Eliza came first with arms outstretched, looking overjoyed.

"Mother," I said as I lifted my arms toward her. Her eyes filled with tears hearing me call her what she had been longing for and she wrapped her arms around me.

"I can't believe how this has all turned out," she said, placing a kiss on both of my cheeks. "A few weeks ago, I would have never thought such a thing possible. But here you are," she said, rubbing my cheek softly before turning to Edwin, "and you have found her for me."

"I have found her for us both," Edwin said, grabbing my hand and bringing it to his lips.

"Don't forget me," Diana said, walking up to give me a hug. "I have been in desperate need of a sister my whole life, and I must say I have chosen well. It is a good thing Edwin is not as daft as I had thought him all this time. It isn't every brother who will adhere to the council of his younger sister, as wise as she might be." She gave Edwin a playful look before the two embraced.

"It seems the entire family was rooting for you, Abigail," Mr. Stanton said, approaching us and placing a kiss on my cheek. "And I must say I am thrilled to welcome you to our family, yet again."

I hardly knew what to say to all the admiring faces, so I did not speak but sat beaming, soaking in a lifetime of love. After Laurence and Mr. Ellis gave their congratulations we sat around talking and telling stories for hours, Edwin sitting near, just like I preferred. Father and Laurence offered every embarrassing experience that involved me they could think of, yet it seemed a worthwhile exchange to hear the ones the Stantons told of Edwin.

When it was time to get ready for dinner, Father escorted me to my room. As I showed him the view from my window, his eyes grew solemn and he turned to me. "I'm sorry if I caused you grief, asking you to keep your past a secret. I am not ashamed of you." He looked forcefully into my eyes, assuring me of the truth in his declaration. "I just didn't want anyone else to hurt you."

I reached up and placed my hand on his cheek. "I know, Father."

"People are too often blinded to a person's goodness because of circumstances they had no choice in. Your mother and I didn't want that for you. We wanted to protect you...we thought others wouldn't understand."

I put my arm through his and rested my head on his shoulder, turning my attention toward the setting sun on the horizon. "And few did understand, but the ones who did are the ones worth keeping."

He kissed the top of my head. "My brave girl."

The door opened, and we turned to find Lydia looking giddy with excitement. "I have heard it is official!" She hurried toward us. "And hello, Lord Blakeslee," she said as he stretched out his arms to give her a hug.

"Thank you for taking care of my girl and for your occasional updates." I looked at Lydia in surprise, and she whispered a quick 'sorry' in my direction. "I scarcely received a letter from Abigail before she wrote of the discovery with Lady Eliza and her love for Edwin. I should have been utterly shocked had you not kept Laurence well informed."

He turned his gaze back to me, but I kept my eyes on Lydia, wondering what she had felt relevant to tell my brother and why she had not said anything to me about it.

"And don't look so betrayed, Abigail, she did you a great service in her explanations, painting you to be quite the heroine of your story. If anything, you should be thanking her and promising to reward her how she sees fit."

My eyes went to her widening smile that I loved so well.

"A sufficient reward would be remaining with you when you marry," Lydia said, her sincere smile turning calculated. "And perhaps a new dress?"

I laughed. "I would not think of having anyone else," I said, grabbing her hand. "And you shall certainly have a new dress, for it would not do to have my bridesmaid in anything but the latest fashion—whatever that is!"

"Your bridesmaid?" Lydia looked stunned. "But I am a servant, surely that is unheard of."

"The Blakeslee's are not people who conform to the shallow ways of Society, or have you not heard?" I asked, grinning. "And besides, at this point I think very few people would be shocked by my choice. You have been my dearest companion since I first arrived at Easton Manor, so it seems a most fitting invitation for you."

"I just don't think—" Lydia looked from me to Father and then back to me.

"You are the maid of a bride are you not? Think of it like that and it might not seem nearly as unseemly."

"I very much agree," Father said decisively. "With you, Mrs. Ellis, and Lady Eliza assisting with plans, Abigail may have a fashionable wedding after all."

"Thank you for your confidence," I said, feigning offense.

"We must all have weaknesses, my dear girl," he said with a

grin as he turned to walk toward the door. "I shall see you at dinner."

When he left, I returned my gaze to Lydia who brimmed with joy. "Thank you," she said, walking to my side and wrapping her arms around me.

"Thank you," I said, returning the gesture. "For everything!"

CHAPTER 20

*T*he next few days were filled with preparations for the ball. It was to be a simple country ball, just as I preferred, with only a few close family friends, neighbors, and relatives. The night of the ball, Lydia performed beyond her typical abilities, and I felt remarkably beautiful as I looked in the mirror at my reflection. She had chosen the rose-pink muslin gown with gold embroidery, and I was pleased with the soft golden shimmer it pulled from my skin as well as the pink in my cheeks and lips.

Diana peeked into the room. "Are you ready, Abigail? Guests will be arriving soon." She walked toward me, a smile growing on her face as she got closer. "I cannot wait to see the look on Edwin's face when he sees you," she said excitedly.

I glanced at Lydia who looked beautiful in one of my gowns, styling her own hair in front of the mirror.

"Would you like us to wait for you?" Diana asked kindly to Lydia. "Or I could send for my maid to assist you in getting ready?"

"Oh no, I am quite practiced putting my own hair up.

Besides, Laurence—I mean Mr. Blakeslee," Lydia said, glancing at Diana who appeared unaffected by the familiarity, "will escort me down before the ball begins." I couldn't overlook the way she blushed when she mentioned my brother's name. "As long as I don't faint in fright, I shall be well enough."

"It will be better to not make you suffer through the monotonous welcoming of the guests, though poor Abigail has no choice." Diana grabbed my arm and began leading me to the door.

"I shall see you down there," I said to Lydia, still thrilled she had agreed to join us with only an extremely relentless amount of coaxing on mine and Laurence's part.

"Of course," she said, still smiling as we walked out the door.

As we reached the top of the stairs, I could see Edwin talking with Mr. Ellis in the entry hall below. He looked especially handsome in his double-breasted tailcoat, his hair sweeping forward. My heart fluttered in my chest as I took my first step toward him. Mr. Ellis nudged Edwin who immediately turned toward us. The look on his face did not disappoint. He stood frozen, mouth slightly opened, watching my every movement as we descended. I blushed under his attentive gaze.

"Mr. Ellis," Diana said as we neared the bottom of the stairs, "surely you could follow Edwin's example and be a little more ostentatious in your admiration of me. Romance is not only for the unmarried!"

A grin came to Mr. Ellis's face. "If you could see my heart, you would not scold me so. It looks very much as aghast as Edwin now does. I have simply had more time to practice reminding my jaw to stay put so I don't look a baffling idiot every time I encounter your beauty."

Edwin did not take his eyes from me but promptly closed his mouth as Mr. Ellis gave a chuckle.

Diana accepted Mr. Ellis's arm, contented as they walked toward the sitting room.

"You are breathtaking," Edwin said, grabbing my hand and kissing it.

"Thank you. I suppose we shall be an equal match for the evening."

"I don't think I will ever be an equal match to you in that regard," he said, tucking my arm under his elbow with an endearing look on his face. "But I take comfort in knowing it would be impossible for any gentleman to accomplish such a feat, so I'm doing you no disservice in my company."

My face was still pink with color as we walked through the sitting room door to join the others.

"How beautiful you look," Father said, stepping up to kiss my cheek as Edwin continued on to speak with his father.

Tears blurred my vision at the look of unreserved admiration in his eyes. "How I wish Mother could be here with us," I managed with a shaky smile.

"But she is, my darling girl," Father said with a gentle expression, lifting his hand to my cheek. "All the best of her is reflected in you. In your goodness. In your abilities. In your love for others. Your mother is here—always—in you."

The truth in his declaration seeped into me and a tear slipped down my cheek.

"Come now, Father," Laurence said, moving to my side with a grin. "Abigail wears most things well, but tears are not one of them. Surely you do not wish for her to welcome the forthcoming guests with a splotchy face and swollen eyes."

I swatted at Laurence, but my laugh betrayed my intended display of exasperation at his brotherly jest.

"Everyone must have a weakness," Father said with a wink before he turned to speak with Uncle Stanton.

Laurence wrapped an arm around my shoulder and leaned close. "I meant to thank you for inviting Lydia to join us tonight."

I narrowed my eyes and appraised him. "She is my best friend," I said simply. "Regardless of what others might think, I want her to be a part of the festivities."

He nodded, but his face began to redden under my persistent gaze.

"Is there something you wish to tell me?"

His eyes held mine for a moment before he shook his head. "Nothing that can't wait. Tonight is about you, dearest sister." I jabbed at his rib with my elbow and he chuckled. "I'm proud of you," he said with a sideways glance, his voice turning serious.

I leaned my head on his shoulder, allowing him to pull me closer. "I'm so glad you're here."

Father cleared his throat and the attention of the room shifted to him. "I believe we should discuss how to proceed this evening."

Mother glanced at me before returning her regard to Father. "I assume you are referring to which truths we should disclose and which ones we should not?"

"Precisely," he said, with a nod. "I think it would be wise for us to come to a unified answer before we separate."

She looked back to me. "What would be easiest for you?"

My face warmed as I felt everyone's gaze shift in my direction. "I think what they know is sufficient. I am an orphaned ward who has been raised as Lord and Lady Blakeslee's daughter."

"I am willing to share my past," Mother said. "I do not want you to bear the weight of it all."

I looked from her to Father, who watched patiently. Here was a chance to officially declare myself the daughter of Lady Eliza, an opportunity to share some of the burden of my past. I would no longer have to hide who I was; I could be liberated.

I looked from Mother to Diana and then into the loving gaze of Edwin and I knew I had already been liberated, that

313

redemption does not come by placating the curiosity of others but by sharing the truth with those that matter. "I value your willingness Mother, but I do not see a reason for it. There will be little change in how I am viewed regardless, let us keep what we know between us."

"But I yearn to make things right," she said, her voice pleading to make amends.

"You have," I said, walking toward her. "Surely the years of torment you have faced have absolved any wrongdoing long ago. And the love you never ceased to have for me has brought me back to you." She wiped a tear from her face and threw her arms around me.

The group sat quietly watching when Baldwin entered. He looked around hesitantly before announcing, "The first carriage just arrived. Mrs. Hanford, her daughters, Sir Wycliffe and Lord Ramsby."

Mr. Stanton glanced at the clock. "They are early," he said, looking to Mother for how to proceed.

"We will come straightway," she said, looking apprehensively at me and Edwin. Baldwin nodded and left the room to inform the arriving party we would be there momentarily. "There is wisdom in the council Lord Blakeslee spoke when he first arrived—it will be easier to enjoy our night if we first handle the more difficult task at hand."

My heart pounded as Edwin walked to my side and offered me his arm, a look of agreement on his face. As the party followed Mr. Stanton and Mother back to the entry hall, I could feel Edwin's gaze on me.

"What if she is livid with me—if she feels as though I somehow tricked her?"

"I think you overestimate her attachment to me, Abigail," he whispered.

As we stepped into the entryway, Helena's gaze fell on my hand placed on Edwin's arm and her eyes narrowed. I shifted uncomfortably but before I could remove it, he lifted his other hand and placed it firmly over the top of mine.

"Marianne," Father said warmly. "How are you?"

She quickly subdued the shock on her face as she welcomed his embrace. "Quite well, though I did not expect to find you and Laurence among our company."

"We couldn't help ourselves with how things have turned out."

She stiffened, and I wondered if the incriminating tone in Father's voice had been an intentional, albeit subtle, rebuke.

"Helena, Hannah, how lovely you both look." His voice lightened as he turned from Aunt Marianne to my cousins.

"Hello, Uncle Miles," they said nearly in unison.

"And who are these charming young gentlemen?"

Hannah smiled at Sir Wycliffe. "This is my fiancé, Sir Giles Wycliffe."

"It is a pleasure to meet you, Lord Blakeslee," Sir Wycliffe said with a large grin as they shook hands.

"I certainly agree," Father replied before turning his gaze expectantly to Helena.

"This is my fiancé, Lord Ramsby of Handsbury Castle."

My breath caught as I looked wide-eyed at Edwin whose face seemed to lighten at the idea.

"Fiancé? Well, well…" I could hear the smile in his voice though his back was to me. "Marianne, it seems your daughters have made exceptional matches."

"Yes, indeed," she said, though her gaze fell to Mother. "I'm sorry for our early arrival but I felt we must share with you our news before the other guests arrive." She seemed to relax as Mother offered a kind smile.

"We have our own joyful news to relay," Mother said, smiling in our direction.

Aunt Marianne's eyebrows lifted with curiosity as Helena's eyes shot in our direction.

"I have asked for Abigail's hand," Edwin said, smiling at me. "And, thankfully, she has accepted."

A small gasp escaped Helena and she quickly brought her hand to her mouth before returning it back to Lord Ramsby's arm. He shifted awkwardly as he tried to avoid looking at us. Hannah smiled in apparent amusement, as did Sir Wycliffe.

"Exceptional news," Aunt Marianne said with her tight voice and typical smug look. "Three weddings. How delightful!"

Conversation seemed to erupt at the idea, and the couples spread out to greet one another.

Hannah led Sir Wycliffe to us and threw her arms around my neck. "I'm so thrilled for you both!" she exclaimed. "Though I do hate to admit when Mother is right. When will the wedding be?"

"As soon as we can arrange it," Edwin said.

"Then you may very well be married before us," Hannah said, looking sympathetically at Sir Wycliffe. "Mother says we must marry at St. James' Church in London, though we are uncertain how soon it can be arranged with so many brides hoping to marry there. I'm at least relieved Helena and I convinced Mother a double wedding was out of the question."

I laughed at the relief on Hannah's face as well as the idea of Helena sharing her wedding day with anyone, especially her sister. "Well perhaps you could find some diversion in offering your assistance as I plan our wedding."

Hannah's face lit with excitement. "Certainly! And who else have you asked? Lady Eliza and Diana, of course...."

I nodded. "And Lydia—"

Hannah's brow wrinkled. "Lydia?"

"My maid."

Hannah processed the fact momentarily before accepting my odd ways. "Very well, anyone else?"

I looked hesitantly at Helena. She was my cousin, in some respect, but it seemed quite an odd choice with all that had passed between us. Yet perhaps there was a possibility for healing. "Helena, though I would not feel insulted if she refused."

Hannah glanced toward Helena and back at me in disbelief. "I should hardly like her to aid me with mine, though Mother says it is necessary. I don't believe you need to feel obligated to ask her."

I questioned myself for only a moment before settling on my decision. We were family. I needed to do my best to make things right between us regardless if she would welcome it or not.

"Are you speaking of me?" Helena asked, pulling a hesitant Lord Ramsby along.

Hannah smirked. "What gave you that impression?"

"Your blatant inability at discretion."

I cleared my throat, drawing the sisters' attention. "I was just asking Hannah if she would assist me with wedding plans."

"How delightful," Helena retorted, her mouth tightening into a smile.

"And I was hoping you could offer your expertise as well? I do believe it will take a team of ladies to offset someone as fashionably ignorant as myself."

Helena's eyes brimmed with suspicion. "You wish to obtain my opinion?"

"You are my cousin," I said with a nervous smile. "And I should very much like you to be a part of my wedding, if you are willing."

She looked back at Hannah with narrowed eyes, as though she was expecting to find herself at the center of some preplanned jest.

"Very well," she said, when she was assured of my sincerity. "Though I'm not confident how much time I can dedicate to the endeavor, as my own wedding plans will take precedence." Helena's gaze shifted to Edwin. "I am amazed at how beneficially things worked out—each of us has certainly found a more suitable match."

I tensed at the slight, but Edwin smiled down at me. "I-believe you are correct, Miss Hanford." His lips curled up to display a most heart-stopping smile. "Undeniably correct."

Helena turned her attention quickly to Lord Ramsby as Edwin wrapped my hand in his, a look of admiration on his face.

As our conversation resumed, I glanced around the room, finding Mother's anxious eyes on me. I gave her a smile and nodded my assurance that all was well. She looked relieved and returned her gaze to Aunt Marianne, taking a step closer to Mr. Stanton. I realized how closely I stood to Edwin and wondered if she was always so near her husband because he provided her strength like Edwin provided me. I squeezed Edwin's hand affectionately and he looked down at me.

"I love you," I whispered.

"And I love you," he whispered, making my heart stutter.

THE OTHER GUESTS started to arrive and were ushered into the ballroom where the musicians had begun playing and refreshments were being served. As the time came to enter the ballroom my legs felt unstable beneath me. Grateful for Edwin's support, we followed the others into the ballroom.

"You are biting your lip again," Edwin whispered looking toward me. "Is something the matter?"

"Have I mentioned I dislike balls?" My voice seemed to quake as I spoke.

"I don't believe you said it so outright, but you did not deny you dreaded the idea of a ball that first morning in the garden." I gave him a look to curtail his wicked smile, but it only made him chuckle.

"Infuriating man!" I said, trying not to laugh.

"But you know the dances?"

"Well enough. Though I have hardly danced them with partners other than Laurence or Father."

A gleam of excitement flashed in his eyes. "Then you have hardly danced them at all."

The room fell silent as Mr. Stanton took a step forward. "How glad we are to have you here with us. As much as we enjoy a ball, this one has a special purpose. My son, Edwin, will soon be married to Miss Abigail Blakeslee, daughter of Lord Blakeslee." Father waved at the mention of his name though all I offered was a nervous smile. "We are beyond thrilled with the match—"

"Here, here," came the booming voice of Uncle Stanton, making the room echo in laughter.

Mr. Stanton nodded before he continued, "As you can see —thrilled, and we truly feel fate has brought them together." I looked toward Mr. Stanton as he spoke, and he gave a wink in my direction. I had always been fond of him. "We will now be honored for them to lead out the dancing."

Edwin led me confidently to the center of the floor. Diana and Mr. Ellis followed, and soon other couples had lined up across from each other as the music began. I was glad to see Lydia partnered with Laurence and looking more composed than myself. It was a simple country dance and I somehow managed the steps, though I knew I did not look nearly as graceful as the other ladies.

"You are doing well," Edwin said, watching me.

"I fear I will be quite a dull partner, as I must concentrate on the steps."

Edwin smiled encouragingly, though I could see mischief behind his eyes.

With each partner change down the row, I grew more confident in the repetition of the movements.

"You are ready," Edwin said, smiling.

"For what?" I asked as we again partnered.

"To begin dancing." Suddenly I felt his hand on the small of my back heavier than he had previously allowed. My breath caught, but my feet managed to continue moving through the pattern. I followed him as we turned and began back in the direction we had just come, feeling warm under his focused attention.

As we joined the other couples and switched partners, I was desperate for him to return. The steps were the same, but the look in Edwin's eyes, his closeness, and the pressure of his hand kept the color in my cheeks, reassuring me the dance I now did differed greatly from the one we started. My body trembled, and my heart raced but my feet willed me on. I wondered how something so public could feel so intimate.

"How do you feel?" Edwin asked as he again circled me, only inches from my face and displaying the same mischievous smile from earlier.

My trembling hands hinted toward the effect of the firmness of his touch, but I simply smirked. "Quite confused."

As we came together again and danced down the rows of couples, he gave me a questioning glance.

"I thought it a simple country dance, even droll, when we first began," I said, turning back toward where we had just come, feeling the heat of Edwin's hand on my waist guiding me.

"And now?"

"And now it has elements of gentleness, grace, and passion I would not have thought possible." I studied the man who personified my feelings of the dance and he smiled at me, his warm handsome smile that made me want to kiss his lips. "To be honest, the thought that anyone could be watching us makes me feel self-conscious," I admitted. "It feels too personal a thing to share with others."

"I hate to disappoint you," he said as we came together again, "but I do believe you cannot be so enchanting without the repercussions."

I glanced around to find countless eyes on us, even the other dancers seemed to have taken notice. The heat rose up my neck until it filled my whole face.

"I do not like to see you discomforted," Edwin said. "But I cannot help but love the way your face colors when you are embarrassed."

I was glad as the music ended, and the attention turned to the musicians.

Mr. Ellis led Diana to where we stood. "I fear Mother will insist upon a chaperon for your next dance," Diana said with a pointed grin.

"It was for the sake of education," Edwin retorted. "I was demonstrating the difference between knowing the steps and actually dancing them."

"The rest of us must have just been stepping then," she said with a weak laugh.

"Darling," Mr. Ellis said to Diana, a look of concern in his features. "I do believe you have exerted yourself stepping about the room with me. I have reserved a chair for your sole use this evening and will happily escort you to it, whenever you desire a rest."

Diana rolled her eyes and swatted at him playfully. "I am not some old matron who requires outlandish accommodations to be made on her behalf, Mr. Ellis." She pursed her lips thoughtfully. "Though, I might change my mind after the next set so don't go about relinquishing it to the use of others just yet." Diana shifted her gaze to me. "I did have one thing I needed to mention to Mother, will you join us?"

"I fear I need a moment longer to catch my breath," I said. "We'll be along shortly."

"Very well," she said, taking Mr. Ellis's arm.

My gaze followed the couple until they rejoined the others —all the people I loved most, standing together enjoying one another's company. I paused to take it in.

"What is it?" Edwin asked, his brow creased with worry.

"When I first came to Timpton House, I was sure nowhere would ever be as dear to me as Easton Manor. I had been given a second chance there, found a family, and discovered love." I looked up at him and a tear slipped down my cheek. "And now I have been blessed with those same things here at Timpton, and I'm certain I could not love either place more."

The pleasure in his expression was undeniable as he reached up and gently wiped away my tear.

"Shall we join the others?" I asked, squeezing his arm and looking toward the group of people watching us with expectant gazes.

As we neared, Diana eagerly linked her arm through mine as Mr. Ellis led Uncle Stanton to us.

"Now this will make for a grand story!" Uncle Stanton said. "That is, if anyone could be made to believe it!"

We all laughed as he reached for my hand. I gave his hand a gentle squeeze, and his smile brightened to match the rest of ours. Mr. Stanton drew near as Mother placed a kiss on my cheek. I glanced toward Father, Laurence, and Lydia who watched with affectionate gazes when Edwin's hand moved to my waist, sending a warming sensation through me. Standing here, enveloped in so much love, I felt truly and completely happy.

THE END

DID YOU ENJOY ABIGAIL?

As an author, reviews are *critical* to my success. It would mean so much to me if you would take a moment and submit a review on **Amazon**, **Goodreads**, or wherever book reviews are welcome. There are so many stories I'd love to write and your assistance is a vital part of bringing those books to fruition. Thank you so much for your support!

If you'd like to receive updates regarding future books, release dates, and giveaways, sign up for my newsletter at JessHeileman.com.

I love connecting with my readers. You can find me on Facebook: Jess Heileman or Instagram: @authorjessheileman

ACKNOWLEDGMENTS

What an overwhelming task it is to thank the countless people who have supported me on this journey. Here is my meager attempt at expressing my eternal gratitude to those who have made *Abigail* possible.

First, none of this could have happened without the unwavering support of my amazing husband. He is my sanity, my strength, my greatest inspiration, my best friend, and my constant support. He is the love of my life and my companion for eternity—how I love him!

My five darlings—Andrew, Hyrum, Eden, Mary, and Edmund—have brought me more joy than I could ever express! Aspects of their glorious personalities are sprinkled throughout my characters, especially Eden whose spunky charm and lovely, dark features helped bring Abigail to life for me.

I couldn't have asked for better parents to teach me that love is unconditional. They started my fan club over three decades ago and haven't stopped cheering for me since. I am forever indebted to them both!

A much-deserved shout-out goes to my mother-in-law,

Sheri, and her skills at making the gorgeous Regency dress for my cover. I'm blessed to have in-laws who I love and adore, and who offer their love, their talents, and their continuous support.

I count myself blessed to have such supportive siblings: Justin, Ryan, Andrew, Matthew, as well as Cindy and Rick. They have been an unwavering strength to me. I am also relieved that they were competent at picking phenomenal spouses—Erika, Brittany, Craig, and Tina—as well as producing beautiful nieces and nephews for me to love.

Love to all my extended family: grandmas, grandpas, aunts, uncles, and cousins on all sides! There are not words enough (nor pages) to express my gratitude to each of them.

I am indebted to my first group of readers who gave me their feedback and the confidence and encouragement I needed to keep going: Tim, Jody, Grant, Tawnie, Cindy, Jenny, Cara, Julie, Jamie, Katie, Wendy, Carrie, Emily, Larissa, Monika, Kim, Kimberly, Pat, Whitney, Sheri, Leilani, Melanie, Lauren, Loretta, Jessica and Terri. I'm also grateful for the countless others who have reached out to receive ARCs or have shown interest in my journey—the support means so much!

I love that some people appreciate grammar, editing down long sentences, and using hyphens correctly. While I'm not one of those people, Whitney Wright and her fondness of editing helped me to appear as though I am.

Lauren Santana was the perfect model for my cover. She is not only beautiful and a blast to be with, but goodness honestly radiates from her.

Ruth Nickle impressed me with her artistic abilities long before she agreed to design my cover. What a privilege it has been to work with her. She is kind and patient and is a master designer.

Kathy Habel has been indispensable in helping to get the word out about my debut novel. She is encouraging and helpful, no matter how many questions I ask. I'm still amazed at her ability to rally her troops.

My formatter, Cora Johnson, has been a pleasure to work with. She has been patient with my perfectionist tendencies and understanding of my many edits.

I appreciate the authors who have inspired me with their writing and, on occasion, their advice and words of encouragement.

Lastly, and above all, I'm grateful to God for His steadfast love and support as well as the innumerable blessings I've been given!

ABOUT THE AUTHOR

In kindergarten, Jess won a first prize ribbon for her original creation *Pigs in Wigs*. The storyline was solid: there was this pig that wore a wig—and it rhymed. Not impressed? Neither were her children when shown the very masterpiece that influenced her to become an author. "You won a ribbon for that?" Yes. Yes, she did.

Thankfully, life has since exposed her to a thorough education with its share of awards and accolades—and, more importantly, to the trials and human experiences that form the heart of a storyteller and the substance of great stories.

Besides her love of writing, Jess is an avid reader, shameless people observer, international café loiterer, and partially retired photographer. She loves being a mother to five amazing humans and a wife to the greatest man she knows.

Made in the USA
San Bernardino, CA
09 February 2020

64252383R00205